THE GOSSIP SPREAD AROUND OLD EAST LIKE OIL ON A MARBLE SLAB, OOZING INTO EVERY CORNER OF THE HOSPITAL UNTIL NOT ONLY WERE THE STAFF TALKING ABOUT IT, SO WERE THE PATIENTS.

'Three suicides in as many days, so they're saying,' she said. 'If it was the patients, you'd understand, what with worrying about yourself the way you do, but the staff ... You read a lot in the papers about morale being low in the NHS and all that, but this is really too much ...'

The staff were most affected. If people they worked with were choosing to hurl themselves prematurely, and to an extent, violently out of life at Old East, didn't that mean they should look a little more closely at what life in the hospital entailed? As the patient in Annie Zunz had surmised, morale was indeed low, and the implication that you might be driven to commit suicide at any moment did nothing to raise it.

Also by Claire Rayner

A STARCH OF APRONS

THE MEDDLERS

A TIME TO HEAL

MADDIE

CLINICAL JUDGEMENTS

POSTSCRIPTS

DANGEROUS THINGS

LONDON LODGINGS

PAYING GUESTS

FIRST BLOOD

SECOND OPINION

THIRD DEGREE

Claire Rayner

FOURTH ATTEMPT

A Dr George Barnabas Mystery

PENGUIN BOOKS

For Judith and Kim,
Katy and Amy,
with love

PENGUIN BOOKS

Published by the Penguin Group
Penguin Books Ltd, 27 Wrights Lane, London W8 5TZ, England
Penguin Books USA Inc., 375 Hudson Street, New York, New York 10014, USA
Penguin Books Australia Ltd, Ringwood, Victoria, Australia
Penguin Books Canada Ltd, 10 Alcorn Avenue, Toronto, Ontario, Canada M4V 3B2
Penguin Books (NZ) Ltd, 182–190 Wairau Road, Auckland 10, New Zealand

Penguin Books Ltd, Registered Offices: Harmondsworth, Middlesex, England

First published by Michael Joseph 1996
Published in Penguin Books 1997
1 3 5 7 9 10 8 6 4 2

The moral right of the author has been asserted

Printed in England by Clays Ltd, St Ives plc

For Judith and Kim,
Katy and Amy,
with love

ACKNOWLEDGEMENTS

Thanks for advice and information about death, detection, fires and sundry other topics are due to: Dr Trevor Betteridge, Pathologist of Yeovil, Somerset; Dr Rufus Crompton, Pathologist, St George's Hospital, Tooting, London; Dr Azeel Sarrah, Pathologist, Queen Elizabeth II Hospital, Welwyn Garden City, Hertfordshire; Detective Chief Inspector Jackie Malton, Metropolitan Police; Dr Hilary Howells, Anaesthetist of Totteridge, Hertfordshire; the London Fire Brigade; many members of the staff of Northwick Park and St Mark's Hospital, Harrow, Middlesex; and many others too mumerous to mention; and are gratefully tendered by the author.

I

The gossip spread around Old East like oil on a marble slab, oozing into every corner of the hospital until not only were the staff talking about it, so were the patients.

'I said to Sister when she was doing my dressing this morning, I said, "Well, Sister, what's going on here then? And who'll be the next? Is there anything worrying *you*?"' The rather fat woman in the peach chenille dressing gown, sitting awkwardly festooned with drainage tubes and IV lines in the shabby dayroom on Annie Zunz Ward, shook with pleasure at her own wit and then grimaced as her operation site gave her a twinge of pain. 'Ooh, you take your life in your hands when you laugh, don't you? Still, you've got to laugh, haven't you? It's the best medicine, I always say.'

The woman sitting on the other side of the dayroom, who had heard enough of Peach Chenille's opinions on everything upon which it was possible to hold an opinion, forbore to answer, but later, when she went back to her own bed, she too spoke to her immediate neighbour about it all, wondering what was going on at Old East and who might be next.

'Three suicides in as many days, so they're saying,' she said. 'If it was the patients, you'd understand, what with worrying about yourself the way you do, but the staff . . . Well, it makes you think about there being something wrong in the place, doesn't it? You read a lot in the papers about morale being low in the NHS and all that, but this is really too much.'

Her neighbour, who knew herself to be dying of her liver disease and already detaching her mind from other people's interests in consequence, managed a faint smile. 'People don't choose to die because of the way everyone feels,' she murmured. 'It's always because of something personal.' She closed her eyes and wondered if it wouldn't be easier to die now herself rather than a few weeks down the line when she'd probably feel even sicker than she did at present – if that were possible. She'd always promised herself she'd choose when to go; but since she no longer had the strength either emotionally or physically to take action on any decision she made, she wisely chose not to think at all any more.

But others did: most of all, the staff. They, after all, were most affected. If people they worked with were choosing to hurl themselves prematurely and to an extent violently out of life at Old East, didn't that mean they should look a little more closely at what life in the hospital entailed? As the patient in Annie Zunz had surmised, morale was indeed low, and the implication that you might be driven to commit suicide at any moment did nothing to raise it.

Sheila Keen, the senior technician in the path. lab and famous throughout Old East for her passion (and great gift) for gossip, seemed excited rather than depressed by what was going on. She was displaying a bright-eyed relish for it all that irritated her colleagues immensely, not least her boss Dr George Barnabas. George had been sitting in her cubby hole of an office, looking over the notes that had been sent down with Pamela Frean's body and the post-mortem request, when Sheila came in, smiling sweetly and bearing a tray with a pot of freshly made coffee and biscuits. Since Sheila was often loudly on record as not being part of Old East's staff in order to make coffee for the head honcho (a piece of out-moded slang which in itself set George's teeth on edge), and the two of them had had a row only last week, the sight of her made George scowl.

'What are you after, Sheila?' she said bluntly. 'And try not to be so obvious about it, for Pete's sake. I'd prefer you to come right out with it and ask instead of all this best buttering-up stuff.'

Sheila's fixed smile became a little more brittle but didn't falter. 'Oh, Dr B.,' she said indulgently as she set the tray down on the desk and set about pouring the coffee, which smelled wonderful to George, who had as usual missed her breakfast. 'You did get out of the bed on the wrong side this morning, didn't you?'

'I did not,' George said, managing not to clench her teeth. 'What do you want?'

Sheila opened her eyes wide. 'I just thought I'd see if there was anything special you wanted done. I'm bang up to date with everything – even the cardiac clinic stuff is ready a day early – so I've got a little time available. I could take your PM notes for you maybe? Just to take some of the weight off you?'

'Oh, balls!' said George. 'Who do you think you're kidding? You just want to be there when I do it.'

'Well, why not?' Sheila dropped her air of innocence and looked avid. 'You can't blame me, Dr B.! I mean, what a carry on! Three suicides among the staff and –'

'Who says they're suicides?' George snapped. 'I don't believe I made any such suggestion about the last two. And as I recall,' she added with heavy sarcasm, 'I think I did do the PMs, didn't I? Not you?'

'Oh, Dr B., come on! They can't just be accidents. Not three times in a row. You might as well expect your lottery tickets to come up as that.'

'The first two *were* accidents. I can't say what this one is. Not till I do the PM. And I don't need your help with it, thank you. I can cope perfectly well with Danny's assistance.'

Sheila flushed. Danny was, after all only the mortuary

3

porter and as such well below Sheila's regard. 'Well, if that's the way you want it. I was only trying to be helpful.'

'Oh, sure,' George said. 'You always are, aren't you? If you've got that much free time, you can help Jerry catch up. He's overloaded with the extra histology I gave him. He needs someone to cut his specimens for him.'

'I'm not here to do Jerry Swann's work, thank you very much.' Sheila made for the door. 'I'm the senior technician here and that means I have a supervisory role over people like Jerry. Take a look at my job description some time to remind yourself.' And she flounced out before George could answer, even if she'd wanted to.

George went down to the PM room, clutching the notes and swearing inaudibly at letting Sheila rile her so much. Sheila had always been the most difficult member of the staff while at the same time being the most expert at her job. She never made mistakes, kept well up to speed with the lab's very considerable output of work and knew the place inside out. If only she didn't have to be so hard to get on with, George thought as she dumped the notes and made for her dressing room to get into her greens. A taste for gossip shouldn't madden me so much, I like gossip myself. But she really is the end . . .

By the time George was ready, her hair tied up in a tight cap to protect it from the unpleasant smells that were an inevitable part of working with corpses, rubber-aproned and with her feet tucked into the oversized boots that protected her from the water Danny always sent splashing so enthusiastically over the slabs, she had managed to push Sheila and her irritating ways to the back of her mind. She had a job to do and she had to concentrate on it.

But all the same, as she and Danny prepared to start, she couldn't help mentally reviewing the previous two cases involving members of Old East's staff on which she had worked in the past few days: Tony Mendez, the theatre porter who had died of alcoholic poisoning, and Lally Lamark, from the

4

Medical Records department, who had been diabetic and who had died in an insulin coma. Both had clearly been accidental, she thought, yet all over the hospital there had been this rush of gossip that they had been suicides. No wonder Sheila had been so eager to come and find out what had happened to Pam Frean. She'd want to be first with the news; just as, probably, she'd been first with the chatter about Mendez and Lamark. Goddamn Sheila, George thought furiously, and then was annoyed with herself for letting her intrude again.

Pushing Sheila out of her mind, George looked down at the body on the slab and felt the twinge of pity that she still experienced whenever the subject for a PM was young. This girl couldn't have been into her twenties for long: her face was smooth and taut with none of the signs of wear that life had scribbled on most of the bodies George dealt with. Her hair was thick and long, and George watched as Danny twisted it into a heavy rope and pinned it to the top of the head to get it out of the way. Had the girl been proud of its soft smoothness and pampered it with expensive shampoos? Probably. And her body, so soft and pretty, in spite of the marble-like effect that was inevitable in the post rigor mortis state: had she taken a delight in that too? Who could know? George picked up one of the flaccid hands and looked at the nails. They were short, unpolished, cut straight across and had clearly never been manicured. So she hadn't been into fashion and self-adornment, George thought, letting the hand go. This was being silly, even sentimental, she told herself. Better to find out the facts instead of surmising like this.

'Right, Danny,' she said briskly. 'Let's get going.' She pulled down the microphone above her head so that it was suitably close to her mouth and began to dictate. 'The body is of a female, height . . .' Danny measured and told her and she repeated the fact into the mike and they were off, slipping comfortably into the routine of a post-mortem, and all musings apart from what she was actually doing and looking at slid out of her mind.

Her knife slid down the belly, from xiphysternum to symphysis pubis, cutting a wake that lay open the whole of the belly from the lowest ribs to just above the smudge of dark pubic hair. She pulled the flaps apart and began to investigate the abdominal contents, dictating continuously as she went. Danny took the various pieces of viscera, weighed them and gave her the details, which she dictated into her mike too before carrying on, checking the stomach for its contents, which she emptied into a stoppered flask that Danny held for her, then the gut, the kidneys, liver ... and her puzzlement grew. This had been a healthy young woman. There was no hint of disease anywhere that she could see with the naked eye, though of course there was still the microscope work to be done. The liver, in particular, she thought, had the pristine look of one belonging to someone who had never tasted alcohol in her life.

But that was a fanciful notion. She set it aside as unworthy of a practitioner who was supposed to have a scientific mind as she set to work on the pelvic contents. Ovaries and fallopian tubes: normal and, to the naked eye, healthy. The uterus: here her gaze sharpened and she looked even more carefully.

Bulky, she thought. Moving even more carefully now, she lifted it over the bony pelvis and set it on the slab where she could do a further dissection. Danny watched her in his usual imperturbable fashion, his lips pursed as though he were whistling, though he never emitted a sound as her knife slid over the membrane and then bit into the thick strong muscle of the uterine wall.

She wasn't unduly surprised when she finally had the uterus open. She had expected it, but all the same it deepened the pity she felt; standing there looking down on the twelve-week foetus that lay curled up and very dead inside its equally dead mother. She could almost have wept for it.

*

6

It took her some time to regain her equilibrium. She finished the PM, finding the cause of death without any difficulty: the lungs were full of water, and there were other signs which made it clear Pam Frean had drowned. Since she had been discovered in her bath under the water, that had been the most likely explanation anyway; but George had deliberately given no thought to that fact when making her examination. It would not be the first time she had found that a corpse which had been recovered from under water had been dead before it entered it. But in this case, it was a true bill; death by drowning. Later, however, the blood-chemistry tests added another dimension: the girl had taken a large dose of diazepam.

But try as George might to stop thinking about the case, she couldn't. She did all she could to keep the facts about the PM quiet, but of course she failed. Sheila had them wormed out of Danny immediately; she might regard him as one of the lower orders, but when she wanted something from him she could turn on the charm to great effect and without shame. So in no time everyone around the hospital was talking of the three deaths – and still calling all three of them suicides. And though George tried not to let the gossip get to her, she found herself wanting more information than she had, certainly about the last case. Because with this one the gossips were almost certainly right.

That was why she went over to A & E to see her old friend Hattie Clements. There had been something in the notes which suggested that Hattie might be able to give her more information about Pam Frean. And that was something George badly wanted.

'I know people are overreacting a bit,' Hattie, the senior sister on Accident and Emergency said as she gave George a beaker full of the department's famous bitter black coffee. 'But it's understandable. I mean, one suicide a day for three days! No wonder people are uneasy.'

'But there weren't three suicides!' George said. 'It's people like Sheila whipping them up, that's all. And it wasn't one a day. That was just the way people heard about it.'

'You're wrong, George,' Hattie said. 'And I don't often think that, you know I don't. But right now Sheila's irritating you so much you'd blame her for the war in Bosnia if you could. But truly, she's not the only one talking. Now, just listen!' She raised her voice to override George's attempt to interrupt. 'On the Monday they found Lally Lamark dead on the floor of her office, stiff as a board and –'

'Which shows she didn't die on Monday,' George said. 'Goddamn it, Hattie, who's the pathologist around here, me or you? She'd been dead since the Friday. Rigor mortis had –'

'They found her on Monday.' Hattie was stubborn. 'And that caused enough drama, the way it happened. And then on Tuesday, there was Tony Mendez collapsing in the middle of a case and frightening the crap out of Gerald Mayer-France so much that he had to hand over the gall-bag he was doing to his registrar.'

'Any excuse to cut short his NHS sessions are balm in Gilead to Mayer-France,' George retorted. 'He's the sort of consultant who gives the NHS an even worse name than it's got. He was probably cuddling up to one of his private patients in Wimpole Street before the poor sap of a registrar had the skin clips in –'

'And then,' Hattie said, riding over George magnificently, 'yesterday, there was Pam Frean. Is it any wonder they're all looking over their shoulders to see who'll be the fourth one?'

George put down her cup with a little clatter. 'Oh, Hattie, really, listen to yourself, will you? This is sheer nonsense! Those first two were accidents! Lally Lamark had been having trouble with her diabetic control ever since they'd changed her to the new sort of insulin. And Mendez, well, they thought he'd kicked the booze and was OK, but he hadn't. And when he took a drink he just overestimated how much he could safely take and poisoned himself. *Accidentally.* I did the PMs on them both myself, goddamn it! If they'd

8

killed themselves I'd have spotted something to prove it. And they left no notes or –'

'But Pam Frean did!' Hattie cried. 'She definitely did, didn't she? And as for the other two being accidents, everyone says that Lally got her insulin right and people who knew Tony well swear he was well and truly in control. I have no trouble believing they were all suicides, no matter what you say!'

'Don't confuse me with facts, is that it?' George said dryly. 'Because guessing is so much more fun? Come on, Hattie, I expected better of you.'

'Fiddle-de-dee,' Hattie said, refilling George's cup. 'You wait and see. You'll come and apologize to me yet. I know a suicide when I see one.'

'Well, you didn't see Lamark and Mendez,' George said. 'So you're guessing as wildly as Sheila and everyone else are.'

'Not wildly.' Hattie insisted. 'Informed opinion based on experience.'

'It's your experience of Frean that I want.' George felt that the argument was getting sharper and the last thing she wanted to do was fight with Hattie. The whole fuss would die down in a few days, the way hospital fusses usually did, and George and Hattie would slip back happily into their old comfortable friendliness. No need to upset her over something so transitory, George thought, leaning forwards to bring her head closer to Hattie in a manner designed to disarm her. 'Tell me what happened when you saw her.'

'Hmm,' Hattie said, only a little appeased. Then she shrugged slightly. 'So you know about that?'

'It was in the notes,' George said.

'Oh, fair enough. OK then. Well, she was brought down here by one of the other nurses on Laburnum Ward –'

'Neurology.'

'Uh-huh. Well, more neuro-research now, since Laurence Bulpitt died and the new chap came. What's his name? Zacharius? Polish, I think he is.'

'Hungarian,' George said. 'Go on about what happened with Frean. When was this?'

'Um, last month. Let me check my notes.' Hattie turned to her computer and began to click keys. 'Here it is. The third of May. Wednesday, May third. Four-fifteen p.m. She passed out, really passed out cold. Not just a fleeting fainting episode but deeply out for several seconds. The nurse she was working with at the time was very sensible, saw it was an unusually prolonged syncope and once she came round insisted on putting her in a wheelchair and bringing her down here. I checked the girl and her blood pressure was . . . let me see.'

Again she clicked keys and, as the screen rolled, re-assembled its data and then settled, nodded. 'Here we are. Look over my shoulder. It's all here.'

George obeyed, squinting at the bluish-white expanse, reading off the information. 'Blood pressure low but not too bad. Pulse rate fast – that figures. Normal temperature, normal reflexes, normal – yeah, I see. Looks like a vaso-vagal episode of some sort.'

'That's what I thought, but then the other nurse went off back to the ward because they were bleeping her and I could talk to Frean on her own. So I asked her, could she be pregnant? Well, you always have to ask, don't you? And she went as white as a sheet. I thought she was going to go out again, and I had to hang on to her because she'd have fallen off the couch. She didn't flake out but she started to cry like a fountain and after that it was all pretty much run of the mill. From the story she gave' – she squinted again at the screen – 'last menstrual period and all that, she was about eight weeks pregnant. Give or take. She denied it all at first but then I got it out of her. She was just at the point of missing her second period. She was frantic about it.'

George raised her brows. 'Wanted an abortion?'

'No, that was the . . . Well, I asked her how she felt about the pregnancy to see if she wanted to terminate. I could have referred her to the right people then, you see? But I don't refer girls unless I know they've made up their minds about the issue. Some of the abortion clinic people are, well, a bit enthusiastic, you know? These girls need time to think. She said she didn't know, she'd never thought about such a possibility, and I told her that if she was having unprotected sex it was a very high one and even then she didn't seem to know what I was talking about. Very naïve, I thought. At first. But then I found out why . . .'

'She can hardly have been uneducated in these matters, surely? You don't get to be a senior staff nurse without learning something about the physiology of reproduction.'

'Maybe so. But you can block it out of your thinking if you want to. Her family, you see, are religious. No, not just religious. Barking mad fanatic. The sort who come knocking on your door on Sunday afternoon and preach at you until you have to slam the door in their faces to get rid of them.'

'Ah!' George said, and let her shoulders relax. She had been right to come to Hattie with her questions. She had no right to dig around in the girl's history, of course; her job had been just the post-mortem. But George being George, her curiosity was, as ever, uncontrollable. And now it was beginning to be assuaged. The puzzle had been why a pregnant girl should kill herself for such a reason in 1995. In 1895 it would have been understandable, but for a sophisticated nurse today, it was surely excessive. An unwanted pregnancy was a problem – even a major problem – but it was not an insuperable one, unless the girl was subject to pressures most modern young women were not. Strict religious parents could be just such a pressure.

'That makes sense of her note, then,' she said now.

'I thought so as soon as I heard about it,' Hattie said. 'People said they couldn't understand it, but I knew at once.'

George shook her head irritably. 'Then everyone's talking about the note too?'

'Of course they are! This is Old East, remember? The mere

concept of a secret is unknown here.' Hattie was amused. 'I told you I knew Frean had left a note. How could I have known if everyone else hadn't?'

'I don't know,' George said. 'You heard where it was found, too?'

Hattie nodded. 'On the screen on the computer in Neuro? Yup.'

'You don't think that's a bit odd?' George said, trying to be casual.

Hattie was not deceived. 'Do you?' she said sharply.

'Well . . . maybe a little. I mean, to sit down at a computer to leave a note rather than grab a piece of paper and a pen seems a bit calculated, don't you think? And the ward computer at that.'

'Calculated?' Hattie said. 'The whole business of suicide is calculated! As for where people leave notes, I had a patient in here once who had written in lipstick on her belly that she was sorry and it was her husband's fault she'd done it. *That* was calculated. For people today to use computers isn't. They're as common at work as pens and paper, aren't they? More common, really. And anyway, what other computer could she use? Unless she had one of her own, and though I know a few of the live-in staff do, they're not all that common. People on NHS pay can't afford 'em. I certainly hadn't heard she had one.'

'You no doubt heard what sort of toothpaste she used!' George permitted herself to be sardonic. 'Ye Gods, is there anything that isn't a resource for chatter in this place?'

'Nope,' Hattie said cheerfully. 'And you be glad of it. If we weren't that way, you wouldn't be here now finding out whatever it is you're trying to find out. You use gossip the same way the rest of us do.'

'Oh, shit!' George went a little pink.

There was a silence and then Hattie said. 'It was a weird note, wasn't it?'

'Not now you've told me about the family.' George

reached into her pocket and pulled out a piece of paper. 'I copied it.' And she began to read aloud.

'"I broke the fifth commandment. I cannot go on. It is a wicked thing I have done. I have to pay for the wicked thing I have done. Pamela Frean, her days are as grass, as a flower of the field so she flourisheth. For the wind passeth over it and it is gone; and the place thereof shall know it no more. The world shall know Pamela Frean no more. Amen."'

Hattie gave a little shiver. 'Poor creature.'

'Yes,' George said. 'Poor creature.'

There was a little silence, and then George spoke again. 'Did she tell you more? More than you've told me already?'

'Oh, yes,' Hattie said. 'Lots.'

'Can you tell me?'

'Why not?' Hattie shrugged. 'She's dead now, so the confidential bit is null and void really. She told me that her parents were very strict members of a fundamentalist group called ... the Enclosed Brethren, I think. You know, no Christmas or birthday celebrations, no TV, no radio, no newspapers – and certainly no romantic entanglements. That was the phrase she used, and I thought it was rather sweet. It certainly made a change from the way everyone blathers on about relationships and "significant others" these days. Romantic entanglements ...' Hattie sighed. 'I talked to her for a long time. They really are as hard as nails, those parents. Not that she complained about them, the opposite in fact. You'd think they were angels incarnate the way she talked, but they sounded so mean, so pinched, so ... They forced her into nursing so she could go and be a missionary in Africa or somewhere – those people like to go to meddle and make trouble – even though she just wanted to be a musician. They told her that was a sinful way to think and prayed it out of her, she said.' Hattie gave a little shudder. 'It sounded a dreadful life, yet here she was, in a "romantic entanglement" and terrified of what her parents would say. That was when I put it to her directly: did she want to go ahead and have the baby? She stared at me and said, "What choice do I have?" I opened my mouth to say a termination and d'you know, I couldn't? Obviously with that background she'd have been appalled at the mere suggestion, so I just said, well, she'd better tell the father of the baby and make their plans, and sign into an antenatal clinic as soon as possible to get proper care. I told her not to come here for it.' She hesitated. 'I think it's grim for staff to be patients in their own hospitals. You're so bloody vulnerable to talk.'

'Tell me about it!' George said. She put the copy of the note back into her pocket. 'Well, that all makes sense now. I couldn't understand why the poor wretch should leave a message like that, just because of a pregnancy, in this day and age. Now I do. Poor kid. And what a way to do it!'

'I didn't know it could be done,' Hattie said. 'I thought the reflexes would make it impossible to drown yourself in just a bath.'

'You'd be amazed at what a really determined suicide can do,' George said. 'And she made sure she made a job of it. She took some diazepam to sedate herself and then inhaled a really big quantity in the first breath she took under water. She was unconscious in a matter of seconds and by then she was lying on the floor of the bath and it was full so . . .'

'So they're both dead.'

'Both?' George was disconcerted for a moment.

'Frean and her baby.'

'Oh, yes . . . Bloody religion!' George said with sudden violence.

'You can't blame all religion for the fundamentalists,' Hattie said and George lifted her chin in disagreement.

'You don't get fundamentalists without it.'

'No? Then what about political ones?' Hattie said mildly.

George stared at her and then bit her lip. 'Sorry, Hatt. I didn't mean to offend you. Though I have to say I never knew you were religious. We never talked about it, did we?'

'Oh, I'm not.' Hattie was her usual cheerful self. 'I'm as

much a pagan as the rest of the people here. I just – well, I like to argue. Almost as much as you do.'

'She's my best friend and I just *hate* her.' George got to her feet. 'OK, thanks for the information. I'll pass it on to the coroner's office, together with my P M findings and then they can have the inquest. And once there's evidence we've had just the one suicide at Old East, people'll shut their goddamn mouths about the other two.'

'Maybe,' said Hattie diplomatically. She stretched as she got to her feet. 'Listen, I'd better get back outside and see what's what. Life's a bit easier here now with those two new nurse practitioners on triage, but I have to keep an eye out all the same. See you later?'

'Uh-huh.' George was at the door. 'At the presentation for old Hunnisett, if that's what you mean.'

'Where else?' Hattie brightened then. 'Maybe we'll pick up a bit of news about who's to be our new Medical Director.'

'I hope so. It'll give people something else to gossip about for a change,' George said. 'Especially Sheila Keen. I'll gag that woman if it's the last thing I do.'

'Phooey,' Hattie said good naturedly. 'You know she's not all that much worse than the rest of us. Just better at digging out the facts and spreading 'em around, that's all.'

'I'm not so sure,' George said grimly. 'I'll tell you this much: if I can't stop her tongue over this poor Frean girl, I swear she'll be the next suicide for people to talk about. I'll drive her to it, see if I don't.'

'Yeah, sure.' Hattie managed a fair imitation of George's American accent. 'I'll believe that when it happens. See you at the meeting then. Now get out of here!'

George got.

2

The Board Room was in festive mode, which George always found rather depressing. The fact that the imposing furniture had been pushed into different positions to clear the centre of the space, and that trays of sad-looking vol-au-vents and sausages and curly sandwiches had been dotted about, didn't make it any less lowering, with its heavy dark-panelled walls and looming deeply varnished portraits of long-dead benefactors and faded red Turkey carpet. The room was one of the relics of the days when Old East had been a famous voluntary hospital supported by public contributions and staffed by lofty doctors in frock coats and subservient nurses in a great deal of starch. Now, as a National Health Acute Trust, Old East had sprouted a shabby array of portakabins put in to be temporary but becoming ever more permanent as the increase in work swiftly outstripped the money available to run the place properly, and concrete extensions which sat sullenly in all their stained grey hideousness against the red brick of the original foundation in a way that made both of them look even uglier and more dilapidated than they were. If that were possible.

But in the years since George had come to work at Old East she, like the rest of the staff, had become inured to the surroundings. It would have been agreeable to work in a wonderland of modern chrome and tile with broad well-windowed rooms and corridors, but since they didn't, they learned not to see the way the place really looked. They settled instead for the fascination of the work that went on inside these unprepossessing premises and an absorbing interest in the people who did it, both of which were very vibrant indeed.

Looking around the room now George could see that two of the research fellows, Frances Llewellyn and Michael Klein, had already arrived and was amused. The Royal Eastern Clinical Research Institute had been set up just a year ago by the now departing Professor Hunnisett, and he had been very successful in attracting both money to run it and good people to work in it. There was no way the research fellows already *in situ* were going to risk losing their plum places at the Institute's table. If Hunnisett was going, the identity of his successor would be a matter of huge import-ance to all of them. George watched as they clustered round the rather pompous figure of the old man and was glad she wasn't into research. Being Old East's pathologist as well as Forensic Home Office Pathologist for the patch of London served by Old East was quite enough for her to deal with. Anyway, her patrons, if she had such things, were not here, but among the police and the civil service, and she rarely had to see any of the latter. What she saw of the former suited her very well.

However, she would not let herself be distracted by thoughts of the police, or more accurately thoughts of one particular policeman: Superintendent Gus Hathaway. There were several things that needed thinking about regarding him. But not now.

Another of the people standing beside Professor Hun-nisett caught her eye, smiled and raised one hand. She smiled back. She'd already met him. He'd come over to her table in the canteen one lunchtime a few months ago, very soon after being appointed, to introduce himself as the new research fellow in Neurology.

'I don't know yet just how much I might want to ask the path. lab to do,' he said. 'I do a lot of my own tasks, of course, but you never know. So I thought I'd better ingratiate myself with you as much as possible to be on the safe side.'

She had laughed at so direct an approach and invited him to join her, which he had, eagerly, and she had found him amusing company.

'My name, heaven help me, is Zoltan Zacharias,' he said. 'Yes, I know it sounds like something out of an eighteenth-century Gothic novel but I can't help it. People call me Zack.'

'Good to know you, Zack,' she had said. 'They call me George, on account of it's my name, just like yours is Zoltan. I wouldn't let them call me Barney just because they couldn't cope with George.'

'Then I guess I just don't have your courage,' he said. She had tilted her head at the hint of an American accent she had heard in his voice. He didn't wait to be asked. 'Canadian. Why George?'

'Because my mother was a feminist,' she said shortly. 'And my grandfather wasn't. He left all his money to any child of hers named after him. She had me and called me after him. Why Canadian?'

He blinked. 'How do you mean, why?'

'All the Canadians I ever met came there from somewhere else. Like Americans dodging the draft and Europeans dodging – well, Europe. The ones who are born there all go to work in the States.'

He laughed. 'That's a gross exaggeration. You've clearly met all the wrong Canadians. But you're right in one way. I'm – I was – an immigrant. Too young to know it at the time, mind you. I went there in '56.'

She nodded, understanding at once. 'The Hungarian uprising? I thought Zoltan was a Hungarian name. And I didn't mean to be rude about Canadians. It's a great country, and –'

'Yeah. Some of your best friends, right?'

'No, really. I was just being a smartass, I suppose. Hell,

what right do I have to be rude about Canada when I come from Buffalo? So, what are you planning to do here?'

'Research.' He grinned widely and it suited him. She liked the way he looked: he had thick hair that was the sort of dusty brown that must have been straw-blond in his infancy, and narrow green eyes that almost disappeared when he smiled. The cheekbones and the jawline were pronounced enough to be almost a caricature of the Slav stereotype, but were over-lain with enough chubbiness to show that he enjoyed the pleasures of the table. He wasn't fat but he clearly could be, one day, if he didn't watch it. Altogether an attractive person-ality, she told herself. And I like his voice. It's very dark toffee and luscious with it.

'I know. You already told me that. What sort of research?'

'I'm interested in motor-neurone disease. And stuff like it.'

She grimaced. 'Nasty. So little anyone can do. And it's so damned fast, isn't it?'

'Sometimes. Some patients manage to live a long time, however. Like Stephen Hawking.'

'Ah, yes. The exception that proves the rule, hmm?'

'No. The exception that proves research makes sense. If one man can live so long with such symptoms, why can't an-other? And is it possible to delay the onset of symptoms once the disease process starts? And can the effects of the nerve damage be reversed? And –'

'Sounds like you've set yourself a major research pro-gramme,' she said, trying not to smile.

He shook his head at her. 'Don't you laugh at me! Sure, it's a big project, but big projects are the sort most likely to win through. My dad used to say "Aim for the sky and you'll hit the top of the tree. Aim for the top of the tree and you'll never get off the ground."'

She had been struck by that and hadn't been ashamed to say so, and they had settled to a long talk about the possi-bilities of the work he was doing with an ease that had made her feel she'd known him for a long time and not just for an hour or two. But he made it extra easy by doing most of the talking. She knew as much about neurology as she had to, and perhaps a little more, but it didn't match his expertise so she listened, fascinated, as he outlined some of his plans.

Since then, they had shared tables in the canteen on several occasions. He always seemed to choose the same time to go to lunch as she did; after a while she had begun to make a point of going at a set time, to make it easier for him, even lingering at the end of the line-up for food until he arrived, if she got there before him. Over the months they'd developed a comfortable bantering friendship that she valued more and more. Especially when she was annoyed with Gus, which seemed to happen rather more often lately.

But now, she reminded herself, was not the time to think about Gus. She concentrated on watching Zack come towards her across the Board Room, and felt a frisson of pleasure. This evening's clambake would be, she had told herself as she tidied herself to come to it, a real buttock-clenching bore, but now she felt much more cheerful about it, even glad she was here; and also glad, at a deeper level, that she'd put on her deep red silk dress this morning, with the matching tights and shoes. It was a racy outfit that looked good on her; and though that shouldn't matter, for after all she wasn't meeting Gus, somehow it pleased her. And hadn't she promised herself not to think about Gus? Dammit.

'Hi,' he said and smiled until his eyes disappeared. Smiling back was a real pleasure.

'Hi,' she replied.

'This feels like a funeral rather than a celebration.' He looked over his shoulder. 'Look at those locusts, will you? If they lick his ass any harder they'll wear their tongues to points.'

'Hey, come on!' she said. 'You were up there with the thick of 'em when I came in. Pots and kettles, isn't it?'

'Ah, hell,' he said. 'I didn't think you'd notice. Care for some white wine? It's actually chilled tonight, or it was when

I got here. It's probably pretty warm by now, but it's not too bad. The old boy's really pushed the boat out.'

He was right. The drink he brought her from the long table in the far corner was cold and tasted good. She relaxed as she drank and happily let him fetch her another, sopping it up with a handful of potato crisps taken from one of the tables. Even they were better than they usually were at these events. Zack's right, she thought. Old Hunnisett really is making an effort. I wonder who will get his job? And will it make a lot of difference to us at Old East? How much will it matter to the researchers? It was somehow important to her that Zack should be safe in his little niche in the offices and little labs of the Institute, which had been carved out of the old medical school building for them; it was none of her concern, of course, but it would be a pity to lose the edge Old East got from having its own research set-up. And she smiled at Zack as she took her drink from him and blinked a little owlishly round the room over the rim of the glass. Yes, it would be a pity.

Hattie moved into her line of sight and she lifted her chin at her cheerfully. After a moment's hesitation Hattie came over to join them. 'I saw you a while back,' she said. 'When I got here. But I didn't want to intrude.' She looked with limpid eyes at George and dared her to say a word.

'It's no intrusion!' Zack said. 'Good to talk to you at any time, Hattie.' He grinned at her too and as she grinned back George felt a stab of – what? Irritation was too strong a word, and yet . . .

'Why should you be intruding?' she said lightly. 'This is the old man's farewell bash, not a private party.'

'Oh, I don't know,' Hattie said, peering up at them with bright eyes. 'You both looked so absorbed in what you were talking about.'

'Probably,' Zack said. 'I've been told I'm at risk of turning into a real nerdish bore because work is all I ever talk about. Right, George?' This time he grinned at George, which made her feel better. They hadn't even mentioned his work tonight, hadn't talked about anything much, but it pleased her that he should speak so; it felt like a defence. Then she drew her brows together for a brief moment. Why on earth should she feel she needed any defence against Hattie, her old friend? This wine must be going to my head, she thought. I'm thinking rubbish.

There was a little flurry at the far end of the room which was now quite crowded as more and more of the staff arrived. Surgeons congregated with surgeons as usual; George could see Keith Le Queux and Robert Gray, the gynaecologist, with their heads together as Kate Sayers, like Le Queux from the Renal Unit, and Peter Selby, an ENT man, talked earnestly to them over Gerald Mayer-France's shoulder, while in another cluster the physicians huddled in exactly the same sort of way. Agnew Byford from Cardiology was standing next to Barbara Rosen, the psychiatrist, as Maurice Carvalho, the diabetologist, talked confidentially into his left ear. Only Neville Carr, the oncologist, stood aloof from his colleagues, though he had found congenial company; standing with an air of eager subservience at his side was one of the young men from Radiology, the senior radiologist, George seemed to remember, and she was amused. The only person no one at Old East gossiped about was Neville Carr. Not any more, not since he'd come out and told everyone in the sunniest manner possible that he was gay, had been gay all his professional life and was damned if he was going to apologize for it any longer.

The only people who weren't talking to each other were the anaesthetists, who had distributed themselves amongst other groups. There was David Denton, chatting up Margaret Cotton, the Head of Finance, and Heather Dannay, the Head of Anaesthetics, scowling into her glass and clearly hating everyone around her, and the most recently joined of the Gasman Team (as they were commonly known), James Corton, leaning against the wall in a brown study, clearly anywhere but here. George felt sorry for him, he looked so lonely; and she had a sudden memory of her own first days at Old East. It wasn't the most welcoming of places to new-comers, and she would, she decided, make an effort to talk to him some time.

Someone tapped a microphone in the maddening manner that microphones seem to force on certain types and there was a booming 'testing, testing, can you hear me?' followed by a cough that made several people with acute hearing wince. Professor Hunnisett looked expectantly at the corner of the room where the microphone was and slowly the chatter died away.

'It's good to see so many of you here tonight!' Matthew Herne, the Hospital Chief Executive Officer, was looking ex-ceedingly dapper, George decided, in a fine houndstooth suit which had the silky sheen that spoke of expensive cloth. I wish he were more thoughtful, though, she thought, looking sideways at some of the other younger men in the room, the registrars and the lesser lights of the administrative staff. He makes them all look so shabby when he dresses so well.

'Very good of you to turn out when I know how busy we all are. We're running at over ninety per cent capacity at the moment, I have to tell you. Pray there isn't a major push on A & E, or we'll find ourselves in the papers again!'

A faint rustle moved round the room, not quite a sigh, not quite a laugh. They'd read the attacks on them in the local paper, and indeed in several of the nationals as well. The NHS was a choice political football at the moment and Old East in particular got more than its share of the kicks. All they needed was one more patient forced to spend the night on a trolley for want of an available bed in a ward and all hell would be let loose. The threat of closure always hung over them, they felt, even though the Department of Health had promised them they were safe. But then the Department had promised all sorts of things to all sorts of hospitals that somehow never quite happened.

'And of course, we have had some unfortunate publicity over the sad – um – loss of three of our staff. *Not* all suicides, of course, though the papers tried to suggest so, using unfounded surmise as a stick with which to beat us.' Herne scowled slightly, as though he were mentally castigating Mendez and Lally Lamark for having the temerity to die accidentally, let alone Pam Frean for actually killing herself. That he disapproved of all three of them rather than pitying them was very clear. 'But we will no doubt weather this little storm as we have weathered greater ones. Yes. Hrrmph.' He coughed, rearranged his facial expression to one he clearly regarded as suitable for what he had to say, and went on.

'Now, tonight we have bad news and good news. The bad news you all know. We're losing our esteemed and trusted colleague and long time medical guru, Professor Hunnisett.' He turned towards the old man and made applause gestures and obediently everyone joined in. 'We wish him a long and happy retirement and fruition of all his plans for the future. You'll hear more about that in a moment. Right now, with the good news that will help cushion us against the loss of Professor Hunnisett, here's our Chairman, Sir Jonathan Spry. Sir Jonathan, let me just move the microphone down a little for you.'

Sir Jonathan, who was a little tetchy about the fact that Matthew was at least five inches taller than he was, smiled in a wintry fashion and firmly took the microphone stand from Matthew's hand and made it his own. For the next half-hour.

What he had to say did matter. He had to announce that Professor Hunnisett was retiring in one sense, but not in another; he would still be part of the Research Institute he had founded. That much he managed to make clear fairly quickly. The rest of his news was less easy to comprehend. But when he'd finished and there was a spatter of applause and the presentations of engraved silver salvers ('Who uses things like that these days?' hissed Hattie into George's ear in disgust),

24

George leaned towards Zack and murmured, 'I need a précis. I'm not sure I got hold of all that.'

'It's not as splendid as he tries to make out.' Zack sounded unusually serious. Generally he was a relaxed and cheerful individual, but now he looked enclosed and tight and George looked at him curiously.

'As I understand it, the Research Institute is to go on working while they look for a new chap to take over from the Professor?'

'Yeah,' Zack said. 'That's what it sounds like, but the fact is unless we can get more money in on all our individual projects, no one worthwhile will want to come. He implied all that without saying it. We have to get more projects in place to make the job a really interesting one for a high-flyer. It's a bastard.'

'What happens if you don't get more money in?'

He grimaced. 'End of Institute, I suppose.'

She was horrified. 'Hunnisett would surely never let that happen?'

Zack looked at her and shook his head. 'He's not the man he was. Tired, to tell the truth. That's why he's announced his retirement. He could have gone on for a couple of years more if he'd pushed for it. But he's – well, he's a weary old man now. We'll just have to fend for ourselves, I guess.'

He seemed to realize that he was saying more than he meant to and smiled at her, and was at once his usual comfortable self. 'But no need to worry. I have a few irons in the fire to get my money in. Here's hoping the others do. Some of 'em need a hell of a lot of capital.'

'Don't you?'

'Uh-huh. But I've got every chance of getting it. I told you, irons in the fire. Nothing like a cheerful cliché to make a point, hmm? Look, let's get out of here and go for a drink somewhere, what do you say? This wine's warmed up now and it's getting very stuffy.'

She hesitated. Hattie had drifted away from them now and

they couldn't be overheard. She could easily accept and go out with him and no one would know, so there would be no gossip. But, dammit, this wasn't a date he was asking for, just a drink. So she smiled at him and nodded.

'Let me do a quick whirl round the room and talk to the Prof.,' she said. 'And have a word with my own staff who turned out, then I'll be ready. Give me – what, twenty minutes? Will that be OK?'

He looked at his watch. 'You can have nineteen,' he said.

She bowed her head ironically. 'Nineteen it is. See you by the main door?'

'The main door it is.' He laughed and she knew he was thinking just what she had: if they left the room together there might possibly be talk. It would be much safer to bump into each other accidentally downstairs on the way out.

She went round the room as fast as she could, nodding at people and stopping for a few moments to ask after Kate Sayers's brood of babies and to talk to Barbara Rosen, the crumpled and always rather grubby-looking psychiatrist for whom she had a particular affection; then she looked round for her own staff before making her final sortie towards the Professor and her way out.

She saw Jerry and Alan Short talking in a corner and made her way through the chattering hubbub towards them. Jerry greeted her cheerfully. 'What ho, Dr B.! Not poisoned by the vol-au-vents yet? I ought to run a salmonella check on them, only I don't dare. We'd have to close the whole hospital down if we really knew how much death and disease lurked in 'em. Have you tasted one? I have and I'm not long for this life, I swear to you.'

'More fool you for risking it,' she said. She tried not to frown as she asked, 'Where is everyone else?'

Alan went scarlet. 'Um, Jane wasn't feeling too good,' he muttered. 'I told her I'd make her apologies.'

'Oh, that's all right,' George said quickly. 'I didn't mean her. It was Sheila I wondered about. She left the lab early

26

especially to go home and change. Which shouldn't have been necessary if she'd remembered to dress suitably this morning.' Her current irritation with Sheila, who was indeed being more than usually captious, spilled over into her voice to sharpen it.

Jerry all unwittingly fed the flames. 'Oh, she always has to go home to change for these shindigs. You never know *who* you might meet,' he said, in a fair imitation of Sheila's rather high voice and pinched would-be upper-class accent.

'Yeah, no doubt,' George snapped. 'All the same, she should be here. I told her I expected all the senior people to turn out. It doesn't look good if the most senior technician cuts the Prof.'s farewell do.'

'She definitely said she was coming.' Jerry now realized he'd put his foot in it and rushed to Sheila's defence, though normally they sparred like a pair of bad-tempered puppies trapped in the same basket. 'She knew it was a three-line whip, because I told her as well as you. Anyway it's not like her to miss a party. She actually likes the vol-au-vents.'

'I'll talk to her tomorrow.' George set her jaw. 'I can't have – Well, thanks for coming, you two. And tell Jane it's all right, Alan, I do understand. Throwing up, is she?' Alan went even redder, if that were possible, and started to stammer. She patted his shoulder affectionately. 'It's all right, Alan. We all know, you know. This is a hospital, remember. No secrets here.'

Indeed, however hard the couple tried to hide the fact that Jane was in the very early stages of a pregnancy, everyone in the department knew about it, and were making snide comments about the speed with which the pair were launching themselves into parenthood. 'Give her lots of glucose and a hint of salt and she'll feel better,' George said.

She said her goodbyes to Professor Hunnisett, who assured her that he would indeed see her again since this was just a retirement from active clinical practice they were celebrating rather than a total eclipse of all his medical activities.

'The work of the Institute of course often involves your special contribution,' he said and beamed in a way that she found quite nauseous. Clearly the old boy was hoping to get cut-price work out of the department. Well, he'd have to deal with Ellen Archer, the Business Manager for the lab, not herself; she smiled sweetly at him and said, 'Of course,' before escaping downstairs to meet Zack Zacharius.

As she went she was planning exactly what she'd have to say to Sheila next morning for her defection of duty tonight. Really, she thought furiously, goddamn Sheila. She's getting too big for her boots altogether. She just took an early evening off and ignored what I told her about tonight. I really must do something about her.

3

Zack wasn't at the main door when she reached it, and she felt a stab of disappointment. He had tired of waiting for her, she told herself; after all, she'd taken rather longer to escape from the party than she had meant to. But all the same, he could have waited a little longer.

Oh well, she thought, and pulled her silk jacket a little closer. The weather was unseasonably cool for June and she regretted not wearing something warmer than the red silk. The sooner she got home and into a thick tracksuit in which she could spend her evening curled up on her sofa watching TV, the better. And again she felt a stab of disappointment, but this time because of Gus.

She'd done all she could to help him get his promotion to Superintendent, and when he'd got the job he most wanted, which was heading the Area Major Incident Team which covered the territory that included Ratcliffe Street nick, she had celebrated with him with enormous glee. But then she'd told him to get the job sorted first and himself well settled before they returned to the suggestion that had been made, in the heat of the investigation that had led to his getting the job, that they should be married. She had felt suddenly unsure of taking so massive a step, afraid of upsetting the status quo in which they were so comfortable. Well, comfortable most of the time.

And now look at what had happened. The job was an onerous one and very absorbing. He loved it, and she was delighted for him, but she saw even less of him than she had during the bad times just before he left the rank of Detective Chief Inspector behind him, all during that awful summer when she had been so frightened for him and he'd been under a cloud. Now the only thing he was under was the warm sun of police approbation. There didn't seem to be a committee on which he didn't sit or a job of any importance that the powers-that-be didn't want him for. And he, damn his eyes, accepted all the invitations with enthusiasm because, 'Well, it's the job, darlin', ain't it? You wouldn't want to hold me back, would you?'

And because she didn't, there she was with more and more evenings to spend sitting watching TV on her own and more and more time to notice the attractions of other men. Gus was the man she wanted, but he wasn't there; and talking – even flirting – with other men could help fill the gap. But would that be wise? Remembering how Gus had reacted once before when he had thought her interested in someone else, she doubted it.

Not that she, as a modern woman, gave a damn about such displays of male jealousy. If she wanted to be interested in other men, she damn well would be. But the trouble was, her real interest was Gus. So, there she was: not for a moment wanting to hurt Gus's career by clinging to him, but missing his company. Not being naturally self-sacrificing, but behaving so. It was a bitch of a situation to be in.

She began to walk towards the car park on the far side of the courtyard, stepping out sharply to warm herself against the cool breeze, as she made herself pay more attention to her surroundings than to her own thoughts. There must be some sort of panic on somewhere, she thought. There was the penetrating wail of ambulance sirens, not an unfamiliar sound here but particularly urgent tonight, it seemed, and one or two people were running across the courtyard. Without intending to, she quickened her own steps until she too was almost running. Maybe there *was* a panic and extra pairs of medical hands would be needed? It did happen occasionally, and she lifted her chin as she ran, trying to hear more.

But all there was in addition to the continuing siren squeals was a drift of shouting voices that became a little louder as she reached the way out of the courtyard, between the pharmacy and her own path. lab, and she hurried through hard on the heels of a little flutter of nurses who were running too, their blue check skirts flying over black tighted legs. She managed to catch up with them as they reached the far side of the corridor and the double doors that led to the nurses' and doctors' residences and the car park beyond.

'What's happened?' George panted. One of the nurses looked back over her shoulder and George recognized her as one of the senior staff nurses from A & E and was grateful. It was always easier to get sense out of people she knew.

'No idea,' the nurse called back. 'Someone said a car had got into trouble in the car park and I want to see if mine's OK.' Then she and the others ran on with George, coming up behind them, now very alert on her own behalf.

There had been a couple of robberies in the hospital in the past few weeks; nothing new for so large and accessible a site encircled by a series of main roads. The half-dozen or so points on the periphery at which people could get into and out of the hospital were impossible to police without very expensive security staff which the Trust couldn't afford, so the management felt themselves to be in ceaseless battle with the forces of wrong-doing, regarding themselves as serving a community made up entirely of thieves and muggers. Not true, of course, but they undoubtedly had more problems with petty and sometimes grand larceny than most establishments had suffered. Twice cars in the car park had been robbed of their wheels in full daylight, and several had been broken into and had radios and stereo systems removed. Now most people had fitted their vehicles with alarms, including

George. But all the same she ran to see if her own beloved if battered and elderly Citroën had been tampered with.

The sirens had ceased at last, but the sound of shouting voices was even louder as she came round the corner into the crowded car park. Then she stopped short in horror.

It was a small area for such a large staff and every corner of it had been marked out to take as many cars as possible. Getting in and out took a great deal of driving skill and tonight the place was even more tightly packed than usual. And on the far side, about halfway along, there were, George could see, flames leaping. Very close to the place where she had parked her own car.

She found her muscles operating again, as she ran even faster now, along the sides and round the edges. It was impossible to get between the cars and go straight across; some of them left hardly any space for drivers to get in and out when their doors were open, so the long way round was the swiftest.

To her shame her first reaction when she got to the site of the flames was relief. There, beyond the little cluster of firemen who were directing the jets of creamy foam over the affected vehicle, she could see her own car just where she had left it, a couple of spaces up from the affected one. And she bit her lip at the shabby flood of gratitude that it was someone else's property which was in trouble, not her own. She moved forwards quickly, as though she could leave the shabbiness behind, pushing her way to the front of the little crowd that had collected.

'What –' she began and again stopped. There, lying on the ground, was a figure with people leaning over it, and she became aware of an ambulance trolley sitting alongside the little group and the ambulance itself at the entrance to the car park, alongside the fire engine from which the foam hoses snaked their way.

'It just caught fire,' someone said. She turned and looked and it was Zack.

'I came to get my car,' he said. 'I thought I'd drive round the outside to the front and pick you up in the street. I saw it all.'

'Who is it?' George asked, as the cluster of bodies around the supine figure shifted and rearranged itself. 'Is it any one I –'

'Sheila Keen,' said a voice on her other side, and she whirled to look. It was the staff nurse from A & E. 'I just found out. It seems she was –'

But George didn't wait to hear. She pushed her way through the ambulance staff, calling loudly above the hubbub, 'Let me through. I'm Dr Barnabas. This is one of my staff. Let me through, will you?'

The crowd shivered and parted and she stopped beside the trolley as the paramedic in charge strapped the blankets in place. They'd already set up an emergency IV line and had wrapped Sheila in a foil cover. There were nylon tubes feeding into her nostrils and she looked ghastly, with a deep pallor and smudged shadows in her cheeks. But her eyes were open and she managed to blink up at George.

'Missed,' she said. Her voice was thick and clearly painful to use. 'Didn't mean to –' She began to cough and the paramedic glowered at George, putting a hand on Sheila's shoulder and saying, 'Slowly now, love. Just breathe slow and easy. No talking. Your throat's been damaged. No talking.' He looked up at George again. 'Sorry, doc, but we've got to get her round to A & E soon as poss. I reckon she's OK but there's a bit of damage what needs looking at.' And then he was gone as they wheeled Sheila away and loaded her stretcher into the back of the ambulance.

The firemen had stopped using their jets now, for the flames had gone. Where there had been a car there was a snowdrift of foam which had spattered the surrounding cars liberally, but nothing of the affected vehicle could be seen at all.

'What happened?' George was stricken with remorse.

There she'd been complaining bitterly about Sheila's absence from the Professor's party and all the time she had been in some sort of trouble here. It was a shameful thing and she needed time to come to terms with it. While she was asking questions she gave herself room to find that time.

One of the firemen looked at her and grimaced. 'A nasty one.' He said. 'Electrics fire, I reckon. You could smell it as soon as we got here. Great plumes of smoke coming out of the car and the driver struggling to get out.' He shook his head. 'It wasn't easy, poor thing. I mean, look at the amount of space there is there to open her door. Bugger all! This place is lethal, you know. And in a hospital an' all! Shouldn't be allowed. You could have had the fire spread – the whole lot could have gone up, and with all these petrol tanks it doesn't bear thinking what might have happened to the rest of the hospital!'

'I can imagine,' George said grimly. 'But what *happened*? Cars don't just catch fire like that, do they? There has to be a reason.'

The fireman shrugged. 'Electrics, most probably, like I said. They can short for all sorts of reasons. You won't know why this one did till someone's had a look and even then, p'raps not. You'll need an expert. The state the car's in under that, it won't have much to offer.'

'What's happened to Sheila?' George turned to Zack who was still standing beside her, though most of the other watchers had drifted away by now, reassured that their own cars were safe. 'Was she burned?'

It was the fireman who answered, a little reprovingly, clearly feeling he was the one to be consulted first. 'I was telling you, madam –'

'Doctor,' Zack said, hearing the fireman's tone. The fireman flicked a glance at him and then at George and relaxed.

'Well, yes, doctor. The thing is, when the electrics go, the first thing you get is this awful smell. Really acrid and thick. And it gets worse if the damage is affecting all the car's wiring. It sends out choking smoke after a while. Now, that's bad enough – does nasty things to the throat and lungs – but the worst bit is that the whole thing can go up. Like this one did.'

He looked mournfully at the snowy heap, which was now drooping sluggishly and looking less pristine than it had.

'If the driver's got time to get out, well, that looks good. Just a bit of breathing damage done. That's what happened here. She got out, and she's got her skinniness to thank for that, I can tell you. Some of us wouldn't have managed it' – he looked briefly at Zack – 'but she did. And rolled away just in time. Someone saw what was happening and called us. Don't know who. We got here just as the flames went up. So we pulled her away and did the necessary. Hope she'll be OK.'

'I'm sure she will,' Zack said. 'As long as she isn't burned, and I don't think she was. It'll just be the fumes. She'll be back on her feet in no time.' And he closed one hand warmly around George's elbow and pulled her back out of the way as the fireman nodded and moved off with his equipment.

'She might have been killed,' George said blankly.

'But she wasn't,' Zack pointed out as though they were speaking of the weather or something equally banal. 'So that's all right.'

'Why should a car's electrics go up like that?' she demanded, standing still even though she knew from the pressure on her elbow that he was trying to lead her away. 'I don't know much about cars – not as much as I should, I suppose. I've never had a case killed in an incident like this, and I thought I'd seen most sorts of violent deaths.'

'Lots of reasons,' he said. 'Too much pressure on the system, so it's overloaded – you know, CD players and stereos and all that. Neglect, or damage or –'

'Neglect? Sheila's car? Never. She loved it like a mother. You'd have thought it was a sentient being, the way she fussed over it. I just don't understand it.'

'Well, the garage will no doubt sort it out when they get it in,' he said soothingly. 'Look, you've had a shock. Come and have a drink as we planned and then we can –'

She shook her head. 'It's kind of you, Zack, but I have to go over to A & E and see how she is. It's such a – it's bizarre! I can't imagine such a thing happening to Sheila, of all people.'

'Accidents can happen to any motorist,' he said, and again she shook her head sharply.

'Not to Sheila. She's been driving for years and never had so much as a scratch, I swear. I told you, she was fanatical about this car. And now look at it. A write-off, isn't it?' George shook her head as she turned and stared at the now fast collapsing heap of foam. 'It's dreadful.'

'I can understand why you're upset –' he began and she felt her face redden.

'You think I'm going over the top, don't you? But I'm not. She's a member of my staff and I feel bad about her.'

'Is she a favourite member of staff?' he said shrewdly. 'Or the opposite?'

She went even pinker. 'That,' she said, 'is beside the point. She's a member of my team and I care about all of them.'

'I'm sure you do.' She had a suspicion he was a little amused now and felt an even higher tide of embarrassment. He was right, of course. She wouldn't feel nearly as bad over this if she hadn't been so annoyed with Sheila before it happened. The doctor part of her mind told her that her technician was probably fine. She'd have a bit of hoarseness and breathing trouble for a few hours perhaps, but she'd escaped a much worse set of injuries. George had no need to be so uptight about her. But she was.

Could this be a fourth incident that would get Old East's gossips going even more? she found herself thinking, and then was irritated. That was the sort of conjecture that Sheila herself would make and use as the basis for a great edifice of talk and surmise projected as almost fact. George was damned if she was going to allow herself down that path, and she tightened her jaw. 'Well, anyway, I'm going to go and see her,' she said firmly. 'Thanks for the invitation but –'

'Oh, I'll come with you.' He linked an arm in hers. 'It's a pleasure to know someone who cares so much about the people she works with. Too many of them here are so stiff about the upper lip they don't open their mouths for fear their lips'll break off. They don't know what it means to be emotionally involved with anyone but their dogs. Come on. We'll see how she is.'

He made a determined move back towards the courtyard and George had to fall in step beside him. She was beginning to feel better. Sheila was, after all, likely to be perfectly all right, as Zack had said. She had been overreacting somewhat, and couldn't deny it. Now she deliberately relaxed her shoulders, took a hard deep breath and then coughed. The smell was awful, acrid and ugly in her mouth.

'It is nasty, isn't it?' He was sympathetic. 'It happened to me once. I had this old Morgan, lovely car, wood frame, the lot. I was fixing it, back in the days when I wasn't as experienced as I might have been, and the wiring went, just like that. I managed to stop the fire starting, fortunately, but it was a close-run thing. Wait till we get into the middle of the courtyard and then try a good splutter. It'll help.'

She obeyed, standing still and coughing hard and feeling the mucus collect in her throat. After a while she nodded at him gratefully and began to walk again. But this time she kept far enough away from him to stop his holding her elbow. Enough was enough.

And no matter what he said, she decided, she wouldn't go for a drink tonight. After she'd seen Sheila and reassured herself that all was basically well, she'd bid him goodnight, pick up the Citroën from that wretched car park and go home. And tomorrow, first thing, she'd send a very strong memo to Matthew Herne about the car parking arrangements, pointing out the danger. She felt better at the thought. She'd enjoy doing that.

4

It was just as well that the path. lab was busy the following morning for, inevitably, when everyone first arrived they stood around in groups talking about Sheila Keen's mishap in slightly hushed tones. Even Jerry managed not to make too many jokes about it, apart from the obvious one about always knowing Sheila was hot stuff but this was ridiculous. However, they soon scattered to their work-benches when George came and chivvied them.

'Sheila's fine this morning,' she reported. 'On Ballantyne Ward, and they're treating her like royalty. And as Peter Selby's looking after her himself, she's in very good hands.'

'Ah!' Jerry said. 'Then she *will* be happy. She's always wanted him to tickle her tonsils.' And he grinned at Peter Claff's shocked expression. 'It's all right, Peter. She only meant what she said. He's the senior ENT chap you see, the *ENT* chap.'

'I know perfectly well what you meant,' Peter said. 'And as usual it was disgusting. Dr B., what's her prognosis? Has there been any permanent damage, do you know?' He looked at George owlishly and she felt a momentary urge to snap at him to stop being quite so stuffed a shirt. But he always had been and always would be, so she contented herself with a crisp nod.

'Not quite yet, but Peter Selby seems to think she'll be fine in a couple of days. That means she'll be off for at least a week, if not longer, and we have a lot of work to do. Jerry, you take on Sheila's stuff as well as your own, will you? And Peter, you take over some of Jerry's histology to even the load. As for the cardiac stuff, well, Alan can do that when he gets back this afternoon – he's in court this morning with that dosser they found under Tower Bridge. Now, let's go through what else there is . . .'

Quickly she set about reorganizing everyone's workloads and to do them all credit they accepted the burden without a murmur, though they were usually very swift to complain if they felt they were being put upon in any way, which left her to deal with her own paperwork as well as some of the stuff Sheila usually handled, before going down to the mortuary to do a post-mortem on a traffic accident victim who had been brought in overnight. Danny Roscoe, her mortuary assistant, would do all the necessary preliminaries, so the job needn't take too long.

But it was difficult to concentrate and after a while she put down her pen and leaned back in her chair, trying to sort out her thinking. Last night, when she'd reached A & E, she'd found Sheila holding court in her cubicle, clearly rather enjoying her status as heroine of a Dramatic Event, and talking far more than she should, George suspected, for the pleasure of hearing her own voice, which was undoubtedly sounding somewhat sexy because of its new huskiness. Sheila was getting increasingly desperate to retain what she regarded as her allure as she reached middle age still unattached. Her ever-more urgent search for a husband was something everyone in the hospital knew and joked about. An episode like this was one she would milk of all possible value for as long as possible. George foresaw some weeks of disruption in her department in consequence, and was ashamed of herself for even thinking about it in the face of Sheila's undoubted misfortune. The fact that Sheila herself was less than warm in her reception of her boss didn't help.

She was all charm to Zack, who came to stand on one side of her trolley while George went to the other, but was decidedly distant with George herself. She responded to any attempt by George to be cheerful by looking lugubrious and producing another painful cough, but when Zack said something lighthearted she flashed him a vivid smile. Clearly, George had told herself grimly as she left A & E, Sheila was going to punish her for being so irritable with her last week. Good technician though Sheila was, there were times when George heartily wished her anywhere but at Old East. As she had told Sheila bluntly when they had their fight last week. Was that why she was being so hateful now? Or could it be that she in some way blamed George for what had happened to her car?

George had stopped short in the middle of the department. What was it Sheila had said to Zack, carefully not looking at George when she said it? 'It's strange the way things happen,' she'd murmured, peeping up at Zack beneath her lashes. 'One week someone wishes horrible things will happen to shut you up, and the next week, there you go! Just like having your fortune told. Do you read your stars, Dr Zacharius? I always do.'

No, George thought, moving again as a patient in a hurry almost careered into her. I'm being paranoid. Sheila was using one of her chat-up techniques. Even when she's flat on her back on a trolley, she's on a manhunt.

She'd already said goodnight firmly to Zack when they'd taken Sheila out of A & E and off to the ward, bearing assurances from George that she'd come to see her on her way into the lab in the morning (to which Sheila responded with a wintry little smile aimed at the gallery) and then had turned to go.

'No drink?' Zack had said. 'By now I was thinking a little supper too mightn't be a bad idea. There's something I'd like to talk to you about, and it would be easier with elbows on a shared table. There's a great fish-and-chip place not too far away that does the best fillet of sole I've ever had.'

George, smarting after Sheila's reception of her, might have wavered, but had immediately stiffened at that. She knew perfectly well which fish-and-chip restaurant he meant: Gus's star establishment, where the engraved glass windows and the silver on the tables glittered and the fish was the most succulent and the chips the most crisp and golden you'd get anywhere in London – where could it be except in one of Gus's restaurants? He owned eleven now and they showed no signs of losing their charm for their multitude of customers.

But she couldn't be seen in one of them tonight. Interested though she was in what Zack wanted to talk about (her native curiosity, always one of her most developed features, had twitched with delicious anticipation at his words) his suggestion of that particular restaurant had reminded her that there was still the possibility that Gus might get home at a reasonable time. She doubted it, but . . . Well, she wouldn't eat at the restaurant, all the same. Not with Zack, at any rate.

'I'm going home, Zack,' she said. 'It's been a bit of an evening one way and another and I'm bushed. See you tomorrow, maybe? And thanks for your help with Sheila.'

'I did nothing,' he said, making no attempt to argue with her. 'I was just there at the time. OK, George. I'll tell you what I wanted to discuss with you some other time. If it's not too late.' He smiled as the shadow of frustrated inquisitiveness passed over her face. 'Goodnight, then.' And to her surprise he leaned over and kissed her cheek briefly.

The fact that she had found it rather agreeable made her thoughtful all the way home, as did her itching to know what on earth he might wish to discuss with her; and when she arrived and found that contrary to her expectations Gus was there, she was even more thoughtful.

He was in the kitchen twiddling with various dishes – as usual he had out nearly every pan she possessed – and

41

happily slicing garlic and ginger into a balsamic marinade. It smelled wonderful and she stood at the kitchen door watching him silently for a moment or two till he looked up and saw her.

'Hi there, dollychops! How's this for a bit of a treat?' he cried and then bent his head to his slicing again. 'This concoction is going to be stuffed inside that luscious bit o' sea bass you see over there looking sorry for himself on the draining board, and then he'll be baked in the oven and we'll have him with a pan of rosti and some wilted rocket and spinach salad on the side. Who needs fancy chefs when they've got me, eh, darlin'?'

She found her voice. 'That fish looks more furious with you than sorry for itself,' she said, for indeed the fish did have an evil glitter in its full round eyes, as well as on its silvery sides. 'I didn't expect you tonight. You didn't say –'

'Surprise, surprise.' He finished the chopping and wiped his hands on the tea towel he had tucked into his belt, showing great satisfaction at his handiwork. 'Give this half an hour, no more, and you will eat a dinner fit for a pathologist.' He looked at her now and his forehead creased. 'Well, you don't have to look so fed up! I thought you'd be tickled I managed to get away so early! I picked up the fish on the way home. I thought I'd have it all ready when you got here and we'd have a lovely greedy sexy evening. And look at you! Face like you've lost a half-crown and found a tanner.' Then his voice changed. 'What's up, love?'

It always infuriated her when she wept. It didn't happen often and every time it did it was unexpected. Now the tears trickled down her cheeks and as she sniffed lusciously he came trotting across the kitchen to take her face between his garlicky hands.

'Hey, doll, what is it? What happened? A nasty bod got to you? Or has someone been coming the old acid? Just you point me at him and I'll break his arm off and bash him with the soggy end. Tell old Gus all about it.'

She shook her head, swallowed and pulled back. 'Your hands stink,' she managed huskily. She sniffed again and drew the back of her hand across her nose. He lifted his hands to his own nose, sniffed hard and shook his head. 'Smells lovely to me. What is it, love? Don't go changing the subject now. What happened?'

She told him about Sheila and he listened, concentrating entirely on what she was saying, then put his arms round her and held her closely, crooning into her ear. There was no joking now.

'It's all right, dollychops. These things happen. You've got a nasty case of the might-have-beens. It's harder to cope with sometimes than the really-did-happens. Sheila'll be all right as long as she got out before she was burned, and you say she did. She got a nasty fright and a throat full of muck, I dare say, but no worse than that. It does you credit to be so upset over her, but honestly, she'll be all right.'

George let herself weep on. It was luxurious to do so, and it saved her having to come up with anything logical to say. She knew why she was weeping: it was indeed stress over the might-have-beens; she might have been having a drink and supper with Zack Zacharius in Gus's own restaurant, while he sat here forlornly with his sea bass and lovingly prepared marinade and chilled wine, wondering what sort of emergency had pinned her down at the hospital. He wouldn't have doubted for a moment that that was where she was; would never have dreamed she was cavorting with someone else, but she would have been. She wept on, feeling almost as though she had actually done it.

After a little while though, Gus had taken the tea towel from his belt and begun to dry her face with it. She had grimaced. It smelled even more of garlic and ginger than he did, and she spluttered at him, 'Stop! I'll smell like the fish all day tomorrow if you go on anointing me with that!'

He laughed. 'Better than smelling of the job the way you sometimes do,' he said comfortably.

Her tears stopped at once and she reared back and stared at him. 'Gus! Are you saying I smell of the mortuary?'

He looked considering. 'I've known you to.'

'Oh, no! I shower and wash my hair and scrub and –'

'Oh, I mean before you've done that,' he said, and grinned. 'There were times I've been there stinking too. It's a horrible job, 'n't it? Garlic's much nicer.'

'I hate you,' George said, rubbing at her face with both hands. 'I'm going to shower now. You get on with your fish, and for pity's sake, wash your hands.'

He did both and by the time she came out of the shower, glowing with the hard scrub she'd given herself with half a tub of the most expensive exfoliating cream she had, her hair doubly shampooed and tied up elegantly in a deep blue silk scarf that matched her housecoat, dinner was ready, spread on the little table which he'd brought into the living room out of the squalor that was now the kitchen.

'Don't worry, I'll clear up afterwards. Not a dish shall you wash tonight,' he said. 'I'm going to spoil you.'

He was as good as his word. The dinner was perfect, ending with a *crème brûlée* that first he swore he'd made himself and then admitted he'd brought from one of the restaurants he'd inherited from his father, and which he still ran in tandem with his police job, with great skill and considerable financial flair. ('And don't it taste unbeliev-ably home-made? I tell you, we're the best restaurants in the whole bleedin' East End!') Afterwards he cleaned up, whistling tunelessly through his teeth throughout, the way he did when he was particularly contented, leaving her stretched on the sofa in a pleasant post-prandial doze, re-fusing to think about Sheila, or her confusion over Zack. All was well. Gus was home and what more could she want?

Now, sitting at her desk in the path. lab office, leaning back with her hands linked behind her head, her lips curved a little reminiscently. When Gus was in the happy mood he had

44

been in last night, lovemaking was something else. And his mood had been particularly happy.

Afterwards, as she half dozed, curled up in the crook of his arm, he had told her why he was so pleased with himself. 'Special new job, sweetheart. You remember Bumble Bee? The all-out effort to prevent burglary? Well, we're doing something similar on our patch to pre-empt some of these buggers who come in with fancy ideas about uniting to make families to run things on the villains' side. They get their ideas from watching cruddy American movies about God-fathers and they've got to be stopped. You remember how it was with the last case.'

She remembered. She'd had to work very hard indeed to sort out the mess he had got himself into and she opened her mouth to say as much. But he rode over her, and she let herself slide back into sleepiness.

'Well, it seems they're trying again. We're getting a bit of a whisper from here and there, so we're going in with all the airy grace of Saddam Hussein with a boil on his bottom to clobber them before they so much as get a packet of paper-clips ready for their first meeting.' He tightened his arm around her. 'I might be out and about a bit more than I usually am. Can you put up with that?'

She had snorted softly, her sleepiness banished suddenly. 'Do I have a choice?'

He was silent for a moment and then said uncomfortably, 'Well, I guess not, doll. But I'll tell you what. I'm going to book us a holiday before I buckle down to all this. Just a week, maybe, in France or Spain? We'll just get in the car, pip through the Tunnel, and then take the route south. How about that? Would you like a bit of French nosh and scenery?'

'Before you start the new project?' George said, rousing herself. 'But I'm not sure I can get the time off that easily.'

'Well, tell 'em you've got to. You haven't had a holiday for ages.'

'That's true, but –'

'So it's high time. Tell 'em we're off – oh – next week.' He began to sing growlingly into her ear an old-fashioned version of 'The Vagabond's Song', which burbled about 'bed in the bush with stars to see, bread I dip in the river – there's the life for a man like me, there's the life for e-e-e-ever', and she'd fallen asleep to it as to a lullaby.

Now she sighed, straightening in her chair as she tried to concentrate again. Life was just a little more complicated than it ought to be ... She had to think of work and coping somehow until Sheila was back, and dealing with Zack next time she saw him, and ... 'Oh, hell!' she said aloud.

By lunchtime when she'd finished her post-mortem and reported death from natural causes to the coroner's officer, and had showered (scrubbing herself extra hard again with the memory of Gus's teasing in her memory's ears) she'd reassured herself that she was being as silly as Sheila was on one of her worst days. Zack Zacharius had only asked her out to dinner last night out of concern for her distress over Sheila (she refused to think about what he might want to talk about; it was probably something minor and just a ploy to get her to make a date) and there was no more to it than that. All was well; she'd just had a silly set of notions because Gus had been away a lot, but now he was back in his old sweet mode there'd be no more problems. If there had to be lonely nights over the coming weeks she'd manage them well enough. I'll put in for a holiday in two weeks' time, then, she thought as she crossed the courtyard on her way to the canteen and lunch. Then I'll be ready whatever Gus comes up with.

Zack was loitering at the canteen entrance and his face lit up when he saw her, or so she thought. 'Hello! How are you today?' he said. 'Feeling better? How's the invalid?'

'Oh, she's doing fine,' George said. 'I saw her this morning, and Peter Selby too. He says she'll be home in a couple of days. No harm done. You were quite right.'

'That's OK then,' he said with high satisfaction. 'We can

talk about other things.' He tucked his hand into her elbow again, the way he had last night, and she stiffened against it. Last night when she had been distressed had been one thing. Now it was something other.

It felt like panic. It was quite absurd, part of her mind told her, but that made no difference. She pulled her arm away and said quickly, 'Oh dear! I'm so sorry! I can't share lunch with you today, I'm afraid.' She looked over her shoulder and saw the long queue stretching into the canteen, normal at this time of day, and swallowed hard. 'I've – er – I've arranged to eat with Dr – um –' She scrabbled for a name as her glance raked the people in the line and finally seized upon a vaguely familiar face. 'Dr Corton. About anaesthetics, you know. I'm sorry.'

And she went in a rush, her long legs swinging her coat behind her and her thick hair bouncing on the top of her head so that it nearly came apart from the bunch in which she'd pinned it up, to slide in alongside a startled James Corton and say a little breathlessly, 'Do you mind if I jump the queue by joining you? Pretend we had a date to meet, you know? I'm in a mad rush and I'd be so grateful!'

5

To say that James Corton was shy would be like describing Mother Theresa as a tolerably well meaning old woman; the label just wasn't adequate. He gulped at her, managed a sort of convulsive nod and then stepped back to let her slide in front of him. She had to share his tray, since she hadn't picked up one of her own and was certainly not going back to fetch one in case Zack was still there at the other end of the queue (she didn't dare look to see), and she chattered absurdly to Corton as she piled a plate with salad and slapped it on to the tray next to his own plate of sausages and chips. She thought that choice said all that needed to be said about him: he had the schoolboyish look that went with such a diet.

She insisted on paying for both of them, since the girl on the till would, she knew, make very heavy weather of sorting out separate bills for the contents of one tray, and the last thing she wanted was any sort of delay or fuss to draw more attention to them (they had already had a couple of black looks from people who had been pushed back in the queue by her intervention). He tried to protest, but she would have none of it and, still chattering, led him to a table on the far side of the massive canteen space, which had all the ambience of an aircraft hangar with none of the charm, where she sat with her back to the room as though that would make her less noticeable.

Beneath her chatter, she castigated herself. She was behaving foolishly. The trouble was she found Zack interesting, the sort of man who, pre Gus, she would have fancied and made a distinct effort to get to know well. Very well, even.

Pre Gus she had been, and she had known it perfectly well, a woman who was extremely susceptible to masculine beauty. And personality and wit and charm. Frankly, as she had told herself once, long ago, after yet another of her hopeful relationships had foundered, she liked men too much as male creatures rather than as people. She was a goddamn pushover for them. Despite her very real championship of feminist causes and her frequent irritation with male domination of almost everything (well, perhaps not everything, but certainly a hell of a lot) she found male attention irresistible.

And Zack fancied her. Of that she was in no doubt, and it alarmed her. She had been genuinely in love with Gus Hathaway for a long time now, two and a half years. He had spoken of marriage and dammit, they nearly had done the deed. Would have done, had she not backed down. He still intended to marry her, she knew, and she also knew that she intended to marry him – eventually. Yet she could still be attracted to a man who was attracted to her, and it was a damned nuisance, to put it at its very least. A downright shameful one if she was to be as honest as she should be with herself.

She became aware of James Corton's steady gaze on her and broke off. She had been chattering about last night's party and how dull it had been, and she had probably repeated herself several times; now she smiled at him rather ruefully.

'Hell, you must think I'm really crazy,' she said. 'I make a pest of myself pushing in and then talk your ears off. I'm sorry.'

'Oh, not at all, not at all,' he said.

She looked at him with sympathy. He was sweating slightly, a faint mist of dampness glowing across his rather narrow forehead and darkening the roots of his fair hair. He had lashes and brows of the same lightness which gave him a sandy look, but he seemed agreeable enough. About thirty, she hazarded, and still low on the ladder to success in his career.

'So tell me,' she said, making an effort not to look over her shoulder and to stop thinking about her confusion regarding Zack. 'How's life in the Gas Fight And Choke Company?'

'I beg your pardon?' He looked startled.

'Hey, don't tell me I get to explain an English joke to an English person! Someone told me when I first came to work here. There used to be a company in London selling gas and coke and so forth called the Gaslight and Coke Company. Like, sixty years ago or more? And anaesthetists came to be called Gas Fight and Choke people. I thought all anaesthetics people knew that.'

He went a sudden scarlet, the colour leaping across his face so fast that she could see it happen, and the sweating increased; with his rather protuberant greenish eyes, she thought, he looks like a freshly boiled kitten. 'I suppose I'd heard it and forgotten,' he mumbled.

'It doesn't matter,' she said kindly. 'Anyway, it's a very old joke and perhaps it just doesn't mean anything to younger people in the field. So, do you like anaesthetics?'

'Er, well, yes,' he said and she stifled a tinge of irritation. Talking to this chap was like walking over a ploughed field in high-heeled pumps. 'I mean, it's the speciality I've chosen.'

'Ah? Then you're staying in it? I mean, you don't see this as a step on the way to something else?'

'Like what?' He looked genuinely puzzled and she explained patiently.

'The pain people – the consultants who run pain clinics and deal with intractable pain problems as well as terminal pain – aren't they always anaesthetists?'

To her relief he became a little more animated. 'Not all of them. There're neurologists in it as well. And some pharmacologists, of course. There was an interesting paper on the use of sodium channel blockers in the alleviation of chronic pain in one of the journals recently . . .' And he began to talk earnestly about the article, as though, George found herself thinking in some amusement, he'd learned it by heart in order to impress his superiors. He was after all a very junior gasman, which would account for some of his tension as he talked to her. She sometimes forgot how intimidating a junior could find a consultant, even one as relaxed and as easy to talk to as she knew herself to be. It was rare that she stood on her dignity or reminded anyone of her status; but he was new of course and wouldn't really know that.

She went to some pains now to make him more comfortable. She questioned him on the research he was talking about and though he seemed able to do little more than quote the article he'd read back at her, he was clearly interested. So she shifted her tack; got down to talking personalities. Might make him more comfortable, she thought.

'How do you get on with the rest of your firm?' she asked. 'They seem a pleasant crew.' It was a clear invitation to gossip.

He didn't accept it. 'Oh, everyone's very nice,' he said a touch woodenly. 'Most helpful.'

'Good.' She smiled brightly. 'And the surgeons, too? I've heard that Le Queux can be a right bastard in the theatre.' It was what some of her stiffer colleagues would label a 'poor show', she knew, to encourage junior staff to speak slightingly of their seniors, but why shouldn't they? Everyone else did. 'And Mayer-France.'

Corton primmed his lips a little. 'They're fine,' he said, looking down at his plate. He'd eaten very little of his schoolboy lunch, she noted, and bent her own head to eat in order to encourage him. This was really getting to be more than a little effortful, she thought a touch irritably. Damn Zack Zacharius! And knowing that it was unfair to blame him for her present situation didn't make her feel any better.

'I – er – don't work much with the consultants,' Corton

said then, seeming aware of her irritation. 'I mean, Miss Dannay does most of their lists so I hardly know them. I usually look after the registrars' lists and, of course, routine obstetrics. And Dr Zacharius and stuff like that.'

She lifted her head, a forkful of cole-slaw arrested halfway to her mouth. 'Oh?'

He seemed to relax a little at her interest. 'Mmm. They won't let me do the really complicated stuff for a while yet, will they? I'd like to work on cardiological anaesthetics really. It was because of – of my father, who had a cardiac condition, that – well, anyway, he wanted me to go into medicine and anaesthetics seemed – and then of course when he had to have his operation and he died they said it was as much the anaesthetic as the surgery that – so I thought then I'd like to learn cardiac anaesthesia.'

'I'm sorry to hear of your father,' she said after a moment. 'It's often the case that it's a family experience that shapes up your own view of your career.'

She remembered with sudden painful clarity her own mother, oblivious of who she was or why she was and probably even where she was, over there at home three thousand miles away in Buffalo, in the care of her old friend Bridget Connor, and wanted to weep. Her Alzheimer's disease had never made George want to work with the demented, but it certainly made her interested in the condition.

She reached across the table now and touched Corton's hand. 'It's not unusual. I'm sure you'll get there, with such an – example.'

He flashed a smile at her, which made him look even younger, if that were possible. 'Thanks. But it'll take a long time for me to be able to do that. So much to learn.' He slid into silence and she returned to her own plate. After a while she spoke with studied casualness.

'So you do obstetrics and – who else was it, Dr Zacharius? But I thought he was a researcher? How come he works with an anaesthetist?'

'Oh, it's for his experiments.' Corton put down his fork and leaned forward with some eagerness. 'He's looking for a therapy for some of the degenerative neurological conditions you see, like motor-neurone disease and Parkinson's. Even post-traumatic nerve injuries. Paraplegics and so on.'

Again he sounded as though he were quoting and she looked at him consideringly. Had he too found Zack an attractive and powerful personality? Was that the cause of his shyness with her, a need that responded to men rather than women? It would explain a good deal, she thought. It also made her feel rather foolish, the way she had felt at school when she discovered that another girl had a crush on the football hero she had picked out for herself.

'So, what experiments does he do?' She shouldn't be asking that, she thought then. I have to keep Zack at a distance, not make enquiries about his work. But if I don't, how can I talk to him about it when I next see him? But I'm not going to see him again. Am I? 'That use anaesthetics, that is. I'd imagined his research was all linked with drugs.'

'Oh, not at all.' Corton was well away now. 'He's been trying different sorts of implants to the brain, you see. Sometimes he uses drugs, but mostly he uses tissue.' He stopped suddenly and seemed to draw back. 'But you'd better ask him about that. I can't really explain.'

'Too complicated?' she said, not wanting to stop the discussion. This time he seemed to flare up with anger.

'No!' He said it so loudly someone at an adjoining table looked over with vague interest. Corton leaned forward to speak more confidentially. 'Not at all. I understand perfectly well what he's doing. Dr Zacharius said I was a great help to him. That I – I had some useful ideas and insights. It's just that – well, it's *his* research. I shouldn't really be talking about it.' He looked at his watch with a rather exaggerated air of hurry. 'I have to be on my way. I have a list at two-thirty.' He looked rather pleased with himself suddenly. 'Yes, a list.' He caught her gaze and seemed to anticipate the question. 'Only varicose veins, worse luck. Still, they have to be done even if they're not very exciting.' He stood up. 'You won't mind if I go, then? You said you were in a hurry yourself.'

Remembering her lie for the first time she felt her face redden a little. 'Umm,' she said. 'Yes. Must be on my way. Thanks for being so accommodating.'

'Thank you for my lunch,' he said and hesitated. 'And – er –' He seemed to seize up and she raised her brows at him curiously.

'Yes?'

'I just wanted to say that – that I really shouldn't have said anything about Dr Zacharius and what he's doing. I mean, I don't know all about it, and I'm sure he wouldn't like to think I talked about him, you know.'

'It's only about his work,' she said gently, wanting to re-assure him. 'It's not personal or anything important.' But he shook his head vigorously.

'But what can be more important than a person's work? It wouldn't be so bad to talk about him privately, if you see what I mean, but his work . . . that's different.'

She found herself warming to him. 'I guess you're right. There are people in this place who prefer personal gossip over all other kinds – I'm not averse to a bit of it myself. But you're right. Work is too important to gossip over. We all talk too much about others as it is.'

'I'm sure if you ask Dr Zacharius he'll tell you.' He sounded eager now. 'Do ask him.'

'I'll think about it,' she said dryly. 'Enjoy your varicose veins.'

He seemed to perk up. 'Oh, I shall. I always do. Enjoy what I'm doing, I mean. It feels so – so special to be able to do it. Er – so long.'

'So long,' she said and let him go, amused. And then was less amused as she thought of how old he'd made her feel.

She sighed and got to her feet as she drained her tepid coffee to the dregs. She'd make a better cup when she got back to the lab, she promised herself. There was work to be done and she really couldn't waste any more time thinking about her own affairs like this.

She had reached the doorway and was almost through it when Zack caught up with her. 'Sorted out your anaesthetic problem?' he said in her ear. 'Though quite what pathology has to do with the gasmen I'm not quite sure.'

'I'm thinking about doing some work on blood gases,' she snapped, grateful for yet another lie that slid so easily from her lips. It was one of her major gifts, inventing useful fibs in a hurry, and this was one of her better ones. 'Who else should I ask but an anaesthetist?'

He fell into step beside her and she could do nothing to detach herself from him, apart from speeding up her own stride, which she did. He seemed not to notice.

'One of the senior people who know more about what they're doing,' he said, amusement in his tone. 'Like Heather Dannay. Or David Denton. Why that little mouse of a houseman? I have to hold his hand all the time.'

She looked at him briefly. 'He said he worked with you.' She couldn't stop her curiosity from bubbling up. 'How is it *you* need a gasman?'

'I'm trying implants for various forms of neurological damage,' he said. 'Didn't he tell you?'

'He mentioned it.'

'He usually does.' He laughed. 'He seems rather proud of working with me. It makes a change from mucking about with epidurals in obstetrics and those eternal minor ops lists he gets lumbered with.'

'Hmm,' was all she said, and hurried on, but still he had no trouble in keeping up with her.

'Are you trying to avoid me, George?' he said rather plaintively after a moment. 'You go and busy yourself with one of the duller junior doctors on the staff rather than share lunch with me, you're going like the clappers now to get rid of me – why? What have I done? I thought we were friends.'

She opened her mouth to reply, not at all sure what she was going to say. But she didn't have to. They were by now crossing the courtyard, and someone was calling her name loudly from Ward Block B, where the surgical wards, including ENT, were.

Gratefully she turned her head to see Jerry Swann running along the walkway to catch up with her. She had never before been so glad to see him and she greeted him with the widest of smiles.

'Hi, Jerry! What's up? Something urgent in the mortuary?' He shook his head, looking at her portentously. She had never seen him so pregnant with news, she thought. 'What is it, for heaven's sake? You look as though someone pinched your winning lottery ticket!'

He shook his head. 'My dear!' he said dramatically. 'I've just come from seeing Sheila. And the poor creature's been as sick as a dog, chucking up like fury, and Sister there thinks it was something she got from some chocolates that you – that were sent to her from the department. I mean, poisoned chocolates, would you believe!'

6

George didn't know how she reached the ENT Ward. She just found herself sitting there in Sister's office, looking at the box of chocolate liqueurs on the desk, and trying to think clearly. Once she had seen Sheila with her own eyes, she had felt better; not that the poor woman wasn't ill. She was. She lay in bed with an IV line up and her head turned to one side on her pillow, her eyes only partially closed – a particularly unnerving feature – but breathing with what appeared to be reasonable regularity.

'She's all right, doctor.' Sister Chaplin, a tall red-headed woman in her forties with a pleasant manner that was very reassuring, had put a hand on her shoulder. 'She's going to do, you know.'

'Do?'

'Be all right. Get better. She'll *do*.'

'Oh. I – But I don't understand. What happened? And how did you know it was the chocolate that was the cause?'

'That was sheer luck,' Sister Chaplin said and then, as Sheila stirred and opened her eyes a little more, leaned over the bed and touched the hand on the counterpane. Sheila subsided and went back to sleep. 'She's pretty knocked out,' Sister said. 'She had intravenous diazepam to deal with the convulsions she started to have and she won't wake for a while. Stay with her, nurse, and if you're at all worried, use the alarm.' She peered at the monitor that was bleeping softly beside the bed. 'Her pulse rate has settled well, and her BP's about right.'

'Shouldn't she be in Intensive Care?' George asked and Sister Chaplin lifted her brows.

'No beds available. And she's fine here with us. I can handle a monitor or two, you know. Don't you think so?'

'I'm sorry,' George said quickly. 'Of course. It was just that I'm so shocked and so worried about her –'

'It's understandable.' Sister led the way to the door. 'Come to the office and we'll talk there.'

So now she sat at Sister's desk, looking down at the box of chocolates, feeling cold with terror. Jerry had managed to tell her, as she ran – and now she did begin to recall the headlong dash that had brought her here to the ward – that Sheila had been poisoned with what they thought was nicotine and that she had taken it in a chocolate liqueur. And here they were on the desk. She put out one finger to touch the box, but stopped before she reached it and pulled her hand back.

'It was these chocolates, Sister?'

'Yes.' Sister Chaplin looked at them soberly. 'I brought them in here at once. I – um –' She lifted her head and looked at George very directly. 'I was wearing a pair of rubber gloves when I picked them up.'

'Rubber gloves?' George said a little dully and felt colder still.

'I assumed they were evidence,' Sister said evenly. 'I imagine you'd know more about that than I would.'

There was a silence and then Jerry spoke. George jumped. She'd forgotten he was there.

'The card's on the outside, Dr B.,' he said. 'Stuck on with Sellotape.'

She turned her head and stared at him. 'What card?'

'You'd better look.' He was very serious now and she frowned, feeling remote from what was going on. What was happening here? She knew in an intellectual way it was something of great importance to her personally and yet she was detached and cool as though none of it really mattered.

She reached into her pocket and pulled out a pen. With the tip of it she flipped over the lid of the box to see the outside. There, as Jerry had said, was a card stuck on by one corner with a piece of Sellotape. She twisted her head to read it. *To help you feel better as soon as possible*, it said in neatly typed letters. *From Dr B. and all in the lab.* And there was an inky squiggle that made George's eyebrows contract. It looked very like her own initials that she sometimes put at the end of office memos.

'Who sent this?' she asked, looking at Jerry.

'Well, we assumed you did,' he said after a moment.

There was another silence. George sat and stared at the box, her mind quite blank.

'It was as well it worked out as it did.' Sister Chaplin began to speak easily, as relaxed as though they were having a perfectly normal conversation about the weather or something equally innocuous. 'I had gone into her little side room, after she'd had her lunch, and was chatting to her. She was getting on very well – her throat was still a bit sore from the smoke she'd inhaled in the fire, but her respirations were clearing nicely. Mr Selby had said she could go home tomorrow. The box arrived – it was wrapped in coloured paper. I have it here.' She looked to the table on the far side of the office and indeed there was a sheet of torn bright red and blue wrapping paper. 'I brought that in afterwards, too. I only touched the corner. Anyway, she offered me one and I said I wouldn't as I hadn't been to lunch yet, and she said come in after I get back and have one then. She said she loved chocolate liqueurs and that you knew that and that was probably why you'd sent them. To –' She coughed. 'To make amends for the way you'd been treating her.'

'The way I –' George began, but Sister Chaplin shook her head.

'That was all she said and of course I didn't ask her to say any more. In fact I dropped the subject as I don't like talking about the medical staff. And I know that Sheila – well, we all know Sheila.'

'Yes.' George looked up at her. She had a friendly look on her face, but there was, George thought, another look behind the agreeable mask; a considering stare. Is she wondering whether I wanted to poison Sheila? Ye Gods. She opened her mouth to speak but Sister Chaplin hurried on.

'So she took one and chewed it up as I tidied her bed and she made a face and said, "My God, that tastes disgusting! It's so bitter! Is she trying to tell me something?" And she made as though to spit it out. I thought she was feeling sick and held out a kidney dish, which was just as well, and she spat out the chocolate. But she'd swallowed some and her eyes began to water and she said, "It's burning, oh, my God, it's burning," and began to retch.'

'She looked ghastly.' Jerry was speaking now, with a certain note of relish in his voice. 'I'd just arrived to visit her, on my way to lunch, you see, and I was saying, "Greedy old you, let me have one," when she started to choke and be sick. It was awful.'

'We got the matter sorted out quickly.' Sister Chaplin was all calmness again. 'We put out a crash call and various people came, including Mr Selby. He says he thinks it might be nicotine from the smell.' Sister wrinkled her nose at the memory. 'I could only smell a rather fishy sort of odour, but he seemed to be quite certain it was nicotine. Said he'd smelled it before, so we did the fastest stomach washout we could, though she was vomiting so hard it was very difficult – and of course we wanted her to vomit, best thing for her. Then her pulse went into a very rapid mode, so Mr Selby gave her some intravenous atropine and diazepam, as I said, because she started to convulse. We set up the heart ABC monitors as there wasn't a bed available in ITU, and they sent us a special nurse for her. It was all sorted in a matter of half an hour or so.' There was a note of pride in her voice at her ward's efficiency, as indeed there was every right to be, George thought. And she said as much.

'She was lucky you were there and saw what happened.'

'Yes,' Sister Chaplin said in the same even voice. 'I think she was. If I hadn't been there, able to act quickly, I doubt she'd have survived. It seems to me there was a lot of poison in the chocolate.'

'But who would send her such a thing?' George cried. She turned and stared at Jerry. 'You can't think I would!'

'I did wonder,' Jerry said candidly, after a moment. 'I mean, she's been driving you up the wall one way and another, hasn't she? Sheila can be a real vixen when she gets in the mood and she's been in it a long time now. But then I thought, and I've been thinking it ever since, that you're not the sort to kill people, you just bawl at 'em. You might even throw things or hit them if you got mad enough, but you wouldn't go in for killing. And even if you did, if you really wanted to polish someone off, you'd do it well, wouldn't you? You wouldn't go in for something as daft as this, where you could be caught out by the first person who came along, because you'd signed the poison with your own initials. It doesn't make sense, not with someone as clever – and as well informed – as you are. So I'm sure it's not you.'

He stopped and looked at Sister. She gazed back at him and then he grinned at George a little shamefacedly. 'Though I have to tell you, Dr B., there'll be enough people around here who will believe it. You know what they're like.'

'Yes,' George said. 'I know what they're like. But meanwhile thanks for your vote of confidence. Even if it is a bit back-handed.'

He had the grace to look embarrassed, then mulish. 'You shouldn't have asked me if you didn't want an answer. You know I don't lie.'

'Only when it suits you,' George snapped. Her anger was rising now and making the cold sensation go away. 'Which it has from time to time.'

The phone on Sister's desk tinkled and she answered it with all her usual crispness. 'Ballantyne, Sister speaking. Oh, hello, Mr Selby.'

She listened and then switched her eyes to George. 'She's here now, sir,' she said. 'Mmm? Oh, I'm sure she will. Just a moment.' She handed the phone to George.

'George?' She tightened at the sound of Peter Selby's sleek voice, which he had cultivated to sound like melted butter mixed with honey. ('One must hold one's own with one's patients from the opera world, mustn't one?' he had once said to George at a Christmas party when in the confiding mood engendered by several glasses of the Professor's white wine. 'I spent hours practising how to speak when I was a young chap. But it's been worth it, hasn't it?' It had.) 'This is a nasty turn of events, isn't it?'

'I didn't send those chocolates, if that's what you wanted to know,' she said. Her own voice was harsh. 'I imagine that's what you wanted to talk to me about?'

'Of course not,' he said soothingly. 'I never dreamed of it. I would not consider such a thing possible. It's a very nasty hoax played out on both you and Miss Keen. It could have been a disaster, but as it is, small harm's been done. Sister coped splendidly. Quite splendidly. I – er – I just wanted to ask you . . . Hmph.' He stopped and George stared at the opposite wall and waited. She was damned if she was going to prompt him. He had quite obviously considered such a thing as an attack by herself on Sheila as perfectly possible, which was a horrible fact for her to contemplate. He harrumphed again, then said, 'Well, my dear, what do we do now?'

'Now? Get her fit again, I imagine. She seems to be doing all right.' Sister Chaplin had gone out of her office, probably back to the ward to see Sheila, and George lifted her brows at Jerry in query. He understood at once and went after her. 'I'll see Sheila myself in a moment. I imagine you'll be back again to see her today?'

'Of course. As soon as I've finished my list. I'm in main

theatres,' he said. 'Look, I'm on the spot here, George. You must understand that, of all people.'

'By all means notify the police, Peter,' she said evenly, recognizing his unspoken question immediately. 'It is right and proper that you should if you are concerned about your patient. I will, of course, be notifying them myself and taking all the evidence we have here to them. The chocolates, the wrapping, the contents of the kidney dish she spat into, all of it.'

'Oh, you won't be doing the forensic work on them yourself?' He spoke with an artlessness that did not deceive her for a moment.

'No,' she snapped. 'I will not. It will go to another pathologist, of course. You needn't worry that I'll be covering up any signs of my criminal actions.'

'My dear!' he cried. 'I didn't for a moment think –'

But she'd hung up on him.

By the time George left Ballantyne Ward, Sheila was well and truly on the mend. She'd had the narrowest of escapes, clearly ingesting only a very small amount of the nicotine (if that was what it was: it certainly smelled like it) and responding well to Sister Chaplin's prompt treatment. But every time George contemplated what might have happened she felt sick. The toxicity of nicotine was high, and there was no doubt there had been enough in the chocolate Sheila had eaten to kill her. And was there still some in the other sweets? Had whoever prepared this revolting thing filled every one of the dozen liqueurs with it? She shook her head in disbelief. No one could be that stupid, could they? This was the stuff of silly TV movies or old-fashioned mystery novels. And then she thought bleakly. Well, I suppose people have to get their ideas from somewhere. She remembered again the way Sister Chaplin had looked at her, the sound of Peter Selby's voice on the phone, and the way Jerry had admitted he'd reacted. Please, she found herself praying to the God she knew did not exist, please let everyone else think the way that Jerry did eventually, that if I was going to kill someone, I'd make a better job of it . . .

She called Sister Chaplin and one of her nurses and asked them crisply to help her bag the evidence to give to the police. 'I need some heavy plastic bags,' she said. 'And labels. Then I can arrange for someone from Ratcliffe Street nick – police station – to pick them up and take them to the other lab, over at East Ham. So, if you'll watch, please, so that you can verify that the chain of evidence is established and that I handled them properly –'

'I'm afraid not,' Sister Chaplin said. 'I'm sorry, but I can't do that. Nor can members of my staff.'

George stared at her. 'Why not?'

'I rather think one isn't supposed to touch anything in cases like this? That it should be left to the police? I'm sure you know the right things to do, but under the circumstances . . .' She let the words hang in the air and George felt her shoulders slump.

'Yes, of course,' she said dully. 'Of course, you're quite right. Do whatever you think is necessary.' And turned and went.

She was sitting in her office in the lab when he arrived. She'd gone straight there, refusing to answer when Jerry tried to speak to her as she left Ballantyne Ward, and had slammed the door to sit at her desk with her hands folded to wait. The only way she could contain her anger was by being very still indeed. When the phone rang she didn't move to answer it, letting it trill its urgency until someone in the main lab realized she wasn't going to pick it up, and took it themselves. Once or twice they rang her on the intercom but she ignored that too, and eventually they got the message and gave up.

She heard murmured voices outside her door at one point and tightened her shoulders, preparing to send them packing if they tried to come in, but they – whoever they were –

clearly thought better of it and went away. She heard cars start up outside as the senior people left and then the revving of Jerry's motorbike and felt a moment's pang. It would have been comforting to talk to someone about all this, someone who understood, and Jerry had always been a good guy. But she steeled herself and let him go and sat on.

At seven o'clock she heard him. The outer door clattered and banged and his footsteps came pounding down the corridor. Then her door burst open and Gus was there, glaring at her.

'You daft 'aporth! What sort of bloody mess have you got yourself into this time? And why the hell didn't you call me yourself, right away? I've only just got back to the nick and heard what's going on. I mean, ducks, if you're planning to top someone, at least ask me for some professional advice before you do it!'

7

The best thing about Gus, she decided, was the way he could make things dwindle down to normal size. Sitting alone in her office, with her rage at being so appallingly misunderstood at boiling point, the situation had seemed horrendous, unmanageably huge: she was suspected of attempted murder by everyone. There she was alone with the whole world against her. But it had all been, she now realized as she sat beside Gus in his comfortable old Austin Van den Plas, a childish overreaction.

'You must have been feeling really crappy,' he said as he switched on the engine and let in the clutch with all the tenderness of a mother caring for a newborn infant.

She blinked at him. 'Eh?'

'You should ha' seen your face.' He laughed, a low fat little sound in his throat. 'Like they was about to drag you off to the nick and lock you up for the rest of your natural. White as the proverbial you looked when I walked in.'

'Well, what do you expect?' she said. 'Sheila coming out with these wild accusations is one thing, but people believing them is another.'

'Who believed 'em?' he said reasonably, easing the wheel to get them out into the heavy run of traffic as they reached the main road. 'You told me Jerry didn't.'

'He didn't believe that I wasn't capable of it. Just that I'd have made a better job of it if it had been me.' She glowered. 'To be thought even capable of such a thing – it's humiliating.'

He pondered. 'Is it? I'd ha' thought it was more of a put-down if no one could imagine you doing anything like that. This way at least you know that they don't think you're a wimp.'

'You're a lot of comfort!'

'Of course I am.' He swivelled his eyes to look at her, laughing. 'You've cheered up no end since I got to you, and you look a proper colour again. I'm the best comfort you've got, one way and another.'

She slid into silence because she couldn't deny it. I'll give them all a run for their goddamn money, she thought. I'll show them what I'm capable of and what I'm not. I'll soon sort out who really sent those lousy chocolates to Sheila and then watch them squirm!

Gus pulled up outside Ratcliffe Street Police Station, arranging the car gently against the kerb with a precise two inches between the wheel hubs and the kerbstones, and got out. 'Come on,' he said. 'Let's get it over and done with. Then I'll buy you a slap up tuck-in, eh? You could do with it.' Not waiting to see if she followed, he ran up the steps to the big double doors of the entrance.

He let her give her statement to another officer, one of the sergeants, a pleasant woman who looked as though she'd been poured into her uniform, it fitted so snugly. George was grateful to see her. To have been faced with one of the CID team she knew well would have been painfully embarrassing.

'I'm Sergeant Friel,' the woman said, smiling. 'Mary Friel. We met in court a couple of months ago, d'you remember? That drowning case?'

'Oh,' George said and felt her face redden. 'Yes. Yes, of course. Nice to see you again.' Dammit all, he might have found a stranger to deal with this, she thought wrathfully. He's got about as much sensitivity as a rhinoceros on heat sometimes. The bastard. 'I'm only giving a statement to make things easier for Gus,' she said defensively. 'I mean, it's nothing to do with me, really. But I just got caught up in a case –'

'Of course,' Mary Friel said calmly, and sat down at the desk. 'Now make yourself comfortable and we'll get through this in no time.'

George's irritation made her stiff at first and Sergeant Friel had to ask a lot of questions to get the story out of her. But eventually she finished and pushed the statement sheet over the desk for George to read and sign.

She checked it carefully. There in neat handwriting was a clear and simple account of the way she had been told that Sheila Keen was taken ill after eating a liqueur chocolate, and the course of events once she reached the ward where Sheila was. She had left out nothing, including her attempt to bag up the evidence and the fact that she had been balked by Sister Chaplin, because Gus had told her she must be completely honest about it all. It hadn't been easy to say those things to the moonfaced sergeant, but she had been dogged about it, even describing her conversation on the phone with Mr Selby and his anxiety that the matter should be reported to the police.

That'll show them too, she'd then thought obscurely. I got it all to the police before they did, didn't I? I'd hardly have done that if I'd been part of what happened.

She read on:

The background to this event is as follows: in my department (the pathology service at the Royal Eastern Hospital) we have for some time been under considerable pressure of work and I have had cause to reprimand Miss Keen for various reasons, including her tendency to waste time in gossiping with other members of staff. We had a disagreement about this last week, on Thursday 1 June, at one in the afternoon, which occurred in the middle of the laboratory. There were a large number of witnesses to this disagreement which became somewhat heated at times. [Ye Gods, George thought, this woman's version makes me sound like a real dumb

68

plodder. I don't talk this way, I know I don't!] During this altercation I became heated and told Sheila I'd be glad to see the back of her if I could. She said I could not sack her since that decision was in the hands of Mr Matthew Herne, the Chief Executive Officer of the hospital, to which I responded that in that case I would have to find some other way to shut her up and I would if it was the last thing I did. I now realize this remark could have been misconstrued and I regret it. It was made in the heat of the moment and was not intended to carry any sort of threat to Miss Keen, although she later behaved as though she believed that I had threatened her. When her car caught fire in the car park and she was taken into the hospital as a patient, she seemed by her behaviour to imply that she believed I had played some part in that accident, which was absurd since I was not there when the car caught fire. I do not know why the car caught fire. I do not know whether it has been examined yet for a cause. I did not speak to Miss Keen about her attitude but put it down to her reaction to her experience.

'It reads rather – well, stiffly, doesn't it?' she ventured, but Sergeant Friel shook her head.

'They all say that,' she said. 'But I only do it the way we're supposed to. I can't put in every "er" and "um", can I? It has to be fit to give in evidence in court if necessary. I'm sure you understand that.'

'Yes, I suppose so,' George said. After a moment she took the pen Mary Friel was offering and signed the statement. She'd heard enough of these documents read out in open court to know that the sergeant was right: lawyers and judges could only cope with this sort of turgid expressionless stuff.

Then she blinked and almost dropped the pen in the sharpness of her reaction which had instantaneously brought back the cold feeling she had experienced earlier. In court? Giving evidence? What on earth was she thinking about? There was nothing to take to court, no case of any kind to answer. Gus had advised her to make the statement, 'just for tidiness. So that afterwards no one can say we didn't do it all by the book, see, doll? You make your statement, I'll look into

69

the chocolates business and find out what halfwit tried that hoary old trick and then we can forget all about it. But, bet your bottom dollar, if I didn't get a statement out of you someone'd want to know why. This way we cover all our exits.'

The coldness of the panic receded and with steady fingers she added the date and then pushed the document back to Sergeant Friel. 'It's all yours,' she said. 'No, I don't think there's anything else.'

'Superintendent Hathaway said to take you up to his office when we'd done this,' the sergeant said, and George managed a smile at her for the first time. She was feeling steadily more comfortable and would have liked the girl to acknowledge that, but the sergeant just opened the door of the interview room to usher her out and then led the way up to Gus's office.

George followed the round buttocks, which swayed and bounced in a way that no doubt all the male officers in the nick found agreeable, in silence. Miserable creature, she thought, with her silly questions about the car. What has the car got to do with me?

She said as much to Gus, exploding into words as soon as Sergeant Friel closed the door on herself. 'I thought I was to make a statement just about the chocolates incident because of the card on the box,' she said. 'Why did Miss Self-Satisfied there ask questions about the car fire and put all that into the statement too?'

'Because she's a good copper, George,' Gus said, shaking his head at her. 'What's happened to you? You're not usually so jumpy.'

'I'm not usually on this side in an investigation,' she snapped.

'That's true,' he allowed. 'And it's a nasty feeling, I'll grant you. I remember it all too well.' He smiled at her. 'But you sorted me when I was in shtook, so let me sort you now, hmm?'

70

'But why did she want to know about the car fire?' George wasn't going to be deflected that easily.

'Because you must have mentioned it,' Gus said. 'I certainly didn't. It was the chocolate incident you were to make a statement about. I gave Mary Friel no instructions in this, just told her you had a statement to make and she was to take it. So it was all down to you, wasn't it?'

She frowned, looking back over what had happened, and then slowly sat down. It had been her own doing, after all. She had chosen to start at the beginning, with her silly empty threats when she lost her temper with Sheila in the middle of the lab; and then she had had to mention the car fire, because why else would Sheila have been in the ENT Ward and in a position to have people send her poisoned chocolates? It had been her own mention of the event that had led to Sergeant Friel's questions and those bald sentences about the car that had ended up in her statement. And that made her think.

She sat up a little more straightly. 'Gus, that makes me . . . Listen, what happened to Sheila's car?'

'I've no idea,' he said. 'Why should I?'

'No reason at all,' she said slowly. 'Of course you wouldn't. I mean, the only people who were called were the fire brigade, not the police. There was no need for police, was there? But maybe . . . Gus, how close are you to the people at the brigade? Can you find out from them what happened to the car afterwards?'

He looked at her sideways, then made a little grimace. 'I'll see what I can do.' He picked up the phone and dialled and after a short wait asked for 'the senior officer on duty on . . .' He put his hand over the mouthpiece and hissed at her, 'When did it happen?'

'Yesterday evening,' she hissed back. 'The eighth of June.'

He nodded and uncovered the mouthpiece, 'Yesterday. Around seven p.m. This is Superintendent Hathaway of Ratcliffe Street Station. Yeah, yeah, I'll hold.

'God, how I hate that tinkling stuff they pour in your ears!'

he said savagely as he sat there waiting. George could hear it to be an unbearably sweet and romantic rendition of 'Greensleeves' and nodded her strong agreement.

The tinkling stopped at last and Gus became more alert. 'Hello? Oh, hi, Paul. How are you? All well with the kids? ... Great. Listen, mate, you had an incident yesterday at Old East, right? Car park ... Uh-huh ...' He listened and then nodded. 'Yeah, that was the story I got. So, tell me, were you at all bothered? Did you ask for any forensic check-ups on the car? ... Mmm? I see ...'

The conversation went on for quite a while, with Gus being maddeningly monosyllabic, but then at last he said, 'Right. What did you say? Yeah, I'll hang on, only for crying out loud, don't put that bloody music on again unless you want me to throw up down the phone.'

He winked at George who opened her mouth to speak but he shook his head. 'What was that? ... Yup. Seventeen? ... Oh, seventy. Right. And the phone number?' He was scribbling on a scrap of paper; George strained to see, but she couldn't. 'OK, Paul. Ta for your help ... What? Oh, yeah, next Friday. You're putting a team in? ... Good. We'll slaughter you, of course, but it's always a pleasure to kill a mate ... Garn! You lot play the worst snooker this side of Tower Bridge and well you know it. Probably see you Friday, then, work permitting.' He hung up.

'So?' George demanded. 'What do they know?'

'Not a thing!' he said and reached for the phone again. 'They thought it was just an ordinary electrics fault and told the owner she'd have to get the car sent to her own garage and assessed by the insurance people. They offered to arrange it with the garage for her – got them to pick it up and so forth – since she wasn't fit herself, and to tell them how to deal with the foam extinguisher they used, so they could tell me which garage it had gone to. He's given me the number. He also said they're going to advise the hospital on the state of the car park as far as fire risk goes –'

72

'Yeah,' George said impatient. 'But about Sheila's car –'

'I'm checking. Listen, George, don't sit there listening. You drive me barmy the way you bounce around when I'm trying to talk on the phone, like you want to join in the conversation. I can't handle that. I'll make the call, you go and tart yourself up a bit. We'll get a bit of supper as soon as I've got what I can here. It's a bit late, so there mayn't be anyone there, but I'll have a go. When you've gone. Hop it, now.'

She was too eager for him to make the call to argue, irritating though it was to be banished like a schoolgirl, but he wasn't wrong. She hadn't tidied herself before she left the path. lab, and, she knew she looked rumpled and a bit drawn. Repairs would be worthwhile indeed, and she tucked herself into the policewomen's loo and began to deal with her hair and reapply some make-up. She was tolerably satisfied with herself as she snapped her bag shut, settled it over her shoulder and went back to Gus's office.

He was sitting staring out of the window when she came in and she stood beside the door, frowning slightly. 'What's the matter? No one there at the garage?'

'Eh? Oh, yes. There was someone there.'

'So?'

'So it turns out that there is something a bit . . .' He sighed and got to his feet. 'Listen, let's go to supper, hey? I'm bloody starvin', and you look as though you could make a nice hole in a good bit o' fish. I'll tell you when we get there.'

He wouldn't take no for an answer. He insisted on driving over to the restaurant. He wanted to use the one he'd recently opened a little further down Shadwell towards Docklands, in Cable Street, instead of going to his biggest place in Aldgate, which added to her impatience. But he still refused to talk.

'Listen, I need time to get this sorted out in my head. Just be patient, will you? We'll be there, we can talk, it'll be easier. Now do me a favour and belt up.'

She belted up. There was nothing else she could do, and

73

she somehow managed to stay silent until they were settled at a window table by his favourite manageress, Kitty, who always had the job of launching a new place, and who hurried off to get him his favourite fried halibut and the grilled sole which was all George wanted.

'Now!' she demanded. '*Now* will you tell me? And what it is that you have to be so – so secretive about it!'

'I'm not being secretive,' he said. 'It's just that I know you. If we talk about things that upset you in a public place, you won't go off the handle the way you do if we're on our own. You're great at flying off into the stratosphere; like a Harrier jump jet, you are. Now ...' He paused and stared at her. 'Keep your hair on, love, and listen. The car had been tampered with.'

'What?' She stared at him with that now familiar and hateful wave of cold fear rising in her. 'In what way? And does it affect me?'

'I can tell you how,' he said soberly, 'but I can't answer the rest of your questions yet. OK. They stripped the vehicle down and it really had been severely damaged. The insurance people won't be able to argue that this isn't a write-off or that Sheila's not entitled to a new vehicle.'

She tightened her jaw and began to look dangerous and he hurried on.

'The problem was in the battery. Someone had pulled a sodding great lump of cable – really heavy stuff – across the battery and fitted it with a solenoid switch. Then it was connected up so that when Sheila switched on the engine, the whole of the electrics shorted and started to burn. The casings of the wires had gone and it's a miracle that the bloody car didn't blow up. It was a very thorough job, according to Trev.'

'Trev?'

'Trevor Lucan owns the garage. He's got a bit of form – the occasional organizing of a ringer, a bit of co-operation with a tda, that's taking and driving away – but he's done his time

74

and he's been straight for three years. Or so he says. But it made him nervous when he spotted this and he wasn't going to do nothing about it. If I hadn't called and asked him direct for chapter and verse, well, he wasn't about to come round the nick to tell us. But since I called, he reckons it was meant – he's got a bit superstitious since he did his three years in the Scrubs – and he told me. So there it is, ducks. Someone does seem to have it in for Sheila. The business with the chocolates was the second attempt to get her. She's going to need a lot of watching over, if you ask me.'

'Yes,' George said slowly. 'Yes.' She stared out of the window at the street beyond, her eyes blank. 'And I'm going to need to do a lot to prove it's nothing to do with me, right? Because I tell you, Gus, she's convinced it is. So now what do we do?'

8

_____

'What we do now,' he said happily as Kitty arrived with her tray piled high, 'is eat. No, don't argue. You need your grub. And we'll talk of everything and anything except this Sheila business. Like our holiday.'

'Holiday!' She'd completely forgotten the plan they'd considered, and it was hard to feel any enthusiasm for it now, but she sat and dutifully ate her supper while he chattered busily about the rival merits of Spain ('The good old Balearics. They all go to Majorca still, you know!'), North Africa ('Come with me to the Casbah, darlin', and we'll find you some exotic Arabian trousers to sit around in at home and get up to erotic Arabian games!'), and even, when she showed no particular interest in those, Hong Kong. 'It won't be there much longer, they tell me, and it'd be great to take a look at it.'

'It's no good, Gus. I can't imagine going on holiday, not till this is all sorted out. To tell the truth, I hadn't even got round to arranging the time off.'

'You promised!' He looked affronted.

'Well, maybe I did. But under the circumstances –'

'What circumstances? You're really going over the top with this, you know.' He put down his knife and fork with a clatter. 'I didn't want to talk about it but if we must, we must, and I'm here to tell you you're being ridiculous. Whatever Madam

76

Sheila says – and remember I know what she's like as well as you do – you've had nothing to do with what's going on there.'

'How do you know?' She put down her own fork with gratitude because she really wasn't hungry, and stared at him. 'If Selby and Sister Chaplin –'

'Bugger Selby and Sister Chaplin,' he roared to the delight of diners at nearby tables. 'What do they know? Just what Sheila spouts at 'em.' He dropped his voice. 'Do shut up, George. You're being a right dummy. Either we talk about goin' on holiday – and you can go and sort out the dates with 'em on Monday – or we talk about the weather, or we talk about what we're goin' to do this weekend. Nothing else. I don't intend to do any more about this business till Monday, because there's no urgency about it, whatever you may think.' He had to raise his voice again to ride over her protests. 'And there's an end of it.'

'Oh, is it!' she snapped, glaring at him even more furiously. 'Well, I'll tell you what's happening this weekend, my friend. You're going to spend it in your own flat, *on* your own. I'm not going to have you sitting around with me and paying no attention to what worries me most. Where do you get off telling me what I can and can't worry about? It's my life still, you know!'

If he'd lost his temper back it would have been all right; she could have handled that. But he didn't. He was all sweet reasonableness and she could have hit him for it.

'Look, doll. I know this is an upsetting business, but really, you don't have to worry yourself. I'm here to sort it and –'

'So don't you worry your pretty little head?' she said with all the venom she could put into it. 'Big Daddy'll take good care of his little diddums? Well, little diddums has other ideas. So forget it. I'm going. Goodnight.' She pushed back her chair, grabbed her bag and marched out, leaving him and half the restaurant staring after her. It didn't do much to resolve her problem but it sure as hell made her feel better.

*

Until she got back to the hospital. She could have gone back to the flat, of course, but the mere idea made her feel heavy and miserable. She needed company, someone to talk to, and she had a sudden image of the senior common room full of cheerful registrars and HOs and thought it would be fun, just like the old days when she'd been a resident herself, to go and sit among them and share the lousy coffee and warm beer and gossip. Well, maybe not gossip, she amended, sheering away from the implications of that, but certainly chatter.

But the big cluttered common room, with its litter of newspapers and journals, of empty stained coffee mugs and biscuit crumbs, contained only a young woman in a rumpled white coat, fast asleep on a sofa at the far end. George stood at the door uncertainly, trying to decide what to do. It wasn't all that late – perhaps nine o'clock – and the thought of wandering home just to shower and watch TV or whatever did not fill her with excitement. Besides, she had an idea that Gus might have ignored her insistence that he spend the weekend in his own flat. Perhaps he would just be waiting there when she got in (and a little bit of her mind whispered, 'You'd be quite happy really, if he did, wouldn't you?' But that had to be ignored) and she was damned if she was going home a moment before midnight. Well, around midnight, anyway.

Behind her the door opened. She turned happily and then caught her breath in surprise. Not at the sight of him – Zack Zacharius had every right to be there – but at the way seeing him made her belly lurch a little. She was delighted and she showed it, producing a wide and glittering smile.

'That's better!' he said. 'Last time we met you treated me with total disdain. How nice to see a welcome on your face. What are you doing here? You aren't usually hanging around this squalid joint.'

'I was looking for company,' she said, embarrassed because her voice wasn't fully under her control. 'I was – I don't usu-

78

ally mind spending an evening alone but tonight I thought –
So I came over to see who was around and what was up.'

'Well, I'm around but there's nothing much up,' he said.
'Everyone who isn't working late on a Friday is off about
their own affairs unless they've flaked out like that poor child
over there.' He lifted his chin at the girl on the sofa, who
hadn't stirred. 'My God, but I'm glad to be through that stage
of being part of the lowest form of hospital life!'

'Me too.' George looked at the girl briefly and then back at
him. 'Though it had its fun side too.'

'Like what?'

She shrugged. 'Oh, there was some time off. Time to
wander off to the local and have a drink and a gabfest and –'
She stopped, suddenly shy. In those old days, she remembered perfectly well, that was the form a date took when you
went out with one of the other members of the medical staff.
You sat in the pub and gossiped and then slid back either to
your or their room and necked like fury until the phone or a
bleeper would ring and drag you back to the real world.

He seemed to be aware of what she was thinking because
his mouth quirked a little and she thought, nice. Then looked
away.

'We'll do just that. Give me a moment to get rid of this.' He
was shrugging out of his white coat, and she put out a hand to
stop him.

'Oh, listen. I wasn't asking for a – I mean, if you have work
to do –'

'I've done it. Enough for tonight, anyway. And I only came
over here for the same reason you did. I needed a bit of company. A chance to come down.'

She was startled and looked it and he laughed. 'It's all
right. I don't mean I've been using interesting substances! Just
that my adrenaline's running high and I'm in no mood to go
quietly off to my room and read myself to sleep. I need
someone to talk to, and how lucky can I get? I find you in the
same frame of mind. And there's something I wanted to talk

to you about, anyway. So it's sort of meant. If we were superstitious we'd say the stars were on our side. Shall we go?'

He linked his arm into hers and she had no choice but to
follow. Anyway, she wanted to. This was precisely the sort of
thing she needed tonight, she told herself; someone to make
her laugh, someone to take her mind off her troubles and
someone to show Gus she wasn't his property and he could
get off her train any time he chose. With which somewhat in-
coherent and thoroughly childish thought she abandoned
herself to Zack and his company at the pub across the road
from the hospital.

It was a new one, part of a chain that went in for silly names.
This one had been a perfectly respectable 'Red Lion' when
she'd first come to Old East; now it had been taken over and
tarted up with lots of green paint and tiles and brass and re-
named 'The Fish and Bicycle' with a suitably arch painting
on a board hanging outside to underline the joke. It wasn't a
very good joke, they agreed, but the beer was excellent, and
the coffee was even better, being hot, strong – almost as
strong as A & E's – and lavish in quantity.

'I hope you're not worrying over this business with your
technician and her mishaps,' he said abruptly as they waited
for their order of a pint of ale for him and a half-pint for her.
(She didn't really like it, but wanted to show some sort of
solidarity with him in such a basic matter of tastes.)

'Um – well . . .' she began carefully and he leaned forwards
and took one hand in his.

'I thought you might be. I hear the chatter that runs round
the place as clearly as the next man. It's all shit, of course. I
can't imagine you ever doing anything so crass as sending a
person poisoned chocolates.'

'I think that's kind of you,' she said, managing a smile. 'You
don't say what I might be capable of, mind you.'

'Oh, something much more sophisticated,' he said. 'If you
wanted to get rid of someone I've no doubt you'd find a way

to do it that would be most efficient. Elegant, even. You're like that, aren't you? Elegant.'

She looked at him, her lower lip between her teeth. 'I think you're coming on to me,' she said after a pause. 'And I think I'd better tell you that I'm kinda spoken for.'

He looked around with elaborate interest. 'Oh? Where is he, then?'

She laughed. 'Not here, you fool.' She waved her hand vaguely. 'At home.'

'It can't be much of a speaking-for if he lets you out on your own on a Friday evening when you don't have to work next day. You don't, do you? I thought not' – as she shook her head – 'especially when you look so good. You do, you know. Your hair, all piled up like that. And those crazy big glasses. Really cute.'

'You *are* coming on to me!'

'God, it's good to talk to someone who understands me! English women say you're chatting them up. It's not as sexy as our version, is it?'

'Well, I'm not up for grabs,' she said firmly, but not entirely believing it, and he laughed.

'So, we'll settle for the way it is right now, hmm? Great.' The beer had arrived. 'Let's drink to friendship, if nothing more. At present.' He clinked his tankard on her glass and smiled into her eyes and she knew he was daring her to go further. And knew also that she was very tempted. Gus had been so very piggish tonight, after all.

'So,' she said hastily. 'What was it you wanted to talk to me about?'

'What was – Oh, yes.' He put down his tankard and wiped the back of his hand across his mouth in an unselfconscious gesture she found endearing. 'You remember that bash they had for old Prof. Hunnisett?'

'Sure.'

'And the way the old man – who was it? The Chairman.'

'Sir Jonathan.'

'Yeah, him. He explained that unless we got some more projects on board, and more important ones at that, we hadn't a hope of getting a good replacement for the old Prof. and the Institute of Research would slide down the tubes.'

'Something like that.'

'Yeah, well, it was true. We've been talking about it for weeks now – those of us doing research, and there aren't as many as there might be.'

'Who?' she said. 'Do I know them?'

'Oh, you'll have seen them about, I guess. There's Frances Llewellyn. She's looking at the brain and chemical changes in women at the menarche and the menopause, post natal and all that – it's a study of depression in women, really. She's a real right-on sister, that one, have you noticed? Wears trousers all the time and never has her hair done.'

'I wear trousers,' George said. 'And I'm as feminist as the next woman. So don't –'

'Oh, she isn't so much a feminist as anti-mannist. There's a hell of a difference,' Zack said blithely, then hurried on. 'Anyway, her research is well on, but it's soft, you know? No outcomes there that'll actually change anything. I mean, there won't be any therapies, new drugs that'll do the business.'

'Is that the only sort of research the Institute's interested in? The sort that brings in new drugs?'

'It has to be,' he said candidly. 'Unless we come up with projects that offer something to the big pharmaceuticals on account of there may be a nice new money spinner in it, like a histamine two receptor – a Zantac – or a great new anti-depressant that doubles as a weight-loss inducer, like Prozac, they're just not interested. So Frances is a non-starter. She's made it clear she's not into filling women with hormones to see their effects, but in doing constant very fine assays of their own hormones. Mike Klein isn't so bad. He's looking at the patterns of addiction to assorted substances in adolescents. He might be able to identify a causative enzyme, he reckons. I think it's pie in the sky, but it's an attractive one because if it is an enzyme, then he could come up with an antagonist, right? So there could be a drug there. But really it's mine that's the best.'

He looked at her sideways and then said a touch shyly, 'I'm not putting you on, you know. This is a real assessment. It's not just mine, either. The Prof. says the same. It's not only motor-neurone disease, you see. If I get what I'm after I should have the key to all the neurological degenerative diseases – the demyelinating ones – brain as well as nerves. Like MS and Parkinson's.' He hesitated. 'And Alzheimer's.'

There was a little silence and then she said a touch sardonically. 'That could be really valuable to the pill-makers, I imagine.'

'As they used to say, "Baby, you blubbered a bibful".' He was elated suddenly. 'The thing is, I've come at the problem from the other side. Most of the research homes in on individual conditions. Me, I'm looking at symptoms. Sometimes the same ones affect people with quite different diagnoses. Like, their loss of sensation and of motor ability in MS and to a degree in Parkinson's, and –'

'Not in Alzheimer's though. They . . .' She swallowed. 'They lose intellect, don't they? I should know. It's happened to my mother.'

He put out a hand. 'I'm sorry. But the work I'm doing *could* apply to Alzheimer's if we can show it really is due to nerve-cell demyelination and neurone degeneration. And if I can find a way to reverse that degeneration – if I can find a drug . . . I mean, dammit, that's what the antibiotics were about. They acted against all the bacteria so they could be used for a myriad conditions. Now it's different, of course, with resistant strains, only that doesn't look likely to happen if it's nerve damage you're dealing with. If I can find the right drug, or drugs, that could be used for a huge range of illness – not just one drug for one condition . . . Do you see?'

He took a deep breath. 'Anyway, that's the thing I'm working on. And the Prof. wants to have a demonstration organized to show them how I'm doing with patients and all, invite one really big name, the top people from a couple of the multi-national drug firms, as well as the people at the top of the profession . . . You see, George? I had to talk to someone about it, didn't I? I can't talk to Frances or Mike because they'll get uptight, not to say screaming crazy jealous. Maybe they'd try to scupper us! And I can't talk to the other clinicians because they don't see it my way. I don't have an easy time with the consultants here. They guard their useful patients from me like I was the devil after buying their souls, or about to make their skins into lampshades. But I've got to get a few more patients and well – I'm hopeful.' Again he reached out and touched her hand. 'I like talking to you about it. I'd like to talk more. I reckon you're the only guy here I can be comfortable with.'

'Well,' she said unsteadily. 'Thank you kindly, sir,' she said.'

'Hell, no, I mean it. And I wanted to ask you if you'd help me when it comes to the presentation. I have to get a whole raft of stuff together, and I just can't make it on my own. I need someone with a bit of pathology in their make-up to see me through. So I wondered . . .'

She leaned back in her chair and laughed with real amusement. He watched her, pleased with her reaction at first, but then a little puzzled.

'Look, if I'm putting too much on to you,' he began, but she shook her head.

'I'm sorry to laugh,' she said. 'I wasn't laughing at you so much as at me. No, I won't explain. So, you need someone to help you with your presentation? Why not? When is it to be ready?'

'Next week,' he said eagerly. 'I have patients to sort out, records and charts to make up, a bit of computer modelling to organize . . .'

'I'm on,' she said. 'Why not? I might as well.' And you can

take that, Gus, she thought with a flash of malice, and wrap it round your patronizing neck. See if I care. 'How about starting on Tuesday evening? I've plenty of time to spare then.'

9

When she got home she found a message from Gus on her answerphone. 'Sorry, doll,' he said and he sounded it. 'I guess I should have been a bit more sensitive, but you know how it is with me. I mean to do it right and then I go and come over all macho. So, sorry, sorry, sorry. Call me when you get in and I'll come right over. If you'll have me. I like the toothbrush I've got in your bathroom better than the one I've got in my own.' He managed to sound very plaintive.

But she didn't call him. Let him sweat, she thought with a flash of anger. It won't do him any harm. He wasn't just macho. He was downright patronizing.

It wasn't until she was standing under the shower enjoying the sensation of the water running over her face that she admitted the truth to herself. She didn't really want Gus to know how late she had got in. To have called him at past one a.m. would have been an admission that she'd been out very late indeed, would have begged a question from him regarding why and where; and she was damned if she was prepared to tell him that.

Although, as she pointed out to herself with some sternness as at last she stepped out of the shower and began to rub her hair dry, there was no reason why she shouldn't. The evening had been a very pleasant and most proper one. They'd gone for their drink, she and Zack – though she'd deliberately tried to chose a different pub from the Fish and Bicycle when he asked her where she'd like to go – and talked at great length about his research (well, he had; she'd mostly listened and asked questions) and then, discovering they were hungry, had gone in search of supper. George had thought a little guiltily of the expensive and uneaten sole which Gus had provided, but shrugged away her shame at such extravagance and settled with Zack on a small Tandoori restaurant in Cable Street where they ate, they both agreed, far more onion bhajis and lamb korma than they should have done, and went on talking until both were amazed at how late it was.

'I'll come to your office on Tuesday, then, and show you the stuff I'm proposing to use at my presentation?' he had said eagerly. 'And then you can tell me if you think I've got it right.'

She had laughed; he sounded for all the world like an excited child with a new toy to display, and when he quirked his head enquiringly at her laughter, she told him why and he'd rubbed his face with both hands in some embarrassment.

'Oh, hell, I'm sorry, I've always been like that. When I want things I go for them baldheaded. My mother said I drove her crazy with it. And then when I've got them –'

'You lose interest?' she said lightly as she turned to pick up her bag. Behind her he caught his breath sharply, and she heard it.

'Oh, no,' he said softly, looking at her very directly. 'Quite the contrary. If I get something it's mine and it stays mine. For always. That's why I stick at getting what I want, you see. It's worth the effort.'

Had she misconstrued what he was saying to her? She didn't know; all she was aware of was the way he had looked at her and the way he had made her catch her breath too.

Now, scrubbing herself dry with a towel that was so deliciously rough it made her glow all over, she castigated herself for being so stupid and romantic and childish. The man wanted her to help him with a research project? Big deal. It didn't mean he had any ulterior motive. So shut up, already. Go to bed; sleep it off; wake up sensible.

She woke up miserable. It felt odd not to have Gus beside her; even though they still technically lived in separate flats he spent more nights with her than away from her, and those when he was away were due to work, which she understood. To know that she was alone on this rainy summer morning because she had been silly didn't offer her any comfort at all.

She spent the day being virtuously domestic: cleaning the flat thoroughly – indeed almost ferociously; then trolling around the supermarket to fill her fridge and freezer, both of which had been sadly depleted; and on impulse buying a number of bedding-out plants from a street trader. If she bought them, she thought, she'd have to plant them; to spend the afternoon busily window-box gardening and perhaps fiddling with a hanging basket to install in her front porch (to match those of others which were blossoming up and down her rapidly gentrifying Bermondsey street) would be fun.

And it was, up to a point, but when she had the alyssum, the lobelia and the small fuchsias neatly in place, fed and watered, there was still a long weekend stretching emptily ahead of her; and still she refused to call Gus.

Instead she sat down at her little desk and did what she had come to find was the best way to handle any puzzles with which she was faced. She would write it all down.

On a piece of paper she wrote ZACK in large letters. And then crumpled it up and tossed it in the waste basket. He wasn't a puzzle, of course he wasn't. A silly idea. So she took another piece and this time wrote GUS. She stared at it, and then, slowly, tore the page into tiny segments before throwing it away. There was more to the Gus situation than she could handle this way.

But she still felt the need to sort out *something*; and this time she wrote SHEILA in capitals. That's better, she thought. This one I can deal with. There are real conundrums there, in what's happening to her, and why.

NATURE OF PROBLEM, she printed carefully, the way she had been used to at school. She stopped for a little more thought and then began to write in good earnest. SHE WASTES TOO MUCH TIME GOSSIPING INSTEAD OF WORKING.

Another heading followed rapidly: SEVERITY OF PROBLEM. Beneath, *It's very irritating but in all honesty*, she found herself scribbling, not bothering with capitals any more, *it doesn't matter unduly as a rule. Generally she gets through all her work and does it well. So why does it irritate me so when she pops off to other departments?*

She thought for quite a long time, and then, knowing she had to be honest, returned to the paper again and wrote, unwillingly: *Because she doesn't tell me all that she knows.*

George contemplated that line for a long time, frowning. It was true and she couldn't deny it. What had really made her angry was the way Sheila whispered to other people and then when she, George, came into the room, ostentatiously silenced herself. George, who had as urgent a desire to know what was going on in her environment as everyone else, found this infuriating, and even more infuriating the fact that she couldn't do anything about it. Yes, she was Sheila's superior in rank at the lab but that didn't mean she could insist the woman told her the same things she told everyone else. Sheila would just look at her with that blank insolent stare of hers and refuse.

But what is she gossiping about that I want to know and that she doesn't tell me? George asked herself reasonably, staring sightlessly at the square of her living-room window down which another rainstorm was now sending its spatter. I'm just being stupid. Childish and stupid and –

And then she remembered. It was the sort of memory that in her childhood had been a common experience: a sudden visual and aural reconstruction of an event which was as vivid an experience as the original. Nowadays it happened less often, but when it did, it was a powerful experience. And one that she learned from, if she let herself. She relaxed her shoulders and closed her eyes and let the memory happen.

She had been sitting in her office six or seven weeks ago, quietly checking over a report she was to take in next day for a special court hearing on a death from a drugs overdose when her phone had rung. After waiting in vain for someone in the lab to take it, she had pulled herself away from her complex calculations about the amount of heroin that the dead boy had taken and, annoyed, picked up the phone. She was greeted by a tirade from the senior administrator of the Medical Records department. George had become steadily angrier, until at last she had managed to get a word in edgeways.

'If you will stop and listen for just a moment, Mrs Ellesmere,' she had said loudly. 'Perhaps we can sort this out. Now, as I understand it, you're worried about one of your staff –'

'Of course I am. When a member of my staff, one I need and pay a good rate for, goes sick as often as she does, I'm entitled to know just how much is genuine and just how much is put on! I know the woman's a diabetic, but other diabetics don't give this sort of trouble to their bosses. I'm entitled to know what's what and I thought I could simply have a look at some of the reports and see where the trouble is. I may not be a nurse but I'm highly qualified, well able to understand a path. report. As head of all the medical records, of course I am! But that madam flatly refused to let me see, wouldn't even talk about it when I've seen her, seen her with my own eyes, head down with the woman herself, gossiping like fury over, would you believe, a lab report! I've had enough of it. Either you, as her manager, deal with her, or I tell you, doctor, I will make this a proper disciplinary affair and make a report to the Trust management and then you'll see what a fuss there'll be. They'll raise hell with you and with that woman and –'

'What woman?' George had been bewildered. 'I don't follow you.'

'That Keen woman from your department! Weren't you listening to me? She comes up here, making a pest of herself, and when I ask her to tell me what is going on, she flatly refuses and makes me look and feel a complete idiot in front of my own staff! I won't have it!'

'Let me understand you,' George said. 'You are saying that Sheila Keen was in your department, showing a path. lab report to someone.'

'Showing a woman her own path. report! You didn't *listen*. She was showing her her own path. report and whispering away and when I demanded to be told what it was all about she said it was confidential so I had no right to know. Me, the manager, no right to know! I have every right to know! If she goes on wasting my staff's time like this and refusing to be co-operative, I tell you, the Trust management will be informed and you'll be up to your neck in a disciplinary.' And she had hung up the phone with a snap.

George had of course gone to look for Sheila and found her in the lab red of face and clearly just back from wherever she'd been, and about to start telling everyone who would listen why she was in such a state.

'Sheila!' George had snapped. 'What the hell is going on?'

Sheila had had the grace to look embarrassed. 'I was just – I just got back from an errand,' she muttered.

'An errand? What do we have juniors in this department for? Why are you running errands?'

'This was sort of a personal one –' Sheila began and then George lost her temper.

'I know perfectly where you've been. I've had that Ellesmere woman on the phone shouting about it. You've been up in Medical Records showing someone a path. report she had no right to see, and refusing to show it to Mrs Ellesmere.'

'The person in question had every right to see it,' Sheila

had said with sharp dignity, looking redder than ever. 'And Mrs Ellesmere certainly did not. It was confidential patient data. The relationship with the patient can't be damaged by professional staff prattling to managers!'

'You go too far, Sheila, sometimes, and this is one of them,' George had said. 'Now, what is this path. report? And who is the person who you've been showing it to? Give it to me!'

Sheila had been standing with her hand in her pocket and now she tightened it into a fist so that the shape showed through the nylon fabric. 'It's confidential,' she said. 'I shan't.'

'Sheila!' roared George. 'Show me! Tell me what this fuss is all about at once!'

Sheila very deliberately had pulled a piece of paper out of her pocket – clearly a path. report – and run across the lab to a bunsen burner on one of the benches, its harsh blue pencil of flame pointing up towards her, and very deliberately set the sheet alight. It had been consumed before anyone had had a chance to reach it, with Sheila standing defiantly by it, staring at George with her chin up.

And that had been that. George had gone storming back to her office to cool down as best she could once Sheila had told her mulishly that the burned paper was only a photocopy of an original, which was now safely filed, and she certainly was not going to tell George or anyone else, unless she chose to, where it was or what was in it, because it was no one's business apart from the person whose path. report it was, and she cared about patient confidentiality, even if no one else did.

And really that *had* been that. The whole episode had simmered down the way fights with Sheila always did, only Sheila herself had gone on sulking longer than generally and been ever more obstructive. Admittedly, George had made it impossible for her to prowl around the hospital as usual picking up her news and disseminating it, by making a new work rota that ensured any message that had to be delivered by a senior person, or any non-lab work that needed a special degree of expertise, fell into Jerry's tray. And ever since Sheila had been behaving as though George was the devil incarnate: no wonder George had become irritable with her. Now she was accusing George of trying to harm her. And in fact very unpleasant things *were* happening to her.

The visual memory faded and George shoved her notes into one of the desk's pigeon holes, though she went on sitting there with unfocused gaze, thinking. She'd forgotten all that fuss until now, and why not? So much happened in Old East that the events of a couple or so months ago were like prehistoric experiences. But this was worth remembering. It explained so much.

But not why Sheila was now being attacked. And that was something that it should be possible to work out. What she had to do, George told herself, was to talk to Sheila about what had happened in the Records department all that time ago, and get a lead from her that she could actively pursue; and a faint tingle seemed to reach her shoulders and give her an agreeable frisson. Perhaps an investigation into what had happened then would lead her to why someone was doing these things to Sheila now? Perhaps once she knew that she'd know who. Anyway, it seemed as reasonable to start in Medical Records as anywhere else.

She cheered up so much at the thought of having a piece of digging around to do that she relented about Gus. She would phone him and forgive him handsomely. Then they could spend this Saturday evening together happily, and tomorrow too. And come Monday, when they both got back to work, between them they'd sort out this Sheila mystery in no time, he working on the car angle and she on the path. lab reports aspect, and she'd be able to relax and enjoy life again. Which might or might not include teasing Gus a little about Zack. Yes, that would be fun; and she dialled his number in a very cheerful frame of mind.

But he spoiled everything, because he was out and his

answerphone said only that if they needed him at the nick to use his bleeper and he'd respond at once; otherwise, his voice said flatly, he wasn't available till Monday morning for *anyone*.

Altogether, it was a horrible weekend for George.

10

The first person she saw when she got to the hospital early on Monday morning was Zack, and she had had so dreary a Sunday that she greeted him with more warmth than perhaps she should have done. She had managed to park her car, in spite of the fact that half of the car park had been closed off to allow the Estates Department to apply new ground markings designed to make the place easier and safer to use, and was about to lock it up when she spotted a heap of detritus – paper wrappers, dead leaves, flakes of street mud and the like – on the floor. She bent to brush it out, her posture far from elegant, only to receive a mild slap on her bottom. She pulled herself out of the car to deliver a blistering reproof to whoever had delivered it, suspecting it might be Gus, only to see Zack standing there and smiling at her.

'I'm sorry,' he said at once. 'I know I shouldn't have but I simply couldn't resist. You have a neat rear elevation and the presentation was more than human flesh could bear.'

'You should be ashamed of yourself, a modern man like you,' she said trying to sound angrier than she was. 'I could have you for sexual harassment.'

'I grovel. Don't sue me this week, huh? Leave it till next time. Only I swear there won't be a next time. Until I'm invited, that is . . . So, did you have a good weekend?'

She looked back at it in her memory and grimaced. 'Oh, sure.'

'Like that, was it? Me too. Busy but no fun. Have you had breakfast yet?'

'I wasn't going to bother.' She locked the car and began to walk towards her department. 'I have a lot to do.' But he steered her away towards the canteen block.

'Not healthy. A person needs her breakfast. A pathologist needs it more than a person does, seeing she has such an onerous burden of work to face.'

'More onerous than a researcher's?'

'Oh, much more. All those PMs and tests and the masses of paperwork and computer fiddling –'

'How right you are!' she said feelingly. 'That's the part I dislike most. Still, it has to be done.'

'Can't you hand it over to your staff? I try to get some other guy to do it every chance I get. Not that I get as much as you.'

'Oh, I don't know. I don't have that huge a staff, you know, and most of 'em have very specific jobs of their own: histology and biochemistry and so on. I can't just drag them away to deal with data just because I don't enjoy doing it.'

'Poor you.' They'd reached the canteen where a flutter of night nurses was making a fair amount of noise over the last meal of their working day. There was a smell of not very good curry in the air which made George wrinkle her nose in distaste.

'Poor me indeed. God, that smells horrible. How people can eat curry at eight a.m. is beyond me.'

'To them it's an evening meal,' he said, reaching for a tray. 'What's for you then? Bacon and eggs and all things cholesterol?'

'Muesli and orange juice and all things fibrous,' she said. 'Anyway, it tastes better. They don't have to cook it. Tea or coffee?'

'Since they both taste equally foul, I leave the choice to you. You find a table, I'll pay.'

'Make a note of my share. I pay my own way,' she said. He

opened his mouth to protest but she just looked at him very directly indeed with her brows up and he subsided.

'Oh, indeed, indeed, She-who-must-be-obeyed,' he murmured.

'Oh, did you read that book too?' She felt a warm surge of pleasure. 'It was one of my favourites when I was a kid. *She* –'

'By Rider Haggard. Of course I read it. It was real sexy.'

'Wasn't it just! If my Ma had known what sort of tale it was, it's my guess she'd have pushed me back at *Little Women*.'

'They made me read *The Last of the Mohicans*,' he said. 'I preferred *Ayesha* and *Sanders of the River* every time.'

They found a table and settled to eat, still talking eagerly of the books they'd read as children, until George spotted Jerry leaving the canteen, having finished his breakfast, and sighed. 'I have to get to work,' she said. 'That paperwork, remember?'

'So what sort do you have?' He sounded only politely curious and she laughed.

'You don't really want to know.'

He straightened up. 'Oh, I do, I do,' he said. 'I'm interested in everything you do. So tell me. I insist.'

'Oh, well, if you *insist*,' she said. 'There are all the assays to spot check, to make sure the staff are up to the mark. There are the costings on all sorts of procedures to keep Ellen – she's the Business Manager – happy and to keep my budget in good shape. There're staff assessments for the personnel department. There're the reports I have to make on postmortems and pieces of special evidence I might have to give in court. There are –'

'God,' he said. 'I'm impressed. But it's very routine stuff, isn't it? Don't you have any of the fun data to play with? Research results, say? I mean, some of the research that we do goes through your department, doesn't it? Institute work?'

'Oh, some,' she said. 'There are hormone assays, aren't there, involved in some of the work? That'd come to us, but I don't handle the paperwork – or rather the computer work – for that. One of the senior technicians deals with it.'

'Well that's something. Sheila?'

'Maybe. Or Jerry Swann or Peter. Why do you ask?'

'I told you. I'm interested in everything you do. You're an interesting woman, so your work is interesting too.'

'La, but you're becoming a deal too particular, sir,' she said, with a mock Restoration flourish of her hand, and got to her feet. 'Like I said, I gotta go. And when a woman's gotta go –'

'May I come over later to go through the stuff I worked on over the weekend?' He sounded eager. 'I have the list of patients ready, and the X-rays and so forth. It'd be a great help to get some input from you before I go on.'

She hesitated, mentally running over her day's schedule in her mind. She wouldn't know till she got to the lab whether or not there were any PMs to be done, but she did have an appointment to go to court to give evidence. She explained how difficult it was to know just how long a case would take once it had started, and even if it would start on time. 'But I should be through by a late lunchtime,' she said. 'I sure as hell hope so. If you don't mind taking a chance that I won't be available, you could phone over around three, and I'll see how I'm doing.'

'Great.' He smiled at her, and once again she felt the little surge of interest she had felt when she had first seen his eyes vanish into slits the way they did when he was particularly happy. This time she rather enjoyed it.

When she got to the lab she found Danny waiting in her office, looking even more lugubrious than usual, if that were possible. 'There's a bit of a flap on in the coroner's office,' he reported with gloomy relish. 'There was a multiple pile-up in the Commercial Road. Three of the drivers are here in intensive care and two in the Royal London, and there was two fatalities and they're waiting downstairs for you. And then there's been some trouble at a school over in Stepney Green with a couple of these bovver boys carving up a Paki. They

98

want all three of the PMs dead urgent, and they keep calling to see what you can do to rush 'em.'

'Not a lot,' she said crisply. 'I'm due in court at – let me see my worklist.' She picked up her folder and studied it. 'Ten o'clock. It's a tricky one, so even if it starts on time . . . Look, I'll call the coroner's office myself. You go and get the first of them ready, anyway.'

'Which one?'

Danny was being wilfully difficult, she told herself and smiled at him as brilliantly as she could. 'The one that the police are most likely to be interested in. I imagine that'll be the knife wounds, don't you?'

'S'pose so,' he muttered, and went stomping off.

George set to work to get through as much as she could before having to leave for court. When she'd made sure that the lab was running smoothly and had dealt with her urgent mail and phone calls, she had a little time left over to tidy her desk, which she did, stacking the files high. And that was when she found the envelope that had come over by hand from Ratcliffe Street.

She recognized Gus's handwriting on the envelope, and bit her lip. Maybe she'd been a bit unfair to him; if this was some sort of peace offering she'd accept it and no hard feelings.

It was a brief note that he had merely initialled, chilling in its lack of any friendly touches.

I can't tell you for some time what happened to Sheila Keen's car. It was checked first thing this morning by CID here and arrangements were made to ship it to the main forensics laboratory for full testing. I've just heard, however, that they've a major overload of work and cannot promise a report before midweek at the earliest. Sorry about this. I'll let you know what there is as soon as I get it. Ditto with the report on the chocolates.

She brooded on that for the rest of the morning: all through her court case (except fortunately while she was actually in the witness box, which was just as well because she had to face a particularly vicious cross-examination by the defence) and even while she did the PM on the young Asian boy who had been knifed in the school playground. But again fortunately the anger that created in her (to see a healthy young body sliced to death for no reason was precisely the sort of trigger to rouse her fury at the best of times, and this was far from that) fuelled her concentration enough to find a fragment of metal in one of the wounds that would, she knew, enable the police to identify the weapon and therefore the perpetrator very fast indeed. Which gave her a degree of grim satisfaction, if not enough to help her feel all that much better.

She was about to start on the first of the traffic accident PMs when the phone in Danny's cubby hole rang down the corridor. He departed to answer it, even as she bawled after him, 'Let it ring!', then came back to find her scowling more than ever. He told her blandly that, 'Dr Zack said as how you told him to phone now, but I told him you was busy and wouldn't be best pleased at being interrupted, so he said not to bother. All right, then?'

She stared at him nonplussed. That would have been exactly the right thing to have said to any other caller, but he'd brushed off Zack, and she wasn't at all happy about that. Talking to him would have soothed her thoroughly ruffled feathers. But she couldn't say that to Danny, who was smirking at her in the most maddening way possible. All she could do was get her head down and finish the job in hand as best she might.

Which she did, including the second traffic accident victim, much to Danny's annoyance, since he had expected her to leave that till first thing the next morning, thus allowing him to get to his favourite pub at his usual hour. Recognizing his annoyance helped George to regain her own composure and by the time she had finished and was in the shower as Danny banged about furiously clearing up, some of her equanimity had returned.

If it was going to take three days or so to get the information on Sheila's car, well, so be it. She'd just have to wait till she had it (if, that is, Gus gave it to her, and the possibility that he might refuse she did not even want to contemplate) and in the meantime get on with another line of enquiry.

Once she was out of the shower and dressed, with her hair brushed up and dried, she'd decided what to do. She glanced at her watch as she ran upstairs to her office: well after seven. She had been working flat out all day and she ought to be both tired and hungry, but she was neither. She knew just what she was going to do, and no one was going to stop her.

In Ballantyne Ward all was very quiet. The big central corridor gleamed in the late June evening and the various bays with their four- and six-bedded arrangements hummed with the quiet chatter of patients and their visitors and the eternal bleating of television sets. It wasn't one of Ballantyne's operating days so there was none of the usual bustle that fills a surgical ward after a long list, and the senior nurse on duty at the central work-station was one George knew only slightly. But that suited her very well. She certainly hadn't wanted to face Sister Chaplin again after the affair of the chocolates. And neither did she want to see Peter Selby who would have been here had he been operating today. Luck was on her side, she decided, and pressed it home.

'I've just dropped in to see Miss Keen,' she said lightly to the staff nurse. 'You know – the patient in the single room at the far end. No need to look up her notes or anything. This is just a social call, not a medical one. She's on my staff, you see.' She smiled confidently and went off down the corridor towards Sheila's room before the staff nurse could stop her, even if she'd wanted to.

Sheila was sitting up in bed, wrapped in a pink silk shawl of oriental description, arranged to show off her rather bony shoulders, which were as bare as she could get them to be – her nightdress was pulled well down to show her somewhat meagre décolletage – and she was staring up at the TV set on a bracket on the wall facing her bed. She looked up hopefully as the door was pushed open, wriggling her shoulders into an even more provocative curve and smiling widely; but when she saw George her smile faded in so ludicrous a fashion that George found it easy to grin back; indeed, she almost laughed.

'Hello, Sheila! I've brought you some flowers.' She held out the bunch of hothouse roses she'd bought at the stall just outside the Accident and Emergency entrance, and Sheila looked at it, her mouth turned down apprehensively. 'It's quite safe to take them. There are no secret nasal poisons unknown to Western medicine hidden in them, nothing toxic applied to the thorns. In fact there aren't any thorns at all, Old Eddie told me so. I said they were for you and he picked out the best.'

That was a patent lie, since Eddie the flowerman, who had been at his stand by the hospital gates for more years than anyone could remember, heartily disliked Sheila, who always fussed outrageously over any flowers she bought from him, but Sheila chose to believe George.

'That's very sweet of him,' she said. She managed a pathetic little moue. 'If you leave them there one of the nurses will put them in water.' She pointedly didn't thank George for the roses, but George professed not to notice that. She sat herself comfortably in the armchair beside Sheila's bed and said chattily, 'Well, tell me, how are you?'

There was a little silence as Sheila stared up at the screen where various soap opera stars were posturing busily. For a moment George thought she wasn't going to answer and that she'd have to take tough measures, but after a moment Sheila said grudgingly, 'As well as can be expected, I suppose. Under the circumstances.' And she shot a look of undiluted venom at George, who smiled sweetly back.

'Sheila, I know perfectly well you couldn't be more pissed off with me. You think I poisoned the chocolates. Well, I didn't do that either, any more than I tampered with your car, though *someone* did.'

Sheila's head jerked round and she stared at George with her eyes so dilated there was a rim of white around the irises. 'What did you say? My car? Someone *did* do something to it?'

It was George's turn to be surprised. 'But you suspected that! You said so to Za – to Dr Zacharius. I remember you said that it was strange how one week someone wishes something horrible will happen to you and then it does, and it made you wonder. I heard you, and thought you were having a go at me.'

Sheila had the grace to blush. 'Well, when you're worried you say things you mightn't exactly mean. I didn't really think the car had been fiddled with. I thought it was just an accident – but now you say it really *was?*'

'Yes.' Briefly George explained what Gus had heard from Trevor the car mechanic, and Sheila sat and stared at her throughout, her mouth half open with concentration. When George had finished she hunched her shoulders so that her shawl slid up them to a more demure level, and seemed to curl herself up to lie lower in the bed. It was the sort of move a frightened child makes and George felt suddenly very sorry for her. And said so.

'I know. It's horrible. To think that someone hates you enough to do stuff like this. But you can't think it's me, Sheila? You and I may have our fights, God knows, but you know as well as I do that I wouldn't do anything like that.'

Sheila looked at her miserably for a long moment and then closed her eyes. 'Yes,' she said in a small voice. 'I know, I s'pose. It was just that . . .' She opened her eyes. 'You've been so horrible to me for so long I thought – well, I was mad at you. And I thought, I'll show you how mad if I – well, if I *didn't* say it couldn't be you who did it. The chocolates, I mean.' She looked suddenly watchful. 'Mind you, who could it be, Dr B.? I mean, there's no one in the lab hates me that much, is there? I'm entitled to think – well, you've been on my back something rotten for months. Won't let me set foot outside the place and —'

George leaned closer. 'Listen, Sheila, that's what I want to talk to you about. Do you remember what started it all off? I'd forgotten, but then suddenly I remembered why it was that I was so mad with you and why you were being as bloody minded as you could be.'

Sheila's lips quirked for a moment. 'I suppose I was a bit awful.'

George made a noise at the back of her throat that was deeply expressive. 'A bit! Ye Gods, woman, you would have driven the Angel Gabriel into a decline the way you've been behaving!'

'Well, a person has to stand up for herself,' Sheila murmured and then laughed. And suddenly it was as though none of the arguments between them had ever happened. She was Sheila again, awkward, argumentative, often tiresome but at heart a good enough soul who was in general on George's side.

George reached out and took her hand and squeezed it. 'That's better.'

'Yeah,' Sheila said and then added in a little rush, 'I've been feeling awful about you, Dr B. I never truly thought you would do anything really nasty to me, it was just that I wanted you to know how mad I was. But then the chocolates . . .' Her voice trailed away. 'I couldn't help thinking about that and what with Sister Chaplin saying things and Mr Selby so carefully not saying anything at all . . .'

'I can imagine,' George said grimly. 'But I intend to sort this out, one way or another. And I'm not bad at that, am I? Finding out what happened?'

Sheila looked at her eagerly. 'Oh, no. Gus and you together have done some great things.'

'I can do it on my own as well,' George replied with a spurt of anger, and Sheila produced one of her sharp little grins.

'Whoops! Trouble in loveland, is there?'

'None of your business – don't you start again, lady! I'm glad we're not fighting any more, but if you start being a smartass –'

'Pax!' Sheila said. 'I just meant that usually you and Gus – Well, anyway, never mind. What are you going to do?'

'I told you. Find out what the hell is going on here. And I'm going to start by talking to you. I need to know a few things.'

'Anything you like.' Sheila moved up the bed again and re-arranged her shawl more elegantly. She looked much better now. 'Fire away.'

'OK. I want you to remember: a while back, April sometime, I'm not sure when, there was this fight I had with the woman up in Medical Records. About you and her. Mrs Ellesmere, her name is.'

'That one!' Sheila said with infinite scorn. 'One of those with bugger all to do and all day to do it in, the way she faffs around. I can't stand her, and well she knows it.'

'Yes, and I know it too. But what I want to know about is that time you had a great fight with her – and afterwards with me – because you showed a path. report to one of her staff and wouldn't show it to her. Or to me, dammit! What I'd like to know for openers is the truth of that affair. Is it significant? Has it anything to do with what is going on now?'

'Significant,' Sheila said in a flat voice, staring at George blankly, the corners of her mouth turning down so that she looked as though she'd been standing in a cold wind for a long time. 'Significant, you say?'

'Yup. I need to know, who was the staff member? Is that what was so important in the affair? Or was it Ellesmere being stupid or – Well, tell me. What was it?'

'I can't think how I never thought of it before,' Sheila said. Her eyes had suddenly gone a little out of focus, as though she were staring through George to a distant point. 'There was all that talk, all that fuss and I just never thought of it! I must be losing my mind, I swear it!'

George looked at her, frowning. 'What are you talking about?' she said. 'What didn't you think about?'

'The staff member whose report it was,' Sheila said. 'She'd asked me to look through the reports in the lab because she thought her test results weren't being put into her notes the way they should be. She used to keep a close eye on her own notes, you see, being she was working in Medical Records anyway and knew a lot about the system, and about herself of course. But she was worried about something – I don't know what, she never said. She just asked me to get her path. reports – our copies of them, you know? – and bring them to show her. So I did.'

'That was what Ellesmere got so mad about?' George said. 'Who was she? The staff member?'

'Oh, Dr B.,' Sheila said, and there was an air of tragedy about her that was almost comical in its intensity. 'That's what's so awful. About me not remembering, I mean. It was Lally, Lally Lamark. One of those suicides –'

'Not suicide. Accidental overdose,' George said. But Sheila ran on as if she hadn't spoken a word.

'I never for a moment joined the two things in my mind after I heard she'd died. I didn't think about what she'd asked me to do all those weeks ago. Dr B., do you think it had anything to do with her killing herself? I'll never forgive myself if it did.'

II

When George got back to the courtyard after saying good-night to Sheila, with many assurances that she needn't worry, that she couldn't be anywhere safer than where she was (for Sheila had steadily become more anxious over what happened to her car, adding it to the chocolates incident), she stopped, uncertain what to do next. There were few people about, so after a moment she sat down on the scrubby grass, clasped her arms round her legs, rested her chin on her knees, and thought.

The reassurances she had offered Sheila had seemed to help her, though deep inside George knew that they were little more than her own efforts to whistle bravely in the dark. The hard truth was that two attempts had been made on Sheila, certainly to harm her and possibly to kill her. And on both occasions she, George, had been set up as the possible perpetrator, at least in Sheila's eyes. Did anyone else think she might have had anything to do with the doctoring of the car? (She squirmed at the way the word came into her head; it was hardly sympathetic to protestations of her innocence.) It was natural enough they should think she had sent the chocolates; there had after all been that card with her forged initials on it. But there was not a scintilla of evidence to connect her with the car's wiring, apart from the fact that she used the same car park, and that applied to a large number of other people in the hospital.

One comfort, she told herself, was that it was obvious the police did not think she had been responsible for either attack on Sheila. She'd made her statement and it had been accepted; there had been no suggestion of further questioning. Could that be because she was known in the nick as the Guv'nor's girlfriend? (What a stupid label that is, she thought sourly. Makes me sound like something in gingham skirts with bows in my hair. I'm his woman, dammit. Or I was till this weekend. Right now I'm not sure how we stand.) Well, even if it was her connection to Gus which had protected her, the fact that she was clear of police doubt left her a free agent to see what she could do herself to unravel this mystery. She'd make the best possible use she could of that freedom, she decided, and jumped to her feet to brush the dried grass from her skirt and make her way, not to the car park and home, which would be the sensible thing to do at this time of evening, but back to her laboratory.

The cleaners were there when she let herself in using her private key, and she blinked as one of them came towards her with suspicion written all over her very hostile face.

''Ere, this is private property, this is. You got no call to be 'ere this time o' night. I got instructions from security that no one's allowed in without reasonable cause.'

'I have reasonable cause,' George said mildly. 'This is my department. I'm Dr Barnabas. See?' She pointed to her office door, which bore her name in shabby white paint.

The woman looked at her no less suspiciously. 'Oh, indeed? And what proof 'ave I got that that is true, tell me? There're always people walking in claiming to be doctors and so forth – or technicians, like the last one said – and I got no way to know it's true, 'ave I? Being 'ere only of a night, I can't get to know people's faces like day workers can. So I needs proof, that's what Mr Bittacy said, and 'e should know.'

'Bittacy knows everything.' George, who had herself had brushes with the self-important Head of Night Security (who had been promoted from Head Porter and bossed all the artisan staff about with an air of lordly grandeur, and tried to do the same with medical staff), was not impressed. 'I have every right to come to my own department at any time. But to keep you happy, try this.' She scrabbled in her skirt pocket and pulled out the swipe card all the senior staff carried, which gave them access to protected parts of the hospital, such as I T U, the Pharmacy and Maternity. It bore her name and the usual sort of hideous photograph which George thought totally unrecognizable as her face, and she thrust it under the cleaner's nose with a certain degree of aggression.

The cleaner took several laborious moments to dig in her grubby overall pocket, pull out her glasses and put them on her nose, then studied the card as intently as though it were her ticket to Paradise. But she handed it back at last and said grudgingly, 'Well, all right, then. I suppose that's 'oo you are. We've cleared that office, let me tell you, so I 'ope you don't go messin' it up and then complainin' tomorrow as we didn't do it. I've 'ad that trick pulled on me before.' And she turned on her heel and marched away back into the main lab, where her fellow cleaner could be heard clattering about in a marked manner.

It was quite the most absurd thing that happened next. George marched in to her office, throwing her jacket on to a chair, and was about to go over to her files to start the search for the notes she had made on Lally Lamark, which she now believed needed very careful study, when without any conscious thought on her part she found herself whirling and bolting out of the door and along the short corridor into the main lab in search of the cleaner. It wasn't until she saw the gawping faces turned towards her by the two women standing in the middle of the floor leaning on mops and brooms that she was able to get her thoughts together.

'Uh, Mrs – Uh –' she said and stood still. 'I'm so sorry. I don't know your name.'

The woman who had stopped her outside now stepped forward and stared at her pugnaciously. 'And why d'you want to know? I done nothing wrong.'

'Of course you haven't!' George opened her eyes wide. 'Far from it. It was just that – I'm impressed, you see. Yes, that's it. I'm very impressed. So few people in Old East seem to have any idea of the importance of security and anyone can wander anywhere in consequence. We've had all those robberies and all, remember? So when someone's as sensible as you were and makes sure people aren't where they're not supposed to be, well, they deserve thanks. And I wanted to tell Mr Bittacy so.'

The woman seemed to melt before her eyes. Her squared shoulders softened as the woman behind her first gaped and then giggled self-consciously. Clearly she too shared in the golden glow of George's approbation. 'Oh, well then, seein' as you ask, I'm Mrs Glenney.'

'Let me shake you by the hand,' George said solemnly, and did so, and Mrs Glenney, now beaming widely to show the silvery glitter of well-filled teeth, preened with pleasure. 'It's such a comfort to know my department's in safe hands when I'm not here. Do tell me ...' She dropped her voice to a friendlier, slightly conspiratorial note. 'Who was it you saw off the other time? Recently, was it?'

'Eh?' Mrs Glenney looked puzzled.

'You said that people are always walking in claiming to be doctors.'

Mrs Glenney's face cleared. 'Oh! Oh, well, I didn't mean always walking in *'ere*, you understand! No, around the place like. Mr Bittacy told me, said as 'ow they pinch white coats and then wander about seein' what they can steal. Or worse.' She looked down her nose more primly. 'Some of 'em even try it on pretendin' to be doctors and examinin' women and so forth.'

George filled with disappointment. 'Oh,' she said a little flatly. She too had heard the tales of wannabes trying to pass themselves off as doctors, but such stories always struck her as apocryphal; she had never heard of such an episode at Old East directly from someone who'd had personal experience of it. 'I thought you meant you'd had someone coming in here.'

'Well, yes, I 'ave,' Mrs Glenney said and George lifted her chin to stare at her.

'But I thought you said you'd only heard about such things from Mr Bittacy?'

'I only ever 'eard about *doctors* tryin' it on,' Mrs Glenney said punctiliously. 'Which was what you asked me about. But I've 'ad that other one.'

'"That other one",' George said carefully. Clearly Mrs Glenney was a lady who took questions very literally.

''S right. 'Im what said 'e was a technician and 'ad some special work to do in the lab. Well, I said to 'im, technician you may be, I said, but 'ow am I to know? I got to phone Mr Bittacy, seein' as 'ow you've got no ID – like what you 'ad yourself, doctor – you stand 'ere, I said to 'im, and I'll go and call Mr Bittacy and see what's what.'

'And what was what?'

'Eh?' Mrs Glenney was puzzled again.

'What happened?' George wanted to shake her.

'Oh, yes. I phoned, like I said, from your office. I left 'im out 'ere, o' course, I wasn't goin' to have 'im listenin' in. An' when I managed to get 'old of Mr Bittacy an' I explained 'e said to keep the fella 'ere and 'e'd come over 'imself. But by the time I got back the fella'd bin and gone, 'n't 'e? Well, 'e would, wouldn't 'e? So I told Mr Bittacy all about it, an' 'e said I done the right thing, though 'e wasn't best pleased bein' dragged all the way over 'ere for nothing, as it were.'

'I can imagine,' George said absently, thinking hard. 'Listen, Mrs Glenney, how long did it take you to make that call?'

'Eh?'

'I said –'

''Ow long? I 'eard you.' Mrs Glenney bridled. 'Well, it was a while, I suppose. Maybe five minutes or so. I mean, they 'ad to bleep Mr Bittacy from the switchboard and I 'ad to 'old on a goodish while. They offered to phone me back when 'e answered, but I know them on that switchboard, a right dreamy lot they are, you 'ave to keep on at 'em, so about five minutes it was.'

'Bit longer'n that,' the other woman said unexpectedly. 'It was one of the nights I was here too, don't you remember, Marlene? I heard you talk to that bloke and then you went off to the office and you was gone ages. I was busy doin' the floor, and I'd done more'n half of it by the time you'd come back, and it always takes at least twenty minutes, more if you're on your own, as well you know.' The woman sounded a touch sharp and Mrs Glenney threw an equally sharp glare at her.

'Well, it can't be 'elped if office business 'as to be done,' she said. 'But like you said, it mighta bin a bit longer'n five minutes. Ten minutes outside.'

'Ten minutes,' George said. 'Hmm. Well, thanks again, Mrs Glenney, for being so watchful and careful. It's really appreciated.' She turned to go back to her office and then said over her shoulder, as innocently as she could, playing being Colombo on the TV show, 'Oh – when did this happen, then? This business with the technician who wasn't?'

'Four weeks ago exactly.' The woman behind Mrs Glenney said it, quickly. 'I remember it perfectly well. It was the fifteenth of May, my birthday. It was why I wanted to get away sharpish, you remember, Marlene? My old man said he'd take me for a drink and fish supper. Only of course that fella held us up like.'

Again Mrs Glenney looked affronted. 'Well, if you say so, I suppose so! I don't remember that clear. I just know it 'appened and there it is. It makes me more careful, even if it does use up a bit o' time. You got to do the job right or why bother to do it at all?' With which Parthian shot she glared triumphantly at her colleague.

'Of course, you're quite right,' George said quickly, needing to settle turbulent waters. 'What sort of chap was he, by the way?' And she glanced at the other woman too, hoping for as accurate an answer as she'd given before. But not this time. Both women looked quite blank.

'Oh, I don't know,' the other woman said. 'Do you, Marlene?'

Mrs Glenney shook her head. 'Blokes in white coats, they all look the same, don't they? I can never tell 'em apart.'

The other woman let out a little cackle of laughter. 'It's true, that,' she said. 'Just like the Chinese, 'n't it? Can't tell 'em apart.'

George, this time casting her a glance full of dislike, tilted her head at Mrs Glenney. 'Nothing you can recall?' she asked hopefully. 'Anything that might help us find him? I mean, he might try again and you never know, someone might get hurt. If the man can be spotted in advance, you see . . .'

Mrs Glenney wrinkled her nose and thought hard, an obvious effort. Then she said, 'I dunno. Sort of ordinary, know what I mean? Nothing you'd specially notice. Not the sort of bloke you'd pay much attention to even if 'e wasn't dressed up in a white coat. Just, well, ordinary.'

'Fair or dark? Tall or short? Fat or thin?' George said.

'Oh, well. It might be that 'e was on the thin side, but then again I didn't really – I mean . . .' She shook her head and turned to the other. 'Did you notice, Evie, seeing you was noticing the time so closely?'

Evie shook her head. 'Like you said, Marlene, ordinary. A sort of – Oh, I don't know. Wispy, like.'

'Thin, then,' said George quickly.

'Well, sort of.'

It was clearly a waste of time. If she questioned them any more they'd start to be suspicious and she'd get no more out of them. So she smiled at them both, repeated her thanks and then added casually, 'If you should happen to see him around anywhere, let me know, hmm? I'm just a bit curious, that's all.'

'Oh, yes, doctor.' Mrs Glenney was now much more eager to talk and George thought, with a flash of amusement, this beats working with that damned mop, and smiled at her once more and went firmly back to her office.

'No, there's nothing else,' she said as she went. 'I won't delay you any longer. Not if I want to see the lab as shining clean as it usually is, hmm?' She closed the door behind her and stood there and listened as they returned to the big lab, talking to each other in high shrill tones, not that she could actually identify any of the words.

So there was something new to add to Sheila's experience. Someone claiming to be a technician had come down here to try to get into the lab for some nefarious purpose or other. It had to be nefarious; why else would he have disappeared when the officious Mrs Glenney insisted on phoning the security office? The question was, had he managed to carry out that purpose?

Ten minutes Mrs Glenney had spent holding on to the telephone. George had no difficulty in believing the other woman. She had every reason, clearly, to have so accurate a recall, and no need to exaggerate the time Mrs Glenney managed to spend dealing with the lab phone and leaving the floor to someone else to do. And in ten minutes a determined person could do a lot.

But then she stopped and stared sightlessly across the room. What could he have done? He couldn't have got into the main lab unseen. Evie was in there, resentfully doing the floor on her own. He couldn't get into her, George's office, because Mrs Glenney would be calling Mr Bittacy. What did that leave?

She stared inside her head at her department, at the doors that ran off the main corridor outside. There were the doors to the main lab and this office, of course; then another to the big Beetle cupboard where all the supplies were kept for re-plenishing equipment of the smaller sort, such as slides and pipettes and refillable reagent bottles; and the door to Sheila's little cubby hole where her records were kept.

Where her records were kept. George went on staring at that inner image. She saw an unidentified hand opening the door to Sheila's little office; pushing it open; closing it behind him; switching on the light? Maybe. Or using a torch. Again, maybe. And then peering inside those drawers where Sheila filed the copies of the path. reports as a special precaution against the computer going down, or floppy discs being lost or whatever other disaster could befall records. Of course all relevant reports were sent to patients' notes and to the doctors, including consultants, who had requested them and were also stored in the hospital's main computer; but Sheila was a nit-picking and thorough person when it came to work. She wanted a third safety net and her files were part of that net. Everything was kept for at least three years, and then shredded carefully.

It had to be there that the mysterious non-technician went, whoever he was. What else was there out in the corridor that could be of any use to him? The only other door led to the loo and the cloakroom, and of course there was the one that led to the stairs and the way down. Could he have wanted something in the morgue? Hardly. What could there be amid the specimens and bodies and the stink of Festival disinfectant and formaldehyde that would interest anyone? She couldn't imagine such a circumstance.

But she could imagine a need to go into that record office, especially now she knew that Lally Lamark had also been interested in the contents of those files. And Lally Lamark was now dead.

'Yes,' she said aloud, 'yes,' and did what she had come here to do in the first place. She went over to the filing cabinet where she kept the records of all the post-mortems she had done and reached for the file. Maybe there she'd find a lead to what had happened to Sheila as well as to the lab's mysterious visitor.

12

Considering how busily her brain had been whirling when she went to bed, she slept very well, which made it all the more shocking when she woke suddenly at the sound, and lay there rigid with terror. The stupid thing was that she knew it was Gus. It had to be, for no one else had a key and it was the sound of a key turning in the lock that had dragged her out of her sleep.

He peered round the door gingerly, but by that time she was sitting bolt upright, her knees up and wrapped in the duvet with her arms linked round them. 'Well?' she said belligerently. 'What do you want?'

'A bit of a welcome'd be nice,' he said plaintively. 'Nothin' elaborate. I don't expect you to go throwing yourself at me all soulful and beggin' me to take you in my manly arms or anythin' of that sort. Just a nice, "Good mornin' Gus, and I'm glad you're ready to apologize", 'll do.'

She stared at him in the bright early morning light. He looked perky enough but she could see there was more to his state of mind than that; she had known him long enough to understand that he was often at his most flippant when he was most concerned.

'What's happened?' she said and then looked at her bedside clock. 'Christ! It's half past five. What sort of time is this to –'

'Something else to apologize for,' he said dolefully. He

sighed deeply and with a couple of economical movements went down on his knees beside the bed. 'Are there any other similar offences you're annoyed about that I can take into account while I'm down here grovellin'? Mea culpa, mea ever so culpa, whatever it is, and I'm sorry and –'

'Shut up, idiot,' she said. 'And I'll think about the apologies. No, stay where you are. It'll do you good. What is it you're so anxious about that you turn up at this time of the morning?'

'Anxious? Just because I want to ask you to forgive me for being such a ham-handed ass on Friday –'

'Ham-fisted and ham-butted as well,' she said. 'And stop trying it on. This is me, remember? What is it that's worrying you?'

He sighed, got to his feet, then sat on the side of the bed. 'I'll never be able to call my soul my own ever again,' he complained. 'From now on I'm obviously as transparent as a TV screen. What sort of life is that, I ask you?'

'I asked a question first.' She refused to be deflected. 'What is it? What – is – the – mat – ter?' She pronounced each syllable with offensive emphasis.

He seemed to settle more heavily onto the bed. 'There was an incident at Old East last night.'

She felt herself freeze. 'An incident?'

'Yup.' He looked at her and shook his head slightly. 'No need to look so worried. It was only a small thing, really. But the way things have been lately they thought they'd better call us. And because I'd told them at the nick to call me if anything happened involving Old East, well, they did.'

'Is anyone hurt?' she asked urgently.

'It's all right, doll.' He reached out and took one of her hands. 'No need to panic. No one's hurt. Not physically.'

'Then some other way – Oh, for pity's sake, Gus!'

He was succinct. 'OK. There was an emergency in Ballantyne Ward at half past midnight. A big flap, lots of doctors flying about. Apparently they had a patient who had – what was it? Laryngeal carcinoma with local spread and an artery went, and –'

'OK,' she said. 'I get the picture.' She did indeed, and could imagine the fuss at once; when a throat cancer erodes a major artery the result can be spectacularly bloody and certainly calls every medical person around into service. 'But what –'

'Listen. While the fuss was on, no one paid much attention to such things as ward security and so forth. When they'd finished and the man had been transferred to intensive care, they could sort themselves out. This was about half past one. The night nurse did a round of the ward and found there'd been an interloper. Several patients' things had been turned over. One man had his clothes taken and strewn around and another had had her jewellery taken from her bed table and dropped in the corridor outside. The only real loss was Sheila Keen's. She had her bag taken. It had her keys in it. The keys of the lab, it seems, as well as her home keys.'

'Keys to the lab?' George was bewildered. 'But why should she have those? I have a set, and of course the security office does, but Sheila?'

'I know. She isn't supposed to have them. She told me that and very embarrassed she was too. Seems she had a set cut for her private use years ago. Sometimes, she said, she likes to be able to work late and it's handy to be able to lock up without bothering people or having to go over to Security to get the keys.'

'Dammit, but she is without a doubt the most inquisitive woman who ever drew breath!' George was furious. 'How dare she have her own keys? Work? Phooey! She just likes to be able to snoop around when it suits her.'

'That's pretty much what I thought. But she does assure me they're never out of her possession. She never leaves them anywhere. When she's at work they're in her pocket. When she's at home they're in a secret hiding place. She swears she's had 'em for several years and there's never been a problem, till now. She said she always had her bag beside her during the day in Ballantyne Ward, but she didn't think there'd be a problem at night, so she didn't hide it or anything.'

'I'll murder her!' George said feelingly and then stopped short.

'I agree,' Gus said. 'Not the best sort of language to use at present, is it? Listen, doll, there's more.'

'More? How can there be more?'

'Easily.' He sounded suddenly grim. 'We went on to her house – she lives in Barking – to see if there'd been any use made of the keys. It seemed to me that if someone was after the place in any way, they wouldn't waste time. And I was right. It had been turned over very thoroughly indeed. We can't know what's missing, if anything, till she gets home and can look and tell us, but whoever it was really did an effective job. Not a stone unturned, as they say.' He hesitated.

'Ye Gods,' George said weakly. 'I think there's more.'

'Yup.' He touched her hand again. 'I tried to make this as easy as I could, sweetheart. That was why the jokes, but I have to say it's not very funny. We went over to the lab then because Sheila was almost hysterical when she heard about her house. Our chap had to go back and talk to her, of course, though Night Sister wasn't best pleased, but she was awake anyway because the thing she was really frantic about wasn't her house so much as the lab. That was when she told us the lab keys had been in her bag. So, of course, we have to go there to see what's what. I sent one of our blokes to make a recce. The main door is unlocked, he says, and he's put a guard on the place, but he had the sense not to meddle at this stage. I need you to come and look, see what's what, OK? After all, you're the keyholder, and if there'd been a burglar alarm, we'd have to call you for that. So if you don't mind?'

'Of course.' She almost fell out of bed in her hurry and was padding across the hall to her bathroom at a trot. He went to the kitchen and put the kettle on and by the time she was dressed had a cup of coffee ready in a mug.

'You can drink it in the car,' he said briefly as she tried to refuse it, and took it with him as he hurried her down the stairs to where his old car was parked at the kerb. Usually it was a pleasure to her to ride in its leathery wooden panelled comfort, but this morning she was too preoccupied to notice. She had finished the coffee and was feeling a good deal more alert and less anxious by the time they reached the hospital, and had driven round the back to reach her laboratory.

The uniformed man outside the door nodded at her in a friendly fashion as she climbed out of the car. 'Morning, Dr B.,' he said. 'Not a sign of anything this last half-hour.'

'Thanks for the report,' Gus said sardonically. 'Glad to see a chap knows how to treat a superior officer.'

The man, a young constable, was deeply abashed. 'Sorry, Super,' he said. 'I just wanted to make it easier for the doctor, like.'

'No need to be so formal,' Gus growled, but there was no animus there. 'Guv'll do well enough for me.' He led the way towards the door and pushed it open. As though he'd called them there, other figures appeared round the side of the building to join him and George blinked.

'Hey, does it take four – five of you to deal with this sort of thing?' she said. 'You must be longing to get in a bit of overtime.'

'Unpaid, though.' Michael Urquhart grinned at her. A recently promoted sergeant and always a good friend to George, he showed clearly that he was pleased to see her, and she was happy to see him. A very reliable guy, Mike.

'I don't want to take any chances, OK?' Gus was in serious mode now, speaking in a low tone with no hint of the flippant chatterbox who had woken her. 'I doubt there's anyone still here, but all the same, you never know. Mike, you head straight down to the mortuary. And don't be squeamish. I want every drawer checked, every body accounted for, get me? You two, the main lab, that way. You come with me, Hagerty, and Dr B., you stay behind me. OK. Easy does it.'

They seemed to vanish into the building like wraiths, silently and with an amazing efficiency. George stood behind Gus waiting for him to make his move, which he did as soon as the others had vanished into the various sections he'd sent them to. Then he made straight for her office.

She had never been unduly fussy about the way her office was arranged. She had the usual Busy Lizzie plant drooping on the window-sill; the ever-present heap of unread or about-to-be-read medical and professional journals in the corner; and the shelves full of her most trusted texts. Her desk, however, piled high though it usually was with the detritus of the busy department, still had some charm about it. A small crystal clock Gus had given her as a Christmas present was there, alongside a rather chipped old glass jug stuffed with multicoloured plastic paper clips; and, in central place, a photograph of her mother beaming out of an antique silver frame with an absentmindedness that George had learned to live with, knowing her mother's illness and how very far away her mind now was as a result. That was the first possession she looked over Gus's shoulder to ensure was there; and its presence helped a lot. The broken plant on the floor, the way the papers from her desk had been scattered everywhere, the smashed coffee cups from her corner tray: she could bear all of that as long as Vanny's picture was safe, and she darted into the room under Gus's arm and seized it. He opened his mouth to protest, caught her eye and thought better of it.

'A bit of tidying up to do, I guess,' she said, keeping her voice as colourless as she could as she slid the picture into the big pocket of her skirt where it sat against her hip heavily and comforted her. 'Let me know when I can start.'

'SOCO'll have to come first,' Gus said in an abstracted sort of voice. 'George, come over here, will you?'

He was crouching on the floor beside her big filing cabinet. She stared down over his shoulder and this time she was angry. Very. There were her files, the records she had kept from the very beginning of her career as a pathologist, waiting for that magic day when she'd have time to write that definitive textbook, which would not only make her name in her field but also a great deal of money, since it would of course be a required text for every student in the entire world, lying in a pathetic heap. Photographs had been pulled out and left strewn around (and even the experienced DC Hagerty blenched at the sight of some of them) and papers lay scattered and crumpled higgledy-piggledy.

'What the hell could he possibly want with these?' she said furiously, staring at what looked like the wreck of the record of her whole career. 'Why on earth should anyone want to do this? It's just wanton –'

'Are you sure?' Gus peered at her sharply, his eyes bright, and for a moment she wanted to laugh even though anger still bubbled in her. There was something so attractively simian about him as he crouched there and looked up with those sharp, warm and very knowing eyes of his. 'Not until you've been through lists and checked it all can you possibly know what's what. If there's anything missing then we'll know what he was looking for. If nothing is then indeed this is mindless destructiveness.'

'Or he didn't find what he was after,' DC Hagerty said, and there was a little silence in the room.

'Oh, very clever, Hagerty.' Gus got to his feet and shook his head in heavy irony. 'Will I ever get accustomed to the lightning minds of the best of the Bill what I have in my team? Will I ever cease to be blinded by their flashes of brilliance?'

'Well, I only meant, Guv –' Hagerty began.

'You only meant to put the fear of God into the doctor here, right?' Gus sounded savage. 'On account of if they haven't found what they want then they'll be back to do so, right? You're a thoughtful bugger and no error.'

'Lay off, Gus,' George said. She was crouching beside her

files. Her training prevented her from touching, but she was using her eyes very carefully. 'He's absolutely right, of course, and I'm not stupid: I had realized the same thing myself. But I'll tell you what. This isn't quite as bad as it looks.'

'Eh? How do you mean?'

'Well, it's funny, but only some of the files have been pulled out and scattered. See over here?' She scrabbled in her pocket for a pencil and, using it carefully, lifted a corner of the uppermost file. 'Under here. They've been pulled out and dropped on the floor, but no attempt's been made to gut them, has there? Not like this one.' She peered even closer. 'It looks to me as though only this one's been pulled about.'

'And that one over there.' Gus was on his knees beside her, also armed with a long pencil. 'And is that another one there? See? You can just see the name on the top piece of paper. All the others are covered over with the mess.'

'It's the M file,' she said. 'M's a huge one of course, it's amazing how many names begin with it. And how many conditions.'

'Conditions?' He looked at her sharply.

'Mmm. I use a filing system all my own,' she said, looking a little defensive. 'I find it works perfectly for me. If I have a special interest in mind, then I'll file the notes under the name of the condition with a cross referral note to the right place in the file lettered by patient names. See this one on top: his name's Gradalski, but he's in the M file because he died of a myocardial infarction. I did him only last week, that's why I remember.'

Gus sat back on his heels and shook his head at her. 'Oh, George, George!' he said disgustedly. 'I might have known it! You've really cocked it up, haven't you? Here was I thinking that once we had the initial letters of the files that had been gutted, we'd at least know this bugger was interested in people whose names begin with M or whatever. But it could be because they had a myo whatsit.'

'Myocardial infarction,' George said helpfully. 'Or myasthenia gravis. Or a myeloid leukaemia, though that's more likely to be in the L file. Or Marfan's syndrome. That's a rather rare condition that may lead to premature death in affected children. I've made rather a study of it, had several cases and –'

'Or Uncle Tom Cobbleigh and all,' Gus said, turning away. 'Well, there it is. It's going to take you longer than you hoped to get this stuff sorted out, isn't it, so that you can tell me what's missing?'

'I suppose so.' She looked mournfully at the mess and then straightened up. 'But dammit, how am I supposed to know what's missing just by looking? There are years of records here. I brought some with me when I came here, and then there are those I've done since I arrived.'

'I don't suppose there's a master list on a floppy disc anywhere?' he said.

She shook her head. 'Why should there be? This was just my private collection. No need to make a great fuss over it. I just had to open the filing cabinet and there it all was.'

'There it all was, past tense, indeed,' he said. Then he growled over his shoulder: 'Well?' as the door opened.

The rest of the team were there, all reporting that there had been no other damage done anywhere.

'The main lab's all right as far as I can tell,' DC Morley said. 'If you'd just come and take a dekko, Dr B., and tell us for sure?'

'Of course.' She escaped gladly, feeling positively guilty because she hadn't protected her files on a computer, if only to make life easy for Gus now. But why should she? It made no sense . . .

It wasn't until she'd taken a look at the main lab and reported that, indeed, nothing had been disturbed, and done the same down in the mortuary with Mike Urquhart, that she remembered. And came belting up the stairs from the basement calling for Gus at the top of her voice.

'Gus!' she called. 'Hey, Gus! I'd forgotten, dammit. It comes from getting up in such a hurry so early. Listen, last night . . .'

'Yeah?' He looked at her hopefully.

'Well, last night, I was looking for notes as well. I was in here late, and I took away one set that I was interested in. I didn't feel up to going through it here, so I took it home. So that's one we haven't lost.'

'So what? I mean, does that help us to know what he *was* after? What you might have lost?'

'Well,' she said, 'I just thought that it might. You see, it was the notes for Lally Lamark's post-mortem. She was one of those three we dealt with last week. The suspected suicide, remember? Maybe if we look for the other two files, we'll get some idea? I mean, if they're missing . . .'

'If they're missing, then we may indeed have one end of a piece of string in our hands,' he said. He grinned suddenly, carving his face into agreeable crags. 'Listen, George, the minute SOCO finishes here, we'll get down to the search, right? And I'll tell you what. I'll help you.'

'I was afraid of that,' she said.

13

Despite his offer of help with the files, in the event Gus had to go back to Ratcliffe Street and leave her to it. The SOCO left her office a little before nine, gloomily telling everyone that they shouldn't get too hopeful on account he'd seen some messed-up prints in his time but this was really ridiculous.

George had been a tad affronted at that. 'Well, what do you expect? I dare say my office is a bit on the undusted and un-polished side, but that's because we've got more important things to do here than housework. People's fingerprints would pile up. But you shouldn't jump to conclusions. I'm pretty well the only person who uses that cabinet so you ought to be able to find something you can work on if you look properly.'

'It's not that easy when they're umpteen layers deep,' he muttered as he went off.

Gus grinned at her. 'Don't be too offended, doll. He's always like that: a real misery. Anyway, I didn't expect to get much from prints. Something tells me this isn't a professional job, which means we won't have the prints on file. It's an enthusiastic amateur who made that mess.'

As George, only partly mollified, settled down on her haunches to start the sorting, the phone rang. Gus took it. The call was for him and he listened, grunted, spoke in a few monosyllables, said, 'I'm on my way,' and hung up.

'I knew it,' she said. 'Left to do it on my own again.' But she didn't really mind. To have Gus around helping with this job might be more trouble than assistance; she had her filing system clear in her own head, but having to explain it in all its labyrinthine detail was more than she fancied doing. He'd probably jeer at it anyway. So she smiled at him happily enough.

'There's a meeting I can't miss,' he said briefly, sounding for once as though he wasn't interested in such an activity. 'But they've got some results from forensic over at the big lab on Sheila's car. I pushed 'em on it yesterday, told 'em I wasn't prepared to wait as long as their first estimate. And apparently they've worked out a report on the chocolates too.'

The smile vanished from her face. 'Well, I sure as hell hope they've found fingerprints there,' she said. 'So that they can compare them with mine and prove I had nothing to do with either one.'

'Fingerprints don't prove absence from the scene of a crime,' he said. 'Only presence. You could have used gloves.'

'Thanks a bunch!'

'I have to think like a devious-minded Machiavellian brief,' he said. 'Or one of said devious Machiavellians'll clobber me and any case I bring from here to hell and back. And you should have known that about fingerprints anyway.'

'I know and I do and get going,' she said. 'I've got too much to do here to put up with your pontificating at me. Let me know as soon as you can about those forensics, will you? I do have an interest after all. It's not just idle curiosity.'

'I will.' He bent and kissed the back of her neck. 'Am I forgiven for being such a bastard the other night? You've proven me wrong again and I grovel, like I said this morning.'

'Too much grovelling and you'll get a headache,' she said. 'Go on, scram. I'll think about forgiveness. The jury's still out on that one.'

'Well, send 'em a judge's message that it's time they pulled their fingers out. I'll be back as soon as I can, doll. Hope you can find what we need there.' He kissed her neck again and was gone.

It had seemed an interminable task when she started but in fact, as her hands moved among the piles of papers, photographs and scattered files, she found it wasn't nearly as bad as she had expected. First, she had to sort the papers into sets, so that she at least knew the content of each subfile in the L and M letter files, and then put them into alphabetical order – or sometimes date order – internally. By the time Jerry came in with a tray of coffee for her, having realized there was no way she'd take time out to make her own, she was in fairly good order.

'No problems inside,' he reported. 'We've had another nose around to make sure everything was ticketyboo and it is. No one was in the big lab, I'd swear to that.'

'Good,' she said absently, setting aside the now tidy and, as far as she could tell, complete L section (except of course for Lally Lamark's file which she had at home) and set to work on her Ms. 'It's obvious that what whoever it was wanted is in here.'

'I hope so.' He sounded uneasy, and hovered at the door for a moment. 'I mean, maybe they were after something else, too?'

'I can't think what.' She stretched her now aching back a little. 'We've nothing here anyone would want, really, have we? No interesting substances to shove up noses or give yourself a trip to wherever; nothing remotely saleable apart from big gear like microscopes, and we're not missing anything like that, are we? That couldn't possibly happen again – not since we put the security in place after the last time.' That had been over three years ago but none of them had forgotten it. The microscopes were now firmly bolted in their places. 'No one after real folding stuff would come sniffing around here now, would they?'

'No,' he said, 'I suppose not. Well, give me a shout if you

want anything else. We're well up to speed with the work inside so no need to worry about that. And I called on Sheila in Ballantyne on my way to work this morning and she said they said she can go home so long as there's someone there to make sure she's OK. So I've said I'll go and sleep on her sofa for a night or two. Thank God she'll be too shaky still to try to entice me to sleep anywhere else.'

He made the obvious joke without any of his usual leering enthusiasm, and she, already half preoccupied with her sorting, looked at him with a brief smile and said, 'You're a good man, Charlie Brown,' and returned to her task. He hesitated just a beat longer and then went.

She let the coffee get cold as she moved more and more swiftly through the job of imposing order on the chaos the interloper had created. When she had finished with the Ms she sat back on her heels and looked hard and long at the array of neatly stacked files before going through them once more, just to be absolutely sure.

There could be no doubt about it. She had been right. The file for Tony Mendez, the theatre porter who had died (she had been sure) of alcoholic poisoning, was not there. And though at the time of doing his post-mortem she had been content to accept that he had ingested the alcohol that had killed him accidentally, inasmuch as there had been no indication of a desire for deliberate self-harm, now she was not so sure. She had badly wanted to read again the notes she had made at the time, so that she could if necessary reassess the situation. It was certainly what she would do with the Lamark file as soon as she got back home. But here she had been halted, and it infuriated her.

There was still, though, she reminded herself with a surge of hope, the other set of notes. Had the intruder found them too? The F section took longer to reorganize and her heart flickered in her chest when she realized that this was the only one left that had been rifled as the M and L files had been. The others needed only a simple stacking. Nothing inside them had been disturbed at all; that much was very clear. Unlike the F files.

Her excitement was justified. All the Fs, with the exception of just one set of notes, fell into order beneath her hands. It was the notes on the post-mortem she had done on Pamela Frean which had vanished. And vanished for good, all because, like those other two, they had not been transferred to the hospital computer. PM notes were regarded as too sensitive for detailed electronic storage apart from a brief note of the last diagnosis of cause of death; which George told herself now, was, in the circumstances, richly ironic.

She was sitting at her desk, finishing the last of her piled-up paperwork, a half-eaten apple on the desk at her side because she had had no time to go to lunch, when her door slid open. She was aware of it, but didn't look up, assuming it to be one of the staff from the big lab, or perhaps Danny.

'Uh-huh?' she said after a moment, still without looking up. 'What is it?'

'I just wanted to check you were still on for this evening.' The voice sounded slightly apologetic. 'I don't want to be a pest, but I hadn't seen you around the place all day, and someone said there'd been a break-in here last night so I thought I really ought to leave you alone. But then I thought, well, you might be just as glad to get away from it all anyway. So here I am.'

'Zack!' she said, not at all sorry to be pulled away from cross-checking a long list of blood-sugar readings from the diabetic clinic that had been carried out for one of Dr Carvalho's more esoteric pieces of research. He was always asking her to do various analyses for him but there was never any sign of a published paper afterwards; one day she intended to tackle him about that. But not today. 'Come and sit down! How nice of you to find the time to come visiting. Coffee?'

'It's my pleasure,' he said gravely. He came in and took the chair she dragged forwards for him. 'Thank you. And I have to say that I have Professor Hunnisett's approval of my asking for your help.'

'Professor Hunnisett?' She was surprised. 'How do you mean?'

'I was telling him how anxious I was about making a presentation to the funders that would be lucid and interesting for them, and it was he who said I should ask your opinion. He has a very high one of his own about you.'

She became a little pink. 'I can't imagine why.'

'I can! But spare your blushes. Just tell me you can help me, huh?'

'I will if I can, of course. It's the time problem, really. I get so – so piled up with work. Every day is packed so tightly, you know? Perhaps it's easier for you to find holes in your day, since your main burden is research so you can plan your own work schedule?' She was babbling, more taken aback than she would have expected at the sight of him, and the fact that he had discussed her with Hunnisett. She jumped up to switch on the kettle to make coffee for him. 'Though, of course, I'm in the same situation too, I suppose. No patients.'

'But I do have patients,' he said. 'I've got my research patients, remember? And I have other responsibilities in neuro. It isn't all the Groves of Academe. I wish it were.'

She came back to sit at her desk while she waited for the kettle, which was of a temperamental nature, to deliver.

'Oh! I suppose not. I hadn't realized that your research subjects were in-patients.'

'Some of them have to be. After surgery, you see.' He saw the surprise on her face and smiled. 'I do some implants. Fetal material into the brain, remember? I did tell you about it, I think.'

'Yes, yes, of course you did. I'm sorry. I've had a lot on my mind lately.'

He looked round the room and nodded soberly. 'I heard

you were burgled. Don't they make a mess? Have you lost anything important?'

She bit her lip for a moment in annoyance. Dammit, as soon as she'd finished with the files she'd tidied the room and brought it back to its usual state; he was as bad as that wretched SOCO with his comments. But then she relaxed, admitting that her office wasn't precisely shop-window perfect and knowing he was making no deliberate dig.

'A couple of files,' she said. 'It's all very odd.'

'Odd?'

'It's just that – well, it's all linked with internal affairs of Old East. Those three deaths we had that made everyone twitch so. Accidental, two of them, I thought, and one suicide. But now the notes have been stolen, I have to wonder why. I guessed last night that that was the way forward ...' She was abstracted for a moment, brooding over the problem. 'It's not an easy nut to crack.'

'Oh?' He tilted his head like an intelligent terrier and looked at her, eyebrows up, clearly waiting for more, but she shrugged.

'That's about it. Missing notes on two cases.'

'What about the third one?' he said. 'You did say you did all three PMs?'

'Oh, yes. No, that's not lost. I collected it last night to check it. But the whole of the relevant file here had been turned over, so I imagine whoever it was was looking for it. As I say, most odd.'

'Aren't there copies of the files you could get to replace what was taken?'

She grimaced. 'That was what Gus said. But no. These are my private files and they don't have any computer back-up – it's hospital policy with PM notes.'

'Gus?'

'Uh – a friend. Local Superintendent of police,' she said. 'I'm forensic, remember, as well as hospital pathology.'

'Oh, I knew that. I just didn't realize you were on such close terms with the police.'

132

'Close?' She made a face, thinking of how rocky things had been with Gus lately. 'There's close and there's close, isn't there? The thing is, we work together from time to time.'

'Ah!' He seemed content with that, which pleased her. It wasn't that she wanted to imply she was available, and yet . . . She refused to follow that thought an inch further, and concentrated on his next question instead. 'So, he's investigating this, then? This break-in?'

'Yes,' she said, eager to explain the easy things. 'Ratcliffe Street nick are good to us at Old East. We have a special relationship, you know? They hang about when there are troubles here, which is good of them. We get more than our share of local baddies, one way and another, and it does help to have the police known on the patch as being particularly vigilant. It keeps a few of the bad guys away. Or so we like to think.'

'I'm sure.' Now he sounded uninterested in matters to do with the police and Old East. He quirked his head again with that same terrierlike sharpness as he smiled widely. 'So, tell me. Are you able to come along tonight as you said?'

'Tonight? Well –'

'Because we really would like to have your input,' he said and his smile widened even more.

'We?'

'The other two in the Institute with active projects are going to rehearse tonight too. I thought you'd be able to advise us all on how we go with them. What do you say? Then, afterwards, we could go and try a different local restaurant for supper. We've tried Indian, right? How about Chinese? Or Caribbean? If there were a Canadian one, I'd take you there, but to tell the truth, it'd only be the same as you get at home in the States. But the choice is yours.'

'Tonight.' She tried to think. Was there any reason why she shouldn't? Gus had said that he was sorry that he'd behaved as he had, but he'd been very insouciant about it. She'd told him that the jury was still out on the matter of forgiveness for

133

his dismissal of her anxiety last Friday over her uneaten supper; well, let it stay out a little longer. It could do no harm to accept this invitation from Zack. She wouldn't renege on her promise to help a colleague with work. I couldn't do that, she told herself a touch self-righteously, and why not have supper afterwards? It might be fun. And if Gus doesn't like it, then he'll know how it feels to be left alone in the evening.

'I'd love to,' she said. 'Have supper, I mean. I said I was coming to help you tonight and of course I hadn't forgotten. I was going to bleep you later to find out where and what time and so forth.'

'Great.' He got to his feet. 'No, don't bother with coffee. I won't wait – but I'm delighted. Say you come over to Neuro at – what shall we say, six? The others'll be there around six-thirty, they said, and each of them wants just half an hour for their presentation. So we'll be free to settle down to some work around seven-thirty or so. I'll book a table for nineish? Which restaurant?'

'Nine it is, and you choose. I'm sorry about the coffee. This kettle really is a bitch.'

She had crossed the room to shake the kettle, as though that would speed it up, so she had her back to the door and didn't hear it open as she chattered. Thus when she turned and saw that Gus was standing in the doorway looking inter-rogatively from one to the other of them, she was so startled she nearly dropped the kettle.

'Oh, Gus,' she said. 'I didn't expect to see you there!'

'I told you I'd be back.' His voice was relaxed, with no undue expression in it, which alerted her. That was never Gus's normal style; clearly he was put out.

To find Zack here? Maybe, she thought, and smiled brilliantly at him. 'Gus, this is Dr Zacharius, a colleague. Zack, this is Superintendent Gus Hathaway.'

'Ah, the famous Gus,' Zack said, holding out his hand. 'Great to meet you, sir.'

Gus shook his hand briefly and then shoved both his own

hands back in his trouser pockets, bunching his jacket behind them so that he had a slightly threatening air about him. ''Ow do,' he said abruptly in his most Cockney manner. 'Dr B., I've got a report for you on the car and – and so forth.'

Zack lifted his chin sharply. 'Really? Sheila's car? Do tell.'

The look Gus threw at him would have felled an ox at thirty paces. Zack appeared not to notice the venom in it.

'Police business,' Gus growled after a moment. 'Confidential.'

'Ah. Then I must be on my way.' Zack smiled warmly. 'Maybe George'll let me know what I'm allowed to later, hmm, George? Seeing I was there when the car went up, I'm interested. I take it it *is* Sheila Keen's car you're talking about?'

'Confidential,' Gus said woodenly.

'Yes, of course. OK then, George. Sorry about the break-in here. Hope you get it all sorted out soon. I'll see you at six-thirty in Neuro, and you can fill me in. Oh, and I'll book that table for nine o'clock. OK? I'll really look forward to that. So long, Super, great to have met you.' And he brushed past Gus and was gone, leaving Gus staring at George and looking more truculent than ever.

'If you'll forgive a technical term,' he said after a moment, 'that fella looks to me what we at the nick would call a right dodgy bugger. Friend of yours, is he?'

14

'That is no way to speak of one of my colleagues,' George said. 'Dammit all, how can you make a judgement like that just by looking at someone?'

'Instinct,' Gus said with sublime assurance. 'You get an eye for a villain in my business.'

'And you get an eye for a bigot and a self-satisfied full-of-himself smartass in mine!' George snapped. 'There is nothing wrong with Zack at all. He's an important researcher doing a lot of good work here, which I've agreed to help him with, and you've no right to jump to your dumb conclusions.' Then she stopped and a slow smile lifted the corners of her mouth. 'Unless it's the old devil speaking in you again? The one that made you do your pieces at Mike that time, because you thought we were having a fling? Jealous, are you, honey?'

'Never heard such nonsense in my life,' Gus came right into the room and perched on her desk. 'Just callin' the shots the way I see 'em fall. So, OK, he's wonderful, Cupid on a rock cake. Let's leave him there. Now, are you interested in the report on the car and the chocolates, or are you not?'

She was interested enough to push his reaction to Zack right to the back of her mind for consideration later. 'Well? What do they say?'

He reached into his breast pocket, pulled out two sheets of paper and gave them to her.

'Great!' She seized the papers and sat down at her desk and read them, and then read them again, even more carefully. 'Well, that doesn't take us any place, does it? Nothing on the car, unsurprisingly. I dare say any prints would disappear under the weight of that foam they used, and the inside of the thing'd have been pretty well fried clean. I'd hoped there'd be more news on the chocolate box and wrappings though.'

He came round the desk to look over her shoulder at the paper. 'Me too. But there you have it. The only prints anywhere on the outside are Sister Chaplin's and Sheila's, and the nurse who took it to Sheila. Nothing in the interior wrappings either, see? There.' And he pointed. 'Just nicotine in every damned chocolate.'

She stared at the paper again and then at him. 'A dangerous person,' she said.

'Very.' He spoke bleakly. 'Things like that could have been eaten by anyone. Mind you ...' He shook his head irritably. 'It doesn't really make sense. The amount of nicotine in each one is very small, it seems. I know people said it was enough to kill but apparently not. Enough to make anyone who ate one pretty sick, according to the people over at East Ham, but not enough to kill – except perhaps a child or a frail old person. A weak concentration of nicotine, they say, see there?' Again he pointed to the relevant section of the report.

'Yeah. And made in the most amateur of ways,' she said. 'Did you notice that bit about tobacco shreds? It's obvious.'

'He soaked cigarettes –'

'Or maybe cigars.'

'Yeah, or maybe pipe tobacco. Whatever. Soaked it for a while in ordinary tap water, boiled it down and there you have it. My old dad used to make a nicotine spray out of fag ends that way for the roses in his garden. Used to chuck 'em into this evil pot of water and leave 'em there till it stank like old fish and looked like elderly pee. I hated it. Mind you, he had wonderful roses. Never a bug on 'em.'

'I'm sure. And see this?' She too pointed at the report.

'Whoever it was didn't even bother to cover over the marks of whatever it was he used to push the stuff into the chocolates. All he'd have had to do was apply a bit of heat to each puncture and it'd have melted closed. But he swished the stuff in and put the chocolates back in the box, just like that. See what it says? It had leaked out into several of the paper wrappers. I've heard of amateur, but this is really the pits.'

He leaned over and pulled forward the other report, the one on the car. 'Yeah. It's the same here, in a way.'

'How do you mean?'

'Well, Chummy used a piece of cable and a solenoid switch, but not of a calibre big enough to cause more than the sort of shorting that'd melt the casings off the wires. Anyone with a bit of nous wanting to make a car go up would have done it much more efficiently, and probably have destroyed the evidence of what they did at the same time. This system smacks of a kid bent on mischief rather than any real intent to kill.'

She was looking at him with her eyes slightly narrowed and glittering. 'Are you saying,' she said slowly after a pause, 'that neither of these actions were an attempt to kill Sheila? Just to scare her?'

'I think I am.'

'Now why should anyone want to do that?'

'How should I know, doll? If I knew that –'

'Shut up. I'm thinking aloud.' She was staring at him now, with her eyes wide and unfocused. 'What would the point be? To make Sheila so scared she'd – what? Go away, maybe? Leave Old East?'

'Perhaps,' he said. 'If I'm allowed to express an opinion, that is.'

She ignored that. 'But why should someone want to drive her out of Old East? What is it about Sheila that makes her – what's the term – *persona non grata*?'

'Maybe Chummy plain doesn't like her. After all, that was why she thought you were involved.' He smiled at the way

138

her eyes snapped into focus and glared at him. 'Just trying to be helpful, doll.'

'If you want to get rid of someone on your staff, you don't do it this way. You start to pick holes in their work, or nag 'em or –'

'Ah,' he said wisely. 'Constructive dismissal.'

'Yeah, that's what the employment tribunals call it. And it works. Lots of people try that on with staff they don't like. Me, if I wanted to be rid of Sheila, I'd go about it more directly. I'd just tell her so. But I don't. I need her, dammit. She's a marvel at her job! We're missing her badly this week. Good as old Jerry is, he can't fill her shoes entirely. No, it's not that. Someone wants her out of the way, but –'

· 'But doesn't want to do her any lasting harm. So, whoever our chap is, he's the timid type.'

'Timid?'

'Mmm. Because if he weren't he'd go the whole hog and just kill her, wouldn't he? It would have the desired effect and end his worries. Use a bigger cable on the car, or a stronger solution of nicotine in the chocolates. As it is, he's no better off than if he never started.'

'Maybe he's timid, or maybe he's just not a killer,' she said. 'Not everyone wants to commit murder, for heaven's sake.'

'No?' he said. 'Well, I dare say not. You do tend to get a warped view of humanity in my job. OK, you have a point. Someone's trying to scare Sheila away from Old East. Let's take that as fact.'

'So, why? That's the puzzle.'

Gus was very interested now and was sitting half crouched on the edge of the desk, staring down at her. 'Yeah. Now, there can be all sorts of reasons for that sort of behaviour as well as plain dislike. Fear is one.'

'Someone's afraid of Sheila? She can be maddening, I know, but not really threatening, surely?'

'Not her personally, perhaps. Something she stands for. Something she knows. Something –'

'Something she has access to!' George sat up very straight in her chair. 'Gus, we're idiots! Here we sit in a room which has been turned over by someone who only showed interest in my files and stole a couple of them – a very specific couple indeed. You said last night that if they'd gone we'd really have one end of the string in our hands.'

'Then you were right? The other PM notes have gone?' He was clearly delighted.

'Yes. I'd have told you sooner, only what with one thing and another –'

'Your friend Zack being one of them.'

'With your reports on the car and the chocolates,' she said. 'Anyway, it's what I said, both files are missing.'

'Is that what you were discussing with Zack when I came in? Or did you ask him to come over so you could?'

'He walked in on me while I was still sorting it all out, for God's sake! So I just said – Oh, Gus, do shut up!' She shook her head at him irritably. 'A joke's a joke, but this is too much.'

'Who's joking?' he snapped.

'Then you *are* jealous! Well, well! I thought you'd learned your lesson about that sort of reaction. You admitted the last time you tried it you were acting like the dumbest of dummies, and now you go and do it again!'

'I just think that when you're an item with someone you don't go making supper dates with a different someone, without consulting the first someone about it first,' he said with some dignity, an effect which was spoiled by his choice of language. She couldn't help laughing and that made him scowl more.

'Oh, Gus, do stop being so stupid. All I'm doing is helping the guy with his research. It's what doctors do, you know? In fact I've agreed to help three of the researchers and he's one of 'em. And we'll have to eat, I suppose, so why not go on with the work over food? It's no big deal. There's nothing mysterious or suspicious about it.'

'I'll take your word for it,' he said, still in his dignified manner. She wasn't deceived; he was jealous, and the truth of the matter was she enjoyed that reaction in him. It both amused and warmed her. Disgraceful, she acknowledged somewhere deep inside, but ignored the thought.

'Let's get back to the business of Sheila and what's happening to her. Two attempts have been made on her that look dangerous – well, they *were* dangerous – but aren't meant to kill her. The motive is obscure but may be closely linked with the three deaths here that caused all the gossip, as demonstrated by the fact that their files have been stolen –'

'Run the stories past me again,' he said suddenly, clearly deciding to be businesslike now. 'I don't recall the details.'

'OK. First was Tony Mendez, theatre porter –'

'What sort of bloke was he?'

'Mmm? Tricky apparently. I didn't know him personally. Bad tempered, not popular. Reformed alcoholic. Well, supposed to be reformed. Clearly he slipped though, and took a drink. Too big a one. He died of alcoholic poisoning.'

'Alcohol? He must have taken a hell of a big drink to actually die of it!'

'Not necessarily. If he'd been on the wagon for a few months and then took a drink the size he'd been used to before he stopped – and had an underlying liver problem which I seem to remember he did – then it could have killed him. I remember at the time I reckoned his death was an accident. He collapsed in the middle of a case he was working on with Mayer-France – a gall bladder – and caused a helluva drama there in theatre.'

'So, he was the first, you say?'

'Well, he was actually the first we knew about. He collapsed on . . . let me see. It was a Friday – I remember it was just before the weekend, because Fridays are hectic anyway and an extra PM was one thing I didn't want because I couldn't leave it till next morning.' She reached behind the desk for her calendar and squinted at it. 'Here we are. The second of June. I know I had to do the PM late that evening. Remember? We were supposed to be going out.'

'And I cried off first. Yeah, I remember. You were good and mad. And then it turned out you'd have to cry off yourself anyway.'

'Well, never mind that. The thing is he died on the Friday. The next case to come up was Lally Lamark. She was found on Monday morning, very dead, on the floor of the Medical Records department. I can remember that I was sure she'd been dead over forty-eight hours. So I reckoned she'd died some time on Friday too, only in the evening, after the department had closed. I thought her death was an accident too: she'd used too much insulin and gone into a coma. And as she was alone, she died very quickly since there was no one to spot she was ill and get her to treatment. Not suicide but an accident.' She shook her head. 'At least I don't have to try to remember that. I can check on her notes when I get home. For the rest, it's got to be memory.'

'Which is usually very good,' he said. 'In you.'

She sketched a bow of acknowledgement. 'Well, I'm delighted I can do some things right. Memory doesn't always work and I've done one hell of a lot since then. Remembering the details as I'd like to isn't as easy as you think.'

'Still, we can investigate in other ways. What about the last one?'

'Oh, yes, Pam Frean. That was a definite suicide. She, I recall very well.' She made a face, angry again for the girl. 'It was so dreadfully sad and unnecessary. She was pregnant, came from a very religious family and couldn't take the pressure. So she killed herself in a most unpleasant way.'

'Oh?'

'Drowned herself,' George said. 'In her bath, would you believe. Goddamn difficult to do, but she was clearly very determined. She took a sedative first to help her do it. She left the sort of note that made it clear how determined she was.' George shook her head as her anger increased. 'Oh, God, I wish I'd kept copies of all those files! I remember the tone of the note she left, though not the detail.'

'I bet you could if you tried,' he said. 'You have that sort of memory, haven't you? Eidetic? I remember the first case we worked on: you were able to reel off all the contents of that man's bathroom cabinet like you were looking at them, ages after you'd first seen them.'

'Maybe,' she said a little dubiously. 'It used to be quite easy. Now I'm not so sure. My head gets so silted up with stuff that digging out a whole visual memory like I used to isn't the pushover it was.'

'Try some time,' he said. 'When you're alone. It's not that it's all that important in itself, but maybe, when you get that back, other things'll come back to you as well.'

'I'll think about it,' she said and he tilted his head at her.

'If you've got time, that is, what with helping colleagues and all.'

'Are you starting on that again? What is it with you, Gus? Are you just trying to be awkward?' She was genuinely annoyed now.

His lips tightened. 'No, not trying. I just am an awkward cuss. I thought you knew that when you took me on.'

'There's awkward and there's – there's like positively terminally bloodyminded!' she said. 'Do me a favour, Gus, and stop it. We have a case here to sort out and it's crass to waste time on this sort of nonsense.'

He was silent for a moment and then leaned over and very deliberately took her chin in one hand and kissed her, hard. 'OK, doll. I'll listen to you. I'll make my own dinner tonight while you work with your pal Zack and I won't feel a twinge of loneliness or jealousy or anything else I'm not supposed to, fair enough? And then tomorrow, maybe, when I've got a bit more evidence to bring to the pot, we'll sit down together and see what we can stew up to explain what's going on here.'

'What sort of extra evidence?' she demanded, refusing to be drawn on any other issue.

'I don't know. I'll just make a few local enquiries about this and that. Maybe look into these people's families, hmm? Mendez and Lamark and Frean. And see if there's any news on the patch about the break-ins at Sheila's flat and here. I don't expect much, mind you. They didn't look like professional jobs. But you never can be sure.'

'OK.' She stood up. 'Listen, are you busy now?' She looked at her watch. It was approaching four, and the pangs of hunger were making her belly rumble, and she wanted, even more than food, to be conciliatory. 'I had no lunch and I could do with a bit of English afternoon tea. They do a nice line in tea cakes over at the canteen. Care to buy me one?'

He looked at her thoughtfully for a moment and then shook his head. 'Um, no, doll, if you'll forgive me. I told you, I want to put some other enquiries into action, and that means I have to be back at the nick right away. I just wanted to bring you those reports, and to hear what your own searches had uncovered. Now we know, we can both get on with work in our own ways, hmm? So, I'll see you. At your place tomorrow, for supper maybe? Let's make a proper date of it, shall we, the way you have with your other colleague? And then we can be sure of where we are. So long, doll.' And he flicked his thumb and forefinger to his forehead as though he were wearing a hat with a brim to be tipped, and went.

15

Neurology, George decided, was the most depressing ward in the whole of Old East. One of the problems was that its need for new paint, modern furnishing and similar trappings tended to be obscured by the demands of other wards which engaged in more glamorous activities, such as Cardiology or General Surgery or the Renal Unit where highly dramatic transplants were carried out every time the surgeons could get their hands on a cadaver kidney. In Neurology, however, there were few glamorous activities; it was a ward where the detritus of patients with damaged brain and nervous systems washed up. Interesting disorders demanding intricately plotted neuro-mapping techniques, heroic brain surgery and suchlike interventions were whisked away swiftly to the specialist unit in the middle of the West End of London to be studied in detail and eventually used to teach up-and-coming medics; all that remained here were the elderly Parkinson's patients, the multiple scleroses, the Alzheimer's and motor-neurone disease sufferers, forced to stay under Old East's battered roofs while efforts were made to find permanent nursing homes to which they could be shuffled, since their families couldn't or wouldn't cope with them any longer. 'Community care?' snorted the daughter-in-law of one such patient in a fury. 'If you think you're sending that poor helpless old bugger back to my house so that I can be turned into a worn-out drudge to help out the NHS, you've got another bloody think coming.' She was far from alone in making such a decision. The place looked, sounded and smelled miserable in every way and George felt a pall of depression settle on her as she stepped out of the lift on the top level of Blue Block and turned left to go into the ward which had long ago been named, with incongruous prettiness, 'Laburnum'.

By the time she got there, the patients' evening meal had been served and the big battered chrome trolleys were standing outside the lift waiting to be taken back to the basement kitchens. The tired smell of minced beef and elderly steamed fish and yoghurt hung over them like a miasma and George almost turned back; why on earth should she spend her free time in such dispiriting surroundings? But a promise was a promise and she took a deep breath, straightened her back and entered the ward in search of Zack.

The nurse sitting at the work-station in the centre of the long corridor looked vague when asked for his whereabouts and muttered that he was probably around the place somewhere; George sighed and set off to make a bay-by-bay search. There were four four-bedded ones on each side of the long corridor, with occasional single rooms between them, and going from one to the other made her feel even lower, if that were possible.

Laburnum was a mixed-sex ward, though each bay had single-sex provision. Sometimes, however, it was hard to tell one from another. In bed after bed, individuals with sparse grey or white hair and pinched yellowish faces which showed few particular female or male characteristics – even the incidence of whiskeriness seemed the same for all of them – lay still, staring blankly upwards, or sat slumped uncomfortably in straightbacked chairs beside their rumpled beds, showing little awareness of what went on around them. Certainly none looked at her as she came in. There was a TV set on in each bay, sometimes turned irritatingly low so that even if a patient should want to watch he or she would be unable to make any sense out of the soundtrack, or, in one in particular, so loud it made George's ears sing. She marched over to the set and adjusted the volume knob to make it more tolerable, but the patients seemed as unconcerned as they had been before she did it, and a sudden rush of anger filled her.

'Why don't you ring for the nurse when someone leaves it deafening you like that?' she demanded of the old woman whose bed was closest to the set. 'You shouldn't have to put up with that sort of din!' But the old woman just looked through her and said nothing, while the patient on her other side turned her head fretfully on the pillow and called in a thick yet high voice, 'Is that you, Charlie?'

George had a sudden vivid memory of her mother, long ago, when she had been young and full of energy: they had gone to see a movie and had shared a huge pack of popcorn, eating it so fast they both started hiccoughing. George's eyes brimmed with sharp tears. It had been a Charlie Chaplin Festival at the local Arts Theatre in Buffalo and they'd had such fun that night, she and Vanny. And now Vanny was in much the same sort of state as these people; only she was three thousand miles away and George was here.

She wouldn't stay, couldn't possibly stay, no matter what sort of promise she had made, she thought. She headed for the entrance of the bay, intending to get back to the lift and away from this horrible place as fast as she could; but was stopped when she ran headlong into Zack.

'Nurse McGreedy said you were here!' he cried delightedly. 'I'm so sorry I wasn't out there to greet you, I'd just gone to my office to fetch some notes. Hey, what's up?'

'Nothing,' she said, swallowing. 'Not a damned thing. So where do we go from here?'

He looked over her shoulder into the bay and seemed to understand at once. 'I'm sorry,' he said. 'These are Alzheimer's ... I should have been here to head you off.'

He slid a hand into the crook of her elbow and led her away, tactfully not looking at her.

By the time they reached the seminar room at the far end of the ward, she had recovered, and was able to speak in what would pass as a normal voice. 'So, what are we going to do? Point me in the right direction. Do I write? Chart? Or what?'

'First, you listen,' he said, arranging a chair for her beside the window. 'Will you be comfortable here?'

'I'll be fine,' she said. She sat down, still ruffled, wanting to be anywhere but here and knowing she couldn't leave now, which made her feel unpleasantly trapped. 'Please, let's just get on with it, shall we?'

'Right,' he said. 'While we wait for the other two – they'll be here in a moment or two – let me just give you a bit of background, OK?'

'OK.'

'I told you it's the demyelinating diseases – the ones where the nerve sheaths are damaged – that I'm interested in.'

'I know what demyelinated means,' she said a little sharply. 'No need to cross every T for me.'

'Oh, but you're wrong! The thing is, the people I have to present to, *they* don't speak the language the way you and I do. I'll have to spell things out to them, but not in a way that makes 'em feel stupid. That's what I need help with, you see. That was one of the main reasons I had for asking you. I've heard you talking to people about your own speciality and it seemed to me you have a gift for clear explanation in that area – for simplifying. So, won't you just listen, pretend you don't know anything, and see if I get it right?'

She took a deep breath, aware that she was letting her own discomfort get in the way of what she'd come here to do. 'Sorry, Zack. Yes, I see what you mean. OK. What's myelin?'

'Thank you for a most interesting question, ma'am,' he said and grinned. 'OK ... And he launched himself into a detailed account of his work with the structure of nerve cells and their myelin sheaths, and their methods of transmitting mes-

148

sages between body and brain. Much of it she knew, of course, but she managed to pretend she was an intelligent but medically unqualified listener and interrupted occasionally to make him use clear language instead of medical jargon, corrections which made him look doubtful.

'But isn't there is a risk of making it sound too . . . I mean, I don't want to oversimplify, do I?'

'I think that would matter less than blinding them with science and making the listeners feel inadequate. As long as you don't fall into the trap of being patronizing you'll be OK.'

She got to her feet and indicated her side of the room. 'You sit down and listen to me. I'll have a try.'

She stood beside the central table for a moment and closed her eyes and then opened them and smiled at him briefly.

'Good evening, Mr Moneybags. OK, let me explain what it is I'm trying to do here. My patient, Mr Smith – you can see his notes if you care to, or I'll arrange for you to meet him. He is a very sick, unhappy man, I'm afraid. He has wide-spread loss of muscle power: can't walk, can't do anything for himself. Has to be tube-fed because he can't swallow, can't control his own bladder or bowels. And, worst of all perhaps, he has no loss of any intellectual capacity. He knows perfectly well what his condition is. He's locked in a body he can't control or use. Can you imagine the hell of that?

'Now, why is he in this state? It's because he has lost the insulating material called the myelin sheath that in healthy people clothes their nerve cells and lets messages from the brain be delivered safely and accurately to the muscles. Generally speaking this insulating material, once it's damaged or vanishes for any reason, can't be replaced. But I have a new system for dealing with the problem. Now, here is my patient, Mr Jones.' She looked at Zack. 'I take it you have Mr Jones who has been treated and is doing well? You've plenty of Mr Smiths for them.' She indicated the ward beyond the room they were in.

'Well enough,' he said. 'She's Dawn Greenwich,' and grinned at her brilliantly. 'Don't stop.'

'So here's my patient, Miss Greenwich. In this case, which was just the same as Mr Smith's, I have performed a small – technique or operation or intervention?'

'Call it operation. They understand that, and it sounds more dramatic,' he said.

'OK. Operation. My operation is thus and thus – here you have to go into a little more detail, Zack, but the important thing is that Miss Greenwich shows us what you did for her. You put her through her paces, comparing her abilities with poor old Smith or any of the other patients in the ward.

'That should convince them of the need for what you're doing. I take it this project has been agreed with the Research Ethics Committee? You've got all your informed consents and so forth?'

He looked reproachful. 'What do you take me for? I'm not an amateur!'

'Sorry I asked. Well done again. There you are. That should help persuade Mr and Miss Moneybags to cough up, I hope.'

'God, you're good, George! I knew you'd have the right answers for me. I've been fiddling round with this stuff for so long I breathe it and eat it and sleep it, so I just couldn't see my way clear to explaining it for lay people. You've really cracked that for me. Bless you.'

He was glowing and for a moment she was embarrassed in an almost British way by his enthusiasm. She said hastily, 'Is Miss Greenwich your only patient suitable for demonstration? And is she here at Old East?'

'She's at home now, she's done so well. And she's not the only patient. There's José too.' He came over to her at the central table and her unease at his excitement made her move away from him a little, but he didn't appear to notice.

'José? Who's he?' she said quickly.

'A Spanish chap. People here can't pronounce his name

properly, so they call him Josey. He was referred to me by his GP, in a dreadful state. Paralysis had started with his feet and the lower part of his legs, and he was sent here via A & E. By the time I got to him the paralysis was spreading fast. I had him on a respirator eventually, desperately ill. As far as I could see, he was going to die in a matter of days. So –'

'What was the diagnosis?' She said it almost in desperation; she was now on the other side of the table, moving in as casual a manner as possible, but he was following her.

'Mmm? Oh, motor-neurone, of course. Anyway, I thought, it's the last chance he's got and it was worth it. Even if I couldn't explain to him properly – his English and my Spanish, you know? But it worked. He's back at his own work, even. He's a barman in a West End hotel.'

He was standing right beside her now and she couldn't move away again, not without taking them both into an absurd ring-a-roses round the table, so she squared her shoulders and said briskly, 'Well, that's fine. What now? Didn't you say there were papers to look at too?'

'God, I'm grateful to you, George,' he said and his voice seemed rather thick now. He put both hands on her arms and pulled her closer. 'I just don't know how to tell you how much help you've been. You've made me believe I really can persuade those bastards to fund me and –'

'Well, that's great,' she said, stepping sideways in as off-hand a manner as possible. 'It was my pleasure. Just make sure you invite me to Stockholm when you get your Nobel.' She tried to make it sound funny but it came out strained.

He laughed and to her relief made no further effort to get close. 'The hell with Nobel. That'd be nice, no doubt, but this could make a fortune for me. Don't you see that? If I can go on from here with the right funding, then I've got one of the biggest pharmaceutical breakthroughs since beta blockers and steroids. Bigger, even.'

She looked at him, feeling a little cold. 'Oh. Is that the

thing that matters most to you? Making a deal with a pharmaceutical company?'

'But of course! It's a pharmaceutical that I'm making the pitch to. I told you that, didn't I?'

'I – Perhaps I didn't register it if you did.' She shook her head. 'I have a – Shall we say I'm not as enamoured of the pharmaceutical people as you seem to be.'

He frowned. 'How do you mean?'

She shrugged. 'Oh, you know. They make all these profits out of sickness: a drug breakthrough in cancer or AIDS and whey-hey, up go the share prices. People make vast profits.'

'You've been in England too long,' he said after a moment. 'Profit ain't a dirty word, you know.'

She sighed. 'I suppose not. But in the context of illness . . .'

'Hey, George, think this through, will you? If I can refine this therapy and it's widely applied to all the people like those out there' – he jerked his head towards the door that led out to the main corridor and the bay full of patients – 'can you see how much money the NHS will *save*? Quite apart from the human misery involved in dealing with these godawful demyelinating diseases, they just soak up money and manpower, you know that. So maybe I'll make a profit – I sure as hell intend to – but it's the sort of profit that no one has to apologize for.'

She stood for a moment and then made a little grimace. 'I guess I've got some more thinking to do,' she said. 'And I suppose the important thing *is* finding a therapy for a hor- rible bunch of disorders. So, like I said, now what?'

He had moved away from her now, to her relief, and he looked at his watch. 'The others should be here soon,' he said. 'We were going to have a complete run-through of our ses- sion with these people, and I think they'd value your input as much as I did. Ah! About time too! Hi, Frances.'

The door had opened and a tall woman was standing there looking faintly surprised. She had rather faded red hair pulled back from a fleshy face and deep lines between her eyebrows that made her look rather fierce. George had a vague memory of seeing her at Professor Hunnisett's farewell party, and the things Zack had told her about the work she was doing on female hormones.

'Oh,' Frances Llewellyn said. Her voice was surprisingly soft, even sweet. 'Am I late? I thought you said to be here about –'

'It's all right,' Zack said quickly. 'No matter. Is Michael with you?'

'Michael?' she sounded surprised. 'Is he coming too?'

'Oh, Frances!' Zack said in an indulgent voice and Frances Llewellyn frowned even more deeply, but it was clear to George that this was with puzzlement, rather than with annoyance. 'You know I arranged all this last week! Anyway, let me phone him. He said he'd be here and –'

Behind Frances the door moved again and George smiled at the man who came in. He too was someone she had seen at the Prof.'s party, and also around Old East's various departments, one of the army of familiar strangers with whom she spent so much of her working life. He smiled back tentatively, and his glasses, big and round and rather thick, glinted in the evening sunlight and became suddenly blank, like those of the cartoon character of her childhood, 'Little Orphan Annie'. It gave him a rather threatening look, but then he moved further into the room and showed himself for what he was: a rather small man with a fussy manner who was far from ominous.

'Hello, Zack,' he said, his voice almost as soft as Frances's. 'I got your message, though I wasn't quite sure –'

'Well,' Zack said heartily. 'As long as we're all here. Now, let's get on with it, shall we? George has already been of inestimable value to me, because she brings such a fresh approach to what I'm doing, and I know she can do it for you. So how about it? Presentation time. Or at least the rehearsal.'

16

It had been a bewildering evening in many ways, George thought as she walked to the hospital next day, through the cool of the early morning streets. She paused on Tower Bridge, as she did whenever she could, to lean on the parapet and watch the river go by, still thinking.

Both Frances Llewellyn and Michael Klein had seemed a little startled by her presence at their meeting, but were clearly too polite to express it. They had done pretty much as Zack asked them to, obediently trotting through the representations they would be making to their potential funder; and she had sat and listened and shared some of their puzzlement.

Because there was no doubt in her mind that their research was of a very different order from Zack's. Frances, in seeking the root causes of a range of psychiatric conditions associated with key events in women's lives involving hormones – puberty, childbirth, menopause – was treading a well-delineated path. Many had walked this way before her, seeking some sort of hormonal answer to the depressions and disorders that so often made women's lives a misery. There had been that fashion back in the seventies for filling women with vast doses of progesterone, in the belief that it would prevent pre-menstrual tension, post-natal illness and menopausal angst. That had been based on minimal science and had foundered; now at least Frances was trying to give the idea a sound theoretical basis, but George had small hope that she would succeed. The therapy had worked unreliably when used empirically – on the basis of its effect on symptoms – and there was no reason why, going by the work she was describing, that it would work any better when used scientifically. Frances Llewellyn, George told herself, as the soft-voiced woman droned on about her samples and her assays, has as much chance of getting a Nobel as I have of going single-handed round the world in a hot-air balloon, and there's no way any pharmaceutical company is going to beat a path to her door with handfuls of money.

The outlook wasn't quite as gloomy with Michael Klein. In his search for answers to the problems of adolescent addiction to various substances, ranging from marijuana to methylenedioxy methamphetamine, aka MDM or Ecstasy, and glysergide phenicilene, popularly called PCP or Angel Dust, to good old-fashioned alcohol, he had come up with an overarching theory that there were in certain people a set of enzymes which, acting together, made their unfortunate owners much more likely to become addicted as a result of experimenting. It was his belief, he said, that the enzymes were as genetically determined as eye colour or body build and that he could, given the chance to work on his theories, come up with proof.

He had stopped then to stare owlishly at George, and she had said, almost without stopping to think, 'And then what?'

'I beg your pardon?'

'Well, OK, you prove that addiction is due to a genetically determined set of enzyme responses –'

'Acting in a cascade. Yes.'

'Well, so you prove it. What value does that have? How can you use your proof?'

He had blinked and looked blankly at her. 'I am involved in pure research. I don't think at all about the application in any direct way.'

Zack had thrown her a sharp glance at that, but she ignored it. 'Well, yes, that's very admirable, but you're hospital based, aren't you? Won't the people you're pitching to expect you to be after some sort of therapy for patients? Or even just a test to identify people at risk?' She stopped then. 'Hell, no. That would never do, would it? That would be ethically impossible.'

Klein said nothing. It was Zack and Frances who showed interest. 'In what way?' Frances asked.

'How would you use it? I can't imagine the average teen-ager agreeing to be tested if he's told it's to find out if he could become an addict. I'm damned sure I wouldn't have done! I'd rather have gambled the way you do when you're a kid and know yourself to be immortal. And as for parents – if they insisted on using the test, then if it was negative their kids would expect a *carte blanche* to go out and try everything druggy they could get their hands on, because they'd be safe from the risk of addiction.'

'A sort of Junkies' Charter,' Zack murmured.

'This is nonsense.' Klein spoke much more strongly now, and his glasses seemed to glitter with new-found energy. 'I am seeking only to find out why some people become addicts after experimental exposure to mind-altering substances, and why some do not. No more than that. As for what use the research will be put to –'

Zack laughed. 'Try Pillpopper and Potionshaker's latest wonder drug! Two tablets twice a day and then go out and get safely stoned! Can't you just see it!' Once more he looked at George, this time with a sort of triumphant expression on his face. But again she refused to pay any attention to him.

'Since I was asked here to offer an outsider's view of your chances,' she said carefully. 'I think I have to say, Dr Klein –'

'Michael,' he muttered.

'Michael,' she said obediently. 'That I can't see what's in it for them. As I understand it, the people you have to get your funds from are pharmaceutical companies –'

'Who want a return on their investment,' Zack said. 'I keep telling you that, Mike. I'm glad George is saying it. And I didn't say a word to her in advance, did I?' He looked again at George. 'What she said was totally unprompted, wasn't it?'

'Yes,' she said a little unwillingly.

'And if they can't see what's in it for them, then they don't fund you. And if they don't, we're all in real trouble here at the Institute. Like Hunnisett said – keeps on saying – it's up to us to keep the place going. If we can attract the funds then we stay in business. If we can't . . .'

He had jumped up suddenly and had begun to march about the room as though there was too much energy in him to be contained. 'It's why I keep on so about this. I don't want the hassle of having to find some other place to set myself up as a researcher. It was tough enough getting settled here, and unless at least one of you two comes up with something the funders will find tasty – like my project – then we could all be out on our ears.'

There was a little silence and then Frances said stiffly, 'I'm as aware as you are of the significance of this funding appeal, Zack, but it doesn't mean we have to cut corners and do bad work just in order to get money. If Michael doesn't feel able to tell the funders that he's after a therapy as such then he shouldn't have to. I *am* after a therapy, of course.' She almost preened for a moment. 'So, maybe between us, you and I, we can do what is necessary, and leave Michael to hoe his own row. But really it won't do to push him this way, you know. I wasn't quite sure why you wanted this meeting, to tell the truth, but now I can see.' She threw a look of pure dislike at George. 'You're worried about your own situation more than you're really concerned about the work Michael and I are doing. It's not purely scientific interest on your part, is it? Just a means to your own ends.'

Goddam Zack, George thought furiously. He's set me up. He wanted to put extra pressure on them, just as she says, and he used me to do it. And she had been so angry that when the others had packed up their work – both behaving rather stiffly now – and gone, and he'd grinned at her and told her he'd booked a table at a terrific restaurant, she had shaken her head crisply.

'I won't, after all,' she had said, her voice as flat as she could make it. 'I've started a pig of a headache. And it's been a long day. Some other time, maybe.' And she had gone, leaving Zack there in Laburnum Ward's seminar room on his own as she fled past the bays of hopeless blank-faced people, trying not to think about what had happened.

She had opted to leave her car at the hospital and walk home and had plodded her way through the dusty tired streets, her head down and her hands shoved into the pockets of her jacket, still trying not to think and failing miserably.

She had always known herself to be easily beguiled by charming people. She was not one of those who announced proudly, 'I'm a great judge of character,' by which they meant they made up their minds swiftly that a person was unreliable and then gave them no chance to prove otherwise. She had always admitted that she needed time to get to know people and had a marked tendency to like everyone she met and to go on doing so until something happened to change her opinion.

So it had been with Zack. He was good looking, amusing, interesting, and she had allowed herself to be more attracted to him than she should, considering there was always Gus. So far it had been an amusing game she had been playing, but now, suddenly, she wasn't so sure.

There had been something chilling, she told herself, about the way he had used her tonight. It was now clear to her that neither Klein nor Llewellyn had expected to see her; that Zack had for purposes of his own set her up to act as a critic of their work, as well as supporter of his, and she was far from happy about that. Why had he done it? What was it all about? And was he trying to use her in any other way? She couldn't imagine one at the moment, but the possibility was there; and she pushed her hands even more deeply into her pockets and scowled as she marched on.

The flat had been hot and unwelcoming and she had gone around opening windows and tidying up in a little flurry of activity designed to keep her mind off Zack and the fact that Gus thought she was having dinner with him *à deux*; she had not been treating Gus well, she knew, these past few days, and for the first time she let herself feel really bad about that.

It had been as she was at last falling asleep that the idea had come to her and been so startling that she had actually sat up in bed and stared sightlessly at her window as she contemplated it. It was absurd, wasn't it? And yet . . .

Now, as she stared down at the river on her way to the hospital, she thought about it again, turning the notion round and round in her head, sniffing at it, tasting it, trying to see if it had as much power this morning as it had in the late night watches.

And had to admit that there was still something there. The various things that had been happening at Old East had seemed quite separate from Zack and her relationship with him; now, she wasn't so sure.

She walked on, still trying to get her ideas clear in her mind and not being able to prevent herself from letting her thinking get convoluted, twisting and turning back on itself. When she got to her office, she promised herself, she'd make notes. That always helped her sort out her confusion properly. Hadn't it been just such an exercise that had led her to the link between Sheila and Lally Lamark? Maybe it would work again.

She let herself into the lab quietly, fumbling only a little with the new keys the locks demanded; it was still very early, not yet eight o'clock. She hadn't been able to sleep and had preferred coming in straightaway to hanging around at home; now she was very glad. The solitude meant she would easily be able to settle down at her desk with a piece of paper and a pencil and see what she could sort out of this tangle regarding Zack.

She took herself down to the basement and the mortuary before going to her office; she had a couple of post-mortems to do that afternoon, and she had remembered just as she left the flat that she was short of shampoo and body lotion for her shower room there; and while she was at it, she had decided to bring in a pile of fresh new underwear. She was whistling softly between her teeth as she took herself into her private changing room and set to work, enjoying, as she always did, the minutiae of her job. It made her feel so much more comfortable when things around her were well organized, just as it had when she had been a child and had found satisfaction in rearranging the coloured pencils in her special pencil box.

It wasn't until she was on her way back upstairs and heading for her office that she felt it: a prickling sensation at the back of her neck that told her she wasn't alone. She stood very still on the stairs, listening hard, but there was nothing to be heard apart from the hum of the big refrigerators and the distant mumble of traffic on the ring road that circled the hospital. She had heard nothing unusual, she knew, yet she was certain someone was there.

She didn't stop to think but turned and went quickly down the stairs again. If she'd used her commonsense she'd have sent for someone from security – maybe Bittacy was still on duty? – and let them search, but she wasn't in the mood to be sensible. Being reckless had a sort of charm, this morning.

At first all seemed well. The mortuary was quiet and empty. Taps dripped, the windows rattled in response to the distant traffic, her heels clacked on the tiled floor, but that was all, and after making a thorough search, opening every door, slowly she made her way back to the stairs.

And again it happened, just a few steps from the top; that certainty she was not alone. Now she knew it had to be somewhere ahead of her rather than behind, and moved forwards. Her shoes clicked on the stair-tread and she bent and pulled them off, then, barefoot, moved very carefully along the corridor.

She saw it at once: the door to the Beetle cupboard was open. It couldn't have been open when she came in, could it? She'd have noticed, surely. She stopped and tried to remember, closing her eyes to see the scene as it had been when she first arrived, and realized that she hadn't looked along the corridor. She had come in and made straight for the stairs; if the cupboard door had been open she wouldn't have known, because she simply hadn't looked in that direction.

Mrs Glenney, she thought, the night cleaner. Had she left it open? Hardly. With her overblown sense of her own importance in the maintenance of security, she would never do that. And she had no cause to be in that cupboard, anyway. It contained stores of various kinds, bottles of reagents, slides, unused equipment, spare parts, stationery: the assorted materials of day-to-day life in a laboratory; and she frowned, trying to think if there was anything potentially valuable there. But then, she reminded herself, she hadn't imagined there was anything valuable in her files and someone had broken in and rifled those . . .

She crept over to the cupboard and looked in. She did not know it as well as the junior staff, whose job it was to see to the maintenance of supplies to each work-station, but well enough, and now she tried again to summon up her special gift of memory by closing her eyes so that she could see in the pinkish dark behind her lids the way the cupboard usually looked. She let her memory range over the shelves, browsing among them, opening her eyes from time to time to check the reality against her memory. As far as she could tell, there was just one bottle out of place, on the top shelf; not hard to see since it had left a gap like that in a five-year-old's teeth. She closed her eyes again to try and read the label.

Hydrochloric Acid. That was what had been in there. Just a Winchester bottle of hydrochloric acid, of which they used a great deal for various purposes; why on earth should she be worried about that? Someone must have taken the bottle out to refill a bench-sized bottle and just not returned it. All she had to do was go into the big lab and look for it. And for whoever else might be there . . .

She went to her own office first, opening the door with great stealth, to arm herself with the only thing she had in the place which might make a weapon: a rather battered but very large golf umbrella she kept in a corner in case she was called out to a body on a rainy day and had to examine it *in situ*. She'd spent enough miserable hours with rain dripping down her neck not to know the value of such an item. Now, as she picked it up and held it tightly round the middle, she was deeply, burningly grateful to her own good sense in providing it.

Then she went as softly as she could, with her heart beating like a drum, to the big laboratory.

17

The door was closed but not locked and she eased it open carefully, her own pulse pounding in her ears so loudly that it seemed impossible that others couldn't hear it too for miles around, a fearful notion she pushed firmly to the back of her mind. The familiar smells came out at her, acrid and caustic at the same time: iodine and formaldehyde and methylated spirits and the faint sweetish scent of Festival, which was the disinfectant applied to floors and worktops, and somewhere deep below all that coffee, and . . . something else. She couldn't place it, but knew it to be unusual in this setting. There was the sound of the refrigerators too, and the soft hissing of various other items of machinery and – she stopped and closed her eyes, listening hard. Another unfamiliarity: a thick dragging sound, swift and roughly rhythmic. She opened her eyes and, abandoning any attempt at being quiet and careful but still clutching the umbrella, shot forwards in the big room and round the front end work-bench end to look into the space beyond. No one was there. She twisted her body and pulled back to run to the next bench end and then on to the last. And there she saw him.

He was sitting on the floor, his legs outstretched and his back to the bench, with both hands flat on each side of him, his eyes closed. He was struggling to breathe, his mouth pulled apart in a great rictus, yet held wide open. The sound was much clearer now, choked and painful. She slid to her knees beside him and leaned over to stare into his face, which was pallid and sweating, with a blueish tinge to the lips and eye sockets, though his cheeks and forehead had sprung a rich red rash. His eyes were closed.

'Jerry!' she cried. 'Jerry, for God's sake, what happened?'

Now the smell was even thicker and she thought she recognized it; indeed her own eyes were beginning to water. She pulled Jerry by one arm so that he opened his eyes and stared at her blearily; he tried to shake his head and speak, all at the same time, as his breathing became even harsher, but he couldn't. She let go of him and ran across the lab towards the big window, one of six which lit the space. The long pole normally used to operate the high section, which was the only part that would open, was, of course, not there. It was one of the lab staff's constant moans that wherever the pole was most wanted was always the place where it wasn't, and she could have screamed with the frustration of it as she looked over her shoulder at Jerry again.

He had slumped a little sideways and it seemed to her that the sound of his breathing was thinner, with even less power to it, and in panic she lifted her umbrella and hurled it hard against the window. The panes shook but held; she cast around for a heavier weapon, and settled on one of the lab stools. She picked it up by one leg and virtually threw it at the window; this time it shattered in a great shower of glass and noise and the room seemed to fill with the outside air.

But Jerry still had not moved. She ran to the phone and scrabbled for the dial, muttering aloud as she did so, not knowing what the words were, but realizing later that they had been in some sort of sense a prayer; and dialled.

By the time she got an answer from the switchboard she was almost screaming with urgency and it took her valuable seconds to make the girl comprehend that she was in the lab, that there was an emergency and she needed the crash team at once, but at last the girl understood and George was able to drop the phone and run back to Jerry.

But there was little she could do as she crouched there except hold him so that his airway was obstructed as little as possible, and listen with every part of herself for the sound of the team arriving. Around her the lab sat serene and familiar except for the shards of glass on the floor, and the smell which she had noticed before; now she lifted her head and, still holding Jerry carefully, craned her neck to look at the bench above them.

Clearly he had been refilling a reagent bottle of his own. This, she thought, must be one of the days on which he chose to come to work early. Jerry often did, she knew, particularly after an evening when he had been left to lock up and therefore had the keys. Yesterday had been such an evening, and she stared at the bottles and tried to imagine how it had been here this morning.

He would have come in with his work plans in his mind, and seen that his bottle needed refilling. It was something the junior was supposed to do, but somehow she never managed to keep up with all of them. Sheila often complained because she had to do her own.

And then George caught her breath because she realized that they were not sitting beneath Jerry's work-station, but Sheila's. His own area was further down the bench. Twisting her head to look, she saw that he had his microscope – the familiar old-fashioned one that he loved to use – already pulled forward, with rows of slides set in all the available space around it. So he had needed to do something with a chemical and rather than rearrange his own area had poached on Sheila's. Why not, when she was off sick anyway? George could almost hear his voice explaining cheerfully that that was what he had done, and she looked down at him and murmured, 'It's all right, Jerry. Hold on, honey. They're on their way.' And looked back up at the bottle.

There was a small one with a funnel beside it. Had it been

used to pour something into the bottle or just opened for that purpose? She sniffed hard and the smell filled her nostrils and she blinked at the irritation, and looked again. Beside the small bottle, which was turned in such a way that she couldn't see the label, was another bigger one, a Winchester. The Beetle cupboard bottle, she thought. The hydrochloric acid. And then she knew just what had happened and how and felt a sense of deep sick terror. 'Not again,' she said aloud. 'Oh, Christ, not again!'

Beneath her hand Jerry stirred and she was at once all attention. 'It's OK, Jerry, they're coming.' Then, as she heard the clatter and the crashing down the corridor, she cried, 'They're here!' She lifted her chin and shouted and went on shouting until the door burst open and they came rushing in.

The next fifteen minutes were, as far as she was concerned, bedlam. There were four of them from the Accident and Emergency crash team and within a matter of seconds they were at work. Adam Parotsky, whom she recognized as the senior houseman on A & E, set himself at Jerry's head as two of the others eased Jerry into position flat on his back with a hard pillow beneath his shoulders and Adam reached out one hand to the senior nurse who was part of the team. At once she slid a laryngoscope into it and then, as Adam set to work, followed up with the necessary tubes and attachments.

The sound of Jerry's breathing shifted, lost some of its harshness and then finally was replaced by the hiss of the oxygen cylinder which was at once attached to the laryngeal tube to take over the breathing task. His face began to become a more normal colour, losing the pinched blueness that had been so terrifying, and after a few moments he opened his eyes and stared up at Adam's upside-down face above him. His gaze was clearly an appealing one and Adam grunted, 'It's all right, you'll be fine now. Just hang on in there.'

Once the breathing was right the team relaxed and George with them. The nurse mopped at Jerry's eyes, putting drops into them, for they were reddened and watering copiously. Adam looked at George and said, 'What happened?'

'I don't know,' she said. 'Or at least – Look, I came in early this morning to do some work of my own and realized after a while there was someone else here. I went looking – I thought it might be another break-in – and found Jerry like this. I broke the window to help him get better air.'

She indicated it and one of the others in the team murmured, 'Quick thinking,' and she glanced at him.

'Oh,' she said and nodded as she recognized the young anaesthetist, James Corton. 'Thanks, but believe me it was a reflex action. I don't even know if it did any good. And then I called you. You've managed to deal with him in good time, I think, haven't you? I was terrified his tissues would swell so much he'd lose his airway altogether.'

'He bloody nearly did,' Adam said. 'Look, is this tube OK, Corton? Even though you couldn't do it yourself, I'd be glad if you'd check before we move him to the recovery unit on A & E to sort out any remaining problems.'

James, in response to George's brows lifted in query, raised his right hand apologetically. 'I twisted my wrist in a difficult intubation last night, so I asked Adam to deal with this one. It looks fine to me.'

George had checked for herself, not waiting for James. It might be his responsibility as the anaesthetist in the crash team to intubate but every doctor worth the label could manage that, after all. Adam had done the job perfectly; Jerry's easier breathing and greatly improved colour were an index of how effective he had been.

Jerry rolled his head and George said quickly, 'No, Jerry. Keep still. And don't try to talk, you ass, you've got a laryngeal tube in. Be patient.'

He stared at her and then rolled his eyes again, upwards this time. She looked at him, frowning, then understood.

'I think I've worked it out,' she said quietly. 'It happened when you refilled your reagent bottle?'

He closed his eyes in an agony of frustration as the nurse tried again to mop at them, but he moved his head once more to push her away. A little affrontedly, she stood back as George came and leaned above him.

'It's all right,' she said softly. 'I think I know what it is you're trying to say. I can smell it too. I'll be careful. I'll check what happened and, Jerry' – he was still staring up at her beseechingly – 'don't worry. I'll keep a close eye not only on you but on Sheila too. I know this is her work-station, as well as you do. And her reagent bottle.'

He closed his eyes, clearly in relief, as the porters arrived. There was another bustle as he was shifted to a trolley and his breathing apparatus carefully stowed, and then he was taken off by the troop of them. But Adam turned back at the door and looked at her just as they reached it. 'Have you any idea what caused this?' he asked bluntly.

'Give me a little time and I might have more than an idea. Proof perhaps,' she said. 'I've got to do some investigating. But I think I can guess. Chlorine gas.'

He nodded. 'That's what I thought. A hell of a thing to happen in a professional lab, isn't it? I thought everyone would know of the risk.'

'Do you think I don't know that?' George snapped. 'This wasn't carelessness or ignorance, believe me. My staff know which chemicals they can and can't mix. Someone did something to make this happen – but, like I say, let me investigate. I'll let you know if I identify anything that'll affect Jerry's treatment. Meanwhile, regard it as chlorine-gas poisoning.'

'Will do,' Adam turned to go, leaving only James Corton lingering.

'Chlorine gas?' he said anxiously, staring at her with that wide shy gaze of his. 'That's very bad.'

'Yes,' she said shortly. 'Very.'

'An accident, though, surely? I thought it was something that happened often, accidents with chemicals?'

'Not in my lab, it doesn't,' George said. 'Anyway, as I say, I'll be checking it out. So, thanks for getting here so fast.'

He went pink. 'Oh, it was just routine. I mean, we were the A & E crash team. And anyway, I couldn't do much, what with my wrist like this and . . .'

He went, leaving behind him the ghost of his uneasiness. Poor bastard, George found herself thinking. He's got to go a long way to get the self-confidence he'll need to be any good in this game. Then she forgot him as she turned to contemplate Sheila's work-bench.

Properly speaking, if she suspected some sort of meddling she should call the police. She knew that. If someone had tampered maliciously with the contents of the Beetle cupboard – she even thought she knew when it had happened – then a criminal offence had been committed, and she had no right to go nosing about before a SOCO had been to check over the scene and to mark the evidence. But that would take so long and by the time someone had come from the nick and mobilized the SOCO, the last vestiges of the chlorine gas she could still smell would be gone. She looked up at the broken window and the scudding clouds that showed there was a brisk breeze out there and made up her mind. She'd be careful and she would make her own checks, and *then* call the police.

She wore gloves, collecting them quickly from the mortuary, and set to work. She handled each of the bottles very carefully, turning them so that she could see their labels and then replacing them precisely as they had been. And then with great delicacy she made a couple of tests of her own on the contents, first of the bottle which had clearly been removed from the Beetle cupboard and then of the smaller work-bench bottle. To make extra sure, she then checked the content of every other bottle at every work-station labelled *Hydrochloric Acid*, writing down her findings at each stage of the process in her own notebook.

She was barely halfway through when the big doors

outside clattered open. She lifted her head and swore softly. It was Alan who appeared at the door of the lab and came round to stare at her in amazement as she crunched from place to place over the broken glass. She looked at him and shook her head quickly.

'No, Alan,' she said as he opened his mouth to release the inevitable flow of questions. 'I can't explain now. You'll have to be patient. Meanwhile, keep everyone out of here till I've finished, will you? Then I promise I'll explain as much as I can.'

He closed his mouth, nodded, and went. She was deeply grateful to him. A good chap in every way, she thought; I'm lucky to have him on the team. I must tell him so. And went on with her work.

By the time she had finished, closed her notebook and bagged the phials of liquids she had collected from the various bottles, all of them carefully labelled in her neatest handwriting, it was well past nine. She came out into the corridor to find it filled with a group of subdued but intensely curious staff. She did the only thing she could and told them as succinctly as possible just what had happened.

'It seems there's been a third attempt on Sheila,' she said. 'Only this time it was Jerry who got into the line of fire. Someone got in here – I think it happened before the break-in, by the way; there was one night, I discovered, when a stranger tried to get in – went into the Beetle cupboard and meddled with the bottle labelled *Hydrochloric Acid*. It had been emptied and refilled with common-or-garden bleach in a strong concentration.'

There was a sharp hiss of sound as several people drew breath and she nodded grimly.

'You're ahead of me. Whoever it was then emptied the re-agent bottle on Sheila's bench of almost all of its hydro-chloric acid, leaving just enough to make a reaction with bleach, but not enough to work with. He worked out she'd have to refill her bottle –'

'And when she put bleach on top of hydrochloric acid . . .'

'Exactly. It released chlorine gas and damned nearly choked Jerry to death.'

There was a stunned silence and then they all began to talk at once, but it was Alan who said it, most clearly.

'It could have been Sheila.' He was wide-eyed with horror. 'What on earth is going on here? Who can possibly hate Sheila that much?'

'That is what we have to find out,' George said grimly. 'I'm calling the police now – I'll tell 'em myself that I've been doing my own checks. No need to – well, dwell on it, though.'

Alan managed a faint grin. 'Not a word,' he said. 'Right . . .' He looked at the others, at Peter and Danny and Jane and Sam and there was a faint murmur of assent. 'Let's get on with it, then. We'll only use the other benches, OK? No one go near the end one.'

It wasn't until they were nearly all inside the big lab that it happened. They all stopped at the sudden loud wail. It was Louise Dee, the junior, standing very still in the middle of the corridor, clutching her cyclist's helmet to her chest with both hands, still draped in her leather jacket and trousers from her motorbike ride into work, and with her mouth gaping to let the sound out.

George took her firmly by the shoulders. 'Now calm down, Louise,' she commanded. 'There's no harm done. Jerry is fine and now we know this attempt has been made we're in a good position to protect him and Sheila in the future, believe me. There's nothing for you to be upset about.'

'But there is,' Louise wept. She dropped her helmet on the floor with a crash and put both hands to her cheeks, staring at George over them with wide-eyed terror. 'It could have been me! Don't you see? If it wasn't that I keep on forgetting to fill those bottles, it could have been me what was nearly choked to death. Oh, Dr B., what shall I do? I'm scared! Is it me they're really after?'

18

'It's all so bloody *clumsy*,' Gus said fretfully after a long silence. 'It's like a bunch of kids are being mischievous, and not thinking through the result of their actions. And cases like that – casual malice, you know? – they're right buggers to deal with. Give me the professional every time.'

'Yes,' George said abstractedly. She too had been thinking hard, and now she lifted her shoulders and looked at him consideringly. He had arrived promptly with a full team when she had phoned Ratcliffe Street Police Station and told them what had happened. Well before noon the SOCO had crawled all over the section of the lab involved as well as checking for prints everywhere else (a little forlornly, however. As he said, 'The world and his bleedin' wife have been in and out of here'): all the photographs and fingerprint tests necessary had been done: everyone possible had been interviewed: and they'd left, all except Gus. Now he sat in her office, crouching over a cup of coffee and staring gloomily at his notes.

'I'm not surprised that poor kid got the collywobbles and thought he was after her,' he said. 'When someone lets off a scatter of grapeshot like that everyone feels like a target.'

'I managed to persuade her there was nothing personal in it. That Jerry had just been unlucky while she'd been the one to benefit from his misfortune.' She made a face. 'I'll tell you this much – from now on I'll never get her to refill bottles, not for a pension.'

'Who'd be a boss?' he said, but it was an almost automatic rejoinder. He was clearly deeply in thought. 'Look, let's just run through it, shall we?' He spoke as much to himself as to her. 'First, the car is doctored in such a fashion that it could kill – but only chokes. Then the chocolates are poisoned, using a very toxic substance but in so low a concentration that all it did was make the person who ate one sick without killing her. And now this business of rearranged chemicals in bottles – you say that the amount of hydro-whatsit left in the bench bottle was too little to make a killing dose of chlorine gas when mixed with bleach, even though it's highly toxic, but just enough to cause a lot of discomfort.'

'Yes,' she said. 'I guess that's a fair résumé.'

'It's like Chummy just wants to play games, frightening people. Like he doesn't want to kill, just to scare.'

'I'm not entirely sure of that,' she said after a moment. 'I think maybe there's been some real killing going on as well as this other stuff.'

He looked up sharply. 'What gives you that idea?'

'I think I might have had a helluva lot of wool pulled over my eyes,' she said after another, longer pause. 'Shit, this is hell to have to admit. It's those three deaths that were put down to – dammit, I can't use the passive sense. *I* put them down to accident or suicide. Now I'm not so sure.'

He said nothing, just staring at her with his eyes wide and bird-bright.

She went on, never more painfully aware of how much of a fool she felt. 'The first one was a chap who was a recovered alcoholic, remember? Well, he hadn't had a drink for a long time, which is as much as any alcoholic will ever admit to. They know they're never really cured. I thought when I did his PM that his death had been accidental – that he'd slipped from the AA ideal and had a drink – only he'd taken a big one matching his previous consumption, not realizing that

that would now be an excessive dose. And died. And now I'm wondering just how he came to take too much.'

'But –'

'No,' she said. 'I've started, so let me finish. Though I have to say the last thing I feel like is a Mastermind. Now, the second one, Lally Lamark – though in fact she might have died first. But let that be. It's not important – at least, I don't think so. She was a diabetic and I assumed that she had in-advertently taken the wrong dose of insulin, or something of that sort – maybe failed to eat after taking her insulin. But I've read her notes again, seeing I'm lucky enough to have them in spite of the break-in, and I've tried to read between the lines, this time, to see what sort of person she was.'

She stopped and bit her lip for a moment. 'Usually when you read notes you just take in factors. You don't think about the personalities involved because there is rarely much guid-ance on that. Doctors aren't encouraged to write down their subjective opinion of patients the way they used to, not now patients have the right of access to their notes. But we should – because when I looked and thought a bit more I got a pic-ture of a woman who knew her own condition very well. She'd had it most of her life, dammit. Probably knew more about her own diabetes, and diabetes in general, than her doctors did. And the fact that she asked Sheila to show her a path. report on her own blood sugar and insulin levels and assorted assays makes me think –'

'She asked Sheila what?' Gus was even more alert now.

George sighed. 'I hadn't told you that yet,' she said. 'It's all been so – Well, never mind. Sheila had a flaming row with the head of the Medical Records department a while back, as a result of which I got embroiled and Sheila and I fell out. That's the background. The reason for the fight with Elles-mere was that Lally Lamark had asked Sheila to show her her path. reports – her own, you understand – because she was suspicious about something to do with – well, we just don't know what. All I know is that Sheila did show Lally her records and refused to show Ellesmere when she demanded to be told. Ellesmere's just nosy, I think, likes to be involved in everything, and got mad when Sheila blocked her. But the nub of it all is, this woman Lamark was suspicious about something to do with her doctor's care.'

'And then died of an overdose of insulin. It was that, you said when you first told me about it.'

'Mmm. I put it down to an accident, but if Lally really was a mavin about diabetes, really understood her condition, there's no way she'd have an accident with her insulin. But maybe someone arranged things so that it *looked* like an accident.'

'So you're saying . . .'

'I haven't finished,' she said. 'I'm saying that I'm no longer sure of my own reports when I did those PMs. I thought one was a stupid overdose, another an accident. And I thought that one, Pam Frean, was a suicide. Now I'm wondering about all three of them. Could they have been deliberate killings? And could they be linked with these other – what did you call them? – clumsy attempts? Are we looking at one set of linked events rather than a series of separate ones?'

There was a silence and then he said, 'Um,' and lapsed into silence again.

She waited but he just sat there lost in a maze of his own thinking, until she said sharply, 'Well? Um, what?'

'Um is all. Except that I've been thinking something along these lines myself.'

She was nettled. 'I see, Mr Omniscient, eh?'

'No,' he said mildly. 'Just Mr Experienced. And I have to tell you it is as rare as hen's teeth to have a series of nasty events, especially including deaths, on the same premises and all with different causes. They have to be linked if only by copy-catting, or so goes my experience.'

'Oh,' she said and subsided. 'Well, yes, I guess so. I was thinking that sort of thing too.'

Now it was her turn to be silent and he looked at her and waited. And then said simply, 'You'd better spit it out.'

'Spit what out?'

'Whatever it is you think you ought to tell me but don't really want to, either because you feel a bit daft saying it or because you want to deal with it on your own. If it's the first, forget it. Nothing you do say or think is ever daft in my eyes. Misguided and due to conclusion-jumping maybe, but never daft. And if it's a case of preferring to do it alone, do me a favour and forget that too. We always do better as a team.' He spoke more loudly as she opened her mouth to protest. 'I know, I know, it was different last time, that business at Connie's factory, but we're not talking about that. I'm talking about the here and now. And right now, you ought to spit it out.'

She shook her head in mingled irritation and relief. 'Oh, you are the – All right. It's not easy and if you make any of your nasty cracks, I'll probably hit you. Just hear me out.' She took a deep breath and tried to find the best way to start and of course it all came out wrong. 'Zack Zacharius. I know you've been a bit jealous of him but –'

He flared up at once. 'Jealous? Me? I haven't got a jealous bone in my body! I may know the difference between what's proper behaviour and what isn't but that ain't got a thing to do with being jealous, and never you say it has! And anyway, what has that cock-eyed sod got to do with –'

'Oh, shit,' she said. 'I knew I'd get it all wrong! Listen, will you? I think maybe . . . I'm worried that he might be involved with all this.'

She almost laughed then. She had never seen him quite so surprised by anything in all the years she had known him and she let herself grin at the sight of his face.

'Bloody hell,' he said after a moment. 'Bloody hell! I thought you had a fancy for him.'

'I did,' she said calmly. 'He's a dishy fella.'

'Well, thank you very much, ducks. What am I supposed to say to that?'

176

'You can start worrying the day I stop noticing which are the attractive men,' she said, feeling better than she would have thought possible. She couldn't remember the last time she'd felt so very comfortable with him; it was an agreeable sensation. 'The important thing is I come back to you, however much I might enjoy the passing scenery. And don't tell me you never notice what other women look like. I've seen you with your fangs dripping, you pant so hard when some bouncy bottom goes by. But I've got more sense than to fret over it.'

He shook his head, as much to clear his thinking as to disagree with her. 'That's something to talk about some other time,' he said with dignity. 'Tell me now what you mean about this fella. Has he said something? Done something? Come on, doll, don't torment me!'

She was sober again at once. 'It's no one thing exactly. Well, maybe it was last night ... Look, he asked me to come and advise him on his research. I told you that and it was perfectly true. I thought that was all that he wanted and maybe a silly flirty dinner afterwards, and what harm would there be there? Especially if you were doing your famous porcupine-in-a-pet act at me. But when it came to it, he set me up.'

He frowned, never taking his eyes from her face. 'How?'

She explained as best she could, but it wasn't easy. 'You don't understand this business of research grants,' she told him. 'The thing is, unless the Institute can get at least two big projects funded from outside, it'll die. The consultants and the people involved – the Professor, the research fellows – will all lose a hell of a lot of face, as well as their income. The hospital will lose a good deal of status too, and in these days of marketing hospital services because the NHS is run like a market, status is valuable. Loss of it could reduce the number of patients referred to us. So the Institute's survival matters. And all Zack wanted to use me for was to prod the other two researchers so that they came up with a research protocol that could lead to the discovery – or development'd be a better word – of a highly profitable drug. That's the bottom line for him. Money. And I hadn't realized that till last night.'

'Is that the only thing that makes you suspicious?' he said after a while.

'Not the only thing, no. It's all a bit nebulous, that's the trouble, but I just feel ... well, look at what facts there are. He's been around all the time when things have happened. When Sheila's car went up, there he was in the car park. He gave me a very good reason for being there – it was the same as my own, in that he kept his car there and he needed to get it out, and also he said he wanted to get it out to pick me up at the Institute instead of having to walk together all through the hospital and make people gossip. We'd arranged to go out for a drink after the Professor's party, you see.' Gus's brows furrowed for a moment, but she just went on, pretending she hadn't noticed, and slowly he relaxed.

'Then, with the business of Sheila's chocolates, he was in and out of Ballantyne Ward to see her as much as the rest of us – as me even, although he'd never even met her before the event. He just sort of latched on. And then he turned up here at the lab the day after the break-in and the messing-up of my files and – Oh, I don't *know*. It sounds so little now I've spelled it out, but last night it seemed to me to be so import-ant ...' Her voice trailed away.

'And it may well be important,' he said. 'I have to agree if that's all there is, then it doesn't add up to much. But I like circumstantial pointers as much as the next man. It's just cir-cumstantial evidence I can't be doing with. But maybe his behaviour can point us towards something concrete. Hmm. Let me think ...'

'I've been thinking too,' she said. 'I've got a couple of ideas you might like to try.'

'I'll bet you have. Like what?'

'I don't feel comfortable about this but – make a deal with me, Gus. If I point you in an actual direction and it turns out

I'm wrong, you'll never let on to him I suspected him, will you? I'd hate that.'

'Why? Don't want to hurt little diddums' feelings, is it?' He sounded extra sardonic and she grimaced at him.

'You see what I mean? You always jump to the worst possible conclusion. It's because the man's a colleague, dammit. I'll have to go on working in this place with him afterwards. If he turns out to be straight up but he finds out I fingered him as a bad lot, then . . .'

'It'd be embarrassing.'

'Yes.'

'Stop his Dishiness from asking you out to dinner again?'

'Oh, the hell with it. If the best you can do is make snide cracks like that, let's forget it!' The good feelings she had about him began to dilute and she scowled. At first he scowled back but then relaxed, slowly.

'Oh, shit!' he said after a while. 'Maybe I am a bit jealous at that.'

'Wow,' she said, staring upwards with studied concern. 'Where are the flying pigs? Watch out below!'

'The time for you to start worrying is when I'm not jealous,' he snapped. 'Isn't that what you said to me? So, goose and gander, OK? And truce, fainites, Tom Tiddler's ground and all that. What is it you want me to do?'

She was mollified. 'It's not what I want you to do. It's just a suggestion.'

'So suggest it.'

'He said he's a Canadian. Trained there, did some important work there. Well, maybe it'd be worth doing a check-up to make sure that all the things he says about himself are true.'

'Is there any reason to doubt they are?'

'Honestly, I don't know. He seems to be abreast of his subject as far as I can tell, though as I'm no neurologist, how can I say for sure? But it seems to me that he's excessively nervous about the possibility of losing this chance for the Institute and I wondered why. I thought maybe he was embroidering his CV, making himself out to be something he isn't? It's hell being in research. You can't be a researcher in the accepted sense of the term till you publish a worthwhile paper in an important journal of record, and you can't get such a paper published until you're a researcher. Sometimes I suspect people cut corners. Scientific fraud isn't unheard of. There was that chap who made claims about fertility research, and got himself struck off the register, remember? Maybe Zack's in that mould. Maybe he's trying something on here. If we check his past and find out he isn't all he claims to be, well, we're on our way.'

He thought for a moment and then nodded. 'OK, doll. That makes good sense to me. And tell me, I contact where to make these checks?'

'I thought you had contact with the Canadian police?'

'Hell, yes, of course. But I have to have some basis on which to work, you know, some reason for my enquiries. Like where he claims to be at university, where he did earlier research, all that stuff.'

She pondered and then brightened. 'Some of it should be here in his files in Human Resources.'

'Human . . . ?' Gus shook his head irritably. 'You mean what you and I used to call Personnel. OK, yeah. But in my experience they won't part with staff members' files unless you have a warrant. And I can't get a warrant without due cause, can I? Is there any other way you can get a lead on this for me?'

She thought for a while and then said uneasily, 'Well, I suppose I could pump him. Ask a lot of innocent questions and see what comes out of it.'

He frowned, clearly not liking the idea one bit. And then, suddenly, he laughed. 'Dolly,' he said suddenly. 'You're looking peaky.'

'Eh?' She was amazed. 'What the hell are you talking about?'

'You look tired,' he translated. 'Off your peak. Short of a vitamin or two. I think you need a nice night out, just as a pick-me-up. No, not alone with the Dishy One, but with a few buddies, people you can enjoy being with.'

'Try being a little denser,' she said acidly. 'I want to go over to see how Jerry is and I really haven't time for all this silliness.'

'It's all right,' he said and beamed. 'I'll come over with you, A & E, is it? I'll be glad to hear how the poor fella's coping. And of course, good old Hattie'll be there, won't she? It'll be nice to see Hatt. Haven't seen her for an age. It'd be really good to have a chance to get my knees under her table again and my belly wrapped round one of her chicken pies. Best chicken pies in the world, hers.'

'Gus,' she said. 'You wouldn't!'

'Oh, wouldn't I?' He laughed and got to his feet, holding out his hands to pull her up too. 'Just you watch me. By the time I've finished with our Hatt, she'll be convinced she had the idea of giving a party for a few mates all on her own. And what's more she'll include your pal with the buzzy name as though it was the most natural thing in the world!'

19

Quite how he would do it, she didn't know, and she didn't want to. Hattie was one of her best friends, and they were on very comfortable terms, but she would never have had the gall to ask her to give a dinner party in her own home in order to help with an investigation. Apart from anything else, Hattie would insist, and justifiably so, on George telling her all the whys and wherefores, who were the suspects and what the investigation was all about, and George knew perfectly well that she would find it very difficult to avoid doing so. Gus, on the other hand, would manage it easily because, as George knew all too well, he could be the most persuasive of people. And it was important that Hattie wasn't told why, because, bless her, George thought, she had the most open and confiding of natures and would never be able to hide from anyone how she thought about them. The thought of Hattie watching Zack over her own dinner table for signs of wrongdoing was more than George could contemplate.

So, when they reached A & E she deliberately detached herself from Gus and went in search of Jerry. He was, she was told, in the A & E recovery room; he might need to be admitted to the ward later, Adam Parotsky told her, but it was by no means certain.

'He's recovering fast,' he said when George put her head between the curtains of the cubicle where he was busily sewing up a lacerated hand on a nervous Turkish woman in late middle age who had brought most of her relations with her to supervise her care. No wonder Adam looked flustered, George thought, glad it wasn't her task. 'Go and have a look at him yourself. I'll see him as soon as I've finished here – Yes, I won't be long.' This was directed at a flood of angry complaint from a man who seemed to feel he was in charge of the proceedings. 'Then I'll talk to you about what we do for him next. Now, Mrs Othman, let me just turn your hand this way. That's it . . .'

George escaped to the recovery room, grimly amused to see Gus disappear into Hattie's office as she did so. Would he get away with it? Probably.

Jerry was the only patient in Recovery, which was a relief. It could have been tricky talking comfortably to him while others were listening. He was dozing and she stood beside his bed for a moment, feeling a wash of affection for the man. He had been one of the staff of the lab when she had arrived at Old East coming up for four years ago, and though he could be maddening, with a chirpy manner and a vein of bawdy in his speech that drove some of his colleagues to despair and often irritated George herself, he was hard working and deeply loyal to her. She knew that and she was appreciative of it. Looking at him now, she felt a little sad. He was still fairly young – well on the right side of forty – yet he had a tired, slightly hunted look that showed more clearly now he was off his guard. She suspected he was a lonely man, lacking any important people in his life, which was why he worked as hard as she did, starting early and finishing late. He had told her a little of himself once, shortly after she had arrived at Old East, but that had been as far as it had gone. He had never spoken truthfully of private matters again, only ever making jokes, and wouldn't have done so that one time if he hadn't inadvertently become involved in one of her cases. I should encourage him to open out more, she thought now with compunction. Maybe he needs a friend. And she touched his hand gently.

He woke at once, turning his head on the pillow to stare at her with very wide startled eyes that had fear in their depths, and then, as he saw who it was, relaxed.

'Hi there, Chief,' he said, his voice husky. 'Gee, the things some guys'll do to get 'emselves noticed, huh?'

'Not at all,' she said. 'How are you? At least you're rid of that laryngeal tube.'

He grimaced. 'I have to tell you that that is the nastiest thing you can have shoved into any of your orifices. And I'm an expert on the subject.' He coughed, a thick bubbling sound, and she held out a tissue from the box on the bedside locker. He took it and turned his head aside so that he could spit into it.

'Is it very uncomfortable?' she asked.

'Oh, a bit sore is all.' He managed a grin. 'Like smoothish barbed wire.'

'It should ease fairly quickly,' she said. 'I don't think you got too heavy a dose.'

'No, I didn't. As soon as I smelled it I sort of knew. I pushed the stuff away and turned my head in the other direction but after that I couldn't do a thing. I just stood there and held on, trying to breathe.' He looked bleak for a moment. 'I'll tell you this much. It must be a hell of a way to go. It's not much fun when you don't go, if you see what I mean.'

'I see,' she said. 'D'you feel up to telling me what happened?'

'Sure,' he said and coughed again but this time less painfully. 'There was bleach in the Goddamn hydrochloric acid Winchester from the Beetle cupboard. There just wasn't quite enough at the bottom of the bench bottle to work with and I stood there, cursing Louise and putting it in and –' He stopped. 'It was Sheila's bottle I was filling.'

'I know.'

'I should have used my own, but to tell the truth, I couldn't find it. I'd spread my slides so much that it was easier to use Sheila's. Only like I say . . .'

'It was a perfectly natural thing to do,' she said. 'Don't feel bad about it.'

There was a little silence and then he said, 'Don't tell Sheila. Poor cow's scared enough.'

'You're a nice fella, Jerry,' George said and touched his hand again.

He managed a wobbly grin. 'I'll bet you say that to all the nice fellas,' he murmured.

She looked around for a chair, found a stool and pulled it over to the bedside. 'Listen, Jerry, could you bear to have a bit of discussion of all this?'

'As long as I don't have to talk too much.' He made a face. 'My throat really is disgusting.'

'I'll try to keep it to yesses and noes,' she said, reaching for the glass of water on his bedside locker. He took a sip, gratefully. 'I was just wondering: has there been anything else that's happened that I ought to know about? Have you noticed anything that worried you? Just say yes or no.'

'Yes,' he said. 'And I'll have to talk. I want to. The break-in, remember?'

'Of course.'

'After that, the Beetle cupboard looked sort of . . . I couldn't be sure. It seemed to me that maybe it had been meddled with.'

She frowned sharply. 'Why didn't you tell me at the time?'

'I tried to, but there was not enough to show. It was only a feeling. I thought maybe I was imagining things.' He coughed, bubbly again, and once more she did the necessary with a tissue. 'I thought I was being neurotic. Thought I'd just keep my eyes open. And then forgot, would you believe.'

'You say you tried to tell me?' She bit her lip. 'How come you didn't?'

'You had other things on your mind at the time I tried. Your files.'

'Oh, shit,' she muttered. 'I'm sorry, Jerry. P'raps I don't

always listen to you as much as I should, but you do rabbit on, sometimes.'

'My fault.' He managed another of his grins. 'Boy who cried wolf, eh? Next time I'll just come out with it. Hope there isn't a next time.'

'There better hadn't be,' she said grimly. She got to her feet to go and then stopped. 'Has there been anything else you haven't told me?'

'Not a thing.'

'You will, though, if anything else bothers you? Even if you think it's your imagination?'

'Yessir, Mum.' He grinned. 'I'll try to be good.'

'Make sure you are,' she said with mock severity. 'OK. I'll go and talk with Adam now. He still hasn't decided whether to admit you or not.'

'I'm OK,' Jerry said. 'Nothing a day in bed won't cure.' He swivelled his eyes and peered at her. 'Feel like volunteering to help with that? I can't think of a faster cure than having you there with me . . .'

'Don't think you can hide behind disability, my friend,' she said with even more mock severity. 'I'll beat you up, you go on sexually harassing me that way. Get better soon, klutz.' And after a brief moment of hesitation she bent and kissed his cheek, then went back to the cubicle to see if Adam had finished his repair job.

He had, and she found him at the main desk filling in some notes. He looked up and said, 'I'll be right with you,' and she nodded and waited, looking about her.

The place wasn't unduly busy, and several of the staff seemed to be standing about talking to each other. She recognized the senior A & E staff nurse she knew best – though she had to admit she didn't know the girl's name, which was horribly typical of the relations between nurses and doctors. She thought, I really ought to try to get to know the nursing staff better. They know more about what goes on in this place than anyone else. Except for Sheila, of course.

She smiled a little crookedly at that thought. No one was like Sheila when it came to gossip; her appetite for it was insatiable. She'd do anything to find out what was going on just for the sheer pleasure of knowing . . .

It was a sort of epiphany. Standing there in the middle of A & E, hearing the commonplace sounds of voices, the distant clatter of bowls and instruments, the clacking of computer terminals and the buzzing of the lift door at the far side, smelling the familiar mix of spirit and disinfectant and anxious people, she saw quite clearly what lay at the core of the situation they were in.

Sheila, she thought. Sheila was undoubtedly the source of it all. Sheila who let people think she knew so much about what was happening here, that she had the ear of everyone, who was indefatigable in her search for titbits of news; not for any wicked reason, not because she had any intention of using her garnerings in a malicious way, but for the sheer delight of knowing. It gave her status in her own eyes, made her feel in control of everything about her in a way that she clearly found comforting. It was a harmless foible, George knew, and there was no need for anyone to get upset over it.

But not everyone realized that. The hospital must, George thought, be full of people who were convinced that Sheila really did see all, hear all, know all. And because someone somewhere had a secret they didn't want uncovered, Sheila became a threat. That was why she had been attacked – and why those other three had died.

Whoever it was who had the secret, George told herself, staring sightlessly across the A & E department, was one very frightened person. Frightened enough actually to kill. But why kill those other people? Why make ineffective attacks on Sheila? Surely the simplest way for the frightened person to soothe his – or her – fears was to get rid of Sheila. The rest – Tony Mendez, Lally Lamark, Pam Frean – they couldn't hurt him or her as much as Sheila could. Or so the criminal must surely think.

Or – and now her mind went into overdrive – or maybe he knew that the three had real knowledge of him and his activities (remember to think *her* and *she* as well, she scolded herself). If he did know for sure that was the case, then he'd have to kill them. It was the only way to ensure their silence. But if he didn't know what Sheila might possibly know, he was in trouble. That she might have damning evidence was clear, but what was it? It would not be safe to get rid of Sheila completely until he knew just what it was she knew that was a danger to him. Then he would be able to cover it up and go on to killing Sheila. But if he killed Sheila without knowing what it was, there was always the risk it would emerge later in some way. Meanwhile, trying to frighten Sheila so much she'd run away – or be off duty sick – could give him space. Space and time in which to look further (where? George didn't know; think about that later) and see just where his danger lay.

Absurdly convoluted, she told herself. Ridiculous. Wasn't it? But it was the nearest she had come to finding a solid reason for the two situations: three deaths and three clumsy attempts at causing a death, but very efficiently causing fear and incapacity. She and Gus had talked about Sheila's role before, but hadn't reached any satisfactory conclusion. Now, she was sure she had, and she focused her eyes again to look eagerly about the place and see if there was any sign of Gus. This had to be talked about.

'Right, I'm all yours.' Adam came out from behind the desk to stand beside her. 'How does he seem to you?'

'Hmm?' She blinked at him, puzzled for a moment.

'Jerry.' He frowned. 'Didn't you go to see him?'

Her face cleared. 'Oh, yes, of course I did! Poor old Jerry. He seems in a pretty good state, overall. Bit bubbly but no real harm done.'

'I think you're probably right,' he said. 'I think I'll try to get him a bed in Day Care, just till this evening, and all being well, send him home after that.'

'Will he be fit to come back to work tomorrow, then?'

He lifted his brows at her. 'Wow! I didn't have you down as a whip-cracking type of boss at all!'

She shook her head, embarrassed. 'Hell no. It's not that. It's just that he lives alone and I think he'd be better off here with us than left alone at home all day. Too much time to fret, you know.'

'Ah! I see.' Adam looked happier. 'Fine. I'll tell him to get back to work as soon as possible. There's no reason why he shouldn't. The worst he'll be left with is a slightly productive cough for a few days. We've had cases like this before: usually it's over-houseproud women cleaning their loos with everything they can think of, all at the same time. And they do fine. I can't remember the last time we had one that didn't.'

'Good,' she said fervently. 'So you think I'll see him tomorrow in the lab?'

'All being well,' he said. 'I'll go and see him now,' and then switched his gaze from her face to over her shoulder. 'Ah, Sister, about Jerry Swann in the recovery room . . .'

George whirled. 'Good morning, Hattie! How's this for another drama then?'

'I know.' Hattie was bright-eyed with interest. 'I've been hearing all about it. OK, Adam. What do you want to do about Jerry?'

'I'll check him over, but it's my guess that after a day in a Day Care Unit bed sleeping it off, he'll be able to go home this evening. George wants him back at work tomorrow –'

'Slave-driver,' Hattie said equably.

'So that she can keep an eye on him,' Adam finished. 'All of which makes sense to me. So, I'll fix that up – unless you wouldn't mind doing the necessary phoning and arranging for me?' His voice took on a wheedling note. 'I'm up to my hocks in paperwork.'

'Oh, all right,' Hattie said good-naturedly. 'Leave him to me.' And Adam linked his hands together in a boxer's salute of victory as he went away.

'Um, has Gus gone?' George said. 'I wanted another word with him.'

'He's in my office still. I came out to find you and bring you in for coffee. Listen, I've had a thought. It's been an age since we got a chance to be matey, you and Gus and Sam and me. I've been lazy, I suppose, what with the kids and school exams and so forth, but I was just thinking: what about dinner this weekend? The girls'll both be away on school trips – how's that for glory? – so I'll have a chance to do some cooking.'

George blinked. 'Oh? Whose idea was that?'

Hattie looked startled. 'Eh?'

'I mean, what made you think of that?'

'I told you! The girls are away, and talking to Gus was fun and I thought – Well, anyway, he says it's OK with him for this Saturday if it is for you. Are you on? And are you fed up to the back teeth with salmon? Because I've got a new recipe I'd love to try.'

'Not at all,' she said, a touch abstractedly, trying to im-agine how Gus had worked the oracle so completely. It was obvious that Hattie was convinced this was all her own idea. 'Whatever you make'll be great, I'm sure. I'll look forward to it. Just us, will it be?'

'Oh, maybe a few more,' Hattie said airily. 'If I'm going to do it, I might as well make a job of it. Cooking for four is no different from cooking for eight. Anyone you fancy?'

'Oh, it's up to you,' George said hastily. 'I mean –'

'Would it embarrass you if I asked Dr Zacharius?' Hattie looked at her a shade wickedly. 'I mean, he was being flirty with you.'

'Of course not!' George said and flushed slightly. 'There's absolutely no reason why you shouldn't ask anyone you like.'

'OK,' Hattie said happily, turning to lead the way back to-wards her office. 'Let me see now. I'll need another female to balance Zack . . . I think perhaps Kate Sayers. Her Oliver's off on some assignment or other and she's fretting over him. He's not precisely in the front line or anything, but it's in the former Yugoslavia, so she's a bit twitchy. She's the last woman who ought to be shacked up with a journalist. And then there's that rather nice shy young chap, who comes and confides his worries in me and makes me feel like a Jewish mother: I might as well feed him like one. What's his name?'

'I really don't know,' George said quickly. 'And it's entirely up to you.' She pushed open the office door. 'Hello, Gus.' She looked at him sitting there with his chair tilted back tottering on two legs, his hands shoved deep into his trouser pockets and a self-satisfied smirk on his face. 'I hear we've been invited out this weekend.'

'We sure have,' Gus said and grinned at Hattie. 'Ain't that nice now? An' she promises me I can have my favourite nosh too. Aren't we the lucky ones!'

20

Hattie Clements and Sam Chanter, who was a tolerably successful novelist for most of the time, and a very successful coach for slow boys needing to be pushed through their A levels for the rest of it, lived in what George had always regarded as intellectual squalor in a large Victorian house in Bethnal Green. She had been there many times and it always seemed to her much like clambering into a deeply upholstered, unbelievably comfortable womb. There was a deep red carpet with scattered Persian-style rugs in the main living room, which ran from front to back of the house and incorporated both sitting and drawing rooms, since the wall once between them had been demolished, supporting an amazing clutter of big squashy easy chairs, cushion-strewn sofas, overloaded bookcases and oddment-laden occasional tables, as well as a small piano, a large music centre of the most up-to-the-minute state-of-the-art newness, and a big square dining table surrounded by a collection of motley but still very comfortable chairs. The kitchen at the back of the house was another amazing clutter of pots and pans and trailing ivy in overhead containers and children's drawings pinned to the walls, and draining boards on each side of the sink piled high with newly washed dishes, and herbs growing in pots and cats' and dogs' baskets, and above all a constant smell of good food. It could not have been more unlike

George's own rather over-tidy flat ('I have to keep it tidy,' she had once protested to Hattie in embarrassment. 'It's so goddamn small I'd never find anything if I didn't') or Gus's beautifully kept, elegant but slightly spartan home. For George the Chanter house managed to be simultaneously the most homelike of homes, and an example of the last way she would want to live herself, which was, she had to admit, highly contradictory.

When they arrived, she clutching an azalea in a pot and he with a bottle of good champagne under each arm, she wondered for a moment if Gus would have a miserable evening of it, finding the house less agreeable than she always did, and then thought a little maliciously, well, it's his fault if he does. All this was his idea, after all.

But he fitted in beautifully and clearly felt as comfortable as she did herself. He presented the bottles to Sam with an assurance that they were still cold enough on account of he'd taken them from the fridge a bare ten seconds before starting the car to get here, kissed Hattie warmly on the cheeks and settled himself in one of the softest of the armchairs to talk cricket with Sam as they both gobbled one of Hattie's specialities, which were buttery home-salted almonds. George, relieved in spite of herself, went off to the kitchen to keep Hattie company as she put the finishing touches to her dinner.

Hattie was flushed and happy as she moved around her cluttered space, a tea towel thrown over one shoulder of her black dinner dress and clearly quite unconcerned when she splashed herself with droplets of sauce as she stirred and tasted and generally busied herself as she chattered.

'It's my version of a Russian koulibiac,' she said. 'See? Filo pastry umpteen layers deep, and all buttered to within an inch of their lives, filled with a layer of poached salmon fillet on a bed of wild rice with olives and chopped mushrooms and a wickedly rich Hollandaise sauce all wrapped up and ready to bake for twenty minutes. It's no wonder my dress doesn't fit properly any more.' And indeed, it was straining a little across her back. 'But what the hell. Sam loves me as I am, so who am I to argue? I've got mange-touts with this and some marrow I've cooked *à la hongroise* – which only means with dill weed and a bit of caraway and soured cream – and an ice cold borscht to start. I hope Gus likes the taste of beetroot?'

'Too bad if he doesn't,' George said. 'I love it.' She dipped a spoon into the jug of ruby richness that sat waiting in the middle of the table and savoured its tart sweetness. 'To die for, hon. My God, they should taste this at the hospital and know what they're missing.'

Hattie chuckled. 'Well, not all of 'em. Not enough here. Still, I think I've got enough ambassadors here tonight to go back and tell 'em I can cook.' She looked pleased with herself. 'You wait till you see the pudding. I made the biggest damned cherry strudel you ever saw! I know it's two lots of pastry, but they taste so different I didn't think it'd matter. There's a lot of good Chardonnay out in the back porch sitting in a bath of ice so we should have a good evening. As long as everyone keeps off talking shop.'

'Oh, I don't know,' George said as casually as she could. 'I rather like shop talk. It's the best way of really knowing what people are like, I think, listening to their attitude to their jobs. Shall I cut up that bread for you?'

'Hmm? Oh, yes please. Except I wondered maybe I should do some garlic bread to go with the starter? No, OK then. I thought it might be a bit too much. Just cut it up and shove it in the baskets. There's butter in the fridge waiting to be curled and then if you really want to be a darling, you'll set the coffee tray. What were you saying?'

'Shop talk,' George said. 'I like it. You don't, you said.'

'Oh, I don't mind it, as long as it doesn't make people angry or critical of each other. That's what gets boring.'

'I couldn't agree more.' George was careful as she carried out Hattie's instructions, thinking hard. She and Gus had talked a little of what he planned to do tonight, but in very little detail.

'You can't plan other people's conversations, George,' he had said. 'Remember the folk tale about the guy who decides as he's going to bed one rainy night he'll mend his roof next day on account it's leaking? Only he hasn't got a ladder, so he thinks, I'll borrow Joe's from down the road. And then, he goes on inside his head, then Joe'll say I have to fix my own roof, so I can't lend you my ladder, and then I'll say well let me have it when you've finished, and he'll say but I promised to lend it to someone else and then the fella thinks – well, to cut it side-ways, he gets so screwed up inside he gets out of bed, rushes out into the rain to his friend Joe's house and bangs on the door and when Joe looks out of his window all surprised 'cause it's round two in the morning, the guy shrieks, 'I don't want your bloody ladder!' See what I mean? It's a daft thing to do.'

'Hmmph,' she had said, refusing to laugh. 'That's as may be, but I still think there's a lot to be said for doing some for-ward planning.'

'Haven't I done that? Aren't we going to dinner at Hattie's home to meet this guy Zack and see him in action? Pump him a little?'

'I wish I knew how you managed that.' She shook her head, mystified. 'Hattie's convinced it was all her own idea.'

Gus opened his eyes wide. 'Oh, it was, it was! I just sort of opened her mind to it. It sounds like a nice line-up she's got. Zack and Kate, to make a pair even though they aren't, and a fella called . . .' He closed his eyes to marshall his memory. 'James Corton. I don't know who he is.'

'Oh?' George said and smiled. 'Nice old Hattie. He's the shyest fella in the place. Scared to say boo to a goose. It's typ-ical of Hattie to take him under her wing. Who's she bal-ancing him with?'

'I gather there's a widowed neighbour Hattie's fond of – what did she say her name was? Heather, I think. Yeah, Heather Pyne. I think that's everyone. Perfect.'

'How do you know it's perfect?'

'Not so many people that the conversation breaks up into little groups and not so few that it would show if you asked the same person too many questions. Ideal number. That's why I wanted eight.'

'Did you tell Hattie that?' She was amused.

'Oh, no. She told me,' and he grinned at her, his eyes so alight with laughter that she had to share it.

'You're a manipulative bastard, Gus, but I love you,' she said.

His mood changed at once, and he looked at her very directly. 'Do you?'

She had been a little flustered. 'You know I do.'

He gave a theatrical sigh, recovering some of his jokiness, but there was behind it some real feeling, she knew. 'Yet you allow these footloose medicos to ogle you? Ah me, if only life were as it used to be, when a man could tie his woman in his cave by her hair!'

'Shut up,' she advised. 'You'll see for yourself at Hattie's how silly you are over this.'

And I hope he will, she thought now as she carried the bread through to the dining table. The last thing I want is any showing off from Zack. Or Gus, come to that. She felt a frisson of anxiety; this had seemed a good idea at first, a great way to get the lead on Zack she wanted, but now she wasn't so sure. She remembered uneasily the way she had undoubtedly led Zack to believe she found him interesting and mentally crossed her fingers.

There was a flurry then as other people arrived. The front door bell rang in the hall and Sam, a comfortable-looking man whose rather dusty-looking hair, elderly check shirt and battered drill trousers (which had clearly never met an iron in their life) gave him an overall crumpled effect, went to answer it.

George stood by the table, listening. She heard Hattie go along the hall from the kitchen, then cries of welcome and

196

the murmurings of, 'You really shouldn't have,' as the usual offerings were made and accepted – more plants? More wine? Probably – and the deeper voices of the new arrivals. George strained to hear words but couldn't and Gus laughed. She switched her gaze to him.

'Patience, girlie. Your heartthrob will get here,' he murmured over the rim of his champagne glass and she thrust her tongue out at him in the rudest way she could.

'Oh, a nice healthy sight for any doctor to be offered!' The voice from the doorway was light and bantering but it hit George hard. Oh God, she thought. I wish I'd never agreed to this. But she turned and managed a smile.

'Hi, Zack. I was just having a normal conversation with Gus here. You've met, I think?'

'Oh, yes, the Detective Inspector? Of course I remember.'

'Detective Superintendent,' Gus said. 'Not that it matters, which is what we always say when in fact it matters like hell. Good evening to you.'

'Whoops.' Zack smiled charmingly. 'Trust me to make a bish. Now, Hattie, are you sure I'm forgiven? I wouldn't normally do such a thing but I hadn't the heart not to.' He turned the smile on Hattie who had come in behind him.

'It's no problem,' Hattie said, looking at George, her face adorned with a bright expression. 'Zack brought along a friend of his, George. I'll just set another place.'

Her expression didn't alter as George caught her eye, but to George it said it all. Bloody man, mucking up the dining table. Who the hell did he think he was, bringing someone else? What was the point of explaining to people it was a dinner party they were invited to when they behaved as though it was a buffet? 'Shove another cup of water in the soup, hon,' George said, gazing at Zack very directly. She could say it if Hattie couldn't, and had opened her mouth to do just that when Sam appeared, bringing someone else with him. She blinked. 'Oh. Hello Dr – Mike – er – we've met before, Hattie. Dr Klein is also researching at the Institute.'

'So Zack told me,' Hattie said, still with that gritted-teeth brightness. 'Now, do give everyone a drink, Sam, while I go and do kitchen things. Uh, George?'

George escaped too, following her into the kitchen where Hattie closed the door carefully and then growled loudly between her teeth.

'It's all right,' George said soothingly. 'You always over-cater to a ridiculous degree, honey. There'll be plenty of food.'

'And bugger all space for people's elbows! I know my own limitations and eight at that table is fine. Nine is purgatory. I hate him. How could you ever have fancied him?'

'I didn't,' George said unconvincingly. 'Here, give me the extra cutlery and so forth and I'll set a place. Calm down, it'll be fine – and it sounds as though some more people have arrived. Didn't you hear the doorbell? Go and make sure they haven't brought the whole of the Bolshoi Ballet to share your koulibiac.'

Hattie growled again but hurried out. George followed her more slowly to re-set the table, and found the four men, Sam and Gus, Zack and Michael Klein, in happy colloquy, all apparently talking at the same time.

She caught Gus's eye and he winked at her. 'Hi, doll! Why didn't you tell me this man was such an expert on ice hockey? I used to know this guy who played in Montreal – way back it was, what was his name?' He turned back into the conversation as George got on with her chore and the last arrivals, James Corton and Kate Sayers, came in, followed by the only stranger to George, a quiet woman in a rather dowdy dress.

'There!' Hattie said brightly behind them. 'Here we all are, then. Now have you enough almonds to go with the bubbly? No? I'll go and get some more and put my koulibiac in the oven and then we can all settle down for a nice gossip till dinner's ready.'

*

198

Whether it was the saltiness of Hattie's almonds or the warmth of the summer evening that made them thirsty, it was not possible to say, but the champagne, both bottles, vanished rapidly and were immediately replaced by very cold Chardonnay fetched by Sam from the back porch, dripping with ice water and welcomed vociferously by all of them. They seemed to succumb to the softening influence of alcohol very quickly, George thought, but was glad of it. The barriers seemed to dwindle so low that even she began to relax.

Zack's behaviour could not have been more perfect. He paid flattering attention to Hattie, his hostess, until she melted like a glacier transferred to the Equator, and seemed completely to forget her ire at being saddled with an unwanted guest. Mike Klein himself was also charming and a very different proposition from the young man George had met at Hunnisett's party and later in Laburnum Ward. He talked as easily of books and films and music as he did of science – and the conversation ranged comfortably over all those subjects – and showed himself to be a much more interesting person than his rather unprepossessing appearance would have led George to expect. It's not the first time I've done that, she thought, staring a little owlishly into the depths of her glass. Judging people by what they look like is asking for trouble. This guy is very nice: I should be ashamed of myself for making snap judgements about him.

The quietest people at the table were Sam and James Corton. The younger man, though he did talk a little to Heather Pyne, who seemed as shy as he was and even more monosyllabic, mostly sat and crumbled his bread and ate a great deal, blinking at people through his round glasses and clearly listening to all that was said, but contributing little to the general conversation. Sam was an observer, too, but in a very different way. George was used to Sam's sort of behaviour in a crowd. The man could no more help observing people instead of joining in than he could prevent himself from breathing. He had tried to explain that once to George, long ago, blaming his novel-writing activities, and George, who found his quietness endearing, assured him she had understood. Now, sitting beside him, she was happy to join in his silent observation.

Kate Sayers was on the quiet side too, lapsing from time to time into little silences, and George felt for her; she adored her Oliver, a most difficult man who had never quite made up his mind what mattered most to him: his job as a radio correspondent for an independent news company, his life with Kate and her children, or the pressures put on him by the children of his first marriage who, according to Kate, did all they could to make his life as complicated as it could be. Kate was often *distraite* when she thought about Oliver. That she should be so now when he was away reporting in the Balkans was fully understandable. George leaned towards her, across the silent Sam, and talked to her whenever she could, leaving the noisy chatter to the men on the other side of the table, and to Hattie, who was, to tell the truth, very slightly drunk, partly with wine and partly with the praise heaped on her for her dinner, which was, quite frankly, superb. Not a scrap of the koulibiac remained and the cherry strudel was a sorry wreck of rich red juice and flakes of crisp pastry long before the coffee came to top it all up.

Sam had found a bottle of good brandy which he set in front of Gus, who looked up at him with a gleam in his eye, and accepted it gracefully, and a bottle of plum schnapps which he offered in general, but only Zack accepted that. He took a small glassful and threw it back in one swallow with an expert twist of his wrist that made Sam laugh aloud.

'The only other person I ever saw drink schnapps like that was a Hungarian,' he said in his unexpectedly deep voice. 'Like you, huh, Zack?'

'Now, how did you know that?' Zack looked at him, his eyes very dark and bright above his flushed cheeks. He didn't look drunk, but he was certainly elevated, George decided. There was an almost dangerous glitter about him and she caught her breath as he shifted his gaze to her. 'Did you tell him, George? You're the only one here who knows my origins. I reckon it must have been you.'

'No,' she said as casually as she could. 'I don't think I've ever talked to anyone about you, Zack. Why should I?'

'Aha,' he said loudly and took another shot of schnapps. 'So, I'm not interesting enough?'

'Nothing of the sort, mate!' Gus said and leaned forwards. He looked relaxed and happy but George knew he was not one whit affected by alcohol. He may have seemed to keep up with everyone else but in fact had taken rather little. 'We think you're fascinating, don't we? Hungarian, huh? And knows more about Canadian ice-hockey players than any Hungarian has any right to! You'll have to explain that to us all, mate, won't you?'

21

'I told you I don't like shop talk,' Hattie said fretfully as she and George made a third pot of coffee. It was now well past midnight but no one showed any signs of being ready to go. The level in the brandy bottle had dropped, but not as far as that in the plum schnapps; Zack had clearly taken to the stuff like a baby to sweet milk. 'All this explanation about his research – I'm sure it's madly exciting to him but for everyone else it's too, too boring.'

'I don't think it is, you know,' George said. 'No one seems to mind. Even your friend Heather, who has nothing to do with medical matters, seems interested. She's been asking as many questions as everyone else.'

'I didn't mind him telling us about his childhood – that was fascinating, all the Hungarian stuff – and getting out of Budapest at the revolution and so forth, but the rest of it . . .'

'He is rather hogging the conversation, I suppose,' George said. 'But –' She stopped short. The last thing she could do was explain to her friend that it was because Gus wanted Zack to do so that he was talking so much. Had she tried, it would have meant allowing Hattie to know just how very controlling of her party Gus had been from the start. He had set out to make contact with Zack and pump him, and that was precisely what he was doing. George had seen Gus in action many times, of course. She well knew his abilities as a man on the ground during an investigation, but she had never really seen him interrogating anyone; if his performance here tonight was anything to go by, he was a master. His touch was amazingly delicate, sometimes seeming not to be asking questions at all, but giving gentle guidance in the direction he wanted Zack to take, and Zack had responded like ... she couldn't think of a simile that fitted well but found images of fish being patiently hauled in from foaming water on the end of a line or a rabbit caught in the glare of headlights coming into her mind.

Yet it hadn't been like that. Zack had been relaxed and easy, a little drunk admittedly, but not in any offensive way. The spirits seemed only to have sharpened him in a way that was rather attractive: his eyes glittered, his face became pleasantly rosy, his very hair seemed to send off cheerful sparks, and he made them all laugh a lot, kept them all rapt in silent fascination at his descriptions of what he was trying to do.

All the time Gus had sat there, leaning back in his chair, murmuring, encouraging and listening, and never for a moment taking his eyes from Zack's face.

But Hattie was in the mood to grumble. 'I'll say he's hogging it,' she muttered. 'Even that chap he brought with him seems nicer than him.'

'Mike Klein?' George was glad to change the subject. 'Yes, I thought he was rather a dull stick, but –'

'I'm beginning to wonder what it is about that Zack you like,' Hattie said fretfully, picking up the tray. 'Too pushy by half for my taste. Stick to Gus, if you want my advice.'

'I am,' George said nettled. 'There was never any suggestion I'd do otherwise.'

'There's an old-fashioned word for you, my duck,' Hattie said as she pushed the kitchen door open with a thrust of her hip. 'Flirt, that's what you are. And flirts get into trouble.' And she sailed off to the dining table before George could answer her.

When the party eventually broke up half an hour later, amid loud protestations over the lateness of the hour and fulsome thanks to Hattie for her superb cooking and Sam for his generosity with the Chardonnay, Hattie seemed to be a little less testy. She pulled George to one side in the welter of farewells and muttered at her, 'Sorry if I was hateful.'

'Hateful? Never that, Hattie. You can be bloodyminded, hon, in the best Brit tradition, but never hateful.'

'He's all right, I suppose. I guess I was just tired when I slagged him off. Now I've got my second wind, I can see why you find him so –'

'Hattie, shut up,' George said firmly. 'I find no one anything, hear me? I'm just me, your old friend and guest this evening. Goodnight, and thanks for a great party.' She kissed her firmly on both cheeks, and moved to the door where Gus was waiting for her.

Everyone else was out on the front path now, and there were final goodbyes as people found their cars and started engines. Sam and Hattie stood on the doorstep, silhouetted against the light, and waved at them all as they went. George, leaning back in Gus's car, waved too, and then sighed.

'I feel really lousy,' she said.

'Mmm?' Gus was preoccupied as he manoeuvred his way down the heavily parked street.

'Using Hattie like that. Not a pretty thing to do.'

'But it worked,' he said as the car reached the main road and he was able to swing out into the traffic – thin now at this hour of the morning – and relax into his driving. 'And let's face it, duckie, you were the one who was worried about the guy and didn't want to start a –'

'I know, I know. I went along with it so I'm as bad as you are. Still . . .' She stopped, 'You say it worked . . . How?'

He smiled into the darkness. 'I picked up a lot of stuff from him, useful stuff. I can do some searches now, get to know a lot more about him. That was what you wanted, right?'

'Yes,' she said uneasily, then frowned. 'I was listening very carefully, but I didn't hear anything that made me sit up.'

'On account of he didn't say anything startling,' Gus said. 'But he gave me a lot of leads. He was at university at McGill in Montreal, he said. He worked later at the Toronto Western Hospital. He did a stint as a researcher at the Banting Institute.'

'Yes, but that doesn't mean a great deal. Plenty of people will have the same sort of history.'

'I'm sure. And maybe we'll find out he's no more than he says he is. But a little quiet chatting up of people around these places in Montreal and Toronto should give us a good deal of insight. Listen, doll. Leave it to me, huh? This is my manor we're on. I know what I'm doing. I've got the basic material I wanted, Hattie had a good party and no one's been harmed at all. Tell me about this guy Mike Klein.'

'Klein?' she said, distracted. 'What's to tell? You saw as much as I did. I hardly know him.'

'Are you worried at all about his research?'

She stared at him. 'Worried? Why should I be?'

'Well, you're worried about Zack's.'

'No, it's Zack's general behaviour that bothers me. I have no difficulty in understanding his research.' She was puzzled. 'Any more than I have Mike Klein's. They describe what they're doing well, and it makes sense.'

'Oh.' He manoeuvred the car into a side street, aiming for the river and home. 'Well, if you say so. I thought it sounded a bit . . .'

'A bit what?' she said, surprised by his hesitation.

'I guess I don't know enough science.' He sounded unusually self-deprecating. 'I just thought it sounds like real pie in the sky. Finding a pill that'll stop kids from getting hooked on crack and pot tobacco. That'll be the day.'

'It could happen,' she said, suddenly defensive of Klein's work and a little surprised to find herself in such a mind. 'He explained it clearly to me. It's a matter of enzyme activity

205

and enzyme production which are governed by gene threads, which in turn —'

'Spare me the lecture,' he said. 'I just asked if in your opinion the guy's work was kosher. It is, so OK. Leave it at that.'

She was silent for a while and then said, 'I hadn't thought enough about it. The trouble is, Gus, all medical research sounds crazy till it's done. If you'd have told my professor of Cardiology, who was already an old guy when he gave me my first lectures, that there would come a time when open-heart surgery would be as commonplace as taking out an appendix, he'd have written you off as a complete dumb cluck. As it is . . .'

'Yeah,' he said. 'I guess so. So, ducks, here we are.' He stopped the car at the kerb and turned in his seat to look at her. 'What shall I do? Go home or stay here?'

She looked back at him, deliberately expressionless. 'It's up to you, Gus.'

'No. I want an invitation. Just for a change. Not an assumption, an invitation. Ask me.'

'Damned if I will,' she said irritably. She stopped and took a breath. 'Why should you ask for an invitation after all this time? You know perfectly well that you always stay here when you want to.'

'Yeah, I know. But tonight I want to be coaxed. So coax me.'

'But why —?'

'Because I ask you to!' He seemed angry suddenly and she peered at him in the darkness.

After a moment she held out a hand. 'Gus, dear, here is my front-door key, all ready, you see? Please will you take it and let us both in?'

He stared at the key and thought. Then he shook his head. 'It's a start, but it's not good enough,' he said. 'I want a proper invitation.'

'This is crazy,' she said. 'It's late, you've had a fair deal to drink and —'

'Not that much.'

'– and shouldn't be driving at all, let alone on your own,' she finished. 'So, please will you –'

'That's punter's law, not policeman's,' he said, still sitting there. 'Do you want me to stay or not?'

'If you –'

'Yes or no?'

'Damn you, yes,' she snapped after a pause.

'OK. So invite me.'

'Gus, I'm too tired for this crap. Come to bed, for God's sake, and shut up.'

'That'll do,' he said in satisfaction. He got out of the car. 'I just needed to hear it from your lips. I'd love to go to bed with you, George, as long as it's really me you want and not that Hungarian big mouth.'

'Ah!' she said. 'Light dawns. This is another attack of the old machismo, is that it? For the last time, Gus. I am not even remotely interested in that man.'

'You're such a liar. You think he's good looking, you think he's interesting and you probably think he's got a sexy bottom. I know you. You like sexy bottoms on men.'

'Sure I do. The same way you like looking at girls in skirts that are shorter than curtain pelmets, so shut up and come to bed. This is a lot of nonsense. I can admire a man without wanting to go any further, for God's sake. That's how it is – was – with Zack Zacharius. Now, come on. It's past one in the morning and I'm bushed.'

They slept till gone eleven the next morning and she woke to the smell of toast and coffee. She stretched luxuriously as she lay there listening to him pottering in the kitchen, and re-membering. It had been well past three when they had finally fallen asleep; she had thought herself far too weary for more than a goodnight kiss, and had been taken aback by the way he had taken hold of her and pulled her close. That his need was urgent was indisputable, and her first reaction was no, not tonight. Too tired. But then another thought had taken its place. He's trying to prove something. That conversation about being invited to stay wasn't just the half-bantering nonsense I'd assumed. He really isn't sure. He needs to make certain that I'm telling him the truth about Zack. It was so chilling an idea that for a brief moment it threatened to douse the faint spark glowing deep inside her. But he had taken her hand and clasped it to his penis and that had been enough to set the spark into a positive firework display. From then on there had been no thinking at all. Just fireworks. Lovely.

He brought a tray and climbed back into bed, balancing it precariously on one upturned hand. She took it from him, just in time to prevent the bed being soused in coffee and they settled to an amiable breakfast, filling the bed with croissant flakes but not minding them too much.

'Sunday,' Gus muttered as at last they finished and he set the tray on the floor beside the bed, nearly falling out himself in the process. 'I love it. Let's stay here all day.' And he tried to nestle closer.

'It's a tempting thought,' she said. 'But –'

'No buts,' he said sleepily. 'Just stay where you are and leave it all to me. I'll change your mind for you. Just like I did last night.'

'It was as much my idea as yours,' she began, but he laughed.

'Like hell it was. You just wanted to go to sleep. But I convinced you, hmm? I can again. Unless you'd rather be somewhere else, of course.'

'You know I wouldn't. I just feel so . . .'

'Immoral?'

'Something like that. Lazy and squalid and –'

'Mmm. Lovely.'

'Make a deal. Get up this afternoon, OK? Do some work on this case.'

'Work?'

'Like decide what investigations you're going to make – you said you were going to look into the backgrounds of the

Mendez and Lamark and Frean cases, remember? – and what I can do at this end to find out more. Let's pool our ideas to see what might be going on with those deaths as well as the three attempts on Sheila.'

'We can do all that much later this afternoon,' he said. 'After it's dark.'

'No. Say about three.'

'Six, and you've got yourself your deal,' he muttered, pushing his face into her throat. 'Get up in time to go out and get some supper, do a bit of work after that.' He was stroking her belly with one hand as he breathed warmly on her throat and it was, she decided, more than female flesh could bear.

'All right then,' she said. 'Make it five, but no later. Oh, Gus, damn you . . .'

The phone woke her this time. She lay blinking into the brightness of the afternoon sun as it poured itself across the bed and tried muzzily to work out what day it was and why it was so bright. I've slept too long, she thought vaguely, and peered at her clock. Four-thirty? Why was it so light so early in the morning? And then she realized, shook her head to clear it and grabbed for the phone, as Gus stirred and mumbled beside her.

'Hello, George? Did I disturb you? Were you out in your garden or something?'

'I don't have a garden,' she said stupidly, shaking her head again to clear the sleep mists.

'You'll have to invite me to your place sometime so that I can see for myself,' he said. 'That was a good party last night, wasn't it?'

'Um, yes, I'm glad you enjoyed it too.'

'It was great. Great.'

'Did Mike Klein enjoy it?' Her voice sharpened a little as she became more alert. Beside her Gus turned over and pushed his head under the pillow to seek more silence.

'I don't know. Should I?'

'You brought him,' she said. 'So I imagined you were close friends and you would have talked to him about it.'

'Oh, we're not that close!' Zack's voice was reproving. 'He's a bit of a dull stick, to tell the truth. I only took him along because he asked me to.'

'He asked you?'

'Mmm. Said he hardly knew anyone and would my friends mind if he tagged along, and I said, well we can only ask. Don't tell me I've broken the rules of British behaviour again! We always take people along to each other's parties in Toronto.'

'Dinner parties are different,' she said. 'Anyway –'

'Anyway, I didn't call you to talk about Mike Klein.' He sounded cheerful suddenly. 'Listen, George, I've been going over my presentation, and with your new input I have to tell you I've made it a hell of a lot better. I have one last favour to ask you.'

'A favour?'

Gus's pillow moved, rose and then disappeared down the side of the bed as he sat up and rested his head against the board behind them, staring at her with his brows raised.

'What sort of favour, Zack?' she said, lifting her brows in return very deliberately so that Gus would feel included in the conversation. And after a moment she leaned towards him, tilting the earpiece so that he could hear Zack's voice too.

'I want to show you my star patient. The one I thought I'd show the funders when they come. See what you think and help me prepare him, huh? George, will you?'

She looked at Gus and he nodded. 'Well, yes, I suppose so.' she said. 'When? Where?'

'Tomorrow night. In the ward again? Just like last week.' He sounded eager. 'I'd really be grateful, George. I'm heartset on getting this funding, and I truly believe you can help me do it. Will you come tomorrow?'

Again Gus nodded at her and she sighed softly. 'Sure, Zack.

Around seven-thirty, then? I'll see you over on Laburnum Ward. Unless you can find somewhere less depressing.'

'What?'

'Nothing. I'll see you on Laburnum tomorrow. Goodbye, Zack.' And she hung up the phone.

Gus wriggled down in bed again and sighed. 'Another half-hour till we said we'll get up,' he said. 'Come on down, doll.'

But she shook her head and slid out of bed. The fireworks had quite gone now, and she had other things to think about.

22

Laburnum Ward seemed a little less depressing this time. There were more nurses on duty and a number of visitors, which gave the place some buzz, and George relaxed her shoulders as she came in through the big double doors, aware for the first time of how tense she had been. Zack was at the nurses' station with a pile of notes in front of him and he jumped to his feet as she came down the wide corridor towards him.

'George! You *are* punctual. Thanks so much for coming. You've even beaten my patient to it. I told him to be here at seven-thirty' – he glanced at his watch – 'so he's got a few minutes before he's late. Come and sit down.' He fussed with chairs as she came round to the working side of the station and accepted a seat.

'I have his notes here,' Zack said, pulling out a folder and setting it in front of her. 'Do read them and get yourself filled in, huh? Then you'll see why I'm so pleased with him. I can show you a video too. You know, before and after? I'll go and see if I can find him meanwhile, hurry him along.'

'That'll be useful,' she said and obediently bent her head to read the notes. The sooner she got her brain round all this stuff, the sooner she could get away. She was still uncomfortable with him, still had the nagging notion that he was deceiving her in some way and was still aware of Gus's lingering resentment of her contacts with the man, even though he encouraged them for the purpose of investigation. She didn't like the way all that made her feel, but it had to be tolerated till everything was sorted out. Dammit all to hell and back, she thought with sudden anger, but she knew that was pointless. She concentrated on the notes.

José Christophe Esposito, she read. Aged forty-two. Occupation waiter/barman. Address ... All the usual basic facts that started off everyone's medical notes were there. Then came the history.

It seemed that Josey, as he was known to everyone (the diminutive was even used in the medical history), had had an uneventful healthy life up to the autumn of 1994. In September of that year he had been referred by his GP to the neurological department of Old East with a history of tremor and rapidly developing paralysis. The GP had suspected a rapid-onset Parkinson's disease, pointing out that the first symptoms had appeared shortly after Josey had been involved in heavy physical activity (he had swum two miles on a sponsored charity event at the local leisure centre). The diagnosis had been borne out by Zack's opinion. George skimmed through the accounts of the examination and the tests Zack had carried out, and moved on to read about Josey's progress.

It had been a terrible experience for him. Given L-Dopa to relieve the paralysis, he had developed the uncontrollable writhing movements that could be a distressing side-effect of the therapy and had had to come off it, only to be very miserable because of the return of the paralysis, and indeed an extension of it. He had, in fact, needed a respirator on occasion because of his breathing difficulties.

By Christmas of '94 Josey had been a very unhappy man, and, Zack wrote, had agreed readily to be admitted to a research programme. George looked at the consent form Josey had signed, which made it clear that he understood the risks as well as the possible benefits of taking part. The signature was little more than a spidery cross, duly witnessed by one of

Laburnum's staff nurses. Clearly he had been too far gone even to sign his name properly. A very sick man.

George turned the page to the account of the treatment he had had as part of the research. Fetal brain tissue had been used (Zack had noted meticulously that he had obtained it from the obstetric department, from a miscarried pregnancy, with the full consent of the mother) and a preparation of the nigral neurones obtained from the relevant section of infant brain had been implanted into the area of putamen controlling motor activity, but not the caudate nucleus. This, Zack noted in his rather sprawling handwriting, was not the same as previous attempts at such therapy in that it used a different sort of tissue preparation, one devised by himself.

Anyway, she read on, it hadn't worked (and here Zack made a cross-reference to another of his patients, Miss Greenwich, for whom it had been efficacious), clearly to Zack's chagrin. Since Josey hadn't responded Zack had tried again with a different idea. This time he had used a preparation of fetal brain that included oligodendrocytes, together with a proportion of macrophage-generating tissue to scavenge for any antibodies that might lead to an immune response that would block the potential benefits of the oligodendrocyte implant. Zack had prepared both as intravenous injections rather than as a brain implant.

George lifted her head and stared, unfocused, into the middle distance. It read very far-fetched but it made a sort of sense that could be the basis of a real breakthrough. If Zack was putting back into the body of a man who was suffering from a disease that stripped his nerves of their vital covering a material that could replace that covering, while at the same time giving him additional cover with an injection that would prevent his own body's immune system turning on the much-needed replacement cells – well, he truly would have done something very remarkable. Especially since it involved simply intravenous injections and not brain surgery.

She could see, hazily, the commercial development of a

pair of injections, given into the blood system rather than deep into the brain like the Parkinson's treatment, and better still, that could be used for diseases other than Parkinson's. Everything that was caused by loss of the nerve covering myelin. Motor-neurone disease, maybe. Ataxias of various forms. Alzheimer's . . .

Inevitably, she thought of her mother and gave a little shiver. Could this treatment be of use to Vanny? The idea sent a surge of excitement through her and with some sternness she flattened it. That was the reaction of an uninformed lay person, not a doctor. She should know better than to expect miracle cures. And yet, what she had read in Josey Esposito's notes had been so exciting and seemed to offer so much. But I must be scientific, she thought, bending her head to the notes again. Find out what happened, examine the patient, and see if the work can be replicated with other patients. One success means nothing; it could be a fluke.

But that in Josey's case there had been a success was undoubted. She read the account of Zack's examinations of him over the ensuing months up to the present. Of the way he had steadily and slowly improved, losing the paralysis, regaining control of his bladder and bowels (which had encouraged him hugely and, according to Zack, had led to a lifting of mood which was very marked), until in late May he had been fit to return to work on a part-time basis.

She closed the folder and sat, still thinking. Around her the ward buzzed contentedly, and she found herself wondering why she had thought the place so miserable last time she had come here. Then she realized: it's Zack's research. It brings hope to a place where there was none. She watched as an elderly man in a short robe over concertinaed pyjamas emerged from the bay opposite the nurses' station, shuffling along on the arm of one of the nurses and clearly finding it very difficult. Would Zack's treatment give life and activity back to people like that? It was a heady thought.

Then she heard Zack's voice from the direction of the

ward's entrance and turned to look. He was striding towards her, accompanied by a man who was at least a foot shorter than he was and much slighter and who had almost to trot to keep up with him; a dark-haired man with a wide grin that seemed to be fixed in place and who was chattering in a steady monotone.

'I tell you, doc, I could work all day and night too, no trouble. They say to me, when you start to work properly, Josey? And I say to them, you ask Dr Zack. No, they say, *you* ask him, so I ask you, when can I work properly, huh? They share out the tronc all unfair because I'm not there all the time. It's all wrong, greedy buggers they are, but that's the Cypriots for you, you should forgive me for talking racist. So, Dr Zack, you let me go back to work huh?'

'Josey, this is Dr Barnabas,' Zack said, totally ignoring the chatter. 'She wants to talk to you about your treatment and how you feel. Come along now, we'll go to the examination room at the far end. Lead the way.' He gave the little man a push and Josey went trotting ahead obediently but still chattering, apparently not one whit disturbed by the fact that no one was listening to him.

'So, you read the notes?' Zack said eagerly.

'Yes,' she said. 'Oh, yes. It's quite a story. From one patient.'

'Oh, sure,' he said cheerfully. He started to follow Josey so that she had to fall in step beside him. 'I'm well aware of that. I've got one other that's done equally well: the Greenwich girl. I'll present her too when the funders come – she couldn't get here this evening, though I did ask her. Her treatment was slightly different – I refer to it in Josey's notes, remember? And yes, I know two aren't much of a sample, but it's not easy to get the right patients, and anyway, I don't have the funds. That's why I'm applying for the grant, for God's sake.'

'You can't get a job until you join the union,' she said, remembering an earlier conversation.

'And you can't join the union till you get a job. Precisely.'

'So you haven't published anything about this yet?'

'How could I? I've only got these two patients, and a few I'm looking at treating in the future, but I have to be so careful. I have to have the patient's full understanding of what the therapy is, and the referring GP and the Research Ethical Committee here has to agree to the protocol – and I had a hell of a battle with them, believe me – so any attempt at publication is way out of the frame at present. But I can rest a while on what I published when I was working in Canada. There's a fair bit of it, so there's no panic to get into print.'

'Really.' She slowed her walk almost to a stop so he had to too. 'I wouldn't mind reading some of those.'

'They're not very good,' he said lightly. 'I was just desperate to get myself into a journal of record. But you can see them if you like. I'll dig some out for you.'

What she did then she was never fully to understand, even long afterwards, when the whole business had been sorted out and explained. It was to mystify her for the rest of her professional life. She opened her mouth and heard words coming out of it and was appalled at herself as she said them.

'Zack, have you had anything to do with the things that have been happening to Sheila?'

He stopped as though he'd hit a glass wall. 'What did you say?'

'I think you heard,' she said, unable to repeat the words. What have you done, she was shrieking at herself inside her head. You stupid, crazy – What have you *done*?

He stared at her, the bewilderment on his face plain; he was completely thrown by her question. There was no hint of defensiveness, not a scintilla of calculation there that she could see. He was completely and utterly amazed.

'I – What?' He swallowed. 'That is one hell of a question, lady! How do you mean, have I had anything to do with it? Do you mean did I *do* them? Did I put nicotine in chocolates, is that what you're asking? Or what? I just –'

She tried to keep her voice steady. 'I had to ask. It's all so – There are things you do that worry me. You hang around me

217

and make a fuss of me and come on to me like – well, you know you do. And, no, don't say anything. Hear me out. You always seem to be where the trouble is. You were in the car park when Sheila's car went up; you were in the ward when the chocolate thing happened; you've been over to my lab and not many non-path. people do that and – and now, you're leaning on me so much to help with this research. I added it all up together and came to –'

'Some crazy total! Now listen here – oh, shit.' The door of the examination room, now just fifteen feet away, had opened, and Josey had put his head out curiously. 'We'll be there in a moment, Josey. I have to explain things to the doctor here. Just you wait there and behave yourself.'

Josey looked a little hurt at the suggestion he'd ever mis-behave, but withdrew his head and closed the door.

Zack turned so that he was standing right in front of her and took her by the shoulders. 'OK. You've been straight with me. Amazingly straight, for God's sake! I feel like I've been head-butted. Yes, I have been coming on to you. You're an at-tractive woman.' He let go of her shoulders then and took a step back. 'But that's not the only reason I've been hanging around you. Not the only reason I've tried so hard to get you involved with my research. And I suppose not the only reason you're here now.'

'Well, that's something to know at any rate,' she said a little unsteadily, pushing her hands deep into her white coat pock-ets to hide the tremor that had suddenly afflicted them. As though I have Parkinson's, she thought with a sudden wild-ness. Stupid, crazy woman you are, coming out with that stuff – what possessed you?

'I'll be as direct with you and hope it doesn't turn you right off me. Right. You're a pathologist. You have control of a large laboratory in which a great deal of investigative work is done. I'm scrabbling for every last cent I can get to do re-search that is the most important thing in my whole life, and I have to get what I can where I can get it. One thing that eats up a great chunk of my budget is pathology. If I can get you interested and involved enough, maybe I can persuade you to do some of my path. work for me and lose the bills. OK? I don't want a joint project, so I'm not prepared to offer you equal billing on this if I pull it off. I tell you frankly that if I succeed, I stand to make a lot of money. I'll patent anything I develop so that I can get my share and the goddamn pharmaceutical company doesn't get the lot. It's my research and no one, but no one, is going to get a glimmer of credit or cash but me. I don't want a shared Nobel. I want a whole one all to myself. I have been coming on to you, yeah, in an effort to get what I want on my terms. It's nice you're an attractive woman, but that's just bunce, frankly. Simple profit. What this is really down to is money. You've got something I want, and I have inadequate resources, so I've been trying to con them out of you. But that is as far as my vice goes. I am not into booby-trapping cars or poisoning candy or hurting people in any way whatsoever. So now you have it.'

There was a long pause and then she said, 'I see.' She was amazed at how steady her voice was.

He shook his head at her, with an almost comic air of exasperation. 'Apart from anything else, lady, you are known all over the hospital as a close friend of the police. Am I likely to mess with something illegal involving you? Do me a favour. All I want to do is get you to do some research work for me for nothing. It's no crime.'

'In the new NHS it is.' She managed a smile. 'Every single item used has to be budgeted for and listed and audited and Christ knows what else. So getting path. work done for you and not billing your department for it the way I should'd be like stealing from the NHS. A crime in anyone's book.'

'Jesus!' He sounded disgusted. 'What is going on here? People who work in hospitals have always had their perks from it! God knows they don't get as much as they should in hard cash! That's why I never heard of any nurses buying things like – like cotton wool or cough drops. There are things you take from the hospital that everyone takes and if you get away with it, good luck to you. That's as true in Canada as it is here – our hospitals are State-owned too, remember – and I cannot believe you're serious if you say you're going to shop me for –'

'Who said anything about that?' she said mildly. 'I was just saying that trying to get expensive path. work done for nothing is stealing. And yeah. I agree with you. It's been done in hospitals since they were invented. And I'm not about to change the world on that score. I just wish you'd asked me straight out, is all, instead of going in for all this flirty stuff.'

'If I had, would you have agreed?'

She hesitated. 'Possibly not.'

'I'm not crazy then. I knew you wouldn't, so I tried it the old-fashioned way, with a bit of soft soap aimed at flattering a female complexion.' He laughed, his voice sounding more like dark treacle toffee than it ever had. 'And the fact that you're such a shit-hot feminist made it more fun.'

'Hey, I am not shit hot! I mean, I don't go around shouting my head off about feminism. I just take it for granted that –'

'That you're as good as the next guy. So you are. But you're also a female and it was fun to see if I could get what I wanted and – well . . .'

'Get me too,' she finished for him.

'Yup. And let me remind you, if I was up to some sort of villainy would I tangle with a woman who hangs around the goddamn police as much as you do? I ask you!'

She gazed at him standing there, he too with his hands deep in his pockets, and wanted to laugh. She'd been crazy to ask him, she knew, but now she was glad she had. It was like watching a thick fog roll back to leave the air and the view crystal clear. He seemed to see the relief in her face because he smiled back at her even more widely.

'Mind you, George, you were taking your chances asking me that, weren't you? If I had been the sort to go around doing nasty things to people like Sheila and I thought you'd tumbled me, I might have tried to do nasty things to you, right?'

She smiled back. 'Right.'

'But now you know I won't, right?'

'Right,' she said again and shook her head in self-deprecation. 'I screwed up. Let's forget it. Your patient's waiting.'

He nodded and pulled his hands from his pockets. 'OK, Dr Barnabas. I take it we're still in business? That you'll still help me?' His face split then into the wickedest grin he'd ever produced. 'Maybe even to the point of a few free tests and suchlike? Have I ruined my chances there altogether? Or can we still be a sort of team?'

23

'You did *what*?' Gus said in amazement.

George felt her face go a mottled pink. 'I know, I know. I was crazy but I – well, it sort of just came out, you know? I felt so lousy, snooping around like that and – anyway, I have to say the relief once I'd asked him was terrific. I felt better.'

'I never before heard you complain that snooping made you feel bad,' he said waspishly and she made a grimace at him.

'That's right. Rub it in.'

'Yeah, well … Honestly, George, how could you be so foolhardy? If the guy's been the cause of all this stuff – the attacks on Sheila, let alone anything else – then you've tipped him off. *And* put yourself at risk. Can't you see that?'

'Of course. I thought that at first, but I don't think I have. I mean, even if I was still in any doubt about him I don't think I'd have done any harm. He said it himself. He knows perfectly well that I work closely with the police. He knows that anything I know, you know, and he'd have to be really stupid to mix it with me. And he certainly isn't stupid. A smooth operator with his eye to his own main chance maybe, but stupid? No.'

'So you no longer think there's any reason to suspect him of the attempts on Sheila?' He was watching her closely and she knew she had to be as honest as it was possible to be. He'd spot any inconsistency very rapidly indeed.

'I've thought and thought about it, Gus, and I have to say, I don't know. But the reasons he's given me for hanging round me and getting me involved in his research make total sense. It's hell trying to do research in this country on the NHS. Money's so tight it squeaks, and you have to pull every stroke there is to get the funding you need. I know that. Everyone who works in the NHS knows that. If he'd tried to make himself look good it might have been different, but he painted himself in very ugly colours, didn't he? He admitted to being a guy who'd use any trick he could to con a colleague, that he wants personal glory more than he wants scientific respect – and you only get that by sharing your work with the whole scientific community – certainly not by patenting your discoveries for commercial gain. He's even admitted he wants a Nobel. People just don't talk that way in medicine, even if they think it privately. He's been so bloody open with me that I don't see how I can *not* believe him.'

'Well,' Gus said. 'What's done is done. Just do something for me now, will you?'

'Depends what it is.'

'Don't come the smartass with me,' he snapped. 'I'm telling you what to do and you'll –'

'Yes?' she said softly, her chin up. 'What will I do?'

'You'll listen and make up your own mind,' he said after a moment with a wry smile. 'OK, so, I'm being over-protective, but you know how it is. I'm used to you and I don't want the trouble of teaching someone else all my little ways. So do me a favour. Do as I ask you.'

She thought for a moment. 'Probably. Tell me what it is.'

'Keep your distance from him till I get the stuff I've asked for from Canada. They've promised me a detailed run-down on his history there, a real digging-out of everything there is. I'll even know how often he went to the loo, once they report.

But till then be careful. That's not an unreasonable request, is it?'

'You're so *changeable*,' she said. 'On Sunday you encouraged me to meet him on Laburnum Ward and now you're saying –'

'That was before you spilled your bibful at him,' he said. 'That's changed everything.'

She took a few moments to answer. 'Well, I suppose so. I don't think it's necessary, as I say, but –'

'Never mind what you think. Let me indulge myself. I won't feel good until I have concrete evidence that this guy has no form, and we can accept him as what he says he is, a nasty piece of work after his own interests the whole time, but stopping short of murder and mayhem to get what he wants.'

'That's putting it a bit strong.'

'Really? How would you put it?'

She thought again. 'Maybe not a nasty piece of work?'

'Selfish then? Thoughtless? Something like that?'

'Oh, well, I suppose … OK. In the work context then, a nasty piece of work. But not a person who'd deliberately harm someone else.'

'Except in their pocket. Or their self-esteem, hmm?'

She pulled a little face. 'You've made your point. So what am I to do?'

'Be too busy to talk to him if he calls, and certainly too busy to meet him or work on anything with him. Would that be difficult?'

'Refusing to talk on the phone might be, if I happened to answer it when he calls.'

'Then get someone else to answer your phone and only put through the calls you want. Stop making difficulties, George, you know I'm right about this.'

'OK, OK, I'll do it your way. Till you hear from Canada.'

'Yeah. And by then – probably next week – I should have some more stuff about those three deaths. I've put quite a few of my people on to it. Fortunately we're not too pushed right now, so I can use them without running into overtime. You think you've got budget problems in the NHS? Try the bloody Bill, ducky, and then you'll know what budgets are about!'

In some ways it seemed a very long week. First of all the weather had changed for good, settling to a series of hot dry days that made being cooped up in the lab far more irksome than it usually was. There were a few post-mortems to do, and the hot weather made a couple of them particularly unpleasant. One was the body of a man who had hanged himself in his top-floor flat three weeks before he was found; the other a newborn infant who had been hidden on a building site: as well as being noisome, the evidence of George's investigation showed that the child had been abandoned alive, and had died of exposure and dehydration which made it the sort of case which upset her most. There was a limit, as she told Jerry grimly, to the amount of professional detachment she could summon up.

Jerry seemed to show no sign of after-effects from his experience. He brushed away any attempts to fuss over him with his usual jokes, and within a few days it was all as though it had never happened.

It was different however when Sheila came back to work. She dressed herself in black, even though the weather was by now exhaustingly hot; the string of sweltering days that had come in the third week of the month had settled to a prolonged and uncomfortably humid heatwave that had everyone drooping about the place and squabbling over which bench should be allowed to use one of the two precious electric fans which were the department's only concession to air conditioning. Sheila would sit in her corner, blonde and pale and wispy, all of it accentuated by the blackness of her dress under her white coat, making everyone uneasy as she sat and suffered bravely. George was glad to see her return and grateful that she had escaped any long-term effects from her experiences, but within two days was as exasperated with her as she had ever been, and so was everyone else.

But at least that meant everything felt normal again. They plodded through the day's workloads, spending their lunchtimes, like everyone else, in the courtyard on a motley array of benches and old chairs and tattered rugs that had appeared from heaven knew where to accommodate them all, and falling off duty at the end of the day to spend the breathless sweating evenings at home. No one had much energy for anything else; even visits to the swimming pool gave little pleasure, full as it was of shrieking children. George learned to settle for long periods spent taking cold showers followed by padding around her flat, dripping wet and naked, to allow the water to dry on her. It was as effective a cooling system as any other she could devise, and taken in conjunction with the consumption of a great deal of ice water (and noisily chewed ice) she got through the heat somehow.

She saw little of Gus. There had been a sudden upsurge of work at the Ratcliffe Street nick, with a decision made to work over one of the local housing estates where drug-dealing was the normal way of life. Edicts had come down from the top, Gus told George irritably, that this particular nest of hornets was to be flushed out. ('Not that it'll make a blind bit of difference in the long run,' Gus growled. 'The buggers'll only move over to the next patch. But at least we'll be rid of 'em.') And that meant he worked late almost every day. He would arrive at her flat after she had gone to sleep and fall into bed beside her, only to wake her with his exhausted snoring. Then he'd be up and gone before she woke again in the mornings. It wasn't much fun one way and another, George decided. She didn't even have the satisfaction of trying to dodge Zack to keep her mind occupied.

Because he made not the slightest attempt to talk to her, or to see her. He was never in the courtyard at lunchtimes like almost all the rest of the hospital's staff, and he certainly never phoned her. Once or twice, in a spirit of contrariness, she went up to the canteen for lunch, thinking perhaps he was taking his meals there, but there was no sign of him. It shouldn't be so easy to keep out of his way, she found herself thinking crossly. Unless he's decided that, for all his talk of still being teammates, he doesn't want to work with someone who accused him of being a malicious type who meddled with people's cars and poisoned their chocolates. A disconcerting thought, that.

But at last things improved. The weather remained as hot as ever – hotter in fact – but at least the workload in the laboratory eased and George was freed to take life a little easier as the last week in June plodded on its breathless way. She was actually able to take some of her paperwork out into the courtyard to sit in the shade of the main block where it was a little cooler – though not a lot – than her stuffy little office.

She didn't notice him coming towards her; unaware until he touched her shoulder and made her jump. She peered up in the bright sunlight, shading her eyes. At first she could see only the outline of his head but then he moved slightly so that he blocked out the direct light and she could see his face.

'Oh,' she said, not sure how to react. 'Hello.'

'I'm not going to be a pest,' he said. 'I just wanted you to know how glad I am that you've made sure about me. I know you'll be reassured when you see it all, and then maybe we can get back to normal, huh? I gather they've collected all they need now?'

'I'm sorry, Zack,' she said, and genuinely was. 'I haven't the remotest idea what you're talking about.'

'Oh, come on, George! You must know they've been making enquiries about me back home! Didn't you put them up to it?'

She felt her face flame. 'Er – making –?' she began and then stopped.

He shook his head at her, clearly amused. 'Listen, hon, you didn't think I left all my friends behind in Canada and never gave them another thought, did you? Especially my girl-friends. I wasn't exactly a monk, after all. We exchange letters

227

all the time, and phone calls. Faxes, even!' He split his face into a grin. 'I knew you were investigating me, on account of so many people were in such a hurry to call me up and ask me what the hell I'd been up to that there were obvious flat-foots buzzing around asking questions about me. And I thought, you can't blame the lady. She needs a bit more re-assurance than just my word for it. So I thought I'd keep my head well down until you had all the info you wanted and we could pick up where we left off. I've got my presentation to the funders coming up and I sure as hell hoped we'd have all this sorted in time for you to help me with that. I heard yes-terday they've gone away – the investigators, that is, gone away from Montreal – and I thought, right. She'll have her report now. If I'm wrong, I'm sorry and I'll vanish into the woodwork again until you have. Call me then, huh?' And as coolly as though they had been discussing the weather he lifted a hand in a sort of salute and went away across the burned and scrubby grass to the main block, leaving her star-ing after him.

She called Gus as soon as she got back to the lab, seething with anger. The embarrassment of it had been intense. That Zack had known he was being investigated was bad enough; that he should think she had instigated it was much worse.

It took some time to track Gus down. First of all he was out with his men on some sort of stake-out, or so she guessed from the guardedness of the policewoman on the phone, so she left a message, fairly curtly making the point that it was important. Then she sat and seethed till late afternoon when, sick of waiting for a return call, she tried to reach him again. This time she was told he was in the building and no, they did not know if he'd received her message but they'd certainly see to it that he did now. Again she sat and fumed, waiting for him to call. At last, just after half past six when all the staff had gone and there was just herself sweating in her lonely office, the phone trilled and his voice filled her ear as soon as she snatched it up.

228

'So what's the panic, doll? Has friend Zack suddenly arrived with a knife between his teeth and a gun in each hand?'

'Very funny,' she snapped. 'You only say that because you know damned well he's OK.' She told him succinctly what had happened that afternoon. 'I never felt such a goddamn fool in my life. It's like being caught out being a Peeping Tom.'

He laughed. 'I suppose it was. Well, no harm done.'

'No harm done!' She was lost for words.

'I've got the stuff here,' he said, seeming oblivious of her wrath. 'I've had it a day or two but frankly I've been up to my hocks in crack-dealers and the like and hardly had time to look. But I took a quick squint so I knew there was nothing to worry about. I've looked again just now before I called. It seems he's as pure as the driven snow.'

'Gus, you've had that for a couple of *days*? And only just got round to – You are the absolute –'

'Listen, doll,' he said, his voice suddenly very crisp. 'I'm dealing with a lot of real crime here. I'm not saying what happened there at Old East isn't a crime – someone made attacks on one of your staff, sure, and you've had a couple of deaths you don't like the look of – but that isn't as urgent as completing a drugs round-up once it's been started, especially when I'd taken a preliminary look like I said and could see you weren't at risk. It's a matter of priorities, right?'

She bit her lip. 'Oh, hell, I'm sorry Gus. It's just that I felt so –'

'I can imagine.' He was sympathetic. 'Now, listen, doll. I'll be finished here in about an hour. What say we meet at the pub, have a drink and then a nice fish supper? Best in town, they tell me.'

'OK. If we can have the drink outside in the shade and a table next to a fan.'

'You're on,' he said. 'And, George?'

'Uh-huh?'

'Even though it would seem this Zack guy's OK, as far as

his history is concerned, do me a favour. Go on keeping your distance, will you?'

'Why? If you felt safe not hurrying to give me the report, then –'

'A clean history doesn't necessarily mean he's as reliable as he might be. People change, after all.'

She chuckled, feeling much better now. 'Dearest Gus, I do so enjoy your jealousy. It warms me in the winter and cools me comfortably in a heatwave. Lovely! See you at the pub.' And she hung up, well pleased with herself. No matter what reasons he gave for his actions, their true nature was quite clear to her. It was almost shaming, she thought, to enjoy it so much.

24

The pub was pleasanter than it might have been on so hot an evening, because most of the drinkers were outside, cluttering up the pavement so that pedestrians could hardly get by, and the interior was therefore cooler since in their absence the fans whirring in every corner could do their jobs properly. He brought her iced mineral water, which was all she could face, and settled himself beside her at a corner table under an engraved window with his usual half-pint. She watched him take a deep draught and shook her head.

'How you can drink warm beer is beyond me,' she said. 'Put some ice in, hon, make yourself comfortable.'

'Iced beer?' he said and shuddered. 'That's a treasonable offence in this part of London. Here. Read the report and shut up. You'll feel cooler sooner if you do.'

She read, quickly but thoroughly, leafing through the dozen or so pages of flimsy fax paper as he sat peaceably watching her and seeming to find some pleasure in doing so. She was aware of his gaze at first, but soon became absorbed in the picture that was formed by the material in front of her.

Zoltan Istvan Zacharius, aged thirty-nine, was, she read, precisely as he had described himself. The details he had given of his history were spelled out here in detail: his departure from his native Hungary as a child with his mother; his settling in Montreal; his success at school and later at college and medical school. There were also encomiums from his teachers and his colleagues, some of them very eminent people indeed; and even grateful comments from patients he had treated or used as research material. There was a list of his involvement in his community, with membership of student committees and inauguration of successful fund-raising initiatives for the hospital's benefit jostling with accounts of awards won and prizes conferred on him. No one, it seemed, had a bad word for him. He had worked hard in his Canadian days, been fun to know, had lived a reasonably virtuous life – there was no hint of any impropriety, financial, political, personal or otherwise – and altogether was exactly what he seemed: an industrious gifted person with much to contribute to his chosen discipline.

She put the papers down on the table. 'Well,' she said. 'There you are, then.'

'Yup.'

'I was wrong.'

'It seems so. What we have here is a picture of a perfect doctor behaving perfectly.'

'So there's no need to worry any more about him.'

'Unless you get too pally with him.' He split his face with a grin. 'Then I'd worry.'

'Oh, Gus, not again.'

'But you like it! You know you do. I've seen the way you preen when I show a bit of the old green-eye, so I thought I'd do it now. There's no pleasing some females, is there?'

'Not if you call us females,' she said. 'So, where do we go from here?'

'Where can we go?' he said reasonably, setting down his beer. 'I have to admit that I've been a touch lax over this whole business. We should have investigated more when the car went up and done a bit more digging around over those chocolates. To be honest, I put it down to a bit of in-house malice. Knowing Sheila as I do, and knowing what a gift she has for getting up other people's noses, I didn't fret over it all unduly. Anyway, you could search that place for months and be no nearer knowing who mucked around with those chocolates, let alone the car. It's not even as though we can trace the nicotine. Anyone could have made it in their own back kitchen.'

'Mmm,' she said a little abstractedly. 'I suppose so. But, Gus, have you done enough investigation into those three deaths? I know I said two of them were accidents, and one was a suicide but now I'm beginning to wonder. If only I had all the notes to go through and not just Lally's! And that's another bit of criminality you haven't sorted out.'

'Hey, don't try and shift that on to me. It was an internal thing, you agreed that at the time! If it hadn't been for the link between you and me we might never have known about it. No one filed any complaint. Nor did anyone make a formal complaint to us about the bottle in the Beetle cupboard that was tampered with. And I've been meaning to ask you, why Beetle cupboard?'

'Excuse me?'

'Why is it called a Beetle cupboard? The place where you store all your materials and so forth?'

She shrugged. 'Why is the sky up and the ground down? I really don't know. That's what all store cupboards are called around Old East. In other British hospitals too, for all I know. I can't remember what we called 'em in Inverness. Is it important?'

'Not in the least,' he said cheerfully. 'I just wondered. Look, let's do a recap, OK? Then we can see where we stand. There have been three deaths at Old East which you think – thought? – well, which you said at the time were due twice to accident, once to suicide. Then as a quite separate thing, or so it seems, there were three attempts apparently meant to hurt Sheila: the car, the chocolates, the hydrochloric acid bottle. The only person you thought might be involved, our friend Zack, appears to be as pure as the driven slush. We've not done a great deal of investigation admittedly, but we do know that we have no information to show us who might be responsible for those three attempts. The cable and solenoid switch in the car engine could have been obtained anywhere – a more anonymous collection of bits and bobs you couldn't find – and the chocolates too could have come from anywhere. As for hydrochloric acid, well, it's hardly a rare item in a hospital, is it?'

'No,' she said. 'Not really.' It was clear she was not really listening to him. 'Gus, what did you find out about the deaths? Do you remember? You said you'd look into the people themselves a little more.'

He nodded. 'I got a couple of our lads to see what they could suss out. The only thing the three of 'em had in common was a lack of personal contacts. They lived alone, each and every one, though we know of course that Pam Frean had some sort of lover in the shadows. She killed herself – or so her note suggested – for him. Lally Lamark was a childless widow who had lived in the same house for many years but her neighbours didn't know her well. They used that phrase, you know? "Kept herself to herself," they said. And the other one –'

'Tony Mendez.'

'Yeah. He'd been married and had a couple of children but the marriage had broken down a long time ago because of his drinking. The wife and two sons emigrated to Australia, and that was that. If he had other relations no one knew of them – he never mentioned anyone special in his life. Same with friends. Lots of vague acquaintances, but no one close. His neighbours had plenty to say about him – mostly because they didn't know very much, but love to have a gossip – and so did your personnel people here. Oops, mustn't forget, they're called the Human Resources department nowadays, aren't they? That always makes me imagine shops with shelves full of spare legs and arms and eyes and so forth, to fit out humans who've lost their own ... Where was I? Oh, yes. Mendez. He had a small council flat in the Doolittle Estate over towards Poplar, and lived there alone except for a cat. He's worked here for twelve years or so. They knew he was a reformed alcoholic when they took him on, but Old East has always had a positive policy towards disability, so they took a chance on him. At first he was only allowed to do pretty menial stuff under supervision, which he accepted without fuss, though apparently originally he'd trained as an engineer. He just got on with things, and showed he was reliable and progressed to being second-in-command of the theatre porters. Not bad at all for an ex-lush, is it? They spoke highly of him over there, said he was a reliable bloke who knew the department inside out and never missed anything important. And that's about it. Oh, yes, one other thing. Lally Lamark was a diabetic.'

'I knew that, of course,' George said. 'I thought I told you.'

'Um. The reason I mention it now is that it seems it was about her only interest. The stuff in her house – there were files of articles and shelves of books about diabetes and nutrition – it's like she'd made a hobby of her health, there was so much there.'

'Some diabetics do do that. It's as good a way of dealing with a lifelong condition as any. Makes you feel in charge of it. Not that she managed that at the end, poor thing. For all her knowledge she still managed to go into an insulin coma.'

'That was the only thing I remember being puzzled about when I saw the report Urquhart sent in on her. If she was so knowledgeable, how come she had an accident? But then I thought, well, maybe diabetes is like that. Unpredictable?'

He quirked an eyebrow at her, making it into a question, but she shook her head. 'Not usually. I mean, getting a patient's insulin levels right, understanding the pattern of their activity so that the dosage can be tailored for them, that's part of the care they get. Some of them had trouble changing from pig insulin to human insulin when it first became available – they found it was less likely to give them warning symptoms of a dangerous change in blood-sugar levels – but as I say, most of them cope very well indeed. I looked into that too as far as she was concerned, and according to her medical notes she was well stabilized. But even the most stable and experienced may sometimes make a mistake. Perhaps she'd been a bit off-colour – had a gut infection with a bit of diarrhoea and vomiting. That can upset insulin and blood-sugar levels. Or, even more likely, she hadn't realized what the time was and forgot to eat when she should.'

'Nothing else possible?' He looked enquiring again. 'Could she have taken too much insulin, for example? A case of simple overdose?'

She shook her head. 'The term overdose is relative in this context. It was much more likely to be an underdose of food or maybe excessive activity that burned off her sugar and left her insulin too high, because it's very difficult for people to make mistakes with their injections. They use pens, you see, not syringes any more.'

'Pens?'

'That's what they look like. Fountain pens. They get their insulin in cartridges, load the pen as it were with ink, and then simply have to push the plunger home when they've slipped the needle into a suitable bit of subcutaneous tissue. The dose is premeasured.'

'So it couldn't be an overdose in the classic sense?'

'I don't see how.'

He was thoughtful for a while. 'These pens. Can I see one?'

'I imagine so. They have them in Pharmacy. You want me to get one for you?'

'If you would.'

'Why?'

'I wonder how they work.'

'I've told you.'

'Yes, but maybe the mechanism that measures the dose can be at fault. I imagine there's some sort of mechanism involved.'

'Mmm,' she said. 'It's a sort of screw arrangement. It's set so that it pushes the plunger in so far and no further, and exactly the right dose is given.' She frowned then. 'I wonder what happened to it?'

'Happened to what?'

'Her pen,' George said. 'When she was found, she had a few things in her pockets – I remember seeing the list Danny made when he prepared the body for post-mortem – but there was no insulin pen among them. But she must have had one with her.'

'In her bag, maybe?'

'Her bag?'

He sighed a little theatrically. 'Dear George, when did you ever see a woman without a handbag of some sort? Only I forgot, you call it a purse.' He pointed to the soft leather tote bag slung on the bench beside her. 'Like yours. What have you got in it?'

'Just the usual things,' she said, looking at the bag. 'Money and keys and – er – a handkerchief and –'

'Let's have a look.' He held out a hand. 'Unless it's a secret, of course.'

'Of course it isn't,' she said. She pushed the bag over to him and he opened it.

'Yes, you're quite right, keys, money, a hanky, make-up – lipstick, powder – and what's this?'

She peered and went a little pink. 'That's personal.'

He smiled and pushed the small square box to one side. 'See what I mean? Things to do with your personal needs, you carry with you. And here.' He pulled out a sheet of pills in a bubble wrap, a few of them already missing from the pack. 'What're these?'

She made a face. 'Analgesics. I get the occasional headache and I don't like to be without 'em. It's harmless and very effective. A mixture of codeine and paracetamol.'

He pushed everything back into the bag, looking no further, although there was still, she noted with a slight sense of embarrassment, a good deal of detritus there. 'So I'm right.

Women carry important things with them, important personal things. Like a diabetic's insulin pen.'

She nodded slowly, staring at him. 'You're absolutely right. I never thought – the body certainly had no purse with it.'

'Was there a coat, an outdoor coat? I mean, she died before this heatwave started, didn't she? So she'd have had a coat or jacket or something to go home in, I imagine. Where would that be?'

She was getting really interested now. 'I don't know. I suppose that she must have had a locker in the office where she worked. Most departments do have them.'

'A locker?'

'Like the one you have yourself at the nick, I imagine. For a change of clothes and bits and bobs.'

'And handbags.'

'Yes, I guess so. And bags.'

'Has a locker been found in the Records department that belonged to Lally Lamark?'

She shook her head. 'I haven't the least idea. It never occurred to me to check, dammit.' She reached for her bag and jumped to her feet. 'Come on, Gus. Let's go and look.'

'Eh?' He gawped at her.

'I said, let's go and look. I want to know what's been happening here!'

'Sweetheart,' Gus said reasonably. 'It's almost nine o'clock at night. Are you telling me the Medical Records department is open at this hour? I thought even in hospitals office employees worked office hours.'

'Of course they do. All the better. We can go and look around without anyone to get in our way. You want to untangle this one, don't you? You admit you haven't done enough work on it so far, so come on!'

He sighed. 'So much for my fish supper.'

'We can eat later, can't we? This shouldn't take long. Do come on, Gus. I really am dying to see what happened to that pen. And you're the one who had the idea that someone might have meddled with Lally's pen and given her an over-dose of insulin without her knowing.'

'Did I say that?'

She was getting even more impatient. 'Not directly, but that's the idea you put into my head. So please, Gus, can we go and *look*?'

He got to his feet. 'I don't suppose it'll make a blind bit of difference what I say. OK, we'll go and look. If you can get me in, that is. And if you can find out which her locker is, once you have, because I'll tell you now, we're not breaking into a whole lot of 'em. But I'm in only on the understanding that afterwards we go out and eat.'

'Don't worry, Gus.' She led the way out of the pub. 'You won't die of starvation yet.'

'No? I already feel as though I am. I didn't have lunch, you know, not like some.' Grumbling plaintively all the way, he nodded at the landlord, flicked his thumb and forefinger at the brim of the hat he wasn't wearing as a gesture of farewell, and went back to Old East with her, through the fading light of the hot evening.

25

It still wasn't dark when they reached the hospital. On these hot nights it seemed to George that the sky never did get really dark. It retained the exhausted glow of the baking daylight hours for so long that it seemed the sun was up again before the previous day had fully faded into peaceful slumber, so each day started as wearily as though the world hadn't had a chance to sleep at all; a fanciful notion for which George scolded herself as they made their way across the courtyard from the main entrance, on their way to the Administrative Block and the Medical Records department.

'Won't we have to get permission and keys from someone?' Gus said. 'I ain't about to do any breaking and entering. I've got no warrant.'

'No need,' she said. 'My swipe card'll get us in.' She reached into her pocket for it. 'Those of us who may need access to notes urgently have special ones. That includes A & E staff and most of the consultants and, through them, their registrars and house officers.'

'Why you?' He was genuinely curious. 'It's not likely you'll be needed to advise on a living patient in the middle of the night, is it?'

'It has been known,' she said. 'Or maybe it would be relevant if there's an unexpected death, hmm? Anyway, it means we can get in now without any fuss. I could go and find Bittacy, I suppose, but to tell you the truth he's a bit of a little Hitler – you know, one of those guys who like to show they're in charge. He can't stop me going in any more than he can stop me going anywhere the card is valid for. I suppose if we're really security-minded we would make sure he knows.'

'You mean you're supposed to tell him, as head of security, if you use these facilities outside normal working hours, is that it?' he said shrewdly.

She had the grace to redden a little. 'Oh, come on, Gus. You know what it's like when you get these self-important fusspots! And you said you were hungry, didn't you? If we have to go and look for him it'll add a half-hour at least to the job. But if you insist, of course . . .'

He wavered; she grinned at him; and he fell. 'OK, OK. You win. We don't tell security and just go in. Where?'

'This way.'

The Medical Records department was stuffy to the point of being smelly: dust and the lingering wraiths of human sweat and tired feet and dying vegetation were the keynotes. George felt her spirits droop a little as she quietly closed the door behind Gus and repocketed her swipe card.

'Someone's forgotten to water their potted plants,' Gus said loudly. Absurdly, she wanted to shush him. There was no need of course; as she had assured Gus, she had as much right to be here as anyone. But for all that she felt a twinge of guilt as though she were prying into other people's property. Which, of course, she told herself as she moved forwards to find the light switches, is precisely what I am doing. But with impeccable motives.

'Not too many lights,' Gus said mildly. 'Unless you want someone, i.e. Bittacy, spotting them and wondering if the place is being burgled.'

'Mmm.' She sounded a little abstracted, but she obeyed him all the same, switching on one of the desk lamps that threw just a low glow on the surface of the piles of papers that had been left on the desk.

'As far as I know, the staff have their own rest room here. Let's see.' She squinted into the dimness, seeing more easily now as her eyes became accustomed to the gloom, and then led the way across the big space and through the ranks of desks. 'Over here. The main records rooms are on the sides, that I do know, so I imagine that the door here leads through – Ah!' She stopped in triumph as she pushed open the door and peered in. 'Black as the tomb, so there's no windows. Great.' She fumbled for a light switch and the room sprang into life.

The air in here was even more exhausted, with a powerful smell of unwashed clothing and old shoes. Gus wrinkled his nose a little as he closed the door behind him and looked around. 'I hope they keep the records in a better state than they keep their own stuff,' he said with strong disapproval. 'How can people be so messy?' The look of distress on his face was almost comical.

'Maybe it's because of having to be so organized with their work,' George said. 'Always making sure everything is exactly where it's supposed to be must be desperately boring, but they have to do it because all hell breaks loose if notes go missing because they're misfiled. But never mind the untidiness. It's the lockers I'm interested in.'

'First things first.' He came forward and set her to one side. 'Let me do a recce first.' He searched with swift deftness through the piles of magazines that littered a battered sofa in one corner, and picked over the assorted items such as old raincoats and umbrellas which hung on a row of hooks alongside it. Then he turned his attention to a little cluster of plastic bags on a table; these contained assorted detritus including biscuits which shed crumbs everywhere and assorted packets of tea bags and sugar. In another bag there were apples and a third contained curled and stale sandwiches which looked, George told him, like the best culture medium for toxic bacteria she'd seen since she got to Old East.

'Never mind,' he said. 'That's their business. I'm just look-

ing for anything that might seem to point to Lally Lamark.'
He stopped and looked again at the sandwiches. They had
been in transparent plastic packs, clearly; the wreckage of
them still lay in the white plastic bag. The sandwiches had
been taken out, but not bitten into; staring at the one he set
gingerly on the plastic bag, he said to George, 'How old
d'you reckon that is?'

'Hard to say.' She peered at it. 'Several weeks, perhaps.
Look, the bread is rock hard.' She poked a forefinger at it.
'And the mould appears to have stopped growing because
there's no real nutrition left there. You can't even see what
sort of sandwich it was. I'd say it was very old indeed. I dare
say I could find out more if I took it to the lab and set to work
on it. Why?'

'Didn't you say that Lally had perhaps suffered not so
much from an overdose of insulin as the reverse? An underdose of sugar, maybe? Food, that is?'

She blinked at him, her eyes wide. 'You think these could
be the sandwiches Lally should have eaten and didn't? You
could be right. She might have given herself her insulin and
meant to eat her supper at the right time afterwards.'

'And for some reason didn't,' Gus finished. 'I did wonder
if it were that. In which case she did have an overdose of
insulin.'

'If you're right, and this is her uneaten supper . . . I suppose
it's possible. How can we be sure?'

'We can't. Not till we have more concrete evidence.' He
became businesslike. 'I suppose we could take the plastic
sandwich wrappers and see if there are any latent prints
there, but it is a very long shot. I wish she'd bought them at
Marks & Spencer's or Boots. Then they'd be labelled with a
date. As it is there is no information here.' He turned the
packs with fastidious care. 'So latent prints are the only hope.
But not much, as I say. What would we use to match them? I
don't suppose Lally's notes had her fingerprints on them?'

'Of course not,' George said. 'But if we find her locker,

won't we be able to check her prints from that? The things inside, I mean? People don't usually let strangers into their lockers, so any prints on objects in there have to be hers.'

'I wouldn't like to count on evidence like that,' he said. 'Would you? But let's look. This is getting more and more interesting.'

He seemed to have forgotten his doubts about breaking and entering; he had pulled from his pocket a small bunch of slender copper-coloured rods, his skeleton keys. 'Old-fashioned, these,' he said cheerfully, 'but these look like old-fashioned lockers. Come on.'

He moved systematically from one to the next, peering at them closely. None had labels on the doors bearing names; clearly the users knew their own lockers. But Gus was looking with beady concentration at each lock as he went and, at last, stopped and grunted happily.

'Here we are,' he said. 'See? That lock's full o' dust. The others have been opened recently, so this is probably hers. But I'd better check the others first to see if there are any other unused ones.'

There were. Of the thirty-two lockers the room possessed, five had dusty locks. Gus grunted and looked over his shoulder at George. 'They've got spare capacity, dammit. Settle down, kid. This could take a while.'

He moved with great delicacy, inserting one after the other of his skeleton keys into the first lock he'd found filled with dust, and twirling it gently, and after a few minutes (which seemed interminable to George, watching) he produced a soft satisfied snort and the door swung open.

The locker was empty, the upper shelf veiled in dust and only a couple of torn pieces of paper screwed into small balls left on its floor.

'Not to fret,' Gus said, seeing her disappointed expression. 'At least I know what sort of locks these buggers have. The chances are the lockers are a job lot and there'd only be half a dozen key designs between 'em, if that. I'll find it soon.'

He did. It was the third locker he opened. The door swung wide and George, staring, felt her throat constrict a little as some of the personality of its owner seemed to emerge from it. It was tidy in a way that was in startling contrast to the room in which it stood. A brown cloth coat set on a neat folding hanger depended crossways from the central rod, and had clearly been arranged carefully, for the collar and shoulders were precisely set in the wooden arms of the hanger. Beneath it, there was a pair of well-patched street shoes in worn brown leather, severe in cut rather than stylish in design, and alongside them a pair of old-fashioned plimsolls. There was also a pair of Wellington-style boots in startlingly bright red plastic. Clearly the owner of the locker tried to be prepared for all eventualities. On the top shelf, George could see bottles of shampoo and hair conditioner and tubes of body cream, and she thought; I ought to keep my locker as tidy as this. It'd save so much time looking for things.

Gus was wasting no time. He had at some point pulled a pair of cotton gloves from his pocket – George hadn't seen him do it – and now, with his hands carefully shrouded, he picked amongst the things on the shelf. 'Nothing here that appears to be an insulin pen,' he said. 'You say they look like fountain pens?'

'Exactly,' she said. She came and crouched beside the locker, close to his side so that she could look at the lower part of it. 'Maybe it's down here – if, of course, this is her locker. We can't be sure yet, can we?'

'No,' he said. 'It seems likely, though. What living person would leave good clothes in a locker for so long – several days at the very least, I'd say from the dust – do you think? Has to be her.'

'Probably,' George said. 'Look, there's a sort of extra shelf down there, at the back, in my locker. I think it's meant to be used to increase shoe-storage space so that they don't get piled up. Yes, see?'

She had reached forwards and lifted the skirts of the coat and pointed.

Gus crouched beside her and peered in. 'A handy little hiding place.'

'Not really. All the lockers have them, so everyone knows they're there, I use mine to store changes of underwear in plastic bags, because there's no room for the things up top. I imagine other people have their own special uses too.' She reached her hand forwards and at once his clamped down over her wrist.

'Naughty, naughty,' he murmured. 'Gloves.'

'I can't imagine prints'll come into this,' she protested. 'You can't even be sure of identifying her own prints anyway, you said, so what's the point?'

'Sometime we might be looking for other people's prints.' He reached in himself and pulled out the soft leather handbag George had spotted. 'And they could be very important. Not that this would matter, after all.' He looked at it ruefully. 'I never saw this sort of material show prints worth looking at. Oh, well, let's have a dekko.'

He straightened up and carried the bag over to the table. Pushing aside the plastic bags and stale food, he looked around for a moment and then reached for one of the old newspapers. 'This'll have to do,' he muttered and opened it, a little awkwardly as he was one-handed, and then spread it on the table. 'I'd rather have something a little more suitable like a sheet of plastic but needs must when the devil drives. Here we go.'

He moved carefully and neatly, and one by one removed the contents of the bag. Again George felt the constriction in her throat. The woman who had owned these things was dead; and the poignancy of her small possessions spread out by another's hands was intense.

A change purse containing around five pounds' worth of coins. A wallet, containing twenty pounds in banknotes and the usual range of credit cards which clinched their diagnosis, since the name L. Lamark was clear on all of them. A small make-up bag with eyebrow pencil, eye shadow, and mascara and lipstick. A separate powder compact of the old-fashioned sort, rather a nice one, George thought, with an Art Deco design. A comb, a small hairbrush and a small can of hair spray. A set of keys. A little pseudo-leather case, oblong, measuring around seven by two inches, with a zip fastening, a side pocket and, sticking out of the top of the pocket, a plastic clip like those on a fountain pen, marked in black letters against a grey background: 'BD PEN'.

They actually argued over it, standing there with the pen in its case, staring at each other mulishly. Gus wanted to take it back to the nick and have it examined under official conditions with properly accredited witnesses, so that the chain of evidence, if it should turn out to be a piece of material evidence, was ensured. George wanted to examine it right away, pointing out that it'd be a very strange thing if a court refused to acknowledge the sworn assurances of a superintendent of police and a police pathologist regarding the finding of the object, and telling him that he was being unbelievably fussy for a man who had just used his own private skeleton key to get hold of the damned thing in the first place.

She won. 'It's the old business of in for a penny in for a pound, I reckon,' he complained, but suddenly grinned. 'And I have to say I'm as eager as you are to have my curiosity satisfied. OK . . .' He reached forwards.

'Not this time,' she said firmly. She pulled the cotton glove off his hand, then imperiously demanded its mate. 'My turn.'

He made a face but didn't argue. 'Since you're more used to this sort of syringe than I am, it makes sense, I suppose.' He took a step back and let her get on with it. She didn't mention that she had had very little to do with this sort of insulin syringe, but bent her head and carefully withdrew the pen from its little compartment. Then she unzipped the side of the case and took out the contents.

Beneath the zip there were three further little pockets, and in two of them were conical plastic containers, each surmounted by a printed paper cover, complete with a tear-off tab.

'Needles,' George said and picked one out of its holder. 'See?'

He squinted at the printing. '*BD Microfine*,' he read. '*296 × 12.7mm. Sterile*, and on the tab, *Needle*. Yup. It's a needle. No need to open it. It's obviously not been opened before.'

'Right,' she said. 'But this is different.' Carefully she withdrew a slender glass tube from the other pocket. It had a brassy-coloured cap with a tiny pink cushion of rubber in the centre and black printing on its opaque side. Again she showed it to him and he read it aloud.

'*Humulin*. Human insulin.'

'OK. So far so good.' George was brisk. 'This is all clearly normal. The tube's empty though, so she was going to need to get a further supply soon. Let's look at the pen.'

She showed him the garish decoration on the body of the plastic with her brows quirked. It showed elephants drawn in rather a childish stylized fashion in bright primary colours, with, in case the point was missed, the word *Elephants!* in cheerful script.

'Not what you'd have expected of someone as sober as that locker suggests she was. Still, maybe she had no choice in the matter. Let's get down to the really important part.' She unscrewed the cap gently. Another glass tube appeared, this time tipped with a long plastic cap. George slid this cap off and there was the needle, glinting in the bright overhead light. She unscrewed the needle and showed Gus how the insulin phial fitted into the glass tube, the red rubber cap uppermost so that it met the entry to the needle.

'Now, look here.' She pulled pack the plunger from the other half of the pen. 'If I twist this, so, there's a little indicator section here at the side, graduated with numbers. The user of the pen just sets the dial for the dose she has to give herself, and then reassembles the whole thing. When she puts the needle into her own body' – she mimed the action against the back of her gloved hand – 'and pushes the plunger home, the device delivers exactly the measured quantity. See?'

'Yes,' said Gus, and he was grim. 'I can also see that it would not be at all difficult to rearrange that central screw so that the wrong size dose would be delivered.'

'Exactly.' George was examining the device even more closely. 'It's hard to tell just by looking. I'd need to do some experimenting, but I suspect that's precisely what happened here. Yes! Look!' She became excited. 'Look closely, can you see? One of the ridges of the screw has been broken off. I can just see the area where it used to be. That means that when the screw turned, it would take a double turn when it reached the broken area. So, the device *was* mis-set.'

'She used it expecting it to be as efficient as usual –'

'And it delivered a massive dose – massive in the sense that it sent her into a reaction before she could get to her food and overcome the insulin that way. This is human insulin, too, and it's faster acting than the older form. My God, what a nasty thing to do.'

'Killing people usually is nasty,' Gus said. George shook her head. 'I know that, but this is particularly awful, isn't it? Using a device that normally keeps the woman alive, making it into a trap and then calmly going away and leaving it as his weapon against her.' She grimaced. 'Horrible!'

'I know what you mean. And I also know that we have to start an investigation into a murder.'

There was a little silence and then she said, 'It's not even as though it would be hard for someone to get in here to do this.'

'No,' Gus said. 'Not hard at all. We're here, after all.'

'Surely, though, normally, she'd have her bag with her?' George was thinking hard, trying out her ideas as she spoke. 'If she was working out there, and a stranger came and went into this changing room, she and whoever else was at work would want to know why. The interloper couldn't count on having the chance to get at the pen. I imagine he'd have to search for it, the way we did, and that would have taken time. When she went home she'd take her bag with her, wouldn't she? We've only got hold of it because it looks like nobody has made any effort to clear her locker. Maybe they didn't like to; people are funny about possessions when someone dies, as well I know. So not only do we have to worry about who did it, but how? And when?'

'That'll take some hard police work,' Gus said. 'Right now, I'm going to put all this stuff back in the bag.' He reached out, took the gloves from her hands and put his words into action. 'Repack the bag, put it back in the locker, close and lock it. Tomorrow I'll get a warrant and come here, open and above board, and clear it. I'll also get my fellas to work, asking questions, doing the necessary. We'll find out who and how as well as when, now we know what happened.'

'*Think* we know,' George said. 'I have to take that thing apart to make absolutely sure it was fiddled with.'

'Do you doubt it was? Surely that broken spiral didn't happen by accident?'

'No,' she said soberly. 'You can see just by looking at it that it was an artefact – a deliberate piece of damage. Get the thing to me as soon as possible tomorrow, will you? After it's been fingerprinted and so forth. Then I'll let you know what I find. Meanwhile –'

'Meanwhile,' he said firmly, pulling off his gloves and looking round the room to make sure he'd left it as they'd found it. 'We go and get some supper. And tomorrow –'

'Tomorrow we do some checking on what happened to Tony Mendez, right?'

'Right,' he said.

26

The next morning Gus left early, already abstracted with thought of the day's work ahead of him. 'I've got an incident room to organize and coppers to get working,' he said when she prodded him to speech. 'I'll set them on to the Lamark case first, and then, as soon as I can, I'll start looking at what happened with Mendez.'

'I'd like to come with you on that one,' she said quickly but he shook his head.

'Be reasonable, ducks. It has to be a solely police matter. You know that. If there's evidence that there was anything the least wrong about that death then it has to be collected by us. I can't see that taking you along with us'll make the investigation any easier over there in the theatres.'

'Hell, I should have guessed you'd do that. Whenever I get really interested you go and shut me out.'

'That isn't fair.' He looked genuinely hurt.

'Oh, I suppose not. But you know what I mean.'

'I know you mean you're dying to get digging, on account of you're without doubt the most inquisitive person I know and I love you for it.' He kissed her briefly. 'Be patient, sweetheart. Get your own work out of the way, and I swear to you on every piece of fish I ever sold that I'll come to the lab and report whatever we've managed to find out. How's that for a deal?'

She considered it. 'And if you haven't found much, you'll let me go and do some looking on my own account?'

'You won't have to,' he said. 'Believe me, we'll have those theatres and the theatre people turned inside out. That's another reason you can't be involved, by the way. Imagine what sort of time you'd have with your colleagues after that.'

She had to admit he was right and said so, which made him grin. 'Great girl. I'll see you when I see you. So long.' And he snapped his non-existent hat brim and went.

In the event it was a quiet morning at the lab. Now that both Sheila and Jerry were back, the lab work had caught up nicely and she actually had some time available. She could easily have gone along on the Tony Mendez searches, she thought crossly. I could have been useful, even though of course I'd have been an embarrassment. I'm ready to bet now that it will turn out to have been a deliberate killing and I missed it on the PM, dammit, dammit . . .

But she knew at gut level that whatever the police found in the background to Tony Mendez's death she had no need to be at all doubtful of the quality of the work she had done on the post-mortem. She had checked every possibility and there was no question about it; the man had died of alcohol poisoning, and as he was a known reformed drinker it had been perfectly natural she should have assumed his death to be due to accidental self-administration and had reported accordingly. Just as she had with Lally Lamark. She brooded over that too for a while. Here again her post-mortem had been as meticulously thorough as always. She had missed nothing, of that she was certain. All she had done wrong was make assumptions about the accidental nature of the overdose.

At that point in her cogitation she sat and stared blankly at her window. Her cup of departmental coffee, which was as muddy as young Louise could make it (and since her scared conviction that there was a murderer after her personally had taken hold, no one ever dreamed of criticizing Louise about anything, in case she dissolved into helpless tears) grew cold beside her as she thought long and hard.

After about ten minutes, she stopped thinking and jumped to her feet. She almost ran out of her office, dragging off her white coat and dropping it on her desk as she went. 'Sheila? Jerry? I have to go out. Something urgent,' she called across the big main lab. 'Can you cope?'

'Sure thing,' Jerry carolled back. He was quite himself again, as relaxed and cheerful as though he hadn't choked on chlorine gas and genuinely believed he'd never breathe normally again if at all. She threw a grateful smile at him and went.

Where to start was the problem. That she had to check the value of the assumptions she had made over the last of the deaths among the three members of Old East staff she had post-mortemed was the one thing in her mind. She had assumed she understood the motive for Pam Frean's suicide, and had therefore reported it as suicide, but suppose she had been as wrong about that as she had been about the accidental nature of Lamark's and possibly Mendez's deaths? There was only one way to find out and that was to go and talk to the parents she had thought so ill of. If she'd been right about them, then her diagnosis of suicide would stand. If not ... But the first problem she had was to track them down, because she had no address for them, and no immediate way she could think of for getting it.

She started with Hattie in A & E, or tried to; but Hattie was off duty, and there was no way George could ask for access to her computer and its records without making everyone in the department very suspicious and therefore likely to invent and spread rumours with great enthusiasm. There had to be another route.

She tried Laburnum, the neurology ward, next. That had been where Pam Frean was working. Maybe one of her colleagues there would have some idea of where the girl's parents lived? But she'd have to be tactful in her enquiries.

It wasn't till she reached Laburnum and smelled again that familiar odour of hopelessness and helplessness, that compound of long-ago cooked food, antiseptics and tired, out-of-order human bodies that was the essence of the place that she remembered: not once in her previous visits here had she considered the fact that Pam Frean had worked here. She made a little face at herself as the realization slipped into her mind; maybe that was really why she committed suicide. Who wouldn't if they had to spend all day on Laburnum? But she pushed the idea away as frivolous, and went wandering in search of a nurse. And, of course, found Zack instead.

He was clearly delighted to see her. He was in one of the bays, doing something with one of the patients, a bulky old woman who was lying on her back staring blankly up at Zack as he leaned over her. She had her nightdress bunched under her chin, and seemed as oblivious to her nakedness as everyone around her. That made George feel quite dreadful, at some deep level, though for the life of her she could not have explained why. So she pushed the awareness away and refused to contemplate it. Zack had been listening to the old woman's chest, but when he caught sight of George at the entrance to the bay he lifted his chin and almost waved his stethoscope at her, as well as beaming from ear to ear.

'Well, hello! What can we do for you today? We're not used to seeing such illustrious personages as yourself in our gloomy groves!' He sounded exhilarated, and she could not prevent herself from grinning back at him. His good humour was infectious.

'Nothing important,' she lied. 'I'm just sorting out a few details about some of my past cases. Just to get my files straight again, you know. They were in a bit of a mess.'

'Ah, yes,' he said and nodded. 'Your break-in. The bastards.'

'Oh, doctor!' The old woman in the bed startled them all. The words came out of her huskily as though her throat had gone rusty from years of silence. 'Language, language!'

'If you never hear worse than that, Mrs Elgar, then you'll be doing very nicely.' Zack bent over her again. 'I've heard you say worse with my own ears and don't you deny it.' As the old woman cackled delightedly Zack looked over his shoulder at George and said, 'Can you give me a few minutes? I'll be out as soon as I can. Don't run away.'

'I won't,' she promised, and turned gratefully away to hurry up the outer corridor to the nurses' station where at last she could see a nurse had arrived. With a bit of luck and a tolerably fast-acting nurse, she'd get what she wanted before he came out. It was important to her that no one should know what she was up to.

The nurse looked blank and then shook her head in response to George's succinct enquiry. 'I only know she had a flat somewhere – well, more of a room, I think it was. She never talked much about her family or anything. Afraid I can't help you.'

'Damn,' George said under her breath and hesitated, unsure what to do next.

The nurse, who had returned to her paperwork, looked up and made a face indicating sympathy. 'You could ask 'em in HR,' she said. 'They might have it. Or maybe OH.'

George looked, blinked and translated. 'HR? Oh, Human Resources. And – ?'

'Occupational Health. Those two know most about our backgrounds. I mean, they don't tell everyone what they want to know but if you've got a good reason – and she is dead, poor thing, after all . . .' She returned seriously to her paperwork now and George turned to go, grateful for the ideas.

'Thanks, nurse, and please tell Dr Zacharius I had to go off, will you? On an urgent call.'

'Will do,' the girl said absently, and George escaped, hurrying to make sure Zack couldn't follow her. There was no reason why he shouldn't know what she was after; but the one thing she didn't want was him to offer to accompany her on her searches. She knew that once he got such a notion into his head it would be hard to dislodge; and this was definitely something she'd have to do alone.

It was a particularly new young clerk in HR who helped her. She looked anxious when George asked cautiously to see Nurse Pamela Frean's file.

'We're not supposed to show them except to the right people,' she said, giggling a little. 'Confidential – confidentiality, you see. It's very important.'

'Of course it is,' George said heartily. 'And I'm delighted you understand that so well. But that rule applies to people who have no right to access. I have. I'm part of the team who cared for Nurse Frean, you see.'

It was only a small lie, just a minor deviation from the straight line, she thought. She was a little ashamed to have used it on so inexperienced a person, for the girl's face cleared, and she said with relief, 'Oh, that's all right then! I'll go and get the file,' and went trotting away.

It didn't take more than a few minutes to find their address. There they were, listed under *Next-of-Kin* in the application form. Mr and Mrs Ernest Frean, and an address way off in Harrow Weald, in the far north-west of London. She made a face as she scribbled the details on the back of her hand. It would take ages to get out there. But get there she would have to.

She took the file back to the clerk, who received it gratefully, and then went as fast as she could – almost in order, she realized, to prevent herself from changing her mind – out to the car park. She'd need to fill up with petrol; I'll get the man to do it, she thought, while I look up the route. It can't take all that long. And Jerry and Sheila can cope.

It was, on the map, not too bad a journey. She just had to cross London to get herself on to the Euston Road, head steadily west and north out along Marylebone Road on to the Westway motorway, thence to Western Avenue on through Wembley, and finally veer off due north to Harrow and beyond it, Harrow Weald. Argos Road, she noted, was just on the far edge of what was clearly a great suburban sprawl. No wonder Pam Frean hadn't lived at home as she might have been expected to with her attitude to life; it was so far from the hospital. She might as well have been in Bombay as Harrow, the journey was so tedious.

It took George almost an hour and a half of cursing wheel-wrenching finger-tapping irritability to get through the crawling traffic and the stink of diesel and oil fumes as the sun beat down hotter than ever, baking the car into a private inferno. I must be out of my cotton-pickin' mind, she thought furiously. A nickel gets you a dollar they'll be out when I get there and it'll all have been for nothing. But she couldn't have phoned first to make an appointment, because they didn't have a phone. It said so in Pam's employment folder. Probably didn't believe in such an instrument of the devil, George reflected sourly, hooting furiously as a black cab deliberately blocked her access to the only bit of free road she'd seen since she left the hospital.

She reached Argos Road just after noon. The street was tight packed with houses, and narrow, with cars parked on each side leaving barely enough space in the middle of the road for two vehicles to pass each other. There was much jockeying for position, she saw, as people tried to find yet more spaces to park, so she made no attempt to find the house itself and park outside. She just looked at the numbers and when she estimated she was within a dozen or so houses of her destination, turned into a cross street, and there, crowded though it was, managed to find a space for her old Citroën.

She began to sweat as soon as she got out of the car and locked it. The sun burned on her neck and she yearned for a hat. The trees planted at intervals along the road offered no shade; each of them had a thick and sturdy trunk but – because they had been pollarded to within an inch of their lives – had only an absurd crop of dispirited leaves on top, so that they all looked like meagre lollipops, almost too small to bother to suck. Again she cursed herself for coming so far for what would almost certainly prove to be a proverbial goose chase.

But it wasn't. Number 357, Argos Road was a neat end-of-terrace house, with carefully white-painted walls in which the windows, each one heavily mullioned and mitre-topped as though they adorned a massive gothic pile somewhere in the depths of the country, looked ill at ease. There was a tiny patch of front garden filled with scrubby grass and a couple of weary bushes flanked by a neatly clipped privet hedge with a gate in it. The front door was painted dark green and a basket of flowers – geraniums, alyssum and a trail of ivy – dangled from a screw eye in the lintel of the miniscule porch that enclosed it. The place looked ordinary and cared for, a home that was important to its inhabitants. It was not at all what she had expected, though she couldn't for the life of her have said what she *had* thought she'd find.

There was no doorbell, so she had to use a knocker to make her presence known, which sounded thick and muffled beyond the door. She waited hopelessly, sure she would get no response, and in consequence was startled when the door opened silently, particularly as she had heard no footsteps from the interior.

A man stood there, tall and stooped, with thin sandy hair sleeked across a narrow skull and rather watery green eyes that peered at her over glasses. He was, in spite of the heat, wearing a thick cardigan over a shirt and collar and tie, and had heavy carpet slippers on his feet.

She had been so certain no one would be there that she wasn't as ready as she should have been with a greeting; and after a moment she heard herself saying, 'Ah, Mr Frean? I'm Dr Barnabas. From Old East – I mean, the Royal Eastern Hospital. Could I have a few words with you about your daughter Pamela?'

For a moment she thought he was going to push the door closed in her face, so she stepped forwards. But he just stepped back a pace of his own, put both of his hands in the air and waved them about in a disconnected, helpless sort of way. She could now see that his face had gone white with shock, and was filled with compunction. 'Oh, I am so sorry! I must have startled you. I didn't mean to, it's just that I – here – hold on there ...'

The man was swaying and his eyes had rolled back horribly. She only just had time to catch him as his knees buckled. She held on hard.

'Ernest?' A childlike little voice came shrilly out from the back of the house. 'Ernest, who is it, dear? Anyone for me?'

'Er – Hi, there' George called, needing to make the woman hear, but unwilling to shout and cause any alarm. 'I'm afraid Mr Frean isn't feeling too good.'

He was heavier than his thin body made him look, and she had to lower him to the floor as carefully as she could; but then he began to come round, moaning softly but at least straightening his knees so that he stood more or less upright again. Behind him she could see a straight-backed chair set against one wall of the narrow hallway beside a hat stand, and she pushed him towards it gently, deeply grateful that he seemed to understand and let her lead him there. He collapsed on to it, to sit with his head drooping forwards, and a hand on each knee, breathing rather noisily.

She was about to reach down and check his pulse when the voice came again, behind her now, and she turned her head to see its owner. A small, thin woman – as thin as the man who was probably her husband; indeed they looked somewhat alike physically, for she too had wispy sandy hair and a drooping expression – stared back at her and then flicked her eyes at the man in the chair.

'What have you done?' she cried accusingly at George. She flopped on her knees beside the man and began to rub one of his hands between both of her own. 'Ernest dear, do give over. No need to take on so, I'm sure it's all right. What did you say to him?' She looked fiercely over her shoulder at George.

And now George saw that she wasn't as old as she had seemed at first glance; forty-five or so at most, rather than the sixty plus she had appeared. She flicked her gaze at the man, who was now clearly feeling better. He had lifted his head and his colour had returned. He was about the same age as the little woman; it was his demeanour and his clothes that had made him look so elderly.

'I'm truly sorry, Mrs Frean,' George said quietly. 'It is Mrs Frean, isn't it? I'm truly sorry to have alarmed your husband. I came out on an impulse, frankly, and wasn't sure you'd be here. And when he answered the door, I suppose I was a bit startled and said the wrong thing.'

'The Lord brings peace to the honest house,' the little woman said, shaking her head severely at George. She got to her feet, brushing down her skirts as she did so. She was wearing an apron tied with a big bow at the back, and looked like a biscuit advertisement from the 1950s. 'And that was what Ernest – Mr Frean here – expected. If you said something unpeaceful to him it would have come as a shock.'

The words, though odd, were spoken in a perfectly normal tone of voice and they made George blink.

'So, what did you say to him? I hope it was nothing blasphemous or evil.' She spoke in the same tone she might have used if she were scolding a door-to-door brush salesman for using a mild profanity.

'Er, no,' George said. 'It was just ...' She took a deep breath. She'd have to risk doing it again. How else could she get any benefit out of this long journey? 'I told him I'd come to speak to him about his daughter, Pamela Frean.'

There was a long silence as the woman turned her head to look thoughtfully at her husband and then, oddly, at the fingernails on her right hand, turning them up to herself and then buffing them with her other hand in a totally unself-conscious way, rather as a child would.

'Ah,' she said. She let her arms drop at her side. 'I dare say you'd better come along in, then. And you, Ernest. No need to sit there like that. It'll do you less harm to get on with it. In the house the Lord has blessed no evil can befall; and we're still indoors, so come along.'

And she walked along the little hallway, opened a door to one side and held it open. 'Will you come this way, if you please, miss. I'll just put the kettle on as Ernest settles himself, then we can talk as is necessary.'

27

When Ernest Frean spoke it came as a shock to George. She had been sitting there for half an hour while Mrs Frean ('You can call me Deborah. She was a judge in Israel you know, and I'm proud to bear her honourable name') spoke about her lost daughter as the tea on the tray between them cooled, untasted. 'She was never a wicked girl,' he said, his voice a plaintive sound in the excessively tidy room. 'Evilly lead and evilly treated but never wicked.' And George realized that these were the first words he had uttered since they had met. He had been sitting there in the neat armchair to the left of the old-fashioned fireplace, his head bent and his gaze directed downwards at the brightly coloured carpet while Mrs Frean talked. And talked and talked.

It had been a flood, a cascade of words which were oddly unaccented as though she were speaking of something as trivial as the weather.

'We reared our child in the eyes of the Lord, to be a credit to Zion and her people, and we taught her the right way to be, but we couldn't prepare her for the wickedness of others who do not walk in the Lord's way, because we do not think or speak as such people do. So it stands to reason when she met with plain wickedness she didn't know its face,' she said, looking at George with her eyes wide and bright beneath a smooth, apparently untroubled forehead and thin but not too lined cheeks. There was a certainty about her that every word she uttered was the plain unvarnished and self-evident truth that George found chilling.

She had to an extent grown up with fundamental religion. Her mother's family had been stern free-thinkers who maintained that all their views, which included a deep dislike of foreigners, city-dwellers and pushy women who didn't know their place – a category which included George and her mother – were based on what George had always considered a very skewed vision of the meaning of the Bible. So Mrs Frean came as no surprise. George recognized in her the same sublime self-assurance that had been so infuriating in her relatives. It should have been easy to shrug her off as another blinkered self-deluding jackass, which was one of the milder epithets a young George had hurled at her much-loathed uncles, but it was not.

For a start, Mrs Frean had none of the passion that had so illuminated the speech George used to hear from her despised relatives when younger. That was what had most alarmed her about their bigotry. But Mrs Frean was different. Ordinary, everyday, a picture-book version of a sensible housewife, albeit one that belonged to the fifties rather than the nineties, she sat with her hands folded on her apron, her head set to one side like an eager puppy, speaking in a way that made all her twisted thinking sound horribly, dangerously, normal.

'We prayed hard and long over her ministry and work. We thought at first that God had intended her to teach the young. Then we would have been able to keep her here to ready her for her tasks, and she wouldn't have met the evil that she did. But God meant otherwise. He instructed us to send her to a hospital to learn to care for the sick and to minister to the souls of the dying.' She shook her head and then went on as though what she was saying were the most usual thing in the world. 'She had had this devil's notion in her head, you see, about learning music, and we thought – God

263

told us to think – that if she was allowed to be a teacher she might think it right to learn music so that she could teach it to the young. She liked music too much. It wasn't fitting to let her do something she wanted to so much, was it?'

'Wasn't it?' George said weakly, unable to find the words to protest.

The little woman opened her eyes widely, surprised at George's ignorance. 'Of course not,' she said reprovingly. 'Let them do what they want because they like it and you never know where it might end. Look at the evil the sad lost child fell into doing what she *didn't* care for. Imagine how she would have been if she had enjoyed the work God sent her to do!'

George blinked. 'Aren't you happy in what you do, Mrs – ah, Deborah?' she said.

The other woman beamed at her. 'I am happy in the Work of the Lord, of course I am,' she said. She took a deep, satisfied breath. 'Oh, yes, bliss is the Work of the Lord. I had an evil past, when I danced and wanted to sing wicked songs, but I learned! Ernest taught me better.' And she turned her head to look at the man in the other armchair.

He had not spoken again since that first sentence, and now George said tentatively, 'Do you agree it was best to – to prevent Pamela from doing the work she wanted to do? From being a musician?'

'He doesn't agree or disagree with the Lord!' Mrs Frean said in shocked tones, as though George had asked him to strip off in public. 'Such an idea!'

George tried again. 'Mr Frean,' she said, looking at him very directly in an effort to make eye contact and trying to turn a shoulder against Mrs Frean. 'Did you get the same message from the – the Lord when you prayed about what Pamela could do?'

He lifted his hands again in that confused don't-let-it-come-near-me gesture he had made when she had first spoken to him and shook his head. 'I don't remember. What the Lord says, the Lord does,' he muttered.

George began to feel anger rising in her. So far the whole conversation had had a dreamlike quality, but now her mind sharpened. 'It would help me get a clearer picture of what happened to your daughter if I can persuade you both to give me a little more sound information. Not about the Lord and what happened when you prayed but –'

'The only thing that is sound is what happens when we pray,' Deborah Frean said. 'If you don't understand that about us, you understand nothing.'

George bit her lip, trying to get her words clear in her head before she spoke them. Then she took a deep breath and tried. 'I need to know: if you had discovered your daughter was pregnant, if she had told you, would you have disowned her?'

There was a short silence and then it was Ernest Frean who broke it. 'Disown her? Our Pamela? Of course we wouldn't. We would have prayed with her and worked with her and done all we could to take her away from the evil she had suffered, but we would never have disowned her. She was our *Pamela.*'

'The Lord's Pamela,' his wife said almost crisply. 'Lent to us by the Lord. And we would never act against the Lord in such a matter. Of course we would not have disowned her, not if by that you mean thrown her out or something.' The sudden ordinariness of her language was almost shocking, and made George look back at the little woman who was staring at her, blinking mildly. 'You don't understand us at all, do you?' she said in a conversational way again, and actually smiled. 'Poor thing, you just don't understand us at all.'

'I don't think I do,' George said. 'Did Pamela?'

Deborah Frean frowned, puzzled, and George tried again, picking her words as delicately as collecting snowdrops.

'Did she think you'd disown her? Punish her, if you knew? Would she be afraid of you and what you might do?'

'Frightened? Of us? But we loved her! Of course not.'

'But she killed herself,' George said, wanting it to be gentle, but knowing it came out brutally. 'For fear of you – and the religion you'd taught her.'

Deborah's face, for the first time, showed real distress. Her soft, smooth cheeks crumpled and her mouth twisted. 'I still don't believe it. I know it's what they said, but I never believed it. We didn't even go to the inquest. Why should we? We're a loving-kindness family with a loving-kindness Lord. We wouldn't have harmed her.'

'But how can you say that?' George said. 'Do you know what message she left when she – when she died?'

'Whatever message she left, it makes no difference. We'd never have spurned her and neither would our dear Lord.' And she set her hands together in the classic praying position and, as casually as though she had kicked off her slippers, slid from her chair on to her knees. 'Oh, Lord, forgive thy sad child who came to you too soon out of the sadness of her heart. Suffer her and her little one to know the beneficence of your kind protection ...' Her voice sank to a low murmur and she went on in a soft mutter George couldn't distinguish. All she could do was sit there and stare at the praying figure as the doubt that had been sown in her now began to grow and flourish.

She didn't wait for the woman to finish her prayer. She just said loudly, 'No, you wouldn't have hurt her when she came home to you, would you? You wouldn't have beaten her, or –'

The woman opened her eyes, looked at George over her clasped hands and then got to her feet, brushed her knees down and sat back in her chair in a state of complete composure. 'Of course not. I keep telling you. And Pamela knew that perfectly well. We'd have had some prayers and a bit of crying, no doubt, but no more than there'd be in any other family who hadn't seen the light. Not so much, perhaps, seeing we understand the Lord's hand is in action, whatever

266

we puny creatures may do. And then we'd have set to work to be ready for a new little soul for God.' Her lips curved, and for the first time George could see regret in her expression. 'It'd have been a joy to me to have another little soul to love, but there it is. The Lord chose to let my Pamela set hands on herself and take that babe with her to Paradise. I can't grieve for them when I know they're under the Lord's wing, but we miss her, Ernest and me. We miss her ever so much.'

George didn't wait for Gus to come home, but went to Ratcliffe Street to see him. They were used to her now, and nodded her past the duty desk and on through to the station proper. She ran up the stairs to the incident room and pushed her way in past the clutter of desks to Gus's inner office.

But he wasn't there. She stood on the threshold for a moment, balked, trying to decide what to do next, and jumped slightly as a hand came down on her shoulder from behind.

'You're lookin' a touch put out, Dr B.'

She whirled. 'Oh, Mike. I didn't expect – Are you working on this case?'

'Cases,' Michael Urquhart said, jerking his head over his shoulder to indicate the big office behind him. 'Would you like some coffee while we wait for himself to get back?'

'Might as well,' she said. 'Will he be long, do you think?'

Urquhart shrugged. 'Who can say? You know how the Guv'nor is. Plays his cards –'

'– close to his chest,' George said. 'Yeah. Tell me about it.'

'Well, he's been gey busy, I'll tell you that much.' Mike fetched the coffee from the machine in the corner and she sat on the edge of his desk to sip at it. 'He had two of us with him when we went over to the Medical Records department at the hospital –'

She brightened. 'Ah! So that's in hand? Great.'

'Oh, indeed it is. And the whole hospital going mad with

excitement, too. I've had yon Sheila on the phone to me twice already with her questions.'

'I'd threaten to kill her,' George said furiously, 'if it wasn't such a dangerous thing to do. Shit, Mike, does that woman never know when to shut up?'

'Oh, she means no harm,' Mike said hurriedly, embarrassed at having dropped one of George's staff into trouble. 'And it's understandable, after all, when you think what she's been through. If Lamark hadna' asked Sheila to get out her path. results for her, she mightn't be dead, or that's what Sheila thinks. So when she calls, I —'

'Well, yes, I suppose so.' George shook her head. 'Though why she should think so I'm not sure. I've looked up the original report, and there's nothing odd about it as far as I can see. Just a routine blood sugar, a bit on the high side but nothing to alarm a lifelong diabetic who knows how to handle her illness.'

'You never can tell how people react to information about their health,' Mike said a shade sententiously. 'Maybe it meant something to her — Lally, I mean — that it doesna' mean to anyone else.'

'I suppose so,' George said. 'And as for Sheila, it's just that she has this gift for making me mad. Well, all right. What progress has there been? If, that is, I'm allowed to ask. Or does Sheila get the info while I'm left to wait for Gus?'

'Oh, no need to get all sardonic with me, Dr B.! Of course you can hear where we're at. Now, let me see.' He sat down at his desk and began to leaf through his notes. 'We went to Old East this morning, collected the property of Ms Lally Lamark from her locker, together with sundry other items of possible evidence from the changing room.' He made a face. 'Including some very nasty comestibles.'

'Ah, yes, the sandwiches. I doubt there'll be much in them for us to work on.'

'Well, it's up to you. They were sent over to your lab late this morning, together with the insulin pen. It's been fingerprinted and there's nothing on it, or on anything else, come to that. All the prints there were so old and so muddled . . .' He shook his head. 'The print lads were fair sickened when they'd done all the work. Not a thing to be shown for it.'

'Who'd be fingerprints?' George said in mock sympathy. 'OK, I'll go back to Old East soon and start on them. Meanwhile –'

He understood at once. 'Meanwhile, he's gone to see what's what about Tony Mendez. He took DC Hagerty with him, and we're just waiting till they get back. But he told me he reckoned there was some villainy there too, so I left some space.' He indicated over his shoulder to the big white formica-covered boards on the walls. One of them was headed 'Lally Lamark' and the one beside it 'Tony Mendez'. 'He wouldna' have asked me to do that if he wasna' pretty certain he had a case.'

'Well.' She got to her feet. 'When he does get back, if I don't see him first, tell him you can get another one ready. For Pamela Frean. Because I no longer think she was a suicide.'

She left him staring after her as she went, which cheered her up considerably, though she had no idea why it should.

She pulled Jerry out of the main lab to help her with the work on the insulin pen and the sandwiches.

'I know this is outside our usual area of work, Jerry,' she said. 'But I told Gus we could do it here, rather than send it to the main forensic lab. I need you to help be sure I flag up all the evidence, and also to establish the chain of evidence. So, let's get down to it.'

He grinned happily at her. 'I'm beginning to feel import-ant,' he said. 'This is the second time today I've been asked to do something forensic.'

'Eh?' She stared at him. 'How do you mean?'

'Well, Gus was here about an hour ago.'

She lifted her chin in surprise. 'An hour ago? But –'

'He asked for you,' Jerry said quickly. 'Believe me, it was you he wanted. But no one knew exactly where you were so we couldn't help.'

'Shit.' She shook her head in irritation. 'I went to Ratcliffe Street first instead of coming straight back here. If I had –'

'You'd have caught him. Anyway, no harm done. Unless you don't want me to do what he asked to have done.'

'Which was?'

'He wanted an assay on this.' He went over to his bench and brought her a bottle of vodka, or rather the remains of one. It had a shabby label, which suggested it was used to being refilled time and again, and the neck had been chipped. As Jerry held it up, she could see an inch or so of clear liquid at the bottom.

'He said I needn't worry about fingerprints, all that had been dealt with. He just needs to know what's in the bottle. So I said I would check it. I was just about to start when you called me.'

She frowned, thinking hard. 'How long will that take, do you think? I'd reckon an hour or so, depending on what he asked for.'

'Just a general look,' Jerry said. 'No suggestions, no questions.'

'OK. That means – Well, look, let's get going on it. I'll start on the insulin pen and then the sandwiches. I don't expect to get much out of them, they're just very elderly. But I have to check 'em, since Gus asked. I'll do the pen first.'

They worked in amiable silence for the rest of the afternoon. George was well content to find, now she could inspect the insulin pen under controlled conditions with a well-lit system of enlargement, that her initial judgement on the way it had been handled was accurate. A piece of the ratchet that controlled the amount of insulin it would deliver via the needle when the plunger was pushed fully home had been deliberately bitten off. She could clearly see the damage inflicted, she suspected, by a very small pair of pliers. 'The sort opticians use,' she murmured aloud.

'Mmm?' said Jerry, equally absorbed by his rack of test tubes, in which the vodka was being checked, step by step.

'Nothing,' she said. 'Tell you later.' The silence rolled back interrupted only by the faint clink of glassware and the occasional click of the shutter of George's camera as she recorded her findings.

The sandwich checks took rather longer than the pen had done. She needed to test for various obvious poisons, as well as setting up culture dishes to test for bacterial infections, which would take rather longer to give a result, but by six o'clock she was pretty sure she had a picture of what she had been looking at.

'Dead, very elderly dead sandwiches,' she said aloud, straightening her back. 'That's all these are, I swear. No hint of poison deliberately added. Just the sort of visible ending of putrefaction you'd expect. They were good sandwiches, though. Once. Cottage cheese and watercress, lettuce and tuna on granary bread, which suggests that they were indeed Lally's because from all accounts that was a very health-conscious lady. Low fat, high fibre would definitely have been her bag.'

'But is that evidence?' Jerry said, squinting at the last of his test tubes. 'Isn't that what they call circumstantial?'

'Not even that,' George said gloomily. 'It's barely admissable at all.'

'Ah,' Jerry said sympathetically. 'This here, though –'

But she overrode him. 'It's different with the pen. That's real evidence. Someone deliberately broke off a piece of the ratchet that controls the dosage. She must have given herself twice what she thought she had.'

'And that would have been enough to kill her?' Jerry said. 'Unless she realized she was getting hypoglycaemic and took some sugar or food to counteract it. Why didn't she?'

'Because human insulin kicks in faster than pig insulin.

She was probably knocked over sooner than she expected and just wasn't fit to get to the sandwiches she had ready to eat. It makes it clear this was murder, doesn't it?'

'Does it?' He shook his head. 'Don't ask me. I'm not much up on what is or isn't evidence. Though this here –'

She didn't hear him. 'If only there had been some usable fingerprints to indicate who had handled the damned thing,' she said. 'As it is, we haven't any pointers at all to who might have interfered with the pen. It'll all have to be worked out by the police checking for windows of opportunity and all that stuff. It takes so long that way – if it uncovers anyone at all, that is. It's hard evidence you need, dammit. And this just isn't hard enough.'

'Maybe this is, then,' Jerry said mildly. 'Seeing it's been spiked to within an inch of its life.'

This time she heard him. 'What?'

'The vodka,' Jerry said with obvious patience. 'It's been spiked with absolute alcohol. The sort of trick crazy medical students used to get up to. Only, much, much worse. Anyone drinking even a mouthful of this would have been knocked for six in a matter of minutes. The question is, where did Gus get it from?'

28

'Where did I get it from?' Gus echoed. 'The obvious place. Tony Mendez's hidey-hole. His locker. I thought, seeing what we'd found in Lally's, it was the obvious place to start.'

He had come back to the flat at shortly after eight, by which time George had had a chance to write up a brief account of her work on the insulin pen and the sandwiches, to attach to the report that Jerry had given her on the vodka. He was barely in the door before she jumped on him with a flurry of questions.

'His locker? Do you mean – Gus, that vodka, according to Jerry's assays, had enough absolute alcohol in it to kill an ox.'

'Ah!' He sounded deeply satisfied as he dumped the three plastic bags he was carrying on to the kitchen table. 'Had it, by God! Look, I've brought some Chinese to save time over supper. Noodles and the lotus fried rice, some prawns, some chili beef and –'

'Oh, Gus, forget your stomach for once, please!' She was in a fever of impatience. 'Tell me all about it. Every word. All you can think of.'

He sighed a little theatrically. 'I tell you what, you go and make a pot of tea – jasmine'll be best – and I'll set this stuff out and we'll eat it while it's hot. You know how yuk it is if you have to reheat it. And when I've got my chopsticks in my hand I'll tell you every last detail. I promise. But I need some supper to loosen my tongue.'

In this mood there was no arguing with him, she knew, so she scurried around the kitchen making the tea and collecting the little porcelain bowls and matching cups Gus had bought for her last year and insisted on using when he brought in a Chinese takeaway, and the ivory chopsticks he'd stolen years ago from a Soho restaurant that had served him indifferent egg foo yong for which he had reckoned he was entitled to a discount, even if he had to help himself to it. And once they were settled at the kitchen table, perching on high stools, he beamed at her, and with his mouth full of bean sprouts, began to talk at last.

'I went to the operating theatres this morning, complete with a warrant and young Hagerty. Oh, you should have seen his face! The smell of the place put him right off for a start, and when they made us dress up in all the gear before they'd let us in, well, he was one miserable copper. Not that it's surprising. He looked a real guy in all that green stuff. Me, I looked rather dashing, I thought. Maybe I should have been a surgeon instead of a copper, come to think of it. I'd have pulled a better class of bird then.'

He ogled her, expertly filling his mouth with another load of noodles, and then added a large prawn, after which he closed his eyes in ecstasy. 'This is what I call heaven. You can't beat a nice bit o' Chinese when you're in the mood for it, can you?'

'I swear I'll stick you with one of your own goddamned chopsticks!' she cried. 'Tell me!'

'I am telling you! OK, we tog up and start looking. It seems there's this big special changing room in the middle of the unit where they all get into their gear – outdoor clothes have to be plague spots the way they carry on. Everyone has a sort of share of a locker there. Not their very own, you understand. Just enough to put their street clothes in. Then if they need them, there's a second lot of lockers in an adjoining room, and people can put stuff there that they want to leave all the time. OK, so Tony Mendez is one of the geezers that has a locker all to himself in this other section.' He shook his head and speared another prawn. 'It's really amazing to me. The man's been dead for weeks and no one, but no one, has done anything about emptying his locker and putting it back into use again for someone else. And they've got a shortage of 'em!'

'It doesn't surprise me,' George said. 'It's typical of Old East. Unless someone somewhere has a chitty to instruct 'em, nothing gets done. It's my guess no one thought to ask for a chitty.'

'Well, I'm delighted they didn't.' Gus put down his chopsticks, picked up his little cup of jasmine tea and plonked his elbows on the table with the delicate piece of porcelain held between both hands. It looked absurdly fragile, framed by his big knuckles. 'He wasn't a very nice man, this Mendez.'

'Oh?' She too picked up her cup and adopted the same posture so that they sat very close together. She could see the flecks of green in the depths of his dark eyes that she so liked, but for once she was more interested in what he had to say than anything else about him. 'How come?'

'I've nothing against a bit of honest porn,' Gus said. 'I'll read a *Playboy* as cheerfully as the next man –'

'I'll bet you will.'

'– but cutting out some of the raunchier pictures and keeping them in an envelope underneath smelly old shoes, that's sick, 'n't it?'

'Is that all you found?' She was disappointed. 'I imagine you'd find that, or some variation of it, in nearly all the male lockers in the place.'

'No,' he said disgustedly. 'Do me a favour! I'm just telling you, because it's a sort of indicator, know what I mean? Like litmus paper. A man who cuts out and hides stuff like that, like some sort of smutty schoolboy, instead of being upfront and honest and just enjoying it – well, there's something about him I don't warm to.'

275

She wouldn't be deflected, much as she'd like to point out to him just how prejudiced he was being. 'So what did you find?'

'He was cannier than Lally was.' He put down his cup and started again on the noodles. 'She sort of hid her stuff on that rear shelf, but she didn't go out of her way to make sure people who knew the design of the things wouldn't find them. Matey Mendez was another piece of fish. He'd rigged up a contraption that hung from the back of his top shelf, down the other side of the back of the locker – there was room, because it was in a corner, and had a box thing tied to it. You never saw such a Heath Robinson affair. The thing about it was, though, that unless someone really searched, and pulled out all the stuff he had hanging in front of the string, you wouldn't spot it. Very ingenious. It could hold a fair bit of weight, and was adjustable too. When he had a lot of gear in it he could sling it high; when it wasn't full, down it went.'

'And that was where you found the *Playboy* cuttings?'

'If it had only been *Playboy*! These were really nasty, believe me. Yeah, they were there. And a couple of envelopes of photographs which were almost as bad as the professional stuff, only uglier if that's possible, and the bottle.'

'The vodka.'

'Yup. That's what the label said.'

'The label was right. Up to a point.' She jumped up to bring him Jerry's preliminary report. 'He'll get all that properly typed up tomorrow. Mine too. But we thought you'd like to see these as soon as possible.'

'Thanks.' He was reading the report with his brows a little tight. 'I take it this means that –'

'I'll explain.' She took it from him. 'The amount of alcohol you'd find in a vodka with a label like the one on the bottle is fairly easy to assay. When Jerry tried to he got this way-out reading. It was much higher than it should be. So he started to do an analysis and came to the conclusion it had been spiked with absolute alcohol.'

'Absolute?'

'Officially, in the *British Pharmacopoeia*, alcohol is defined as ethyl alcohol, or ethanol BP, if you like the name better, and it's –'

'I know that. Every copper does. It's ninety-five per cent ethyl alcohol and five per cent water.'

'Right. Absolute alcohol, which we use in the labs, is much stronger. It contains no more than one per cent weight of water.'

'So its proof is –'

'No, the proof is double the alcohol per cent. So one hundred proof whisky is fifty per cent alcohol. Absolute alcohol is damn near two hundred proof. And exceedingly toxic at that level.'

'I've always known more about the effects of the stuff than how it was measured,' he said, concentrating hard. 'Remind me how he died. Was it consistent with alcohol poisoning?'

'Oh, yes. Especially in a man who had a history of heavy alcohol abuse. I said as much in my report on his PM. What happened to him was textbook. He collapsed. He wasn't too big so the amount needed to knock him out was smaller than it might have been for a huskier guy. Anyway, in the middle of a case in theatre, he began to stagger severely, lost his balance, fell and went into a convulsion. By the time he'd been pulled out of the theatre – they were in the middle of operating, remember – he was in a coma. And he just never came out of it.'

'How come no one thought of alcohol then? He must have smelled of it.'

'Actually they did, even though alcohol of itself hardly smells at all. It's the flavourings and congeners and suchlike put in it so people can take it that give it fragrance. Vodka is popular with secret drinkers because it doesn't smell and absolute alcohol smells even less. But for all that they did think it could be alcohol – someone remembered his history – but no one mentioned that fact when they sent him down to

277

A & E. So no one there tested for alcohol at the time, before he died. Not that it would have mattered if they had. He was gone in under an hour. It wasn't till I got him that alcohol was looked for and found.'

'Could you tell from the tests you did whether or not he'd had this absolute alcohol?'

She shook her head. 'The reading of the blood alcohol I got was high, but it didn't tell me what sort of alcohol he'd swallowed. It's very hard to judge, after death, how much was taken. There are so many factors involved in making an assessment, you see. I could tell you what his BAC – blood-alcohol concentration – was, but to deduce from that how much he'd had was impossible. The parameters of calculation, like his weight, his basic metabolic rate, his drinking history, the timing, the rate of absorption: they were much too woolly to give me hard answers. All I could be sure of was that he'd died of alcohol poisoning, and that it could have been the result of just one unguarded *ordinary* drink! That's what my report said, anyway. I'm sure I told you all this, Gus.'

'Probably. I'm just checking. Here was someone regarded in the place as a recovered alcoholic who dies of alcohol poisoning . . .'

'Yup.'

'And everyone just accepts that as an accident.'

'Well, why not?' She was defensive. 'It was a logical conclusion.'

'It's all right,' he said soothingly. 'I was recapping, not criticizing. So how did you know he was a recovered drinker?'

She blinked. 'It was general knowledge,' she said a little uncertainly. 'I had the impression he was in AA.'

'Oh, it's hell getting any info out of Alcoholics Anonymous! But I suppose it's worth a try.' He got to his feet. 'Let's see if he carried an AA contact number on him. Some drinkers do. I haven't gone through all his stuff in detail yet. It was getting late, so I packed it all into my briefcase to deal with tomorrow. But hang on a bit.'

She followed him into the living room. He'd thrown his briefcase on to the sofa in his usual fashion and now he emptied it on to the cushions. 'The fellas from prints and photo and so forth have all done their bit with this stuff so there's no reason why I shouldn't go through it now. I've an odd feeling that I spotted something when I first took a look.'

He was picking up one plastic envelope after another and tipping the contents out on to his lap. There were the sleazy cuttings from magazines he'd mentioned, and the photographs, but he shoved them back into their covering quickly. She was a little amused by that: as though she hadn't seen much nastier stuff in her time! Then she forgot the amusement as he let out a little yelp of satisfaction.

'What is it?' she demanded.

He had a pile of cards in his hand, the sort that clutter most people's wallets: a cheque card from the Midland Bank, an Access card, a Union membership card; a card from a taxi firm, assuring holders of their Best Attention At All Times, Just Call This Number; a battered green and black phonecard from BT; an RAC membership card – and another, at which Gus was staring.

'Have you ever heard of something calling itself the SDAW Club?' he asked.

'SDAW? I don't think so. What does it mean?'

'It just says it here. SDAW Club. Now, what do you suppose that's all about?'

She reached over, holding out her hand, and he gave it to her. It was a small piece of buff card, with rather uneven lettering on it which looked slightly amateur, as though it had been designed and printed on someone's not very good word processor. The letters 'SDAW' were large and slightly off centre, and beneath them was an 0836 phone number. A mobile phone. That was all. The reverse was bare of printing but carried another phone number in scribbled pencil, which was so rubbed it was virtually unreadable.

Gus took the card back. 'I think a phone call,' he

murmured. 'What's the time? Nearly ten? A good time to be ringing people, don't you think? Especially those with poser phones. They never switch 'em off.'

'It could be.' She was excited suddenly and followed him eagerly to the small table on which her phone sat, and watched him dial.

The phone rang for a long time. For a moment she thought, we've struck a dry well, but then he lifted his chin and spoke.

'Hello? Is that the – um – SDAW Club? Oh, hello. Am I – er, could I speak to the – um – someone in charge? The membership secretary, perhaps?'

He listened. Slowly the expression in his eyes sharpened and became fixed and after a while he nodded. 'I see. So there isn't precisely a list of members,' he said and listened again. 'If I mentioned a name to you, would you perhaps know who – Oh, me? I'm just a friend. Another friend, you understand.' Again there was silence as he stared blankly at the opposite wall. George felt she'd burst with curiosity but then he grinned, a small conspiratorial smile. 'I see,' he said softly. 'I *see*. Very. Now, do tell me – What? – Oh. Well, that's kind of you. OK, I'll give it some thought.' And he hung up and turned to George.

'So tell me! What is this SDAW Club?'

'I still don't know what the letters mean precisely,' he said. 'But I can tell you this much. It's just a group of friends.'

'A group of –?'

'Friends. Well, she admitted they were accidental friends.'

She shook her head at him in exasperation. 'What's that supposed to mean?'

'She was cagey, the lady on the other end of the phone. But I think I might have worked it out. Or be on the way to working it out. She admitted that it was a club of people who had all been ill together. In St Dymphna's hospital.'

'St Dymphna's?' That was an old hospital not too far away from Old East which dealt mainly with the handicapped and the pyschiatrically ill. It was the centre for the local Community Initiative for the mentally ill and as such highly unpopular with the local people, who blamed the hospital for every wino, mugger and beggar in the local streets. The fact that there were no more than there always had been in Shadwell for the past half-dozen centuries escaped the complainers; they preferred to hate St Dymphna's. 'What on earth,' she said, 'would a person like Tony Mendez be doing belonging to a group of . . . Oh!'

'Precisely! People who have been ill together, she said. Not a real club, just a group of mutually supportive friends. That was all.'

'So, Mendez had some sort of psychiatric illness –' George said. 'In the new thinking, that is. In the past, he'd have been considered weak and in need of AA –'

'But nowadays you send drunks to a psychiatric unit. That's what happened to Mendez. And when he got better he joined the club.'

'Is that what the S and the D part is? St Dymphna's?'

'I imagine so. She didn't say, so we don't know what AW means. But it is a club. The idea was, the woman told me, that they could help each other through crises.'

'Hmm,' George said. 'Pity he didn't call her that morning before he took his vodka.'

'Indeed. And also, why was he using vodka regularly at all? He clearly was.' He looked happy suddenly. 'This is getting exciting. To find out more about Mendez and what happened to him we'll need to go along to St Dymphna's and make a few enquiries, won't we? It's getting more and more tangled. Just the sort of case I like best.'

29

They went to St Dymphna's together. There was no way she would be deflected. The fact that she had work to do in her own department, that properly speaking it was not normal practice for a police pathologist to accompany investigating officers on their enquiries, that Gus would have preferred to get the visit over and done with on his own: none of these counted. George was going with him and that was an end of it. He gave up arguing very early on.

'It feels odd coming here again,' she said as the wheels of his old car squealed on the newly tiled driveway that led up to the front of the Victorian building, a ten-minute drive from Old East. 'It's looking a bit glitzy, isn't it? Lots of new paint and a new drive. It must have cost a fortune. I wonder where they get their extra money from? Surely not the NHS. If they do, though, we could do with some of it at Old East.'

'Monty Ledbetter gave them a big gift,' Gus said in a flat colourless tone as he switched off the engine. 'After Maureen died.'

'Oh.' She sat silently staring out at the bright flower-beds that adorned the sides of the pathway. She had got to know Monty and Maureen Ledbetter a little too well during their last big case, when Gus had had so many problems and she had to deal with them almost single-handed. It had been a difficult time; and now Gus leaned over and squeezed her hand. 'I'm glad you've come with me on this one, George,' he said quietly, 'No matter what I said before we started.'

She grinned at him sideways, a crooked sort of grin that had some irony in it. 'Thanks sweetheart. Remind me to write to Monty when we get home. I wrote after Maureen died, but –'

'I know,' he said. 'It's always harder to help when it's a suicide. Well, that's the way it goes, I suppose. Come on. We've got work to do.' He got out of the car. 'Hagerty should be here in a minute. I told him to use his own transport; I have to go up to the Yard right after this. Got a meeting.'

'No!' she said with her eyes wide. 'How novel!' He made a face at her and, as they walked up to the front door of the hospital, pinched her bottom so hard that she squealed. It felt good to be with him; there was a closeness that wrapped them today that filled her with good humour. Even investigating death was fun when she did it with Gus.

Hagerty had already arrived and was sitting in the hallway under the white marble statue of a long-dead Victorian benefactor of the hospital, staring gloomily at the vast brass plaque which bore the names of other citizens who had given the hospital money.

'Morning, Guv.' He got lugubriously to his feet. 'I was just thinking, pity we don't run hospitals the way they used to, with people giving money out of the goodness of their hearts instead of us having to nag the bloody Government all the time to look after the NHS. Oh, sorry, doc. No criticism of you or Old East meant, of course.'

'What do you mean, of course?' she said. 'Of course you *were* criticizing us, and you've got a point. Old East is cruddy, falling down around our ears. Not like this, all shiny and well polished.' She looked around at the thickly beeswaxed parquet floor and fresh paint. 'But it's what we do in the old buildings that matters most, not what they look like. And I can tell you, buster, from bitter American experience, it's better to be sick in the UK than the US. Disease doesn't put you on the breadline here the way it does some people at home.'

'This is a hell of a time to talk health politics,' Gus said plaintively. 'Ain't I ever to get peace from you both? Come on, let's sort ourselves out.'

A large man in a porter's uniform, well supplied with bright brass buttons, was sitting in a sort of cubby hole by the main entrance, contemplating them with a severe look. Gus arranged his face into one of its most agreeable expressions and quirked his head at him.

'Good morning, squire. And a very nice one too, 'n't it?'

The porter, clearly mollified by Gus's familiar accent, bent his head forwards in a lordly acknowledgement. 'Very nice, sir. Now, can I be of help to you, gentlemen? Madam?'

'I was just wondering,' Gus said, standing with his hands in his trouser pockets so that the skirts of his light raincoat – which he had insisted on wearing in spite of the continuing blazing hot weather – bunched out behind him. 'I got this mate, told me about a club they've got here. Um, the SDAW Club.'

The porter looked at him and then slowly opened his mouth. There was a glint of silver tooth and then a faint rumble from deep inside him. He was chuckling. 'Did he indeed? You got some interesting mates, then, mister. If he's a member, that is, this friend of yours.'

'I got the impression he was,' Gus said, jovial now as he leaned confidingly against the side of the little cubby hole. DC Hagerty hovered behind him and George stood a little back, just watching. Gus in action was always a delight to see.

'Well, now, was he suggesting you ought to be a member 'n' all?' the porter asked, his grin now much more pronounced. He was clearly enjoying this conversation.

'Funny you should say that,' Gus said admiringly. 'How could you know? He did say as much. Now, why would that be?'

The porter let the chuckle become a throaty laugh. 'On

account of maybe you're a bit too fond of the sauce, mister. Mind you, I'm not sayin' that, I'm just saying that maybe your friend is suggestin' that. Yes, bit too fond of the old sauce.'

Gus managed to look peeved. 'Well, really, I don't see as how that's anyone's business but mine. I like a drink as much as the next man, and I don't deny I've had my noisy days, know what I mean? But to suggest I'm *too* fond, that really is a bit much, don't you reckon?'

'Not for me to say, mister. You asked me about the SDAW Club, and I'm just tellin' you what I know of it. Which is not for public consumption, you understand.' He laughed again. 'Quite the reverse, in fact.'

'Hmm.' Gus leaned a little closer. 'Well, I made a deal with him that I'd come here and ask about this here club. He says I could do it a bit o' good, seein' I've got some funds at my disposal for givin' away – being involved in charity work as I am from time to time. So I'd better do it. Can I talk to whoever runs this club then?'

The porter stopped laughing and looked watchful. 'Didn't your friend explain it to you?'

'Not what you might call explain,' Gus said. 'He just said to come along and sort it all out.'

The porter sniffed sumptuously and at last got to his feet and emerged ponderously from his cubby hole. 'Well now,' he said. 'I think this has gone far enough. It's been a nice joke, but it's far enough.'

'Joke?' Gus looked scandalized. 'What do you mean, joke?'

'Didn't you never get sent for a long stand when you was in the army, mate? I imagine you was at some time, you look old enough to have done your national service.'

'Thanks a bunch,' said Gus bitterly, who was not, and looking for the first time genuinely put out.

'Well, when you was a junior at whatever job it is you do then. You send the lads to someone for a long stand and when they've been kept hanging around half an hour or so, the one they're sent to says, 'You tell your boss you've had a long enough stand for anyone, and get back to work.' Well that's 'ow it is now. The joke's gone on long enough, and anyway' – he made an effort to look menacing – 'it's not right to mock the afflicted, and while a joke's a joke, it's over now. On your way, friend.'

Gus looked at him for a long moment and then shook his head. 'Well,' he said conversationally. 'I tried to do it the nice way.' He reached into his pocket and pulled out his warrant card. 'Superintendent Hathaway, Ratcliffe Street. This is DC Hagerty and Dr Barnabas, police pathologist. We'd like to see whover looks after this club we've been talking about, if you please. And sharpish.'

The porter looked at the warrant card, then at Gus's face, and then at Hagerty, who was also displaying his card. He blinked, opened his mouth and closed it again.

'As soon as you like, squire,' Gus said pleasantly, but with an edge to his voice. 'Haven't got all day, you know.'

'But there ain't no club,' the porter said. 'Don't you understand? You've bin sent on a wild goose wotsit. There ain't no club. Only the ward.'

'Try again,' Gus invited. 'Make me understand.' He put away his card, but there remained an undertone of steel in his voice. 'Fast.'

'It's the addiction ward 'ere.' George bit her lip. AW. Addiction Ward. How stupid they had been not to see something so very obvious. Too obvious perhaps. The porter was still talking. 'It's where the boozers go to get dried out. Everyone knows that. We've 'ad some well-known people up there, very well known. But they don't like outsiders knowing where they are, do they? So they gets their letters and that addressed to SDAW and then we know where to send stuff, but people outside don't know they're in a dry-out place. There ain't no club as such, though I believe the patients get very matey up there. So when some geezer comes in 'ere asking for the SDAW Club, o' course I see at once 'e's bin set up by a mate. Stands to reason.'

Gus shook his head sorrowfully. 'Not what I'd call reason, but I see what you mean. So, now, who do I talk to? Who will know about this club business?'

'I keep telling you there ain't no –' the porter wailed.

'Who do I talk to on this addiction ward then?' Gus said sharply and the porter gave in.

'Miss Chambers,' he said sulkily. 'If she's there and o' course I don't know that, do I?'

'Then find out,' Gus snapped, pointing at the phone in the cubby hole. The porter sniffed with all the modest delicacy of an adenoidal elephant and, moving much like one too, turned and went back into the cubby hole and picked up the receiver.

It took some time and considerable forcefulness on Gus's part to enable him to get across to whoever it was he spoke to on the telephone that this particular enquirer was not going to go away, and at length the porter cradled the phone and pointed across the hallway to the flight of handsome curving stairs.

'The ward's on the third floor,' he said. 'And,' he added spitefully, 'the lift's not available to visitors, only patients.'

'No problem,' Gus said sunnily. 'We enjoy the exercise. Thanks for your help, squire.' And he was off, taking the stairs two at a time, with the others hurrying behind him.

The third floor was as well polished and handsome as the hall-way had been, and the two intervening floors too, and they stopped for a moment when they reached it, panting slightly and looking around.

A long corridor stretched away ahead of them, with doors on each side of it. Gus led the way along it, peering in at open doors as he reached them. They led to three- and four-bedded rooms for the most part, all of them with neatly made-up beds which were empty of people, though the oddments, cards and other litter lying around made it clear they were not unoccupied. Almost at the far end there was a closed door and Gus stopped outside it and listened. There was a faint buzz of voices, and after a slight hesitation he reached for the doorknob.

The voice that stopped him seemed to come immediately into George's ear, and she jumped in surprise even more than Gus did.

'Whatever you do, don't interrupt them,' the woman who had appeared behind George said. She sounded alarmed. 'It takes long enough to get them started without you spoiling things. Now, I'm Sonia Chambers. You wanted to see me, I understand. Which one is Superintendent Hathaway?' And she looked from one to the other accusingly.

She was a bulky woman, tall and well muscled, with rather faded red hair arranged in elaborate curls and waves and an impeccably made-up face. She seemed to be wearing a well-cut skirt and silk shirt under her white coat, which was short enough to show a considerable expanse of black stockinged legs. About fifty, George thought, pretending she's still in her flighty thirties.

'Good morning,' Gus said smoothly. 'I'm Superintendent Hathaway. This is DC Hagerty.' There was more flashing of cards. 'I'd appreciate a few words.'

'So I understand,' Miss Chambers snapped. 'This way, if you please.'

She led them back along the corridor to another closed door, this time on the other side, opened it with a key attached to her waist by a long chain and held it open so that they could all file in ahead of her.

'Well now, Miss Chambers,' Gus said. He looked around for a chair, found one and immediately sat in it. DC Hagerty went and stood behind him and George, after a moment, closed the door behind Miss Chambers and leaned on it. Miss Chambers looked slightly alarmed, but controlled it well. She went to sit on the other chair behind the desk, crossing her legs as she did so to provide a goodly view of them. George had to admit they weren't bad, but found the display irritating, though she wasn't quite sure why.

'Well?' Miss Chambers said crisply. 'What can I do for you?'

Gus set down in the middle of the desk the little buff card he had found among Tony Mendez's things in the locker at Old East. 'Tell me about that,' he said.

She leaned over, looked at it but made no attempt to pick it up. 'A joke,' she said calmly after a while. 'A sort of joke to gloss a service we offer here at St Dymphna's.'

'Perhaps you could explain the joke?' Gus said.

'Why? Where did you get the card from?'

'I asked first,' he said. 'If you're helpful now, you might get to ask questions later on. Maybe. So, the joke?'

She sighed and recrossed her legs. 'It's really very feeble. This ward is for the treatment of people with addictions. Alcohol mainly, but also recreational drugs. We get a number of well-known people who need their identities – um – protected, so we use the initials of the unit in all our dealings with patients and outside. Now, when they are stable, shall we say, and can function normally with adequate control of their alcohol intake, and are able to leave us, we don't leave them. We make sure they have a lifeline back here. Each and every patient is given my mobile phone number so that in an emergency, at any time of day or night, someone is available to ensure they have someone to talk to. Not necessarily me. Sometimes I put them on to other people in the team – it depends on, well, whatever. Anyway, I make sure they can handle their crisis. That is what the card is about.'

'Yes. That's what you told me last night,' Gus said, staring at the card. 'But I'm still not entirely satisfied.'

Miss Chambers sat up more straight, uncrossing her legs and setting her feet firmly on the ground, for the first time forgetting what she might look like. 'That was you who called last night?'

'It was,' Gus said and beamed. 'But it's this club bit that puzzles me. And what's the joke? You still haven't explained what's funny.'

289

'Oh.' She threw up one hand in a gesture of irritation. 'It's silly. It's just that we don't enjoin total abstention from alcohol here. We teach social and controlled use of alcohol. So they – the patients – years ago came up with a different meaning for SDAW.'

'Which is?' he prompted.

There was a long pause, and Gus lifted his brows at her. She bit her lip. 'Small drinks are wonderful,' she said unwillingly at last.

Gus stared at her and then looked over his shoulder at George. 'So he hadn't been dry! Does that make the difference?'

'I think it might,' George said slowly and came forward. 'It all depends on how much he was drinking. I know everyone at Old East *thought* he was dry. That was what was said about him. I think they all assumed AA.'

'There's more than one way to skin a cat,' Sonia Chambers said crossly. 'And to treat alcoholics. We think they can be safe social drinkers, and we have excellent results. We're not in the never-more approach like AA. And we're not the only workers in the field who think this. There's Drinkwatchers and –'

'I'm sure,' Gus said absently, clearly uninterested in any debate over methods of treating alcohol addiction. 'But it explains why he hid his tipple the way he did. To make them think there he was a total abstainer. That was probably a condition of his employment.'

'And someone who knew that was able to spike his booze,' George finished. 'Which makes it murder, undoubtedly.'

Sonia Chambers sat up very straight. 'Murder?' she squeaked. Everyone ignored her.

'It's why I assumed, I have to admit, that the fact he'd taken any alcohol at all was an indication that he'd simply slipped from the path of virtue and it wouldn't take much to knock him out. I didn't look much further for any indications that he'd been given a heavy dose of alcohol. Dammit, dammit, dammit. I'll *never* let previous assumptions affect me like that again!' She spoke almost violently, ashamed to have been caught out in such a professional blunder. 'I put it down to accident simply because –'

'No need to whip yourself,' Gus said mildly. 'We've got it sussed now, that's the thing.'

'I didn't know,' Sonia Chambers said. She looked from one to the other, clearly put out. 'You'd think one of them might have told me.'

'Who? Told you what?' Gus said.

'Why, that someone, one of my people, had died. I'm the senior co-ordinator of the project – the support project – and you'd have thought someone would have told me there'd been a death.'

'Well, who would have told you? Maybe they didn't know about the club. And I don't suppose, even if they had, the murderer would have phoned and said, "Oh, by the way, let them know at the SDAW Club that I've just bumped off Tony Mendez."'

'Tony Mendez?' she said, and her face tightened. 'Oh, no! He was one of our best successes! He'd been in steady employment for years and managing to control his drinking beautifully. Oh, they should have told me!'

'*Who* should have told you?' Gus said again patiently.

She looked at him vaguely and then away, still lost in her own sense of outrage. 'Oh, someone who knew he was one of mine, of course. Someone from Old East. They could have told me. When did it happen?'

He ignored the question but sat up very straight and stared at her. 'Someone from Old East? You've got other people who are involved with that hospital working here? Who?'

'I can't betray confidences.'

'You bloody can!' Gus said in a sudden barely controlled rage that made Sonia Chambers blink and move back a little. 'This is a murder enquiry, lady. So tell me, *who*?'

'The doctors,' she said lamely. 'The doctors could have told me.'

'Which doctors?' He almost roared it.

'Well, there's Dr Klein. He might have said – only of course not being surgical, p'raps ... But Jim would have known. He's always in the theatres and that was where Tony worked, wasn't it?'

'Jim who?' Gus said in the dangerous tone of a man whose patience was wearing rather thin.

'Jim Corton,' Sonia Chambers said. 'The anaesthetist, you know. Jim Corton.'

30

'I've got to go, damn it,' Gus said fretfully, looking at his watch. 'I've got to talk to this woman till she turns inside out and there isn't an atom of information left in her, but I'm due at the Yard and I can't muck about with that. Listen, Hagerty, make a date with her to come into Ratcliffe Street when I can talk to her. Take a gander at my diary and fix it up with Mike Urquhart, OK?'

'I can talk to her,' George said eagerly. 'Let me try and find out –'

He shook his head. 'Got to be a proper statement, ducks, you know that. She'll have to come in. Is she on her way back, Hagerty?'

DC Hagerty poked his head out of the office door and looked both ways down the corridor. 'No sign of her, Guv,' he reported.

'Then go and haul her out of wherever she is. I won't be mucked around like this.' He sounded wrathful suddenly. 'Going off like that – who does she think she is?'

'A hospital social worker on duty called to deal with some sort of crisis, perhaps?' George said. 'Other people do have their jobs to do, you know, even if they are needed to assist the police with their enquiries.'

'Hmph,' said Gus, unimpressed. 'If she doesn't get back here soon I'll have her for interfering with the police in their bloody enquiries.'

'Klein,' George said almost to herself. She had walked over to the window to stare down at the gardens below, where a few patients were sitting out in the sunshine, which was still comfortable enough to enjoy; by mid afternoon no doubt it would be sweltering again with temperatures up in the eighties, making everyone irritable. But at present it looked peaceful and pretty down there; not remotely like Old East's battered exterior. 'Klein. I never thought of him as a possible suspect, but he could be.'

'Tell me about him,' Gus said, looking irritably at his watch again.

'You remember him. He was at Hattie and Sam's dinner party, the one Zack brought along because he had nowhere to go that evening.'

'Oh, that bloke!' Gus lifted his head, clearly forgetting the press of time for a moment. 'He seemed pleasant enough. Shy, quietish type.'

'That's as may be,' George said. 'But he's a researcher and he's got his own fish to fry. Maybe he had a reason to go after Tony Mendez ...' Her voice drifted away as she thought.

'What sort of reason?'

'How can I say at this stage? I need time to think.'

'And it isn't just Mendez we're concerned about. There're the others. Pam and Lally and of course our Sheila.'

'Yes ...' George went on staring sightlessly down into the garden. There was a lot to think about. Sonia Chambers's information had changed everything; she frowned as she considered it.

'And this other chap, Jim Corton, was it?'

'Yes.' George had been thinking about him too. 'That really doesn't make any sort of sense.' She turned back into the room and looked at him. 'He has to be the most nerdy and helpless of characters I've ever met. I can't imagine that boy having the nous to argue with a storekeeper who gave him

294

short change, let alone spiking someone's drink or fiddling with a diabetic's insulin gear.'

'It's always the most unlikely suspect what dunnit in the best TV 'tec drama,' Gus said. He got to his feet as footsteps came rattling up the corridor outside. The door was pushed open and Sonia Chambers came in looking ruffled and tense, followed by Hagerty. Gus smiled at her charmingly, all signs of his earlier rather hectoring manner quite gone.

'Sorted out the emergency?' he said sweetly.

'Well, in a way. For the moment, at any rate. That man has been known to go berserk before, and for some reason I'm the only one he'll listen to.' She almost smirked, but her pride in her ability as a soother of angry patients vanished under her anxiety about Gus. She looked at him warily now, and edged her way back behind her desk as though it were a bulwark that would keep her safe from danger. 'Is that all then? You'll be on your way?'

'Oh, I'm on my way.' Gus smiled the same cheerful grin. 'Because I have an urgent appointment. At Scotland Yard, you know.' He bared his teeth even more widely and she seemed to shrink a little as she stared at him, almost mesmerized. 'But we haven't finished, of course. Oh, no. There are lots of things I'd dearly love to discuss with you. So, my DC Hagerty here will take you back to the nick – to Ratcliffe Street – and make a proper appointment for you to come in and make a statement for us. I'm sure you'll be happy to do that?'

She blinked. 'A statement? But I don't know anything.'

'Oh, I'm sure there'll be something,' he said reassuringly. 'And it won't take too long. A few hours.'

'A few – Look, I can't – I mean, couldn't I just do it on the phone?' She sounded almost in despair. 'I'm the senior social worker here and I really can't go gadding about, you know. You see what happened just now when Ishmael took one of his mad turns. I was the one they had to send for. I really can't

waste the hospital's time, you know, and anyway, my clients
need me.'

'I'll tell you what,' Gus said handsomely. 'You don't need to
go to the station now. I'll get DC Hagerty to phone and make
an appointment for you to come in that way. There! That's
better, isn't it? Now I must go. I'll see you as and when, Miss
Chambers, as and when! Hagerty, see to that appointment,
right?' He looked at the DC with mock severity and then
turned to George. 'I'll let you see yourself out with Hagerty,
Dr B.? I really must skedaddle. See you later.' And he flicked
his thumb and forefinger at his forehead and went, like a
flurry of March wind that leaves everyone breathless in its
wake.

There was a silence in the small office and then Hagerty
coughed. He looked from one woman to the other. 'We'll be
going then, doctor?' he said.

'I'll follow you.' George smiled at him in what she hoped
was a relaxed yet winning manner. 'You go ahead. Don't let
me hold you up.'

Hagerty looked at her doubtfully, opened his mouth to
protest that he was sure the Guv expected George to leave
with him, caught a glint in her eyes and decided to be pru-
dent. Any rows the Guv wanted to have with the doctor were
his affair, he thought, and gave a small shrug. 'I'll be going
then. I'll – er – phone you when I get to the station, Miss
Chambers, and make that arrangement.'

'Yes, I suppose so.' Miss Chambers had settled in her chair
now, sitting in a slumped sort of way, not posing her handsome legs at all and looking rather smaller than she had, as
though she had been air-filled and some had leaked away.
'Goodbye.'

'Good morning,' Hagerty said. He gave one more uncertain look at George and went. George stayed where she
was, leaning against the window, saying nothing, just looking
at Sonia Chambers.

It was almost a full minute – an unconscionable time,

George felt as it ticked away -- before she stirred and raised her head to look at George. It was clear she had been hoping George would follow Hagerty, and now she stared up with a wary expression on her face.

'Was there something else?' she said, her voice carefully controlled.

'Well, yes,' George said. 'I'm glad you asked that. There are a few things I'd like to talk to you about, now the guys have gone. It's so much easier when it's just a couple of women, don't you reckon? You know where you are with women.'

Sonia Chambers looked unconvinced by this attempt to create cosiness and George tried again.

'I'm so thirsty, I could kill a cup of coffee. Is there somewhere here we could go to get one?'

Sonia looked at her a little more sharply. 'I've got work to do,' she said.

'Well, of course you have! And it's important work. The trouble you had with – what did you say his name was? Ishmael – I can see you have to be close at hand. How about I go and fetch some coffee then and bring it here? I'm sure you could use it. There's nothing that makes you feel a bit better than a decent cup of coffee.'

'It's not very decent in our canteen,' Sonia Chambers said with a flash of what must be her usual brightness.

George laughed appreciatively at the joke, such as it was, and crossed to sit in the other chair, settling herself quite obviously for a long session. Sonia gave up stonewalling.

'I suppose I could make you one,' she said ungraciously. She got to her feet and went over to the corner of her office, where a small table held a kettle and the apparatus for making hot drinks. George, who had seen it as soon as she came into the room, relaxed even more. She had won, she told herself. Now, go easy, softly softly and all that . . .

'It's a nasty business this, hmm? About Tony Mendez?' she said when Sonia had brought her a mug of coffee, which was in fact very good, being filtered rather than the usual dust and hot water.

'What — what exactly happened to him?' Sonia stirred her own coffee with jerky movements, staring hard at George all the time. That policeman did say it was murder, but . . .

'Overdose of alcohol,' George said succinctly. 'Collapsed on duty and died soon after.'

Sonia closed her eyes. 'Oh dear,' she said weakly. 'I suppose that is always a risk, even after so many years.'

'What is?'

'That the control will slip. That's what the AA total-abstinence types say, that it's more likely that people allowed controlled drinking will slip back than that teetotallers will, but I always say — and our people here say — what's the difference? If they're going to drink then they are, and there's not a bloody thing we can do about it. It's not us who cure them, they have to do it for themselves. We can only stand by and help them while they try to do it.'

'Yes,' George said. 'But that's true of all medical care, isn't it? What was it that French war surgeon had on his epitaph? Paré his name was. Ambroise Paré. "I dressed his wounds. God healed him," or something like that. Replace the word God with nature or whatever you like, and it's true of everything we do.'

'Oh, philosophy, is it? Bit early in the day for that I'd have thought.' Sonia had regained a little of her spirit now and at last stopped stirring her coffee and began to sip it. George congratulated herself. She'd managed to chip away some of the woman's defences. Now to see how far she could get over them.

'So, tell me, what sort of work does go on here? I may work at the next-door hospital as it were, but I don't know very much about you and I suppose I should.'

Sonia shrugged. 'Oh, the usual stuff. We have wards for mental handicap, or rather learning difficulties as you have to call it these days, though if you tell the parents of some of our people who weigh fifteen stone and have to be carried everywhere, who are doubly incontinent and have to be spoonfed and have the minds of ten-month-old babies that they just have learning difficulties, they'll spit in your eye.'

'And they'd be entitled to,' George said warmly. 'All that dumb PC stuff drives me crazy.'

'Tell me about it,' Sonia retorted, softening by the moment. 'Then we have a certain amount of long-term psychiatric illness which just can't be put out into the community; severely damaged burnt-out schizos who just can't cope and a few very labile manic depressives who don't respond well to drug regimes and need a lot of ECT.'

'And people with addictions,' George said softly.

'Yes.' Sonia tightened a little.

George risked pushing her. 'Mostly alcohol?'

'No, that'd be too easy! We get a lot of drug-users: heroin mainliners and people trying to get off crack and a few who've overdone the ecstasy. You know, the usual mix. Well, I *suppose* you know. You're a doctor, aren't you? What's your speciality? Are you just a police surgeon or do you –'

'I'm a pathologist,' George said. 'At Old East. I do forensic work for the local nick – Ratcliffe Street – but I also look after ordinary path. stuff for the hospital, or quite a lot of it.'

Sonia nodded, understanding. 'Yeah, I see. So we know some of the same people.'

'If they work in both hospitals, sure,' George said, trying not to hold her breath in over-hopefulness.

'Well, we do see a few from there. The registrar from General medicine does regular checks on our long-stay people, makes sure they're in good general health,' Sonia said. 'He's here quite a lot –'

'Yes,' George said, very casually. 'And what about Dr Klein? And Dr Corton?'

Sonia rode over her, pretending not to hear. 'And we have someone from the gynae. unit from time to time to check over some of the girls in the mental handicap wards. A lot of them have IUDs because they can't be trusted on the Pill. Of course it's imperative they have contraception, and they have to be checked. We haven't had an unwanted pregnancy here for the last five years. Not bad, eh?'

'Not bad at all,' George said. 'But what about Dr Klein? Why does he come here? He doesn't have anything to do with mental handicap, does he?'

Sonia was silent for a moment. 'No,' she said flatly.

'Then why does he come?' She still sounded relaxed and calm, but there was a steeliness there. She was determined that Sonia Chambers was going to tell all she knew.

Sonia looked back at her so thoughtfully that George could almost hear the ratchets in her brain turning over. Sonia was trying to calculate how much to say and what she could get away with; George was quite certain of that, and she deliberately relaxed her own shoulders. She had to be as casual and offhand over this interrogation as she could be, in case the woman realized that that was what it was.

There was another silence and then Sonia sighed. Clearly she had made up her mind that there was little she could do but answer. 'He's doing research,' she said. 'Into addiction.'

'I know,' George said. 'Not that he came here to do it, but that he's been at it some time. He's looking for some sort of enzyme effect that leads to rapid dependency, especially in teenagers. If he finds it he could be on to a major breakthrough in therapy. Maybe even, one day, a pharmacological remedy.'

Sonia stared and set down her coffee cup with a little rattle. 'You know that?'

George opened her eyes wide. 'It's no secret. Most of us – the consultants at Old East – know about the research that goes on in the Institute. Some of us know more than others. I'm one of the researchers' advisors, so I know more than most. I help them sort out their presentations to the funders, all that sort of thing.'

Sonia was visibly relieved. 'Oh, well then! You'll understand what it's all about!'

'I think so. But explain what he does here so we can see if there are any ... problems about it. Then when you go to talk to Gus – Superintendent Hathaway ...' She left it hanging delicately in the air and felt the flash of fear that attacked Sonia, or rather smelled it. It was as vivid as a burst of spirit from a newly opened bottle.

'He's, er, he's checking out some of his theoretical work,' Sonia said carefully. 'As he says, you can't do it all in test tubes and on a computer. Now and again, you have to deal with real people, with real symptoms.'

'I see,' George said slowly. 'Real people. You mean he investigates patients? Examines them and –'

'Yes,' Sonia said quickly. Too quickly? George thought perhaps so. 'That's what he does. Examines patients.'

'Is that all?'

Sonia's lids covered her eyes and she looked down at her coffee cup. 'Pretty well.'

'But not entirely.'

'He takes some blood sometimes,' Sonia said after a moment. She lifted her lids again and looked at George with apparently limpidly honest eyes. 'Stuff like that.'

I'll bet, George thought. There's more to this than she's saying. Try a new tack.

'What about James Corton?' she said bluntly.

'Jim?' Sonia was visibly pleased at the change of subject. She sat up a little straighter, and even crossed her legs again. 'Oh, young Jim, bless him! Well, he helps us with our ECTs.'

'Indeed? How?'

'Well, they have to have an anaesthetic, you know, before they have their treatment. In the old days we used to give it to people when they were conscious, but these days we're fussier. Now they have a mild general anaesthetic and then their shocks.'

'Yes, I did know they did that, though I can't pretend psychiatry is something I'm that well up in. But I thought the psychiatrist himself, or whoever administered the shock, was the one who looked after the anaesthesia? Just a little intravenous valium or something of that sort.'

'I don't know all the details, I'm a social worker, not a nurse, of course.' She seemed to lift her shoulders in pride. 'But I do know Jim wanted to improve his experience and skills, so he comes here to do it.'

'Improve his –' George stopped and stared at her. James Corton was one of Old East's junior anaesthetists, admittedly, but he should be experienced enough not to need to go moonlighting elsewhere to do what sounded to her like very simple forms of anaesthesia. There was more than enough complex work at Old East on which he could hone his skills, she thought. Why should he care about a few intravenous jabs and airway monitoring? She frowned. It was very puzzling. Another idea came to her and she lifted her chin and looked very directly at Sonia.

'Is Jim paid for the anaesthetics he does?' she said softly. 'Is that why he does them?'

Sonia went scarlet and George thought, that isn't embarrassment! It's something else. Relief almost. 'Heaven's no! Of course he isn't! This is an NHS hospital. We couldn't ask people to pay for their relatives' anaesthetics and we certainly don't have a budget. Oh, no, Jim isn't paid.'

It was the slightest of emphases she put on the word, only the most fleeting of giveaways, but George knew, suddenly, exactly what had been happening here at St Dymphna's – as far as one part of the puzzle was concerned, that was. The second part she would solve by going and talking to the man himself.

Now she said softly, 'I see. So . . .' And she repeated Sonia's words exactly, including the slight emphasis she had put on

302

one word. 'So, it's "oh, no, *Jim* isn't paid", which suggests that Dr Klein *is* involved in paying. Well, well. But who is doing the paying, Miss Chambers? And above all, who gets the payments?'

31

George had to take a cab back to Old East, since she had arrived at St Dymphna's in Gus's car, and she sat in the back sightlessly watching the streets outside pass by, trying to collect her thoughts. I need to do some writing, she told herself, get it all clear that way. Maybe tonight when Gus gets home and we pool our information? She felt the delicious tingle that came when she and Gus were well set on a case that was beginning to crack. The cracks so far were very fine, and it might be tough to prise them apart, but they'd do it somehow.

There were two people she had to investigate, she told herself. But which one first? Maybe she wouldn't have a choice; it could depend on who might be accessible. Well, fair enough, but one thing was certain. She had to clear her decks of other preoccupations first so that she could concentrate with uncluttered attention on the investigation. That meant calling in at the lab to catch up with any work and news and making sure they were all comfortable about how they were to spend the rest of their day.

She found the place in a mini uproar. Louise was perched miserably on a tall stool in a corner of the big lab, sodden with tears, her head shoved against Jane's bosom, who was crooning and trying to soothe her while at the same time throwing angry glares at Sheila. She, in her turn, was arguing fiercely with Jerry, who was, unusually for him, getting more and more agitated. The usually easygoing Alan was shouting at both of them and as George walked in, her face a picture of amazement, he was the first to see her and throw his hands up in eager surrender.

'Thank God you're back,' he cried. 'See if you can get any sense out of this lot and settle them!' And he turned away from the hubbub to go over to his wife, who was still holding on to Louise.

'What on earth's the matter?' George called above the noise of Sheila and Jerry's shouting match. They both stopped yelling, whirled and looked at her with almost comical synchronicity.

'He won't listen!' Sheila roared then. 'I don't care what he says, this was deliberate and it was aimed at me. Everything else has been, so why is this different?'

Not to be outdone, Jerry shouted at the same time: 'She just won't listen. I told her this time it was a genuine accident, that it was an oversight by the cleaner and no harm was intended to anyone –'

'Shut up!' shouted George. She glared at them and even took a menacing step forward. They duly shut up and stood looking sulkily at her but both were clearly still steaming with rage.

'Jane.' George looked at the little group in the corner of the lab. 'You tell me what happened. Oh, Louise, for heaven's sake, honey, stop crying so that we can hear ourselves think! What happened, Jane?'

'Louise slipped and fell,' Jane said. At the sound of her own name, Louise started to wail even more loudly and Jane half hugged her, half shook her. 'Now, Louise, do stop. You've been X-rayed and no harm's been done. If you just relax, then the painkillers they gave you in A & E will take over and you'll feel much better. The taxi'll be here soon, I'm sure, and you can go home.'

'What *happened*?' George cried, her own voice rising so that she contributed as much noise as any of the others, and Alan shook his head in exasperation.

'All right, I'll explain,' he said crisply. 'Jane, love, help Louise out to the corridor, will you? Jerry, take the stool with them so that Louise can sit down when she gets there. Wait with them till the taxi comes. It shouldn't be much longer. I'll explain it all to Dr B.'

Jane obeyed and, after a moment, so did Jerry. Sheila, who was now looking less agitated but still belligerent, relaxed a little and arranged herself on a stool by her own bench, sitting with folded arms to listen.

'It's really very simple,' Alan said wearily. 'Louise slipped on the wooden floor outside, on the bit at the top of the stairs. She came down rather hard, I admit, and screeched blue murder. So I got Jerry to take her over to the A & E department and report it as an accident to a member of staff, and went and had a look at the floor myself to see if there was a reason for the fall. I found a wide patch of floor that had been coated with wax polish but hadn't been buffed off. So, I sent for the woman who supervises the cleaners – you know, Mrs Fletcher – and she said it was clearly down to the night staff, since we don't have daytime cleaners, and she'd look into it. She rang me back a little while ago full of apologies and said she'd phoned Mr Bittacy, who's in charge at night, and he'd said the usual cleaner, Mrs Glenney, is off sick, so they had a temp here last night and it was one they knew to be unreliable and who's done precisely this before – put down polish on a patch of floor and forgotten to buff it off. So she's for the chop, and Mrs Fletcher says Bittacy'll probably get his knuckles hard rapped too for not supervising better. And that's all there is to it, honestly. Louise is all right, just a slightly bruised buttock and no bony injury at all, but you know our Louise – calls herself highly strung. Bloody silly little fusspot, if you ask me. Anyway, she took it into her head it was another attempt at killing people in the lab and was sure *she* was the intended victim, no matter what I said. And then Sheila came in –'

'And when I heard what had happened, I agreed with Louise,' Sheila snapped, unable to keep silent another moment. 'We don't have accidents in this department, dammit. It's always deliberate and it's always people after me! And as for Louise thinking it's her they want, who does she think she is? The Queen of Sheba?'

'Now you can see why Louise was still bawling,' Alan said, even more wearily. 'She took it hard that Sheila didn't sympathize with her conviction she was a target.'

'As if she would be!' Sheila fumed. 'What possible reason could anyone have for trying to hurt *her*? With me, it's different. I know all sorts of things about all sorts of people. I am in charge of all the path. records here for staff as well as patients and it's understandable someone thinks I have a secret about them. But her? God, do me a favour!'

'There's no need to show off about –' George began and then stopped and stared blankly at Sheila. 'What did you say?'

Sheila was startled in her turn. 'Eh? What do you mean, what did I say? Just that Louise is stupid thinking anyone has it in for her, the way they have for me.'

'Staff as well as patients,' George said, her eyes glazed as she concentrated. 'Staff as well as patients. Of course. I've known that all along but not really thought about it. I just thought it was the way you gossiped that got to people. But storing path. records, for staff as well as patients . . .'

Sheila looked at her and then at Alan, clearly totally mystified, and then shrugged. 'Well, of course we do. We always have.'

'Yes,' George said, still thinking. Then she pulled herself out of her reverie to concentrate on the here and now. 'Yes! Alan, are you satisfied this was a genuine accident?'

'Oh, absolutely! This woman who worked here last night is famous for slipshod work. The only mystery is why she wasn't sacked ages ago. It's just our bad luck our regular Mrs Glenney was off.'

'Mrs Glenney,' George said and slid back into her own

307

thoughts. Mrs Glenney. She could see her, standing there and pontificating about the way she managed when people who shouldn't be in the lab came there, after she'd been so unwilling to let George into her own office. She'd said something then, something that at the time had meant nothing, but now it had enormous significance and George felt elation burst into her chest as she realized what it was.

'Sheila!' she cried. 'I love you!' And startled the little woman by hugging her extravagantly. 'You too, Alan. You're great!'

'Delighted to hear it,' Sheila said acidly. 'I'm sure we're both very gratified.' Alan said nothing. He just stood stolidly looking at George.

'It's all right, I haven't gone crazy.' George was jubilant. 'It's just that I've suddenly realized – Well, jigsaw pieces, you know. Jigsaw pieces.'

Jerry came back into the lab followed by Jane. 'She's gone home,' he reported. 'I thought she'd calmed down. What do you think, Jane?'

'Oh, she'll be all right. She just needs people to make a little fuss of her. She has a rotten time at home and she regards us as a sort of surrogate family. So when people here don't pay attention when she's upset she takes it hard.' It was Sheila she looked at as she said 'people'.

Sheila ignored her, speaking purposefully to George. 'So, what is it that we've jigsawed for you, Alan and I?' she demanded.

'I couldn't possibly explain.' George smiled brilliantly. 'I'll tell you in due course, though, I promise. Look, I have some more – other places to go. Can you hold the fort here for a while longer, you lot?'

'Of course,' Alan said quickly. 'It's really rather quiet. Or was till this fuss blew up.'

Sheila let her face become wistful. 'It's understandable that I should get upset,' she said. 'I've had a lot to put up with.'

'We know you have, Sheila,' Jerry said. 'And you're not the

only one. But making a lot of noise and being unsympathetic to poor old Louise helps no one, least of all you.'

Still squabbling but a little more amiably now, they drifted back to their benches. George went off to her office with Alan in tow. 'Alan, something's come up that I'd like time to look into. If I take my bleep – and I promise not to ignore it the way I have sometimes in the past – do you mind holding on here till I get back?'

'I've got plenty to do,' he said. 'And Jane and I had planned to go out to eat tonight so that's all right. No hurry to get away if there's no cooking to do.' He stopped then and said a little shyly, 'You're investigating this case, are you? The attempts on Sheila?'

'I certainly am.' She was glittering with it, she was so sure she was on the edge of the answer. 'And the other three as well.'

'They really were murders then?'

She sobered. 'Yes, I'm afraid they were. There seems little point in pretending otherwise. Though quite how Pam Frean was murdered I'm not sure. That she hadn't intended to commit suicide I'm sure of now. That note she was supposed to have left must have been a – Well, it's all too easy to forge notes on computers, of course. And she certainly had drowned. There was no evidence in the body to suggest any other method of killing as I recall. She'd taken a lot of diazepam before she did it – Perhaps I should reword that: before it was done, but I'm not sure how . . . I suppose he held her under. Though there were no bruises I can remember . . . but I can't check her notes because of course they were stolen.' Her words drifted away as she slid back again into her own thoughts.

'We're turning into a regular chamber of horrors here,' Alan said. 'We'll be able to open the doors and show them our own black museum any day now. Roll up, roll up, see the car park where the car didn't catch fire. See the poisoned chocolates that didn't work. See the bottle of hydrochloric acid that didn't kill the technician! See the patch of polish that wasn't a trap!'

'But some people *were* murdered, Alan,' she said gently. 'Lally Lamark died and so did Tony Mendez as well as Pam Frean.'

'I know. It's all the other trimmings that seem so silly. Better you than me looking at it, that's all I can say. Give me a nice mucky post-mortem any day. I've got one down there to do this afternoon, if that's all right with you? Traffic accident yesterday, died in the ward this morning, less than twenty-four hours after admission.'

'Yes, please, Alan,' she said, fervent in her gratitude. 'You're an angel.' And she kissed his cheek lightly and he laughed and went away, leaving her free to get on with her own work. Or rather, she thought as she tucked her bleep into her white coat pocket, checking punctiliously to see she was switched on, Gus's work. But he'll be pleased, I know he will, at what I'll sort out. And I know all the way through to my middle that I'm going to.

She started in Laburnum Ward in a spirit of contrariness, because she was sure she'd do better chasing her other line of investigation. But then she reminded herself, as she hurried through the courtyard along the walkway, grateful for the little shade it threw at this, the hottest time of the day, I was always the same. Saving the favourite part of my dinner to eat last. Except it wouldn't be precisely last. After the business of talking to people she would have to search Sheila's files of staff test records. But until she knew more about those people involved she wouldn't know what she was looking for. So, she told herself frankly, get on with it, lady!

She walked up to the nurses' station on Laburnum as casually as she could and nodded her head at the duty nurse. 'Dr Klein about?'

'Sorry, no. He's away, I think.'

'Ah. Any idea where? And when he'll be back?'

The nurse shrugged. 'He's not really one of the staff, you know. I mean, he spends most of his time on his research, so I don't keep track of him the way I do some of the others who do more with patients.' She hesitated. 'Dr Zacharius might know where he is.'

George hadn't thought about Zack much lately, but now she did. She stood there, her eyes slightly narrowed as she pondered then, nodding briskly at herself, she said to the nurse, 'Where is he?'

'Mmm?'

'Dr Zacharius.' She tried not to snap, but the nurse wasn't being very helpful. She was standing with her head down over her paperwork, with her shoulders hunched and her lips pursed. A nice-looking girl, George noted, with rich red hair pulled back into a tight pigtail pinned on top of her head and a thick pale skin dusted prettily with freckles; or she would be pretty if she didn't look so sulky. 'Where will I find him?'

'Oh.' The nurse looked up and her face filled with the ready flush that afflicts fair-skinned people so easily. 'He's around, I s'pose. You'll have to look for him.'

Now what, George thought as she set off to look in all the side bays and treatment rooms of Laburnum Ward, was that all about? If I didn't know better I'd say that girl had a thing about Zack. Maybe he's given her reason to? Has he been flirting with her the way he flirted with me?

She explored that thought to see whether she minded, and whether it hurt, much as one might press a dubious tooth with an exploring tongue to see if it was still painful. To her relief, it wasn't, and she went on with her searches cheerfully. Let Zack have all the fun in the world with his red-headed nurse, if that was what was going on; it mattered not a whit to George. She had Gus and an interesting case to look into. What more could any woman want?

It was a comfort to feel so free of what had been an irritating experience, like having a burr caught in your hair which refused to be dislodged. It shows too how much more comfortable I am again with Gus, she thought as she reached the end of the ward and the room the researchers used as their special office, if I can be so relieved to be free of other entanglements. As the word came into her mind she remembered Pam Frean and felt a deep twinge of pity for that poor dead girl. And angry on her behalf, as well. Oh, this case had to be cracked. And soon!

Zack was in the office, his head bent over a microscope, but he straightened as she came in and welcomed her warmly.

'Well, hello! I thought you'd banished me to the outer wastes.'

'What crazy notion is that? Why should you think that?'

'Because I haven't seen you since last Monday week, that's why,' he said at once. 'I've been counting the days.'

She felt her lips quirk. 'Really? With that nice little red-headed nurse outside to help you do it?'

'Hey, hey!' he said. 'What is this? Jealous, I hope and pray? Or just –'

'Just observant,' she said.

'Well, even if you were right – and I take the fifth and refuse to answer any questions on that issue on the grounds I might incriminate myself – so what? You don't want me, do you? You've got your policeman, haven't you? What do you say to that?'

She treated him to a brilliant smile. 'The answer is no and yes. I don't want you, not in that sense, and I do have my policeman.'

'In the Biblical sense, I hope,' he murmured.

She flushed. 'None of your business.'

He grinned lazily. 'I guess not. OK, to something that is my business. Did I come off with a clean bill of health after all your policeman's check of me back home?'

She went a little pink with embarrassment. 'Hell, yes.'

'I knew I would.' He sounded smug. 'But I guess it was reasonable for you to do it.'

'Once the idea – Once we were worried, of course we had

312

to. But truly' – she held out her hand – 'no hard feelings, I hope?'

He seemed to consider for a moment and then held out his hand. 'Not at all. Friends again?'

'Of course.'

'Still ready to help me with my research?'

She laughed. 'Wow, you're single-minded, my friend! Sure, if I can. Are you ready to help me with my investigation?'

His eyes sparkled suddenly. 'Try to stop me! What can I do? Crawl over the floor with a magnifying glass? I always fancied that.'

'No, of course not. Just answer a few questions. Um, off the record.'

'I'm not a journalist! I don't make records.'

'I mean, don't tell anyone else I asked you these questions. This is meant to be in confidence.' She gestured. 'These four walls and you and me, just the six of us, OK?'

'OK.'

'I'm trusting you.'

He held up both hands in mock submission. 'I promise you can!'

She nodded. 'All right. You'll see – well, Michael Klein, what do you know about him?'

He stared at her, nonplussed. 'Mike Klein? You can't mean he's – I mean, *Mike Klein*? He wouldn't bite the cherry off the end of the cocktail stick, for Chrissakes.'

'Maybe not. But just tell me, how much do you know about him?'

He shrugged. 'Not a hell of a lot. I mean, I saw his CV when he joined – we all saw each other's – and he has a respectable history in his field. And we're colleagues, working for the same Institute. More than that, what can I say?'

'Is he' – she tilted her head – 'honourable?'

'Well, you sweet old-fashioned thing, you! What does that mean?'

'You know what I mean! Is he straight up, would he cheat

or cut corners to get what he wants? To do what he wants?'

He thought for a while, clearly treating the question with respect. Then he said, 'Wouldn't we all? If you're doing research you care about it. And if idiots get in your way . . .'

'What then?'

'Well, you, um, push them aside. Or climb over them.'

'And Mike's like that?'

'He might be. I have no evidence that he is, or that he isn't. It's just the way researchers are in my experience.'

'Would he . . .' She swallowed. 'Would he experiment with human subjects without full permission from a Research Ethics Committee?'

There was a long silence and then he said, 'Oh, shit! Is that what you've discovered about him?'

'I don't say I have. I'm just asking.'

He sighed, a genuinely sad sound. 'It's possible, I suppose. He might.'

'Let me ask you another hypothetical question. If he had, and if he was found out, what would be the result?'

'All hell would break loose,' Zack said confidently. 'Unsanctioned human experiments have overtones of Nazi Germany and the way Stalin treated political dissidents as psychiatrically ill and dosed them into idiocy. No one nowadays would stand for that.'

'And here at Old East, at this Institute? What would happen?'

'Out on his ear,' Zack said succinctly. 'Christ, George, is that what lies behind all this? Has he been illicitly experimenting?'

'Zack, I don't know. I just wanted to get some information. You have to understand that I wasn't making any sort of accusations. Just asking in a general sort of way.' She had a moment of inspiration, a vision of how she could reduce the light she was shining on Klein. 'What about Frances, for example? Could she ever cut corners that way? I'm checking up on all research people, you see.' Would he see what a tenuous

314

link that was? She hoped not. Fortunately he was far too self-aware even to think about it.

He grinned at her sideways on. 'Me included?'

'I've already had you investigated,' she said, 'haven't I? And you're in the clear. That's why I can talk to you about the others, as long as you remember your promise to bite your tongue on it. And I need to know, could Frances Llewellyn behave in a way that would put her at risk of being pushed out of her research here?'

Again he thought carefully and again sighed. 'Honestly, George, who can say? She cares about her work, cares quite desperately. I don't know though ...' He got to his feet and began to prowl round the room, dodging desks and chairs and the trailing wires from computers and word processors as he went. 'I'm one of those that couldn't enjoy cheating in research. It's tempting maybe, as a way to get the funds, but what's the point? You'd know you hadn't managed to do anything worth while, and it's got to be worth while if you're to get your prizes and your big bucks, hasn't it? Cheating is such a *negative* activity. It ruins your chances. But not everyone can see that. There have been people who've gone in for scientific fraud – remember that fuss over Piltdown Man? And that chap not long ago who claimed he'd done something incredible in the gynaecological line – re-implanting an ectopic pregnancy in a woman and cherishing it till she reached term? Look what happened to him when he was caught. It was horrible, he was struck off. But even if he hadn't been caught where'd the satisfaction be in claiming something and knowing yourself to be a liar? I couldn't do it and I don't think my colleagues could.'

He lifted his head. 'But I have to tell you, George, it's possible. I can't deny it's possible. Does that help you at all?'

32

She worked out the best lie to use to prise the information she needed out of the Human Resources department on her way back through the courtyard from Laburnum Ward, but then found that in the event she hardly needed anything so elaborate.

The HR office was a buzz of chattering word-processor keyboards and equally chattering staff; she had to stand at the window marked 'Enquiries' tapping on the glass for some time before anyone noticed she was there. Under normal circumstances she would have delivered a blistering reproof for such inefficiency; this afternoon she didn't risk it.

Fortunately the girl who came hurrying over had a guilty conscience about the fact that she had been gossiping when a senior member of the staff was asking for attention, and was almost pathetically eager to please in consequence. She listened to George's rather unlikely explanation of wanting to check on someone's academic and employment history because she had to provide a reference for him for an academic journal in which he wanted to be published, and went away cheerfully willing to pull the record out of the file, even though normally files were not shown to anyone outside the HR department. She even provided George with a small room containing a chair and a table at which to sit while she did whatever it was she wanted to do with it.

'Would you like a nice cuppa?' she asked solicitously as she bustled around, offering pens and pencils and notebooks, none of which George needed. 'Or I could get you a coffee from the other office.'

'Not a thing, thank you,' George said. 'Just let me look up this information and I'll be on my way.' Then a thought hit her. 'Um, there is just something – not to do with this file, of course.' She set her hand on it as it sat invitingly on the table in front of her. 'But out of general interest. We were – um – having a discussion about it in the senior common room the other night. This thing about being a referee for people, we're often asked, all of us.' She warmed to her concocted tale. 'And one of the surgeons was saying that he only agrees to have his name put forward to provide a reference for people he really cares about, because otherwise he'd spend all his time writing them and he really is much too busy. But someone else said that really we don't have a problem because more often than not people – new employers – don't bother to take up references. The mere fact that someone gives a well-known and reliable name is good enough. So, do tell me, who was right? Mr – the surgeon who won't let people use his name as referee unless he likes them a lot, or the one who said employers don't bother to take up references? What happens here at Old East, for example?'

The girl leaned against the table, her arms folded against her ample bosom, and settled herself for a nice prose. Clearly George had struck gold: getting someone who liked nothing better than a chat, no matter what the subject.

'Well,' she said. 'They're both right and they're both wrong.' She beamed with satisfaction at her joke. 'It all depends, you see. Here we take up some references – write to the person, you know, and ask for a form to be filled out, what we send them. But others, well they attach copies of written references to their application forms when they first write in, and we just go by that. As long as it's a reputable place they've come from, you know.' She nodded sapiently. 'Like Mrs

Gosling says, you get a nose for what's what in this department. I work a lot with Mrs Gosling. She says I'll make a good HR director one day, on account of I like people.'

'Yes,' George said, amused as well as grateful for her garrulousness. 'I'm sure you will. So, you don't always get in touch with referees. Um – there's something else I've always wondered, as we're talking: what about qualifications? Do you check with medical schools? Ask to see certificates and so forth?'

The girl laughed merrily. 'Oh, no! We'd never get a thing done if we had to do that. We deal with over five hundred staff here, you know. And not just the doctors. There's the nurses and the PAMs – Professions Allied to Medicine, you know,' she added helpfully.

'I know,' George said dryly.

'And the clericals and the administrative people and the cooks and the cleaners. You have to be all things to all men and women when you work in HR, and you have to have your antennae well up.' She nodded, pleased with herself. George could almost hear the voice of her mentor, Mrs Gosling, prompting her. 'So we couldn't possibly look at every certificate and contact every referee. But, like I said, we don't really need to, do we? You know when someone is a reliable referee, by their name and where they are. A good hospital is a good hospital, 'n't it? As for qualifications, well, a lot of people have them framed and hanging up in their houses. Their loos, usually.' She giggled. 'That's where I keep my certificate what I got from City and Guilds. But I only have to tell people I've got it and that's good enough.'

'And I'm sure you'll get lots more to put up in your loo,' George said handsomely, beaming at the girl. 'Well, thanks a lot. I'll just collect the information I need from this file and bring it out to you when I'm done. Will that be all right? I don't want to waste your time while I do it.'

The girl, who had clearly been happily settled for a nice long wait that would keep her away from whatever else it was she was supposed to be doing, opened her mouth to protest that she didn't mind a bit, but George lifted her brows at her in what she knew was one of her more unattractive expressions and the girl closed her mouth again and made for the door.

'I'll wait till you bring it to me, then,' she said. 'You know where I am – in the reception office.'

'I know.' George waited, sitting with her hand on the file, till the girl had opened the door and gone. Not till the door reluctantly closed did she pull the file closer to read it.

The home address was a northern market town, and the school history there, it seemed, had been exemplary. Good O levels, A levels and acceptance at a medical school in the Midlands followed. Odd, she thought, I never heard any hint of an accent in his voice. Still, maybe that's because my American ears aren't as finely tuned to regional variations as they might be, in spite of rapidly learning the differences between various Scottish accents when living and working in Inverness. But that's irrelevant now; think about this file, she told herself firmly.

So, a routine medical background: good first job in a hospital in Birmingham, a second one in suburban London, well south of the river, and now here at Old East. A commonplace enough career resumé, she thought, and then automatically translated the American term into English: curriculum vitae, CV.

Her mind was wandering, she knew, and she brought her attention back to the file. She read the references that were attached to the application form, and frowned a little as she went through them again. Then she realized what it was that bothered her and settled down to read them more carefully, checking one against the other. It was, indeed, a very revealing exercise.

She got home at seven, later than usual because she had stayed late at the lab out of guilt, making sure that all the work she had neglected was done. And it was. Alan was turning out to be a classic tower of strength and she told him so.

'Glad to do it,' he said. 'I need the experience anyway. And of course if it means you'll give me a glowing reference when I go, then it will all have been more than worth while!'

References again, she thought, and made a little face. 'Of course I will. Not only will I give you a written one when the time comes, but I'll tell you to insist that future would-be employers actually contact me so that I can really sing your praises the way they should be. Or give you a bollocking, of course . . .'

He laughed. 'Ah, but people don't, do they? If they can't say something good about a person, they usually say nothing at all.'

'Yes.' She stared at him for a long moment. 'Yes, indeed.'

'So, here's the work schedule for tomorrow. There're two bods waiting for PMs – routine stuff, I'll gladly do them.' He tried not to look too eager, but she wasn't fooled.

'I'd be grateful if you would,' she said graciously and watched him go happily home, still thoughtful. Everything seemed to point in the same direction. All this talk of references . . . There would be a lot to talk about when she and Gus got together tonight.

He arrived a half-hour after she did, so she had had time to organize some supper. Nothing special, some pasta with a pot of pesto she had in the freezer, and a salad. It would be enough to stoke them for an evening's hard talk, she thought, and barely gave him time to wash his hands when he came in before thrusting a steaming plate in front of him and instructing him to: 'Get on with it. We've got work to do.'

'So,' he said mildly, picking up spoon and fork and beginning to twirl the strands of fettucine on to the fork with expert turns of his wrist. 'What sort of time did you have at your meeting, Gus? Was it interesting, Gus? Well, well, how nice to hear that, Gus. Tell me more, Gus.'

'Oh, pooh,' she said and joined him at the table, pouring

wine for them both. Gus could no more eat a plate of pasta without an accompanying glass of something red and cheerful than eat dry toast without butter. Although he should, she told him sometimes, as she noted the way his already generous girth had softened and spread since he had become a more deskbound superintendent than a bustling detective chief inspector. 'I've got other things to think about than your committees. I've made progress today, let me tell you. Very good progress.'

He cocked an eyebrow at her and packed his mouth expertly. 'Mmm? What?' he said indistinctly.

'When we've eaten and washed up. Then you can have the lot.' And in spite of his demands for information she made him wait until they were sitting side by side on the sofa in the living room. She had prudently armed herself with a clipboard bearing a large thick pad of lined paper and a handful of coloured pencils, and he looked at them warily.

'We're really going to work then?'

'We are,' she said. 'We have to write things down to get our heads clear. Look, like this.' She headed the first sheet of paper in ordinary blue ink: SUSPECTS, and alongside it, MOTIVE. 'We'll get on to the other bits later. Like opportunity and so forth. Right. Let's see who and why. Because when you're dealing with three murders and one attempted one – and it is only one attempted one even though there have been three goes so far – then working out the times and places the suspect would have had to be to be responsible for all the events'll take a lot of doing. And we're agreed, aren't we, that there is only one perpetrator here? That we're not dealing with the coincidence of a couple or more murderers whizzing around Old East?'

'You know that perfectly well. I never believe in coincidences like that. Synchronicity sometimes, maybe, when two things happen together because – well, because they do. I've read my Jung and my Koestler with the best of 'em. But I doubt any synchronicity here. We're looking for one person.'

'So, let's start with the first column. Who do you want to see written down as a suspect?'

He thought for a while. 'It's hard for me to say yet. I haven't been able to question the Chambers woman. Maybe she'll have more to tell us.'

'She has.' George put the board down on her knee again. The next little while was going to be a tad difficult, and she knew it. But she'd overridden Gus's instructions before now and got away with it. No reason, she thought stoutly, why I can't again.

'Oh?' He looked at her accusingly. 'Don't tell me. You stayed on and talked to her, right?'

She lifted her chin defiantly. 'Right.'

'George, you really are the end,' he said with a sudden surge of real anger. 'Christ, I'm grateful for your input, have been from the very first case we worked on. In the last one, well, I'd have gone down with all hands if you hadn't jumped the gun on me, more than once. But there's a time and place, for Chrissakes.'

'There was a time and place this morning,' she said. 'Listen.' She told him calmly all that she had got out of Sonia Chambers, and he listened silently, not taking his eyes from her face.

There was a little pause when she'd finished and then he said, 'Will she repeat all that when she makes her statement?'

'That's up to you, isn't it? You have to get the information out of her. Or get that police sergeant of yours to do it – the one who took mine over the chocolates.' She made a little face. 'That one would get a full confession out of Bluebeard, given the time.'

'So, let's assume she does. And I suppose we can still act on her information even if she doesn't. From what she says, both Michael Klein and James Corton work at St Dymphna's when they shouldn't. And money changes hands which in the NHS is the crime of all crimes.'

'Money usually is anyway,' George said. 'But yes. And this

afternoon I talked to Zack about Klein to see if Klein was the sort of guy who would do unauthorized tests on patients, the way Chambers said he did, and Zack said –'

Gus went red. 'You did what?' His voice was thin and controlled and she looked at him swiftly and then away. Dammit. This was always going to be the most dangerous area.

'I talked to him in general terms,' she said carefully. 'Not just about Klein. I asked him whether any of the people he worked with, which includes Klein and Llewellyn – Frances, remember? – were the sort to behave that way. Where else would I get that sort of information? He knows them both better than anyone.'

'Talking to a suspect about other possible suspects is hardly the way to run a proper investigation, George, and you should know that by now. You're too fond of going off half-cocked like this.'

'Hey, hey!' George said. 'Is Zack a suspect? I understood that all the research on him you had done in Canada had exonerated him. And, remember, it was I who thought he might be involved, not you. When we investigated here, it was clear he wasn't the man we're looking for, so why shouldn't I talk to him about the case? He's got an interest in seeing it cleared up as much as we have. A hospital – and a Research Institute – with unsolved murders hanging around the place isn't going to be attractive to potential funders, is it? The only thing Zack Zacharius cares about is getting the resources to complete his work. If he thought one of his colleagues was messing up his patch he'd be the first to co-operate with us to get them sorted out.'

Gus was gazing at her, his eyes a little narrowed, but she could see his first angry reaction had muted. 'OK,' he said after a moment. 'I suppose you have a point. We did agree he was out of the frame. But all the same, it goes against all my instincts to discuss a case with an outsider who might –'

'But he couldn't be more of an insider!' George said. 'Can't you see? Where else would I get the sort of info I – we need on Klein? Which is, by the way, that Zack thinks it unlikely that Klein misbehaved the way Chambers says he did, though he admitted that it could happen. It's not out of the range of possibilities. With Chambers's evidence and his we ought to be able to nail Klein. If it's him, of course.'

'Yes ...' He sighed. 'Well, you've done it now, so we're stuck with it. If he tells Klein you're investigating him and Klein is our man, then all that will happen is that Klein will run into cover. And we'll never nab him.'

'Are you sure?' she said and looked at him sharply. 'Didn't you once tell me, a long time ago, that people under pressure make mistakes? Reveal themselves? Couldn't having Zack warn Klein help us? Not that I think he will, mind you. I asked him to treat my questions in confidence.'

He laughed then. 'Oh, George, you are funny. You asked him, did you? So that means of course that he'll do as you asked.'

'I believe he will.' George was defensive. 'He said he would.'

'Let me tell you a secret, ducky,' Gus said, leaning over to whisper in her ear. 'He might have lied.'

'Well, even if he did,' George said crossly, pulling herself away from him, 'it's like I said. Maybe that'll make Klein less careful, according to your creed. So either way there's no harm done.'

'Is he your prime suspect?' Gus asked. She looked at him sideways, and slid down a little on the sofa. 'Dammit,' she said after a pause. 'No, he isn't. I wish he were. He's not really a likeable man.' She stopped.

'So, what have you discovered about the other one? Who, I take it from your reaction, *is* a nice man. Which shouldn't carry any weight, but I know how you feel. I gather it's the same man Chambers talked about.'

'Yes,' George said. 'And I thought he was – Well, what I thought of him doesn't really matter, I guess. Maybe he's a good actor. I suppose he has to be to do what he's been doing.'

'How do you mean?' He was sharply curious now, seeming to know that she had a very special piece of information for him. 'Have you got some hard evidence?'

'No,' she said. 'Not yet. But it'll be the easiest thing in the world to get. The thing is, Gus, I don't think Jim Corton is a doctor. He's a hoaxer with no qualifications to be dealing with patients at all, either at Old East or at St Dymphna's.'

33

Gus sat very still and stared at her, and then, to her amazement, leaned back and opened his mouth wide to roar with laughter.

'I don't see what's so goddamned funny,' she cried. 'We're going to have to gather evidence and if – no, dammit, *when* we do, I'm in one hell of an ethical quandary. And you're laughing?'

He pulled a handkerchief from his pocket and wiped his streaming eyes. 'I'm sorry,' he said huskily and managed to calm down. 'It was just that I got this sudden set of images. I mean, admit it, George, it's like one of the corniest of *Doctor in the House* gags, or some seaside comic card joke. You know, "Big breaths," says the doctor. "Yeth," says the sexy girl. "And I'm only thirteen." And then the so-called doctor leers at the audience and says, "I'm really a fishmonger, but a white coat comes in handy." Oh, dear.' He shook his head, wiped his eyes and stowed his handkerchief. 'Sorry, ducks. I'll be sensible now. So, how do you know?'

'I got the idea because of a lot of things. Things people said, but particularly the night cleaner on my department. A Mrs Glenney. She talked about people in white coats all looking the same and how people sometimes pretended to be doctors. I didn't pay much attention at the time, but later . . . Well, I won't detail it all. Just say I went to HR –'

'Personnel,' he muttered. 'I hate these new labels.'

'Call it what you like. I went there, and conned a girl into showing me his file. All highly improper, of course. And there's nothing there that they've checked. Not his qualifications, not his references, nothing. Apparently, employers don't.'

'They do in the police force,' Gus said.

'I'm not surprised. Some very flaky people get involved in the police,' she retorted. 'I mean, if you got past their vetting, what are the ones they discard like?'

'Oh, lovely,' he said approvingly. 'That's more like my girl. OK, so no one checked his references. But this alone doesn't make him a fraud.'

'The references are all written in the same sort of way, same tone of voice. It's hard to explain but you know how different people use different speech rhythms? These are all matching. Also some of the words used are repeated, like saying he has "perceptive judgement". That one was used in every reference, and that has to be unusual. It's not a phrase you normally find doctors using about other doctors. They might say something clichéd like "sound judgement", but "perceptive"? In three separate references supposed to be from three different people? No way. And there's more. The way the paragraphs are indented. The use of semi-colons – I mean, who uses semi-colons in letters these days? There's no individual personality behind them either. I know doctors, and you can spot the sort of guy most of 'em are from the way they write. Add it all together, I plain didn't believe those references weren't all written by the same person.'

'It'll be easy to check, of course,' he said. 'All we have to do is ask the named referees if they know him and wrote those references. If we can get the names and addresses, of course. But we'll have to get his consent to seeing his employment file. Data protection and all that.'

'Do you have to?' she said uneasily. 'Because as I told you I got a peek at it kinda illegally. But long enough to take note of the names and addresses of the referees in question. Can't you just use the stuff?' She picked up her clipboard and raised the pad. Underneath it, tucked against the back, was a sheet of paper with her handwriting on it. 'Here you are.'

He looked at it for a long moment, thinking. 'This is tricky,' he said. 'Here I am with information to use, but can I legally use it? And more to the point, if I go into court with evidence gathered this way, will it be admissible?'

'Can't you make discreet enquiries?' she asked. 'Send a chap to these hospitals and get them to snoop about the way a private detective would? Then if we find we're right, we treat him as a prime suspect and act accordingly. Once we start watching him properly, surely he'll do *something* that'll give us the evidence we need without ever letting anyone know I – er – bent the rules a bit?'

'Hmm,' he said and was silent again for a while. 'I suppose so. It's highly improper, but this is a murder enquiry after all, and I'm not above crossing the boundaries occasionally if it's in a good cause. You genuinely think he could be our murderer?'

It was her turn to be quiet. 'It's hard to say,' she said at last. 'He seems such a nerd, so shy and – not helpless, exactly, but very vulnerable. But that has to be an act, of course, if he's a hoaxer. That alone takes enormous chutzpah. In which case, his whole manner is a con and he could well be our man.'

'Mmm.' He looked again at the sheet of paper. 'Birmingham,' he murmured. 'And ... well, the London one'll be the first we do. See what we can find there and then go on if necessary. When was he supposed to be there? OK, I'll put someone discreet on to that first thing in the morning. If he draws a blank there we'll have scored, and I'll send people on to Birmingham to check what happened there, and also to the medical school. We'll do it as a mispers search.'

'Mispers?' she said.

'You know that! Missing person.'

'Sorry, I forgot. Of course.' She sat up a little straighter then and smoothed the paper on the clipboard, not looking at him. 'Gus, I've one hell of a problem if you do find out that he's a fraud. An ethical quandary, in fact.'

'I'd have thought the reverse,' he said. 'It'll be a direct pointer to a piece of behaviour which, if it isn't usually murderous, certainly gives us reason to suspect he has a possible motive to murder. Someone finds out — maybe the theatre chap Mendez spotted something in his behaviour which gave him away? Or Lally Lamark noticed something in a patient's medical record? It makes sense.'

'I'm not sure I can see why Pam Frean should have died,' she objected, momentarily diverted. 'If that's the criterion.'

'That one's horribly easy,' he said. 'Easiest of the lot. They were lovers, right? They got together because they're both these shy, nerdy types. Or at least he's pretending to be like that, which is what attracts her. He plays along 'cause a fella has to get his jollies where he can, so they become lovers. She gets pregnant and demands marriage. He knows the chances of her finding out the truth about him are higher if they marry — when people call the banns and get marriage licences and so forth, it's amazing what information shakes out of the branches. And she gets too demanding, maybe. Whatever it is, he's already got his head round killing two people, what's one more?'

'And Sheila?'

'Ah! Again she knows something about him. Or she *seems* to.'

'Then why doesn't he just do the same to her as he does to the other three? Why mess about with abortive attempts that seem to be designed deliberately to fail?'

That stopped him. He narrowed his eyes as he looked at her, though his stare was glazed. Then his vision cleared and he opened his eyes widely, and said, 'Because he wants to know what it is that she knows! No good getting rid of her if there's evidence lying around that could be found by her successor, right? So he wants to frighten her off so he has time and space to look around for whatever it is she might have.' He jumped up and began to prowl the room, too excited by his thinking to sit still. 'That makes a lot of sense, George. The fella who went spying round in your lab, dressed in a white coat, the one Mrs Glenney scared off. The theft of Sheila's bag and the keys, and the break-in at her flat and then into your office to steal the notes of the people he's already killed – maybe he got more than that. Maybe he found something somewhere else in the department that he was looking for.'

'Sheila has a file that she calls her own. It isn't really, it's a sort of back-up, only it's on paper and not on disc. She stores a lot of past path. results and reports on staff and patients in these files in a little cubby hole of her own. Most of our later stuff's on computer, of course. So, whatever he's looking for would be from the past, not the present.' She shook her head then and subsided. 'No, I don't think it's that. I've looked around Sheila's files. Believe me, no one's been interfering in there. I could tell at once if they had.'

'Then it's what we said before. It's what the guy *thinks* she has. He hasn't found it yet, but he'll carry on till he does.'

'It's all falling apart in my head,' George complained, uncertain now of her original conviction that James Corton was indeed the object of their search. 'Why go to all this trouble just to cover up a hoax, like pretending to be a doctor when you're not? Let's face it, it happens a lot. It's not a capital crime – there are always cases being reported. Sooner or later they're flushed out because they display ignorance of an important subject that every doctor knows. That's his big danger. Unless . . .' She went off into a brown study of her own.

He waited a while and then said, 'Well? Let's be having you.'

'Unless,' she said slowly, 'he's already done something that's led to a patient's death. Maybe in one of his other hoaxing adventures – and we've no way of knowing where else he's worked, of course – he's done something that led to a death. Which means he's got a hell of a lot to hide, right? That would account for him being so willing now to risk deliberately killing people, in case one of them lets it out that he's a hoaxer and that starts a search for previous activities. After all, if you've killed once, what can they do if you do it again? No one gets executed any more, glory be. How does that sound?'

'It sounds sound,' he said gravely. 'A sound judgement. Listen George, we could be on to something good here. I'll start the wheels rolling in the morning.' He sat down, leaned back and stretched. 'What was the ethical quandary?'

'Mmm?'

'You said you had an ethical quandary: one hell of a problem, if we do find out he's a trickster.'

She'd forgotten her words in the thrill of the deductive chase but now it all came back to her. She bit her lip. 'Ideally no one lets him know if we find out he's a hoaxer, right? We just stake him out and watch for actions that could be evidential, right?'

'Of course,' he said, sounding almost shocked. 'You wouldn't rush off and tell him we've rumbled him, would you?'

'I might have to,' she said flatly.

'What?' He stared. 'Why on earth – oh Gawd!'

'Precisely,' she said. 'I wondered when you'd see it.'

'You can't let an unqualified fella loose on your patients any longer than you have to. In fact, you ought to report your anxieties to the hospital right now, yes?'

'If not to the management, at least to the Three Wise Men.'

'Who?'

'It's a rather neat system they have here in Britain. If a doctor spots something about a colleague's behaviour that worries him and doesn't want to alert management or make waves, he goes to one of the people – doctors, you know –

appointed by all the medical staff to be one of the Three Wise Men and says, "Say, Jack, old boy, I'm a touch bothered about old Fred. Tends to drop his tools in theatre, don't you know. Could be because he's always pie-eyed. What do we do about him before he kills someone and gets us all in the soup, hmm?"' She managed a creditable imitation of a drawling Oxford accent and he grinned fleetingly.

'Well,' she went on. 'I could go and tell them what I know, getting myself in trouble no doubt for snooping round the employment records, but I can wriggle out of that, I dare say. Once I tell them I'm off the ethical hook.'

'What would they do?'

'It's my guess they'd go straight to him to have it out. They wouldn't go to the management, not till they knew, in case he really is a doctor. But once they did he'd be out faster than you can say "hang about a bit", even though we're looking for a murderer here. And then we'll never get our evidence and these cases get listed among the great unsolved.'

'Then don't tell your Three Wise Men,' Gus said, sounding very reasonable.

'I've got to do *something*,' she said. 'There's no way I can let the guy go on working as an anaesthetist when I suspect that he isn't trained to do so! People die in operating theatres because of good anaesthetic practice, for God's sake. When the anaesthetist isn't a good one, the risk is enormous.'

'Has anyone died after one of his anaesthetics since he came here to Old East?'

'No,' she admitted. 'Not to my knowledge, though maybe there've been some near misses, and that was what alerted people like Mendez. Or Lally when she saw from the notes what had happened in a particular case? Hell, Gus, what do I do? Whether there's been a death already isn't what matters. Preventing a future one is the important thing.'

'I can see that,' he said. 'Shit! Have you no ideas apart from telling these wise monkey doctors? We all know what doctors are – when they're under threat, they close ranks tighter'n a duck's bottom, and that's watertight.'

'Like the police don't?' she said, firing up. 'I remember what happened when you were in trouble.'

'OK, OK,' he said hastily. 'No ancient history, please. Is there no way you can get him relieved of duty that won't make him suspicious?'

'I'm a pathologist,' she said. 'Not occupational health. And even they couldn't do anything unless he came to them with symptoms. Except when –' She stopped.

'Except?'

'Except when there are special pushes on infection control,' she said slowly. 'Do you remember? When we were looking into the baby case, a couple of years ago, I used the ploy of saying I was checking infection control and had to swab all the noses and throats of people in the maternity unit. I did it to find out where everyone was on a particular day, without actually interviewing them.'

He was grinning widely now. 'I remember that very well. So, a variation on a theme?'

'Indeed. Let me think.' He looked at her and then got to his feet and padded out to the kitchen to make them some coffee. When he came back with the tall cafetière steaming gently on a tray, she was scribbling furiously.

'So,' he said. 'What's the remedy?'

'MRSA,' she said.

'Ah.' He waited but she offered no more, still scribbling, scratching out and scribbling again.

'So, explain already!' he said plaintively. 'MRSA sounds like something to do with World War Two, like – like – ENSA, Every Night Something Awful. Or the NAAFI – Nasty Attacks of Awful Flatulence Immediately. Only they didn't say flatulence. So what's MRSA? Let me see – Make Randy Superintendents 'Appy?' And he leaned over and slid one hand into the neck of her shirt.

She wriggled and said absently. 'Shut up. I'm trying to

word this announcement right.' She went on writing as he sipped his coffee, but at last stopped, read over what she'd written, and then, satisfied, leaned back. 'Got it.'

'So, what is MRSA? Could it possibly be I was right?'

'Not at the moment,' she said crisply. 'It's Methycillin Resistant Staphylococcus Aureus.'

'Serves me bloody right for asking.'

'It means a dangerous pathogenic – disease-causing – organism that can make people very ill, which is resistant to treatment by the toughest of antibiotics, that's all. If it gets into a hospital – especially the theatres and surgical wards – it's the very devil to get out. We're always doing checks for it. If I set up a random sampling operation no one'll be a bit surprised. And after I do it, if I tell James Corton sadly that I'm very sorry, he has a dubious result and I'll have to keep him off duty until such time as I can clear him –'

'You mean he can have this disease without being ill?'

'He can carry it. Like typhoid or hepatitis or HIV – there are lots of things people can carry while being symptom-free themselves. And they can pass them on, that's the thing. I'll put this in hand tomorrow, send this note to all theatre staff and get the job done quickly. I'll have him off duty very fast indeed. How's that?'

'Great.' He slid an arm across the back of the sofa to rest on her shoulders. 'So, we've done a good job tonight. Let's go to bed and rest after our labours. Or rest eventually, anyway.' He leered sumptuously.

'I'll be glad to,' she said. 'Eventually. But right now, we've got to finish the paperwork.' And she flourished her clipboard at him.

'No point,' he said. 'We've got two suspects in there. First Corton, who has to be our main man, and, secondly, Klein.'

'I think Frances Llewellyn too,' she said.

'Why? She wasn't involved at St Dymphna's, was she?'

'The St Dymphna's connection only points at a link between the murders and Mendez. But she could have had

334

links with some of the other victims. She was researching gynae. matters, remember, so she might have treated Pam Frean.'

'That rabbit won't run, ducks. Frean has to be dead because she got pregnant. And with the best will in the world, even the cleverest of female gynae. researchers can't make other women pregnant.'

'Tell that to the infertility unit,' she said, laughing at him. 'No, fair enough. Her apparent motive is not obvious. But I have a gut feeling strong enough to put her down as a suspect.' She duly did, but didn't tell him she'd got the gut feeling from talking with Zack Zacharius about the case. It seemed wiser. 'And now we've got the three suspects, in order, with motives for three of the deaths. Next we have to look at some more headings. Like OPPORTUNITY and MEANS, and –'

'Bugger that for a game of soldiers,' he said with a sudden burst of energy. 'There's a lot of work before we can even begin to fill those columns in. We've done very well for tonight. I told you, come to bed!' He twirled an imaginary moustache and flashed his eyes at her. 'Come, my fair maiden, I will not be balked of my desires. I demand that you part with your womanly virtue instantly!'

'Oh, Sir Jasper,' she cried, throwing her clipboard on the floor beside her, 'spare my maiden blushes!'

'Some maiden!' he said and kissed her.

34

Getting the MRSA testing for theatre and other surgical staff set up the next day was less easy than she had hoped it would be. First of all she had to get financial consent from Ellen Archer, the Business Manager for the Investigations Unit as a whole, and since she had recently had some major expenses for the Radiology Unit (who were clamouring to get their hands on a Magnetic Resonance Imager) George almost had to go on her knees to do it. The only way she could persuade her was by lying freely about an increase in cases of infection in post-operative patients sent home, about which she had heard in an informal manner from local GPs. And she prayed inside her head that Ellen wouldn't take the time to check up and find out what a dreadful fabrication (and, incidentally, an insult to Old East's surgical care) that was.

'I'll tell you what I'll do, Ellen,' she said then, inspired. 'I can take a close look at the bit of forensic which is part funded by the police and Home Office, and see what I can push in there that belongs to us. It's not exactly honest, but what the hell – if the police can't take care of the sick occasionally it'd be a pretty poor show.' She produced the very English phrase with aplomb and grinned broadly at Ellen who cheered up considerably at the thought.

'If you can manage to do anything to stretch the edges of this bloody budget, I'll be one grateful lady,' she said.

'It's getting harder to do all I have to with the pittance I get.'

George promised to do her best and went off guiltily aware how much NHS cash she was spending on an operation that was more designed to help the police than Old East. But she comforted herself with the reflection that, after all, keeping a suspected hoaxer anaesthetist well away from patients while he was being quietly investigated had to be to the patients' benefit.

And then the actual work had to be done. She played with the notion of collecting all the swabs and then not culturing them, not even Corton's, and just telling Corton he was a possible carrier, but she rejected it. Suppose there really was a MRSA carrier in the place? If she didn't spot him now and he was noticed on a future screening . . . it didn't bear thinking of. So she set to work grimly.

Jerry looked surprised when she recruited him to help, as well as some of her junior staff, but went off obediently enough with his trays of swabs and specimen bottles, marshalling his assistants like an amiable sheepdog. He did very well indeed. When she checked with him at lunchtime, needing to know where she herself should take over, he grinned at her with great self-satisfaction, and reported, 'I've done the lot. Every surgeon, every technician, every surgical nurse. I know the uvulas of the staff a great deal more intimately than I want to, and I've been retched at and coughed over like a right 'un. If I wasn't afflicted with MRSA before I started and one of that lot has it, then I'll sure as hell have it myself now. Lots of luvverly sick leave, hmm, while I get cleared of it?'

'In your dreams,' George said. 'Seeing I can always put you on non-infection-area work if you happen to have a problem. Which I doubt. No Staph. organism would dare to come near you for fear of what it might catch.'

'Thanks a bunch,' Jerry said without ire. 'Listen, how essential was this? I don't think we have a problem here, have we? I've been asking around and I'm mystified. So're the staff. I know there's a lot of MRSA at some of the neighbouring hospitals, especially the geriatric ones, but us? The surgeons were a bit surprised too. Put out, I'd say.'

'I'm trying to make sure we stay that way. Clean as the proverbial,' said George quickly, mentally cursing herself for not telling Jerry some anecdotal tale for use with the staff before he set off. 'Do tell them all if they ask. It's a policy of perfection. I'm the sort that likes to mend the plumbing in good time rather than keep on mopping up puddles on the cellar floor.'

'Good thinking,' Jerry said. 'I'll put that about. Or ask Sheila to do it. You know how she likes a nice opportunity to gossip.'

They were sitting in George's office as she looked through the lists of people he had swabbed, making sure that the sole object of her search had in fact been caught in the net, and she looked up at that. 'Sheila,' she said thoughtfully.

'It was a joke,' Jerry said, holding up both hands in mock surrender. 'I wasn't trying to finger Sheila, believe me.'

'It's all right. But you have a point.' It could be an idea, one way and another. But she said that to herself. 'On your way, Jerry. Set up the cultures, will you? We really need fast results on this, and the sooner it's out of the way, all of it, the better.'

He went, and a short while afterwards George followed him oh-so-casually to wander around the lab until she 'happened' to find Sheila, who was in her little corner office filing some reports. For her own files probably, George thought crossly, and bit her lip. She would say nothing about it at present, but after all this was over that special file of Sheila's, she told herself, would have to go. It just made no sense to waste time on it, not in a lab where her own files were so extensive, and which in any case was properly computerized. And Sheila's collection appeared to act as a honey trap to the ill-intentioned, which was something they could all do without.

She perched on Sheila's desk as though for a comfortable

gossip. Sheila, a touch suspicious at first, took some time to realize what George wanted, but once she did, relaxed wonderfully.

'Oh, things are all right,' she said in response to a question about the state of morale at the hospital. 'It's a bit better than it was when we first became a Trust, which is reasonable, I suppose. I mean, it couldn't be worse! People seem to be getting used to the idea that we can do better things when we handle our own budgets, though they get fed up having to count the paperclips. And they get really fed up if they see other units wasting resources.'

'Mmm,' George said, with an air of having had a new idea. 'I wonder if the surgical lot will see my MRSA tests as a waste of money?'

'Probably,' Sheila said. 'They hate being swabbed anyway. Well, doesn't everybody?'

'Yes,' George said. 'Look, Sheila, do let me know if anyone says anything to you about it, will you? I'd hate to upset any of them, and I do want them all to know we're doing it for the best possible reason. To maintain Old East's high standards. We don't have any MRSA at present, and we have to be really vigilant to keep it out. Do put that about, won't you?'

'You're *asking* me to talk to people?' All Sheila's suspicions came back in a rush. George could see them glinting on every line of her sharp little face. 'After all the fuss you made about my not having my nose to the grindstone here every minute that God sends?'

'Well, why not?' George slid off the desk and headed for the door. 'It's quicker and I dare say cheaper to let you tell people than to get posters printed and shoved up on the noticeboards to be ignored or scribbled on.'

Sheila's face cleared. 'Well, yes, exactly. That's what I always say. You can't beat word of mouth. And you never know what sort of news I can pick up. It can come in useful, general information. I'll take a little stroll around later, shall

I? Just to see how people are talking about the MRSA swabbings. Would that be a good idea?'

'Why not?' George said. 'Why not? I'll be most interested to know. And,' she added as she reached the door, 'I'm sure people are dying to hear how you're getting on after all your awful experiences. And to know the police are hot on the trail.'

'Are they?' Sheila said eagerly. 'Do they have a suspect?'

'Oh, several, I believe,' George said. 'Of course, I don't know any details, but I do know they're hard at work on your case.'

Sheila nodded seriously, looking hard at George to be sure she wasn't just making soothing noises. 'Someone tried to kill me, after all. Three times!'

'So it would seem. Anyway, the police are really digging deep into every aspect of the situation. I think they're on to something – they've got an air of suppressed excitement about them. I wouldn't be surprised to hear they've really cracked it in the next couple of days.'

'Well, it's high time they did,' Sheila said. 'I'll tell people that – they'll be delighted to hear it. Ta for the information, Dr B.'

'You're welcome,' George said sweetly.

'She won't be able to resist embroidering,' George said to Gus when she reported her progress on the phone. 'It seemed to me that getting our suspects stirred up could be no bad thing, I mean, unless they think they're being suspected they'll do nothing to cover their tracks, will they? Having Sheila going around talking artlessly about the progress of the investigation and how much effort you're putting into it and how far you've got does no harm at all.'

'I just wish it were true,' Gus said. 'But we've hit the buffers on it. No leads anywhere. We've tried, God knows, but –'

'I know,' George said. 'But she'll still say you haven't, and that's the purpose of the exercise.'

'I thought you asked her to talk to people about this testing you're doing.'

'Gus, for heaven's sake, don't you understand Sheila at all? She'll have that at the bottom of her list. If she mentions the MRSA tests at all, I'll be amazed. It's the murders and what happened to *her* that excites her, and the more she talks the more uneasy our man will get, right? And the more likely to do something that'll reveal him.'

But the Sheila ploy didn't seem to work. The week ended in the usual flurry of extra activity in the lab as they caught up with their workload and the weekend crawled by with no sign of anyone running for cover or being anxious about possible discovery. Gus had put all sorts of things in hand, with his detectives checking facts about Corton in every part of the country he claimed to have worked, and all medical schools where he might be known, and could do no more. And George fretted.

Gus tried to persuade her to fill the time with some sort of pleasure, ranging from swimming ('Too many people at the pool. It'll be like Wall Street on a Bull market day,' she said) to a concert at the Festival Hall ('Too hot — and I can't pretend to really enjoy Harrison Birtwhistle.') and his favourite standby activity, bed ('Gus, you're verging on the obsessive!' 'Oh? And you're being obsessively virginal.') which last exchange at least had the virtue of making them both laugh. But laughing or not, she was restless, and it seemed to infect Gus too after a while.

'Shall we go back to the checklist?' George said after lunch on Sunday when the long afternoon seemed to stretch interminably in front of them.

'Not enough information,' he grunted. 'We'll have so many blanks on it that it'll be like doing the crossword with yesterday's clues for today's grid. We just have to be patient. Did you know that's a definition of great leadership? "Courageous, patience." And everyone says I have great leadership qualities.'

341

She ignored that. 'This is killing me,' she said and jumped to her feet to go over to the window-box to see if it had dried out. Since she had watered it just last night, it had not.

'I doubt it,' he said from the sofa and held out one arm. 'Come and sit down, do. If it's killing anyone, it'll be our man.'

'How do you mean?' She came and sat beside him, leaning back on his shoulder.

'I think he knows he's very near the end of his road,' Gus said. 'Let's do a recap and you'll see what I mean. We can do that much, at least, if it'll make you behave less like a giraffe on heat.'

'How do giraffes on heat behave? And how would you know? You've never seen one.'

'I can imagine, and they'd be like you. Long necks all aquiver with frustration. A recap, then?'

'I'll settle for anything that feels like doing *something*.'

'OK. This person has over the past few weeks been killing people. Why?'

She pondered, but not for long. 'He has a secret.'

'He or she.'

'Stick to he or we'll drive ourselves potty. On this occasion I'm prepared to allow man to embrace woman.'

'Thank you. OK, he has a secret, obviously. And it's also obvious that it's a secret that other people have found out. So, he has to kill them to keep his secret. Um, what sort of secret is it?'

She peered round at him. 'Does that matter?'

'I think so. If it's just a shameful secret, then I don't think he'd have gone so far to hide it. Actually, I'm not sure there is such a thing as a shameful secret any more. People come out about their sexuality and their dabbling with drugs and drink and whatever, their prison records and assorted other pecca- dilloes like bullets out of guns. It's getting very boring. Cer- tainly no one's ashamed of anything any more. So I reckon this has to be a profitable secret. Something that means big rewards if the secret can be kept.'

'That sounds reasonable enough. OK. A profitable secret.' She took a breath, unwilling to name him. 'I suppose that includes young Corton. If he is a hoaxer, that is, and we can't know that till your fellas report back on him. Though I'm not sure it does include him.'

'I would have thought it did. Look what he gets from his posing. Status. Money. Security.'

'What, as a junior doctor? Jesus, Gus, where have you been hiding for the past ten years? Junior doctors are paid less than peanuts and work all the hours God sends. As for security, there are fewer and fewer top jobs and more and more qualified doctors coming up for them. You really have to be the hottest of hot stuff to get a consultancy these days; most of the young doctors we get'll be lucky if they finish up in good general practices. That's where the real NHS action is these days. And the GPs don't earn a whole lot either. Not like back home where all doctors are rich. Here they're mostly struggling to keep up their mortgage payments. No, it's not money with Corton. And all he has to do if someone spots he's a fraud is get the hell out of Old East. He doesn't use real references after all. So if he thinks he's about to be fingered, he just hops it, gets a nice new name and applies for a job at some other sucker hospital, and starts all over again. Though why anyone should want to beats me! As you can see, there's not a lot in it for real doctors, let alone for hoaxers.'

'Hmm,' he said and stared at the ceiling thoughtfully. 'But maybe he's invested a good deal of effort into this particular bit of hoaxing? Perhaps he's trying to equip himself with a real set of references? If he can get out of Old East with them he's well on his way, surely? The old place has quite a good name in the doctoring trade, I'm told. And however few jobs there are, maybe he'll be contented with a nice ordinary job as a very average GP somewhere, since he didn't put in the ten years plus of studying to prepare him for it.'

She was silent for a while and then said unwillingly, 'OK, I guess it's just I don't want it to be him. There's something so, so –'

'I know. Nice and vulnerable about him. Forget it. Let's move on to the next. What's in it for Klein?'

'Money,' George said promptly. 'And professional disgrace. If he's been using patients at St Dymphna's as experimental material without the proper consents and protocols, then he'll do anything to hide that fact. I believe the pharmaceutical people can provide a fortune for anyone who looks as though they're going to produce a really new drug. He's got a lot to lose if anyone spots him in some sort of misdemeanour. The big drugs people are very smart cookies – they won't go anywhere near anything that's dubious. He'd be out without a hope of a future with them if he was discovered, and he's put something like ten years into this research of his, remember. It's a major investment.'

'What about Llewellyn?' Gus said. 'You were determined to include her.'

'The same,' George said. 'Her investment in her work is just as big. You've no idea what they put themselves through, these researchers. They live on a corn cob and a dish o' grits for years, they work all the hours there are, and at the end of it, what do they get? Either they hit the really big time and live high on the hog for the rest of their lives, or they just sink without trace, as someone else beats them in the search for whatever it is. For every Salk or Pincus who got there first with polio vaccine or the Pill, there were umpteen others who were left gasping on the beach. So she's in the same position as Klein.'

'And Zack.'

She thought about that carefully. 'Well, yes,' she said at length. 'I guess, yes. But you said –'

'I know I did. I've investigated him and everything about him checks out. He's bright to the point of being brilliant, according to the people at home in Canada. They're convinced he'll be a major high-flyer and –'

344

'He talks about getting a Nobel,' George said unhappily.

'Well, maybe he will. So hasn't he as much to lose as the other two?'

She shook her head. 'I don't think so. Because he's a true researcher and gifted with it. He won't want to take any short cuts. Not like Klein who tries his stuff out illegally on helpless patients.' She went a sudden red. 'That makes me sick, you know? Really sick to my stomach, just thinking about it. It's a disgusting thing to do.'

'I know,' he said and hugged her. 'It's ugly. But it doesn't mean he's a murderer.'

'It means he's more likely to be such. Isn't it easier for people who already behave reprehensibly to kill than for people who are essentially honest?'

'You may be right,' he said. 'But me, after all these years in the Bill, I'll tell you I'm never surprised, not by anything people do. So though your Zack got a clean bill of health from Canada, for my part, he's –'

'He's not my Zack,' George said, still pink. 'Don't hand out that sort of stuff. He's just a colleague. No more. A *colleague*.'

'Of course,' he said soothingly, looking down at her. His face was laughing. 'I just love to see you angry. Gee, you're beautiful when you're angry, Dr B.'

'And don't you patronize me with your dumb movie clichés, either!'

'Would I dare? Shall we go back to our recap?'

'I think we'd better.' She settled down again. 'So, how far are we? We've looked at Corton, at Klein, and at Llewellyn. And Zack. Anyone else?'

'You tell me,' Gus said. 'You know the place and the people in it much better than I do.'

She was silent for a moment and then jumped to her feet. 'Let's look in the Lamark file,' she said. 'It's the only one I've got since the others were stolen, and you never know, there may be something I've missed and that you'll spot. Or that I missed last time I looked and that'll jump out at me this time.'

She was rummaging at her desk as she spoke, and after a while she took hold of the big pile of *BMJ*s and *Lancet*s that lay on the front of it and took them over to Gus. 'You look through them,' she instructed, 'and see if you can find it. A buff folder – you know the sort of thing. I'll see if it's in my drawers.'

Ten minutes later, by which time Gus had got to his feet and was hunting round the room too, they had to admit the truth. Lally Lamark's file, which had been left tucked away in George's desk, had vanished. Completely and utterly.

35

When the phone rang, George was too abstracted in her anger and confusion over the disappearance of the file to answer it at once. She stood there, trying to work it out in her head: could she have taken it somewhere else? Could she have mistaken where she put it? But she knew perfectly well she hadn't forgotten. Her memory was as clear as iced water; she had put it at the back of her bottom drawer after reading it the last time. She had thought for a while when she started looking that she had left it on top of her desk but had then recalled perfectly well where it was. Except of course that it wasn't. And there were no signs of anyone interfering with the drawer, no indication that anyone had come to the flat to meddle with the desk apart from herself and Gus, neither of whom could for a moment be considered to blame for the file's disappearance. So, she told herself, staring at Gus with glazed eyes as the phone rang on, someone came in and took it. But how? And who? And how is it I never knew I'd been burgled?

Gus moved across the room towards the phone, and automatically she shook her head at him and reached for it. They had both long ago made a deal not to answer each other's phones, unless it was unavoidable, not only because inevitably it delayed the caller, who of course wanted the person he or she expected to answer, but also because they saw no need to put bellows of fact to the flames of surmise about their private lives which flickered and flared constantly around both Old East and Ratcliffe Street nick. When she picked it up it was a second or two before she could clear her mind of her preoccupation with the missing file to take on board what was being said to her. But once she did begin to understand, considerations like unnoticed burglars in her flat vanished like cockroaches when a light is switched on.

'Dr B.?' The voice was thin and shrill yet whispery, an odd effect that filled George's ear with a fear that was almost tangible. 'Dr B.? Oh, God, thank God you're there. Please do something. You'll have to do something – I tried to pretend I didn't know, that I didn't understand, but I do. I know now and he's – Oh, God, Dr B. you've got to come. Right away, please, I don't know what he'll make me do. He says we have to go out, he has a treat for me, he says, and oh, Dr B., please come –'

'Who?' George began, but she knew who it was. The voice was far too familiar, however distorted by anxiety right now. 'Sheila? What is it? Where are you? What's the matter?'

'It's – I think he blames me for it all, Dr B. I don't know why it is he's so – but he means it this time. I know he does. It isn't just – It isn't like the last three times. He *means* it. Oh!' She caught her breath and the sound became muffled, as though Sheila at the other end had put her hand over the mouthpiece. George felt the tension rise in her so quickly she was almost frantic.

'Sheila!' she cried. 'Sheila, for Chrissakes, what is it?' Gus moved closer to her, alerted by her voice. The muffled sounds stopped and Sheila's voice came back, bright and artificial now. 'Oh, yes, Suzy, of course. I'll do it for you – next Friday? I'll see if I can get a day off. I'll have to ask Dr B., but I dare say she won't mind ... Yes, do call me on Thursday to confirm it ... Sweetie, I have to go now. I'm so sorry, someone's waiting for me. I'm on my way out ... Bye-eee, sweetie.' And then, so softly that it was barely a whisper that George couldn't be sure she had heard, the sound changed, became a breath. 'Aldgate East,' it said, and the phone clicked and the dialling tone buzzed in her ear.

She stood there for a fraction of a second staring at Gus. He reached out and took her shoulder and shook it a little roughly. 'What was all that about?'

'It's Sheila. I can't . . . She was in a panic. Talked about a he, said he was taking her out and – Gus, I think she thinks whoever it is is going to try again. And this time succeed.'

'Is that what she said?'

George had hurled the phone back on the rest and was heading for her jacket and the front-door keys which were in the pocket, together with her bleep. 'Not in so many words, but she's terrified. And there was someone there. She covered up the phone and then came back pretending to make a date with a girlfriend, and then she whispered, "Aldgate East." Oh, come *on*, Gus. We must hurry. There's something Godawful going on. You should have heard her – you'd understand then.'

Gus was blessedly quick on the uptake. He was shrugging into his own jacket, pulling on his shoes and following her to the door in a fraction of a second. They both went rushing down the stairs to the street as though half a dozen Rottweilers were after them. He opened the car door and had the engine started almost as she scrambled in. He turned the wheels with a loud screech of protesting tyres and headed for Tower Bridge and the tangle of streets going north that would bring them to Aldgate East underground station.

It was quiet in the street, at first, a typical Sunday summer afternoon in London. Children in minimal clothes ran around, but listlessly, because the sun was still relentlessly beating down in what was turning out to be one of the longest and hottest heat waves in London's records, and mothers sat on doorsteps watching them in a lackadaisical fashion. Once the car left Bermondsey behind and crossed the river, which glinted with eye-piercing brilliance, and reached the City streets, peace descended; there wasn't a pedestrian in sight, let alone a car, and they'd get there very quickly now.

And so it was until they reached Whitechapel High Street and Gus took a screaming right turn to bring them up to Aldgate East Station. Then it all changed. The road was suddenly full of cars, very slow-moving cars which had been polished to a gloss so high that every building they crept past was reflected in bonnets and wings and side panels, and each of them packed solid with people, women and children and old men with, generally, one proud younger man driving with infinite care. The pavements too were thronged with people; the glitter and flurry of every possible colour as well as gold and silver and bronze threading and embroidery from sumptuous saris jostled with somewhat tightly fitting but clearly much prized Western-style suits worn by the men who accompanied them. All the people they could see were Asian, and if George and Gus hadn't been so filled with anxiety, they'd have enjoyed the spectacle of a shabby bit of London pretending to be a smart corner of Calcutta; but the charm of what they could see made no impact at all on them, except to fill them with a desperate frustration.

'Christ!' Gus swore. 'It's Brick Lane out in force.'

'Oh, Gus, can't you push? Shout at them, make them move! Haven't you a siren? No, don't – that's the last thing we want. Oh, hell!' She leaned out of her window, trying to peer through the hubbub as her belly knotted with impotent rage.

She managed to last another five minutes, no more, during which Gus had at least been able to insert his car into the stream of traffic. He was using his hooter as hard as he could but it made no difference because so was everyone else, responding to his vicious stabs of noise with their own, clearly assuming he was offering a greeting. The resulting cacophony was head ringingly loud. Eventually she could stand it no longer.

'I'll get there on foot,' she shouted, wrenching her door open. 'Get to me when you can – and maybe see if you can

350

call up some help too?' And she almost fell out of the car even as Gus, swearing again, reached to try and pull her back. But he was too late and she hurled the car door shut and dodged across the stream of traffic as the hooters started up again, this time reprovingly, and headed for the pavement.

She had since childhood suffered from nightmares in which she was being forcibly held back from something desperately important, or in which she couldn't find the place she urgently needed to get to, or couldn't move her limbs properly so that she felt like a character in a slow-motion advertisement for hair spray, and now, pushing and twisting her way through and past these gloriously clad people it became very dreamlike. Some of them moved aside with reasonable speed as she gasped, 'Pardon me,' at them; others took offence – especially, unfortunately, the larger and heavier women – and stood firm, glaring at her and shouting incomprehensibly as the folds of their lovely clothes shimmered and glinted, making impossible barriers. She reached such a stage of fury that she shrieked at full blast directly in the face of one such woman who was being more obstructive than most; the woman stared at her, and then, her face crumpling into frightened tears, stepped aside. At last George could move, because the little altercation seemed to have sent a message rippling out that someone needed to get through fast. A swathe seemed to open in front of her and she went streaking along it in the direction of the station.

And reached it almost in surprise, her breath painful in her chest and her pulses pounding. It was not the most handsome of underground stations, and at this point consisted simply of a pair of staircases plunging downwards. Both staircases were again filled with dawdling saried figures, most of them coming up from the depths, and she thought somewhere deep in her mind, Oh, no, a train must have just come in. Maybe she's already gone – and gone where? She almost hurled herself bodily into the throng.

Again the crowd parted to let her through, and she

realized, without having to think about it, that they were behaving as London tube passengers always did by making way
for someone perceived to be an anxious traveller; and she was
able to reach the booking hall below very quickly.

The crowd was less thick here as the recently arrived passengers disappeared to join their friends on the streets overhead. She thought briefly, Wonder what's going on? A festival
day? A religious day? And then dismissed it. It wasn't important enough except inasmuch as it meant there were too many
people about getting in the way.

But as she stopped just at the foot of the stairs, by the big
bank of self-operated ticketing machines, she thought again.
The crowds were in fact a protection and a help, surely. If
Sheila and he – whoever he might be – were here and the
place were almost empty, not only would she see them easily,
they would see her. Suddenly she remembered vividly Gus's
face and voice talking about evidence. Over and over again
he'd said, in case after case, 'It's not enough that we think we
know who did what and with which and to whom, we have to
have hard evidence.' If she were seen now by whoever *he* was,
he'd immediately pull back from whatever it was he planned
to do and then where was the evidence?

But if he didn't know he was observed, then what about
Sheila? The thought of Sheila as a tethered lamb acting as
bait in the middle of the lion's clearing was more than
George could bear, and she peered around, while staying as
close to the wall and ticket machines as possible. She couldn't
exactly melt into them, but at least she wouldn't be as visible
as she would be standing in the middle of the shabby little
concourse.

The people in the area were still mainly Asians, but there
were a few more who were not. There were Afro-Caribbeans
and some whites too, even a couple of Chinese, which made a
more anonymous crowd, greatly to George's relief. She must
have stood out like a pimple on a billiard ball in that glorious
Asian crowd up above.

There was no sign of Sheila, George saw very quickly. Nor were there any station staff about, and the ticket office was closed. She cursed under her breath. No one she could tip off to watch out for Gus if she moved away from here. She looked across the concourse towards the stairs that led down to the platforms and realized gratefully how well suited Aldgate East station was to her needs. Both platforms, for trains going either east or west, could be observed from the top as though from a minstrel's gallery. This was one of London's older tube stations, designed, no doubt, to allow steam to escape from the old engines used before electricity took over. It meant that she could move closer to the stair-head and see who was on the platforms almost certainly without being seen herself.

She moved with great casualness through the people in the concourse. There were more now arriving to catch trains; clearly the traffic of people dressed-up for a Sunday outing was a two-way effort, but now she was grateful for them. Their presence meant she would be less noticeable, she told herself hopefully as she went to lean against the barrier at the top of the stairs that led down to the trains, and looked down.

Below her, two pairs of rails gleamed in the dull electric light; the platforms, with their edging of posters and the fa-miliar circles crossed with a line on which the name of the station was clearly written, made a handsome perspective as they stretched away from her to the mouth of the tunnel at the far end. She couldn't see the near tunnel mouth because that was virtually under her feet. She could however read the sign on the electronic indicators easily. 'Next train Ealing Broadway', she read over the platform that took the trains travelling west and she thought, Ealing Broadway? Why should she want to go to Ealing? She tried to recall the names of the stations on the way; the train would go through the city first: Tower Hill and Monument and Cannon Street, and then ... but her usually reliable memory collapsed. She couldn't see any further, remembering only vaguely that the train went through fashionable areas like Sloane Square and South Kensington as well as less attractive ones.

She stood there staring down at the platform, trying to be systematic in her observations. She started at the far end of the eastward-travelling platform, mainly because it was the least crowded, and raked it with her eyes, moving her gaze across from side to side as neatly as though she were a ploughman in a very narrow field. She registered a couple of shaven-headed, earringed and tattooed boys with cans of lager staring pugnaciously at a very large group of chattering Asians, clearly loathing them but, happily, outnumbered and unable to get vicious in consequence. Good, George thought and carried on.

Some nondescript women in dull clothes, lost in a middle-aged reverie; a trio of pretty girls in skin-tight pelmet skirts that displayed interminable lengths of leg which were beginning to distract the lager-drinkers. No sign of Sheila or anyone else she knew.

She glanced over her shoulder looking for Gus: no sign of him either, and she bit her lip and returned her attention to the platforms, now looking at the westward-bound and more crowded side. Clearly a train was due very soon; people were moving towards the edge of the platform as people always did when they were regular users of the underground, seeming to know instinctively just where in the system their train was and how soon it would arrive.

She started her raking efforts again, this time beginning at the other end of the platform and the tunnel mouth from which the approaching train would emerge. She saw a woman with a small child in a baby buggy; a couple of older children who were squabbling over something George couldn't see, but which made them wail loudly as their angry mother tried to distract them; some more Bengali men, this time wearing the pyjama suits that had once been their comfortable dress in their home village; a cluster of teenagers with knapsacks, jabbering to each other and looking very foreign in the dimness with their glinting yellow hair and broad shoulders. Scandinavian tourists, George thought. Two people standing fairly near the edge, looking at each other and –

It was like a douche of very hot water hitting the back of her head and trickling down her back. She caught her breath, and the hot water immediately became icy cold.

Sheila, standing near the edge with her back to the railway line, her head tipped up and chattering vivaciously with a man, a tall man. A man George knew. She felt sick. She had been so sure and now she knew she was so wrong, so very, very wrong, and it hurt.

Zack, his hands in his pockets, looking down at Sheila with an oddly quizzical expression on his face, seeming to concentrate on her chatter, but now and again looking over her head towards the tunnel from which the train would arrive, large, noisy and sparking with electric power.

Somehow George stopped herself from shouting, from warning Sheila to move away from the edge, to get closer to the back of the platform where she could press herself against the big posters advertising some banal pop concert. She did so by biting her tongue and looking round more urgently for Gus. Still no sign of him, nor of anyone who might possibly be a policeman. She was alone and would have to cope alone. Somehow.

She pressed forwards to go down to the platform and then realized with a shock of horror that she had no ticket. She couldn't get past the barrier, and she looked over her shoulder at the platform below, trying to estimate how long it would be before the train came, holding her head up as she tried to identify the breath of fetid air that an oncoming tube train pushes ahead of itself. There was none, yet still the people on the platform showed their readiness for it. They knew it was close.

'Oh, shit!' She ran for the ticket machines, scrabbling in her pocket for a coin. She had managed to make the machine discharge a ticket, and turned to run back to the platforms, leaving her change behind her, when someone pulled on her arm. 'It's all right,' she gasped. 'I don't want the change. You take it.' She tried to pull away, but whoever it was held on. She whirled, her mouth open to shout her fury; and then stopped, amazed.

James Corton was standing there, his face white and glistening with sweat and staring at her with eyes so wide she could see the whites all round the pupils. She thought for a moment he was ill, but it was agitation. He shook her arm and said breathlessly, 'Thank God, there's someone here. You've got to help. Something awful's going to happen. You've got to help. Come on.'

'What –' she began, pulling away from him, wanting to run down to the platform. He seemed to be pulling her in the other direction. 'I can't go –'

'This time it's for real!' He almost wept it. 'This time it really will happen! You've got to help. Please listen to me – he was down there with her and this time it'll happen, I know it will.'

She gaped at him and then managed to speak. 'Zack,' she said. 'Zack is down there with Sheila. And you say that –'

'Yes, oh yes! Please, get the police to do something. I don't know what but –'

'Come with me. Get yourself a ticket and come on.' She whirled and ran to the barrier.

He didn't stop for a ticket as she pushed hers into the slot and the barrier arm let her through; he just took a flying leap and was over easily and then the two of them were running down the stairs towards the platform where as far as George could see nothing had changed: Sheila was still standing with her back to the tunnel and Zack was still standing in front of her as the other people on the platform went on pushing closer still to the edge. Because this time there was no mistaking it. That long sighing breath of air came towards them from the tunnel, and a glint of light and the distant sound of an approaching train, and George ran as she never had, pushing past the people at the back of the waiting crowd who had, blessedly, left a space between themselves and the curving wall, aiming for the far end of the platform.

James overtook her, running with long easy lopes. She saw him come up to the waiting pair and reach forwards just as the train came bursting out of the tunnel. George shouted but she couldn't be heard above the noise the train was making, except by people near her, who turned to stare and then turned back the other way as a scuffle developed.

George couldn't see what happened then. Only that all three of them, Sheila and Zack and James, were struggling in a heap on the platform ahead very near the edge. Or was it all three of them? she thought as she desperately covered the last few yards. Surely there are just two there? Who then is on the line? Because the train had pulled to a shuddering wheel-screaming stop well before the far end of the platform and all around there were loud cries and expostulating voices and inside her head a shriek of rage and pain and misery as she realized she was too late and Sheila wasn't there.

36

Lights, she remembered. Lights and noise and people shrieking and chattering and children bawling and then Gus and the police and paramedics and trolleys and onlookers being herded away before the work of clearing the ghastly mess that had been Sheila from the line; and then, at last, long after, sitting there in the awkward yet oddly comfortable chairs at the nick, listening, nodding, asking questions and listening again as Gus made notes, and both of them, Zack and James, filled in the holes that no amount of thinking on her part could ever, she knew, have managed to get on to her own clipboard. And she felt the shame of her own failure to see the truth sweep into every last corner of her.

Sheila, the architect of all that had happened at Old East these past weeks? Sheila, the gossiping, sharp-tongued yet tolerable colleague, a murderer as cold and calculating as any murderer ever had been? It seemed impossible; but she had listened to all that Zack and James had told Gus, and the truth of it was inescapable. It had been Sheila. George's fury at the way Sheila had behaved added to her own sense of failure in not recognizing the woman's true personality warred inside her to a point where she felt downright sick to her stomach.

But she drank the coffee that kept coming – Gus had clearly trained his staff well on that issue – and watched the two faces, Zack's and James's, as the light changed with the ending of the daylight and the slow ascendancy of the electric bulbs, until, by eleven o'clock, they both looked washed-out, grey and haggard – but that was as much exhaustion as shock and, as she told herself a little wryly, a form of post-traumatic disorder.

She interrupted then. Gus had just asked James what he promised was the last question, and James had managed, somehow, to answer it, though between stiff lips that could barely move.

'That guy's at the very end of his rope,' she said. 'I know you have to do your job and all that stuff but there comes a point when it's sheer cruelty to go on, whatever he did.'

Gus looked at her sideways and made a grimace. 'Does she bully you fellas at work the way she bullies me?' he murmured at Zack. 'Never a decent word to say to a bloke doing his best as best he can, like what I am right now.'

'I doubt you have much of a problem,' Zack said, trying to smile but failing. 'And she's right. He's about to keel over.' He too looked across at James, who was sitting upright, glassy-eyed, pale and sweating, staring at nothing at all. 'And I'm not feeling up to much myself, thanks to everyone for noticing so kindly.'

'You'll get over it,' George said, more unkindly than she had meant to. 'You're older, and anyway you're not in the sort of shtook he is.'

'Oh, aren't I? Aren't I really?' He was very sardonic. 'I must have missed something you worked out and never told me. Like that the entire bloody research side of Old East *isn't* about to collapse. Like I *haven't* got to start all over again somewhere else, if I'm not too old and past getting any sort of post. Like I *don't* have to try to get my bloody research started up again when no one'll touch a guy who's worked with crooks like Klein. Jesus, that man was actually *paying* a social worker at St Dymphna's to let him do illicit testing on live human subjects! And if that sort of association isn't bad

359

enough, I let someone help with some of my procedures who was a lousy phoney con artist.' He threw another look at James, this time with anger and loathing mixed in with his pity. 'I can't exactly see the funders falling over themselves to keep us going, though maybe you can. I'm left with shit, after all these years of –'

'At least you're alive,' Gus cut in quietly.

There was a little silence and Zack dropped his head and stared down at his hands, loosely linked on his lap. 'Fair enough,' he said at last. 'I suppose I should be more grateful.' Then he looked up at George, 'I'm very grateful to you, George. Believe me. Without you –'

'With me you'd be a piece of chopped meat, the way Sheila is, and waiting in my mortuary for a post-mortem,' she said loudly and very clearly. 'I wasn't the one who got to you in time. James was. He arrived first. He stopped her from shoving you on the line under the train. Her idea was just to get me there to be a witness, see what had happened *after* it had happened. To see that the last attempt by her mysterious assailant had only failed because somehow she'd managed to overcome him and push him on the line as he'd intended to push her. RIP Zack Zacharius.'

'She was a bloody clever bitch,' Gus said, lifting his sheaf of notes. 'Only, on this last effort, she got her timing wrong. George got there too soon and buggered it up for her. So you did your share, George, more than your share. Now, stop squabbling. Put that boy down on the couch over there and then let's go over what I think is my case. It'll never get to court, except for the inquest, of course. But I want to get it all clear in my head, and in yours, both of you. You need to know, Zack. Fair enough? I've sent for sandwiches, by the way. You might be ready for them.'

Obediently, they put James on the couch. He didn't demur. He didn't do anything, simply co-operated like an automaton in any way they wanted, moving his legs when they propelled him forwards, lying down when George put a hand on his chest, lifting his head to accommodate a cushion when she put one there and then just lying staring upwards at the ceiling and saying not a word throughout. He was still pale and sweating, but his pulse was reasonably strong when George checked it. She put his condition down to his mental state rather than to any immediate physical problem, and went back to her own chair to listen to Gus, while still keeping an eye on James.

Zack was already sitting waiting; Gus looked over George's shoulder at James and then nodded. 'OK. Here we go then. Here's the scenario as I understand it. The complete story we'll never get, I don't suppose, since the only real witness is a very dead person. But between you two you know enough to add to what we've got. Like I said, here goes.'

He took a deep breath, reached out to switch on his desk light, and at the same time lifted his chin to bawl something incomprehensible. A policeman on the other side of the glass wall that separated Gus's room from the main incident room reached a hand in and switched off the overhead light. The room became softer, more relaxed, and George felt her weary shoulders sag a little. But not too much. She had to listen.

'All right,' Gus said. 'Sheila Keen, whom I thought I knew and had the measure of, and have done these past four or five years, was a desperate woman. I always knew she wanted a man, we all did. But it wasn't just sex, as some people suspected – like Jerry at the lab. No, she wanted much more. She wanted to settle down and marry. Wanted status. I also knew she was a gossip, liked to know what she could find out and enjoyed spreading it around.'

'We thought we knew all that too,' George said in a low voice. 'But there was so much more to it.'

'Indeed there was.' Gus shook his head at her. 'No more interruptions, George. This is my patch, OK? Now, Sheila had allowed these two needs to become obsessive. To get a husband, that had become the be-all and end-all for her. She'd always been on the lookout for a man, of course, but when she was younger, I guess she was like a lot of self-important pretty women: too choosy. Too – calculating, I suppose. Anyway, here she was, old in her own eyes – she was fifty-one by the way, though she'd managed to keep that pretty quiet – been lying about her age for years – and obsessed with getting a husband, and with using the information she collected to help her do it. She started on blackmailing people, first for money, I suspect, simply because she could. It's so easy, I'm afraid. Once people know someone has found out something bad about them, they try to bribe their way to safe secrecy. They set themselves up for it. We don't know when it started, none of us do. But she must have been at it for some time from what James told us.'

They all looked at James, but he showed no reaction at all. 'She'd nosed out within a couple of weeks of his arrival that he was a phoney, that he wasn't qualified, that his references were totally naff. But she told him if he played the game her way she'd help him. And she did. Introduced him to her friends at St Dymphna's to get some extra experience there. Did all sorts of things, it seems, to make him aware of any gaps in his knowledge, really coached him in the sort of hospital background stuff you can't get from books, only from actually living the life. Fun at first for James. Till she started to ask for money. First he had to give her his extra earnings from St Dymphna's. He did it. Then she wanted some of his money from Old East. She must have had a hell of a nest egg squirrelled away somewhere. But that wasn't enough. She also got him to spy on other people and to do other little jobs for her. Right, James?'

Again there was no response from the wide-eyed figure on the couch. Gus sighed softly and went on. 'She got him to, among other things, pinch the files she wanted from George's office.'

'I can't understand that,' Zack said. 'All she had to do was go in and help herself, surely?'

'And be an immediate suspect with all the rest of the lab

staff? Do me a favour,' Gus said, and George, who had opened her mouth to make exactly the same point, subsided.

'No. It was better to have a faked robbery that gave her a complete alibi. She was pretty pissed off, of course, when she only got hold of the notes of two of the people she'd killed.'

'How can we be sure of that?' Zack said, suddenly argumentative. 'I mean, she's dead and she can't be asked, and –'

'I'll come to that,' Gus said, very magisterial all of a sudden. 'Hear me out. She was, I said, pretty pissed off to find one of the files missing. Took her a while to get it, but she did eventually, the easy way. She had copies of George's personal keys, just as she has of every key she ever got her hands on – or could borrow for an hour or two. She simply used them to nip into the flat and help herself. She's probably been in and out of your flat, George, umpteen times.'

'It makes me feel sick to think of it,' George said. Her voice shook with controlled loathing. 'I'll have to move. I'll never feel comfortable there again.'

'I know,' Gus said. 'There's time to talk about that, and I promise we will. I have a few thoughts of my own on that subject. Right now back to my case. Let's get this clear. She gets James to steal the files because she wants the records of what happened to those three people. She also made him help her stage the threats on her life, which were designed solely and wholly to make sure no one would ever suspect her of any involvement in those other killings, if ever there was any doubt about them. The thing is she was a fool, really – the sort of clever-clever fool who ruins it by over-egging the pudding. Because of the ways she used to kill both Tony Mendez and Lally Lamark, they would never have been labelled as murders if she hadn't added so many fancy touches. Overdramatic, that was the thing. Well, there you go. She *did* overdo it, so we investigated more than we might have done. Thank God.' He brooded for a while. 'I wish I had enough staff and enough money in my lousy budget to treat every case the way I'd like to. But there isn't that much manpower and bloody money in the whole stinking system.'

'Watch it, buster,' George murmured. 'Your politics are showing.'

'Eh? Well, all right, I'll go on. So, she kills Tony on account of he was getting fed up with paying her so much of his money, and also was concerned he was drinking too much again. He might get talkative when he was boozed – a hell of a risk. So he had to go. That's my guess, and it can never be more than a guess, I know. But it strikes me as bloody obvious. He probably threatened to tell all and admit to the people at St Dymphna's that he'd been knocking back the old booze, and ask for their help and support. Even if he didn't threaten to tell all, he was a risk. When he was afraid of losing his job at Old East he was vulnerable. When he stopped being vulnerable, there was nothing to keep him giving her money the way he had all those years. Poor bastard. Once he'd decided to throw in the towel and confess then she'd had to kill him. She'd have gone down for blackmail. And she knew it.'

'*You* can't know that,' Zack said, sounding mulish.

'James said she did,' Gus reminded him. 'He was the one who had to do her cover-up, remember. It's been killing the poor little bastard. All he wanted was to play doctors, without having to do all the academic work for seven years, or however long it is. Probably just wasn't up to it. Not enough brain power. But he wouldn't have killed anyone. Once she'd done it though, and got him sucked in by making him do errands that had seemed innocent enough to him till afterwards, well, he was unable to extricate himself.'

'Making him an innocent victim?' Zack jeered. 'Robbing George's office of files? And breaking into Sheila's own flat?'

'She told him that the robbery of George's files was a gag. Ordered him to mess the files up a bit, just to annoy George, and to take out the ones she asked for as much as a joke, as anything else. She also asked him to rob her own flat as an insurance scam. That upset him too, but he felt totally helpless.

Like I said, a clever bitch, Sheila. She also gave him the box of chocolates to put in the ENT Ward, said she wanted the staff to know how kind George was being. He did that gladly, imagining she'd been given them directly when she arrived in the ward after the car fire, which again, she fixed herself. Sheila knew precisely what she was doing, and though she took risks, she knew how far she could go. Which was as far as risking other people eating those chocolates too — Sister Chaplin, say.'

'She poisoned those chocolates herself?' George shook her head unbelievingly. 'It's crazy!'

'Crime is,' Gus said. 'This sort. It's hardly the activity of a rational person. Sheila wasn't rational. She wanted what she wanted and she'd kill to get it. Remember, she'd been building this up for years. She'd had a hospital reputation as a husband-hunter for ages — everyone knew that, really, even if they did imply it was just sex she was after. And when a desire gets unsatisfied for years, it can literally drive people crazy. I think that's what happened to Sheila Keen. She'd reached the stage of desperation. She was getting old, so old that every month that passed made her more and more fearful she'd never get her man, and she'd do anything to get what she so badly wanted. And used dumb innocent idiots like that boy over there to help her do it. He was just a handy weapon to her. Corton isn't the brightest, is he? If he were he'd have got himself into medical school.'

James still lay silently on the couch, but now his eyes moved and he looked appealingly at Gus.

'Sorry, mate,' Gus said to him. 'But whether you like it or not, it's true. You've been a right Charlie. Let me spell it out more. You fiddled with that bottle in the Beetle cupboard in the lab and changed the chemicals. A gag, she said. I bet. Her and her gags! It must have been obvious it was dangerous. You saw afterwards what it did to Jerry. You must have felt pretty Godawful about that.'

This time James closed his eyes. It was clear he accepted all that Gus said as accurate.

'So there you are. She killed Tony to stop him turning on her. She killed Lally Lamark because she was a smart lady, almost as smart as Sheila, who spotted something in a set of notes that alerted her. Not her own notes at all probably, but some others – the fact Sheila said it was her own notes she wanted to look at doesn't mean it was true, does it? Sheila showed her someone else's notes, secretly – and burned the evidence when you caught her, remember. But when she got the request from Lally, for whatever it was, she realized this was a potentially dangerous opponent. And knowing how to fiddle with the woman's insulin pen, she did just that.'

'You can't know that,' George protested. 'That has to be surmise.'

'Tell me a better one,' Gus said.

George was silent and Gus nodded. 'See what I mean? Some of the time we have to use a bit of informed imagination. Not with Pam Frean, though. No need for imagination there.'

He stopped and Zack lifted his head, and then bent it again. He seemed to thrum with tension, and for a moment George felt aware of embarrassment, as though she knew Gus was about to strip him naked, and she'd have to sit and let him do it.

'Poor Pam Frean,' Gus said gently. 'Poor little Pam. That one is down to you, Zack, isn't it? You didn't kill her, of course, but if you hadn't played your games with her, she'd be alive still.'

Zack said nothing. He sat very still with his head down, staring at his hands on his lap as though he'd never seen them before.

'So let's get it out of the way. You're the man Sheila had her beady eyes on, isn't that so? You flirted with her, and she chatted you up like a right 'un, making it very clear she wanted you. It wasn't only sex, was it? She wanted a clever, successful husband with a good future and the promise of a good income she could fiddle with. She wasn't above having a bit of fun with a man like Jerry Swann' – George made a grimace – 'but she wanted her own way when it came to the real business of marriage. It took her a long time before she realized that you weren't up for that. That you chatted up every reasonably attractive woman just because she was a woman.'

'Gee, Gus, thanks for making me feel real good,' George murmured.

'Don't be daft.' Gus was sharp. 'It's not your fault, it's not any woman's fault when men behave like that, any more than it was Zack's fault, except for swanning from one girl to another, letting 'em think he cared about 'em.'

'Get on with it, friend,' Zack said. 'You might as well make a job of it.'

'OK. Well, for you women are like a box of toys. You play games with them until you don't want them any more and fancy a new one.' He didn't look at George, but she knew she had reddened. 'But one of your toys fell heavily in love. This to Pam Frean wasn't a game but a grand passion. Zacharius was her God-given man, not to put it too high. And when you'd had your fling and wanted to move on, she found she was pregnant.'

'I thought she used a contraceptive, for Chrissakes!' Zack burst out. 'What girl doesn't, these days? The girl was so sweet, and eager, so –'

'So much in love,' Gus said, 'that it seemed to her the right thing to make love. No matter what her religious training and education. She loved you. And hers was a loving religion, not the cruel one everyone thought it was. Strict but loving. That's your problem, you see, Zack. They simply fall on their backs for you.' Again, he didn't look at George. 'As Sheila did too. Only when she found out she had a pregnant rival, she didn't panic. She was much cleverer than that – her sort is. She *befriended* her. Found out that she was planning to go home and have her baby and learn to live without the love of her life, while devoting herself to God and her child. At first Pam felt guilty – when she was first diagnosed by Hattie – but after that, she was OK about it. Had plans for the future, once she got over her initial shock. So, Sheila had to act. She couldn't be sure you wouldn't get more involved with Pam, under the circumstances. The birth of a baby does have that effect on people, even Don Juans like you. And she couldn't risk that because you were to•be *her* property. If she couldn't have you, no one would.'

'But Sheila took it so well when I told her I wasn't – that I already had a wife, and had no notion of being divorced because my wife's a Québecois and a Catholic.' Zack said it almost despairingly.

'Oh, took it excellent well, i'truth,' said Gus in rolling Shakespearean tones. 'So well she invites you to come out with her for a last farewell party and has every intention of pushing you under a train. Once George told her we were close to cracking the other two killings, she had to cut her losses, to keep us off her trail, didn't she?'

'It was my fault then, that . . .' George looked stricken, but Gus shook his head at her.

'Don't blame yourself. She'd have done it eventually, now she was convinced Zack wasn't going to come across with a wedding ring. And if she hadn't been so cocksure about her hold over James, and made no effort to hide from him how she felt about things, she'd have done it too. And you'd have gone down in history as a triple murderer who got done in by the person you'd meant to make your fourth victim.'

'So I'm not so stupid after all.' James's voice came thick and cracked from the couch. 'Am I?'

'What?' Gus said.

'Not so thick. It was me who realized what she was going to do, me who realized she'd killed the others, so she was going to kill Zack. And me who stopped her.'

'Yes,' Zack said. 'Thanks.' And he meant it, painful and spare though it sounded.

'I'm ashamed,' George said. 'I should have spotted it – Pam Frean's death being definitely murder, I mean.'

'Why should you?' Gus said sensibly. 'Jesus, no one would have, in your position. I reckon she used George Joseph Smith's method – the Brides in the Bath guy from a hundred years or so ago. Nice girlfriend comes round to spend the evening with preggy Pam and all that stuff, and then when she gets tired she says she'll help her in her bath, wash her back and so forth. In the tub Pam goes, and Sheila, who must have spiked her whatever-they-drank with Valium, takes her by the ankles and pulls hard, and down she goes, and stays down, because Sheila keeps her legs in the air. That's all there is to it, apart from tapping out a suitable message on the ward computer as soon as she got back to Old East. And because people are so used to seeing Sheila all over the place, they pay no attention to her.' He shook his head with a sort of admiration. 'You've got to hand it to her. She got the tone of the note spot on, didn't she? And found the ideal way to kill her. It wasn't hard, not even for a small woman.'

'The girl died at once of a sort of shock reaction,' George said. 'I'd better read up some Victorian forensic pathology, I guess.'

'Don't be ashamed of being conned by the likes of Sheila Keen,' Gus said. 'I was too. And I've been dealing with bad 'uns a lot longer than what you have, lady. And don't forget, you knew her so well, had known her for years.'

'Which is something I couldn't forget,' George said in a low voice. 'Not ever.'

'Any more than I could,' Zack said. He suddenly stood up. 'Am I being charged with anything? I'm dead on my feet, I need bed. I want to go.'

'You're free as air,' Gus said. 'As long as you come back to give me a statement when I ask you.'

'Sure,' Zack said. 'I'll be back.'

He made for the door and then looked down at James, who was now lying fast asleep. 'Do you need help with this fella?'

369

'I'll look after him,' Gus said. 'I have to arrest him for the hoax doctor bit. Poor little bastard.'

'Let me speak in his favour at his trial, will you? He saved my life, after all.'

'If you can help him, I'll let you know,' Gus answered. Zack nodded and turned to go, but then came back. 'I'm sorry, George,' he said. 'I – Listen, I'm sorry. It's just I like women, you know? I can't settle for one, and get sort of – I suppose you could say I'm knicker-happy.'

'If you have to use such a phrase,' she said icily.

'Well, all I'm trying to say is sorry. At first I thought I'd try to get you into bed. It'd have been fun. But after a while, well, I guess I liked you as a person better. I'm glad we never got between the sheets.'

She looked at him, her eyes wide, and behind them Gus coughed. 'Is this a private discussion, or can anyone else get involved with a few penn'orths of their own? Something along the lines of if you'd tried really hard, I'd have pushed every tooth you've got in your head so far down your throat you'd have needed a haemorrhoidectomy to get them back. If you get my meaning.'

'And I'm much too old to need two men discussing who or who will not take me to bed, goddamn it,' George roared. 'So shut up, the pair of you.'

'Fair enough,' Zack said, grimacing. He went to the door. 'And so you shouldn't think too badly of me over young Frean, I'd have paid upkeep for her and the baby, you know. Only I couldn't have married her.'

'The Québecois wife?' Gus was sardonic again. 'Remember who you're talking to. I know bloody well there was no wife in Quebec! I researched you very carefully!'

'I had to tell the woman *something*,' Zack said. 'Didn't I? Oh, shit, what a mess.' And he looked across at James. 'Remember, I'm here if he needs anyone. Goodnight.' And this time he really did go.

There was a long silence and then Gus picked up his

phone and gave some terse instructions about arresting and booking James Corton on a charge of deception and theft of hospital property and anything else they could use to keep him safe in a cell while being looked after. 'Tell him,' he ended, 'when he's woken up enough, that we'll see if we can get him into some sort of training scheme somewhere. When this is all over. He'll probably make a useful – Well, I dare say some sort of hospital job can be found for him.'

Long afterwards, when a couple of police, one of them a woman, had come and taken James stumbling away down to the detention cells, they sat in silence as the clock ticked round and they thought their own thoughts. Then Gus stirred and stretched and grinned at her.

'Ho hum, George, me old darling,' he said. 'Shall we go home to my place and go to bed? And then, tomorrow, talk about that holiday we planned to take?'

'Oh, Gus,' George said. 'Yes, please.'

Read on for a taste of

FIFTH MEMBER

The new Dr George Barnabas mystery from
Claire Rayner.

Published by Michael Joseph

By the time Detective Superintendent Gus Hathaway, head of the Area Major Incident team, arrived, Bob Pennington had finished. The photographers had recorded every inch of the yard and the alley and the pavement on Durward Street outside, and Bob had taken a sample of Mr Wilson's body fluid, an unusually pernickety step, but one which he felt necessary with so terrible and bizarre a killing. 'Anything could be evidence,' he said heavily to Mike as he stoppered his bottles.

'What's all this I hear about weirdies?' Gus demanded almost before he was out of the car. He was looking very dapper. Mike thought, with his usually all-over-the place dark curly hair smoothed down and an expanse of white evening shirt between black satin revers. Gus caught his appreciative glance and reddened slightly. 'Bloody hospital dinner,' he growled. 'I came straight here.'

'And – er – the Doc?' Mike murmured.

'Sent her home to change first. She's wearing a dress that cost her the best part of three hundred quid and if you think I'm going to let her muck that up you've another thing coming. She won't be long. So, fill me in.'

Mike did, swiftly and with much graphic use of language as well as gesture. Gus listened, his eyes glinting in the meagre light from the one remaining set of rotating blue lights.

'Getaway!' he said. 'You're makin' it up.'

'Would I do that, Guv?' Mike shook his head. 'Come and see for yourself.'

'Well,' Gus said, when he stood beside the body and stared down. 'Well, well, well. Makes you hold your knees together, don't it? Jesus, what a thing to do to a bloke.'

'What I can't fathom,' Mike said, 'is why.'

'Hmm?'

'I mean, I ask myself, why should someone do a thing like that? Cut off his wedding tackle. All right, take it away or something, but arrange it all neat and tidy like that, on his shoulder? It's crazy. I mean, it's not that he, well – threw them up there, is it? That's arranged, sort of planned, I'd say. Wouldna you?'

'Now you point it out, maybe so.' Gus seemed abstracted. 'It reminds me of ... Oh, so you're here at last!'

'I'd have been here sooner if you hadn't been in such a sweat over my dress.' The figure which had materialized beside them was wearing jeans, a loose sweatshirt with 'Buffalo' written on it in faded letters, and battered trainers. Her hair, which was thick and dark and as curly as Gus Hathaway's but much longer, was piled on her head and pinned in an untidy but beguiling knot. She was wearing large round glasses and carrying a square attaché case, which she stooped to set on the ground beside the body. 'What's the story?'

'Look for yourself,' Gus said, pulling the torch from Mike's hand. 'Mike, go and organize some lamps here, will you, so Dr B. can see what she's doing. I'll give her the details.'

Mike lingered, clearly torn. 'Are you sure you wouldna – that the Doc wouldna prefer ...' He subsided as Gus turned and stared at him.

'Prefer what?'

'Well, maybe some help. From one of – from a chap, mebbe, from the Home Office backup team. I mean, it's a very nasty –'

'Mike, go and take your mealy-mouthed wee kirk notions away and fetch those lights. If Dr B. couldn't handle this, she

374

wouldn't be in the business, right, George?' And he almost leered at the tall woman as she looked from one to the other.

'What is all this?' she demanded. 'Give me that torch, Gus. Let me see what the hell it is you're all on about.'

'Mike thinks it might upset your nice female suscept-ibilities.' Gus grinned ferociously. 'Me, what knows you so well, has no such fears. I'm not sure you've got any female susceptibilities at all, whatever they may be.'

'Oh, Gus, do shut up,' George said. She grabbed the torch and turned its beam on the body at their feet. She made it travel from one side to the other, slowly, letting it linger as it illuminated the horrible grinning throat, but making no sign or sound in response. The beam moved on, downwards, and then stopped as it reached the belly and she saw the mutilation; that brought out a short sharp intake of breath and Gus, at her side, said sardonically, 'As they say in the movies, dolly, you ain't seen nuthin' yet. Up and a bit to the right – no, your left, it's the corpse's right – yeah. That's it. What do you think of that, then?'

There was a short horrified silence and then George said, her eyes wide and her voice low, 'Jesus. Jesus H. Christ.'

A man came out of the darkness of the alley into the yard and George felt her face stiffen as he, for his part, gave her the sketchiest of nods, barely looking at her. She had never been able to get on to anything but the most frigid of terms with Rupert Dudley. He'd been a sergeant when they'd first met and almost from the beginning she'd managed to step on his toes. Now he was an inspector, because Gus thought highly of him and had worked hard to get him on his team; but in spite of that George still couldn't like the man.

'Hello, Roop,' Gus said. 'You didn't have to turn out of your bed an' all. We've got most of Ratcliffe Street's CID here, as well as some of my own people from area office.'

'My patch, Guv, my case,' Rupert said, primming his lips a little. 'Now, listen, I got here in time to see the body loaded in the van, and I took a look at him. I think I have a notion who he might be.'

'That's handy,' Gus said, suddenly exhilarated. 'A local toff of some sort, is he? Or just a sprounced-up chancer?'

'Local, my foot,' Rupert said, with a certain relish. 'National, more like. In fact he might even be international, seeing his job, as I recall, was to do with export ...'

'So?' Gus said sharply. 'No riddles, if you don't mind.'

'MP,' Rupert said. 'Something to do with the Department of Trade and Industry, I seem to remember. Sam Diamond. I'm pretty sure that's who he is, though he doesn't exactly look the way he does in his pictures in the paper, or how he was when he came to speak to Mrs Dudley's Ladies' Lunch Club. She was President last year, so she got me to turn out. You know how these things are ...' He blushed a little and it was visible in the poor light. 'So, I met him. That's why I'm so sure.'

'An MP?' Gus said. 'Oh, for crying out loud! We'll have every lousy hack in Wapping here. Christ Almighty, that's all we're short of.'

'I'll work tonight,' George said quietly into his ear. 'See you at home.'

As she drove through the almost empty streets she was smiling a little. It had been a good evening up till now, and even this case wouldn't spoil it. It was clearly going to be a real honey of a job; a bizarre style of murder and a VIP victim to boot. She shivered a little with agreeable anticipation of the work that was to come, tracking this one down. It was exactly the sort of puzzle she, and she knew Gus too (though he would never admit it in so many words) enjoyed.